Katrina awoke with a start and ▓▓▓▓▓▓ ...m as a
dark shape clambered ov▓▓▓▓▓▓ ...nd moved
toward her bed. A▓▓▓▓▓▓ ...e bed a hand was
clamped over ▓▓▓▓▓▓ a familiar voice spoke
urgently in her ▓▓▓▓▓▓

"Don't cry out, Katrina. 'Tis me, Jamie. Be still a
moment and just let me hold ye."

Her breath came in ragged gasps as she came fully to
her senses to find herself in Jamie's arms.

"Oh, Jamie, is it really you? I've dreamed of ye so
often. . . . Am I still dreaming?"

He held her so tightly she could hardly breathe, but it
hardly mattered, for he breathed new life into her by his
presence.

As he kissed her soft lips and tasted their honeyed
warmth, all the male desire in him came to the fore. He
could feel her tears on his cheeks, and they were his
tears too, mingling together in shared joy. . . .

SCARLET REBEL

JEAN SAUNDERS

Pan Books

First hardback edition published in Great Britain 1991 by
Severn House Publishers Ltd of
35 Manor Road, Wallington, Surrey SM6 0BW

First hardback edition published in the U.S.A. 1991 by
Severn House Publishers Inc of
271 Madison Avenue, New York, NY 10016

This edition published 1997 by Pan Books
an imprint of Macmillan Publishers Ltd
25 Eccleston Place, London SW1W 9NF
and Basingstoke

Associated companies throughout the world

ISBN 0 330 37017 0

1 3 5 7 9 10 8 6 4 2

A CIP catalogue record for this book is available from
the British Library.

Printed and bound in Great Britain by
Mackays of Chatham PLC, Chatham, Kent

Author's Note

There are a great number of published accounts of the 1745 Jacobite rebellion, when Charles Edward Stuart might have won a monarchy and in losing his cause became the fugitive prince romanticized by legend. I studied many of these works and found that they showed as many different facets of the turbulent fourteen months in Scottish history. Whether Bonnie Prince Charlie was foolhardy, or fired with a doomed ambition, or a truly glorious figure is for the individual to decide.

The main historical events of the novel are true, but there were frequent discrepancies in my research sources. Where it was impossible to verify them I have chosen what I consider to be the most likely occurrences. I have also taken liberties with the wordy royal speeches of the time.

That Charles Stuart was a serious threat to the course of history is indisputable. As for my characters—who is to say whether Katrina Fraser and Jamie Mackinnon ever lived? In the writing of this novel they lived in my head and still live on in my heart.

JEAN SAUNDERS

CHAPTER 1

Sunlight *pinpointed the tumbling waters of the burn like* glittering diamonds. Verdant grasses in the glen rippled in the summer breeze in undulating waves of ever-changing green against a background of distant, blue-misted hills. The girl in the window seat of the crofter's cottage leaned more industriously over her work, trying to ignore the beckoning warmth outside.

The crystal-clear Highland air would be infinitely preferable to the fog of cooking and the nose-tickling stuffiness of wool from old Margret's spinning, but the girl knew she must finish her work. The long fine strands of her coppery hair cascaded over the linen she stitched so lovingly. A birthday gift for her mother, and almost done. Only the final crossstitches of the date, and she could flex her slender fingers and admire her handiwork.

The cushion case was worked more in the nature of a sampler, even though, at seventeen, Katrina was past the age for such schoolroom needlework. But her mother had a special fondness for gifts that were personally worked. She would also be doubly pleased at seeing such diligent attention to detail from the daughter she sorrowfully called "her wayward one."

Katrina gave a thankful sigh as the work was completed and spread the wool-stitched linen across her apron.

"For my mother, with love," she read aloud. And then her own name and the date: Katrina Fraser. July 24th, 1745.

A rustling of skirts behind her made her look up quickly and straighten her face, knowing she had best not show any vanity at her own achievement. Margret had scolded her enough times for such self-conceit.

1

Katrina's oval face relaxed into a smile as the homely wife brought her a drink of squeezed fruits and honey, and oatcakes still warm from the baking. When Miss Katrina called, the woman's spinning ceased awhile, and the old favorites of the nursery were prepared.

As always, Margret was momentarily dazzled by the sudden beauty of the girl's smile. She had known Katrina since babyhood, but the girl had fair blossomed of late into a flower of Scottish womanhood. In repose her face was lovely, but calm as a madonna, belying the fiery, impulsive spirit within. But when she smiled she was positively radiant, and it was a rare body or scene that could make Margret Blainey so lyrical. Others might wax poetic over purple heather and sweeping vistas of the glens, but not Margret, nor her man.

The hills and glens were a place for those such as the Blaineys to toil and scratch a living, and even now, when Margret's nursery duties in the Fraser household were long over, her knotted hands were rarely idle. Hers would never be the life of easy-living folk. She left that to the lairds and their ladies. Margret Blainey still preferred walking the tussocky hills in stout boots, wrapped warmly in good woollen shawls she had spun herself, a solid stick her only companion as she gathered the rubbed sheep's wool from bracken and branch to fill her canvas sling.

Then home to the remote hillside cottage to dye the gift fleece in dramatic hues from dyes she made herself from herbs and wild plants and mossy lichens, followed by the spinning and the weaving into plaids for herself and her man, to the soft accompaniment of the old Gaelic songs that traditionally blessed the work and wove the luck into it.

"I'm almost sorry the cushion case is done, Margret," Katrina said suddenly. "It was good to come and see ye every afternoon. The sewing could never have been done in secrecy otherwise, and it had to be a surprise for Mammie."

"And did your mammie really believe ye came here so often just to see your old nurse?" There was a twinkle in Margret's old eyes. "Did she no' suspect ye were also slipping out to see your laddie?"

Katrina laughed, her blue-green eyes glowingly alive as if lit from within by a thousand candles. Margret could only envy the lad who could put such a glow in them and bring such fire to Katrina's petal-soft cheeks and full, mobile mouth.

"What if she did?" the girl countered mischievously. "There's no secret regarding me and Jamie Mackinnon!"

Yet her heart skipped a beat and then hammered twice as fast as she thought of Jamie . . . Jamie Mackinnon . . . and of herself in the future role of Mistress Katrina Mackinnon. The dreams that Katrina wove in her head always ended with those magical words that would mean she belonged to him, irrevocably . . . and between a lad and a lassie there were always secrets. . . .

"Miss Katrina, I'm thinking 'tis a fine thing I'm no' mind reading at this moment," Margret severely chided her. The blush in Katrina's cheeks deepened even more. "Now then, show me your mammie's gift and prove my worth in the teaching of ye."

Katrina dutifully handed the linen to her, too steeped in the ways of the nursery and Margret's control of it to do otherwise, despite the passing of time between then and now. Margret had been too much a part of her formative years to rebuff her, especially when she knew it was deserved; her thoughts had been deliciously wandering to the moments she would be with Jamie again. Margret was a friend as well as infant nurse.

Yet Katrina sometimes wondered if she really knew all there was to know about the woman. Ever since she was a wee bairn, Katrina had heard the smothered whispers from servants in her parents' household and from others that old Margret had the sight. And it was something that Katrina had never quite dared to ask about.

While the gnarled hands examined the cushion case, Katrina's gaze strayed again to the small square of window in the cottage, as if she expected to see Jamie's tall, powerfully masculine figure appear there out of her own imagination, his long, rough-tangled hair as wild a color as her own atop the firm-jawed, handsome face, the plaid over his shoulder caught with the silver of the Mackinnon brooch, the kilt swinging as he strode through the heather in search of her. . . .

Katrina caught her breath at the image, her fine young breasts rising and falling more rapidly in a way that did not escape Margret's sidelong glance. The sooner the lassie was wed the better, Margret thought sagely. Especially now, in these troubled times. The more kin a body had around him or her the better, and it was time the lassie's future was settled—wedded and bedded and safely brought to childbed in due course. And the notion of more lusty bairns for Margret to spoil and scold was not unpleasing either. There could not be many years left for her to do so. . . .

"Well, Margret?" Katrina's impatient young voice broke into her thoughts. "Will Mammie be pleased?"

"Aye, my dearie, of course she will, and well ye know it!"

She bent to kiss Katrina's soft cheek with fond affection.

"What mother would'na be pleased to have a bairn as bonnie and loving, who was prepared to spend such time on a gift?"

"Ye didn't always say so, Margret!" Katrina teased her, folding the cushion case and wrapping it carefully. Tonight it would be presented at table in the little family ritual always observed on birthdays. Her father avowed that the patience needed throughout the day by the receiver was good for the soul. It might be good for the older ones, but for Katrina and the young ones it was torment. Katrina was always hard-pressed to remain without her gifts until the end of the day when it was her turn, just three weeks before Christmas, and invariably she finished up exasperating most of her family by her wheedlings as to what the parcels might contain.

She gave a chuckle at the thought, once more the bright-eyed child instead of the young lady she was fast becoming.

"Ye'd often wear your cross face with me, Margret, and call me naught but a young rebel!"

"So I did, my lamb, and not without good reason. But now ye're a fine young woman and a credit to us all." Margret spoke generously, with the frankness of one who had given a family long and faithful service. "So when are you and Jamie Mackinnon going to tie the marriage knot?"

"He's not asked me yet!" Katrina retorted, but there was no lessening of the glow inside her, despite the words and the sudden petulant pursing of her mouth. Their two families had arranged things long ago, betrothing them while they were still in their cradles. At least, Katrina had been in hers, a wee scrap of red-haired humanity, when three-year-old Jamie had leaned over her in awe as he'd examined the tiny flailing fingers and angry face, and asked if it was a doll to play with.

"Aye, lad!" Duncan Fraser had roared with laughter and slapped his palm against that of Callum Mackinnon. "She'll be a playmate for ye in twenty years or less! What say ye, neighbor?"

The glory of it was that it had been so easy for Katrina and Jamie to fall in love, as effortlessly as night following day. It had only needed the years to nurture them before the promise of their union was fulfilled. Yet Katrina still had a perverse wish to hear Jamie say the words of the marriage proposal correctly, on bended knee, the way she heard that the gentlemen in England did it.

Jamie's own wild ancestry was at once outraged and stubbornly resisting when she was careless enough to mention the fact to him, and he'd bellowed that she would wait until the moon turned blue over the mountains before he'd ape the powdered fops of King George's court!

Of course, it was only to be expected that he would react that way! And in her heart, Katrina would have him no different. Jamie embodied all the strength and powerful heritage of the clans, their allegiance to each other, their kinship, and he would naturally pit his wits against a mere woman, however beloved. It was no more than a delightful game they played, and the banter always ended one way, in each other's arms.

Katrina turned her head again, fearful that Margret would guess her innermost thoughts from the rosiness of her face. The old nurse would be shocked to know how often the sweet grasses of the glen had pillowed Katrina's head, her hair flowing around her like a rich russet blanket. The crushed wildflowers beneath her body, and Jamie's, had been as evocative for their embraces as a scented bed.

As yet, Katrina had not submitted to the ultimate desires of her strong and vigorous lover, but the needs he aroused in her and the awakening of her own femininity were becoming more and more difficult to restrain. She loved Jamie so much, with a wild free passion that was as much a part of her as the dramatic Highlands in which she lived. A passion sometimes so fierce it almost frightened her.

The cottage door opened with the arrival of Margret's husband, who was as creased and gnarled as she but with a fine growth of luxuriant beard still, gray-flecked as his hair. If the sheep he tended were canny enough to grow their wool to warm them, then why not a man? Angus Blainey would grunt comfortably.

His appearance reminded Katrina that it was time she made for home if she wanted a little private time with Jamie before the formalities of the evening. The Mackinnons would be sharing the birthday meal with the Frasers, but in company the two betrothed ones must smile and talk and observe the proprieties, with only the accepted fond glances to show that they shared more than friendship.

"Well then, bonnie lassie." Angus smiled at her, showing blackened stumps of teeth. He stamped his sturdy boots on the flagstone floor as if to put his mark there, for the boots were his pride and joy and had been bestowed on him by Katrina's father. The old man placed his knotted shepherd's crook in its niche by the fireplace. The small familiar actions Katrina had seen so often gave out a feeling of warm security, of continuity.

" 'Tis good to see ye look so blooming, lass. Does the world treat ye well?"

"It does, Angus," she told him. "It surely does. But my mither won't, if I don't get home. Today is her birthday, and she'd not have me dawdling for too long."

"Aye, well, ye'd best be off, then," he said easily. The folks at the big houses had social occasions unknown and unwanted by the likes of him and other tacksmen, the tenants of the lairds who owned large estates. His Margret sometimes wistfully remembered them from the old days when she nursed the young Frasers, but to Angus, dour and practical, to dwell on the past was a waste of a man's thinking time. Far better to look to the present, however humble. It was still home in this cozy cottage with the peat fire burning in the hearth and therefore more precious to a man than all the rubies in a king's crown. He lived by his own simple logic and was satisfied with it.

Now he stood at his own door and waved their visitor off as she ran lightly away down the glen with the sheen of sunlight on her hair. Once, Margret had been as bonnie a lassie as Katrina, Angus reminded himself, and then he asked for some of those oatcakes he could smell fresh from the baking. In the ways of a wife, Margret was as bonnie still. . . .

Katrina breathed in deeply. The pure air of the Highland glen was like wine in summer. The glen was beautiful now, at once awe-inspiring and breathtaking, but in winter devilish enough in trapping the unwary in its gorges and bleak clefts, fit only for the rough-hewn clansmen who inhabited it. Or so said the Lowlanders in the south, Katrina thought scornfully, and the soft English. To those born to such unpredictable weather, the mists and snows that transformed the country from summer to winter, often in a single night, made the land more beautiful by contrast. And those who called it home were no less predictable. She had heard it said that the barrier of their own wild mountains and glens made even the Scottish Lowlanders think them a strange and different race.

Katrina paused, craning her eyes toward the smooth contours of the summer hills, smothered now in brilliant purple heather, and her fine brows drew together with impatience. It was the meeting time, and Jamie was not here. She scanned all around her, to where the glittering waterfall hurtled down to the tumbling, dancing burn. Away in the distance, to where a single high mass of mountainous rock hid the inlets to the sea and the islands beyond, with the twin hillocks to the north of where she stood. Land that was fashioned on the grand scale, but as familiar to her as her own hand. Her gaze roamed on around the panorama, toward the tracks leading to her home, the impregnable stone-built Frashiel House near the edge of the shimmering loch.

Katrina heard Jamie just fractionally before she felt his imprisoning arms about her waist. Her heart seemed to leap in her chest as she spun around, the laughter welling up inside her as she felt the bristle of his whiskers on her skin and heard the teasing words he spoke.

"Ye look so lost and lonely standing there so poised in the sunlight, my lassie. Is it a laddie ye're wanting, and will I do for ye?"

She had no time to answer before she felt his possession of

her mouth. His kiss was as hard and passionate as ever, dizzying her for long moments while it lasted, and she felt herself shaped toward him by his clasping hands. So close to his body that she could breathe in the urgent masculinity of him, know every sinew of his taut, powerfully made frame. He was exciting to her senses, her Jamie.

Then she pushed him away with a little teasing glower that he had caught her unawares like that, looking up into his face where he was shadowed against the sunlight. The thought sped into her mind that he could truly be likened to a magnificent red deer of the glens, his hair tangled and unkempt, his face momentarily darkened in contrast to the bright sunlight behind him. And just for a moment, the words she intended to say were halted. She suddenly had the strongest urge to pull him close to her again, as if some primitive force told her to hold on to this moment, this day, this oneness they shared.

Jamie knew none of that, only that his lassie thought to resist him. He caught her roughly in his embrace once more, his fingers tangling in her hair, his mouth seeking hers again. Arched against him, Katrina could only thrill to the powerful sensations his maleness evoked in her, and thankfully, the fey images faded from her mind. She wanted none of them. She only wanted this, to be held and loved . . . and only when it seemed that Jamie had had his fill of her kisses for the moment did she manage to chastise him a little.

"I began to think ye weren't coming today! I thought this evening was going to be enough for ye, Jamie, when we'd be in the company of our kin." She knew she deliberately provoked him, her eyes sparkling up at him and as deep-hued as the sea. Nor could she stem the laughter in them, because as always she felt such joy to be with him. It was hard to pretend anger when she was held so deliciously close in his arms.

"And how often do I have to tell ye that a lifetime of being with ye won't be enough for me, ye little witch!" His voice was deep, thickened with desire for her. His was a lusty clan, and he would have her here and now . . . but he had a fine and healthy respect for his father and hers, and knew he must restrain himself. But the nearer the time came for their nuptials, the more impatient he was to know the full beauty of his

8

Katrina and to share the delights of the flesh with her. Jamie
wanted his wife.

"Then ask me properly!" She twisted away from him and
sped away, her skirts flying, the long hair streaming in the
breeze like burnished copper tassles. Jamie strode after her,
his long legs quickly covering the ground, the ease of the kilt
unhampering his movements. A man didn't run after a lassie,
but his breath would outlast hers, and soon she paused, one
hand on her side, her breasts heaving.

Jamie caught up with her, pulling her to him, and the next
minute they were tumbling headlong together on the soft
green carpet of grass, rolling over and over in triumphant
laughter, neither knowing who was the catcher and who the
caught.

"What do we want wi' fine words and fancy gestures, my
bonnie lass?" he whispered against the softness of her mouth
as earth and sky merged in one vivid kaleidoscope of color.
She felt the hàrd weight of him caressing her body, then
heard the sudden huskiness in his voice as he spoke her name.
"Ah, Katrina, my Katrina, do ye even know what agonies ye
put me through?"

She looked at him in astonishment at the unexpected words.

"Agonies? What agonies are these? Do ye think I would
knowingly hurt ye, Jamie? I would'na, not ever!"

He smiled ruefully at her glowing face, loving the sweet
innocence of her that didn't yet recognize how the life-force
within a man could be such exquisite pain. The sight of her
now, with those lustrous widened eyes, and the full rosy
mouth, glistening and parted . . . and beneath the slender
white throat the rise and fall of those glorious mounds in
which he would bury himself. . . . He gave a low groan and
eased himself slightly away from her loveliness. He lay on his
back for a moment, staring fixedly at the sky, fighting to
regain his composure. She seemed so self-assured, his lassie,
and yet he knew that he must go gently, for she was totally
inexperienced in the needs of a man.

Katrina leaned up on one elbow, looking down at him and
suddenly troubled. To her, men were unknown creatures at
times, going off into some secret world of their own, where
even their dearest ones couldn't follow. Shutting their women-

folk out. She bent and kissed Jamie's mouth beneath the rough-tickling whiskers. The fall of her hair made a scarlet veil through which he could see the sun.

"I love ye, Jamie." Katrina said the words softly, too often used between them for her to feel any modesty at uttering them. "I'd never hurt ye."

"Nor I you," he said fiercely, his hands gripping her shoulders. "But I'm thinking your faither will be none too pleased wi' me if I keep ye away from home too long this day. Pick up your parcel and get away to your home, lassie, and I'll see ye in a while."

Katrina knew the sense of it. One last kiss and then her feet were skimming over the springy turf of the glen, turning for a last wave before Jamie was out of sight and going toward the home he shared with his father. Katrina's mother pitied them, those two big men rattling around in that great house of theirs, with no woman to grace it these ten years and only a handful of menservants to attend them.

All that would be changed when she and Jamie were wed, Katrina thought. And tonight she would be seeing Jamie again, and all her dear ones would be gathered at the same table. Ahead of her now was Frashiel House, solidly imposing, its mellowed stone reflection going deep down into the waters of Loch Shiel. It was a welcoming house for those generations that had always known its protective walls, and she slipped inside it with her precious birthday gift.

Her young brother and sister were squabbling, and their mother was trying to pacify them. Katrina hid a smile at the familiarity of the scene. Hamish at thirteen thought himself almost a man, and eight-year-old Iona was forever baiting and teasing him. It was good to be the eldest and past the age for such nonsense, Katrina thought loftily, completely forgetting how easy it was to slip back into childhood ways in their company!

But there were more exciting things in life than the pettiness of the nursery. She felt a mild pity for Hannah, the schoolroom tutor. The woman had a nimble brain at the teaching and knew plenty of Scottish history to impart to the bairns, but when the two of them plagued her at the same time, she was little more than useless at sparing Mammie's temper. Then it would be only Mairi Fraser who could deal with the tantrums.

But by the appointed hour, the scene at Frashiel House was one of harmony and anticipation for the evening. In the dining hall, the scrubbed table was piled high with succulent meats and soft crowdie cheese, with scones and shortbread and a fine boiled salmon and new-baked bread.

"A meal fit for a king," Hamish said with satisfaction. His father gave him a friendly cuff about the ear and told him laughingly that in a few years from now he would be thinking of other things besides his belly, with that gleam in his eye.

"Now, Duncan, please!" his wife, Mairi, said with mock reproof. "We'll have less of that kind of talk on my birthday. Our guests will be arriving at any minute—"

"Guests! The Mackinnons are old friends, wife! What do we want wi' calling them by fine words? They'll not thank ye for putting on airs, woman. Leave that nonsense to your Lowland kin!"

Mairi flushed in annoyance at the reference to her sister and her family living near to Kirkcudbright in the gentle rolling country nearer to the border with England. According to Duncan Fraser, the Lowland family lived the soft life, so near to the English it was likely they were all completely Anglicized by now.

They may well be, Mairi thought a trifle sadly. It was years since the two families had seen each other, and Duncan and her sister's man had had little in common. She knew better than to argue with Duncan right now. Let tonight be free of friction at least! What with the bairns' fussing and squabbling, and the household dealings, and the way Katrina was running wild these days, Mairi had more than enough to worry about without adding more.

And especially not tonight. The birthday gifts were beside the earthenware plates, and the goblets would be raised to her health with good Frashiel whiskey inside them, proportionally diluted for the children. In the huge fireplace a log fire burned, for in the Highlands even a summer night could be chilly, and for all its grandeur a large house didn't have the coziness of a wee cottage.

The walls in the dining hall were decorated with the claymores and ox-hide shields and the crossed pistols of the Fraser household, together with the great broadswords used in past battles, a tribute to the warrior nature of the Highlander. Above the blazing fire was a portrait of a past Fraser in all his warlike stance, a slain deer at his feet. Farther around the walls were hung the magnificent antlers of such deer, their enormous heads proud even in death, the sightless eyes gazing blankly down at the impatience of the three younger members of the present family. In other rooms there were tapestries to soften the walls and rugs deadening the ring of the flagstone floors, but it was in the dining hall where Duncan Fraser showed his mastery and his heritage.

The sounds of hoofbeats heralded the arrival of the Mackinnon men. Katrina's heart beat pleasurably faster, and unconsciously she smoothed down the fine linen dress she wore for this evening. The dress was square-necked and tiny-waisted, flaring out over her hips and proving to her mother, at least, that she was fast becoming a woman.

The copper glow of her hair gleamed in the firelight, its heat coloring her cheeks. Mairi Fraser registered fleetingly that her daughter was a real beauty, and that was something that her sister, Janet, far away in the south of the country, could not deny! Why Mairi had even thought of Janet at that moment she couldn't have said, except that it was probably on account of Duncan stirring up old memories.

But this was no time for dreaming. Their man was showing in the Mackinnons, and their old friend Callum was stumping toward her for a birthday kiss, his stiffened leg, the legacy of a bad fall in the hills, scarcely hindering him when such a vision awaited his embrace. He had always had a special fondness for Mairi Fraser, as he never failed to tell her. In looks he was very much an older version of Jamie, red-haired and whiskered, only in Callum's case the hair was silvered. The determined chins were the same, and so was the dark brown of the eyes, and tonight it was obvious that there was a particular light glowing in both men's eyes.

"Mairi, ye're a sight for sore eyes," Callum told her as he hugged her. "So, too, is the rest of your bonnie family, including my bonnie Katrina, the fairest of them all."

"And ye're an old rogue, Callum Mackinnon!" Mairi

began to laugh as his huge arms somehow managed to embrace both her and her daughter. "I keep telling ye it's time ye took a wife, and then ye'd have no need for your eyes to be roaming."

"There's none I'd be wanting, except for your bonnie self, Mairi, and I'm too old to be fighting Duncan for ye."

"Then we'll have no talk of fighting tonight," Mairi said caustically. "I'll not have it on my birthday!"

"Aye, well, ye just might change your mind about that when ye hear what's afoot, then." Callum's voice had changed, suddenly serious but with a strong undercurrent of excitement that none could fail to perceive.

"Faither, would ye not wait until after the meal?" Jamie spoke warningly. "After going to such trouble to prepare a feast, and on Mistress Fraser's birthday . . ."

He glanced toward Katrina, and she felt an odd little thread of fear at the look. It conveyed nothing to her, but she knew her Jamie too well . . . and besides, the seed had been sown now. There was something the Mackinnons knew that was apparently of some interest or importance to them all, and her father brushed aside any more arguing with an impatient gesture.

"Out with it, man. What's afoot?" he demanded.

Katrina dragged her gaze away from Jamie as her father seated himself and folded his arms, and the rest of them followed his lead. There would be no more talk of eating now until Callum had explained himself, and once he began it was clear there was much to tell. A growing tense excitement began to fire the Frashiel dining hall, far greater than any heat thrown out by the fire.

" 'Tis a tale brought to us by a fisherman." Callum spoke quickly, as if needing to spill everything out at once. " 'Tis a wild and fanciful tale if ever I heard one, and yet too much so to be aught but true. What do ye say to it, neighbors? Do ye believe the Stuart cause is to be revived again for Scotland!"

The few words alone were enough to stun his listeners for a moment. Each had his own thoughts. For Katrina, the lessons learned in the schoolroom were still clear enough in her mind to know immediately what Callum's words implied. The Stuarts had been kings of Scotland since the first James inherited the throne of Great Britain from Elizabeth, his first cousin twice removed. Now known as James the First of England, he was Scotland's sixth king of that name, and so caused much confusion in childish heads when trying to keep account in the schoolroom.

Katrina thought swiftly. Tension between the nations of Scotland and England had always existed, with religion often the catalyst that made it erupt into outright war. The Stuart religion was Catholic, and to have a Catholic king on the throne of a Protestant England had only fueled the flames. The support of the Catholic Church in Rome for the Stuart line had alarmed the English even more and antagonized many toward their new king. From the day James Stuart succeeded to the English throne in 1603, the uneasy peace between England and Scotland had been fractured several times.

"In some hearts I'd say the Stuart cause was ne'er in doubt, man," Duncan growled meaningfully. "But explain yourself quickly. How does a fisherman come to know such a tale? And in what form is the cause to be revived?"

When—and where? The questions seemed to hang on the pungent, wood-thick air, and now Jamie took up the explaining.

"The man got the tale from a kinsman on Eriskay. They fish between the islands, and the man, Dougal Maclean, whom ye'll know, came to the house as usual to supply us wi' fish. He told of how a nobleman and seven men had landed on Eriskay and were all that remained of two small ships. One was the French *Du Teillay*, and the other an armed frigate, the *Elizabeth*. It seems that these ships set sail from France on July thirteenth."

He stopped and let his words sink in. All there knew the significance of them, save perhaps the small Iona, who looked curiously from one to the other of them and would be wanting to know the reason for the half-serious, half-excited looks in due course. Katrina knew already and felt the beat of her heart quicken as Callum interrupted his son's flow of words.

"The two ships were in combat wi' an English man-o' -war, the *Lion*. The frigate had most of the arms and ammunition on board her and had to return to France. Both French ships were damaged, and Dougal Maclean was reliably informed that the nobleman who landed with the seven men gave his name as Charles. In full, it was Charles Edward Louis Philip Casimir Stuart, and by all accounts a bonnie, adventurous lad of about twenty-five years. Some of his men were talking free with the whiskey and said that so great was his wish to sail for Scotland on a mission he held dear to him that he sold his mither's jewels to raise money for ships and arms.'' Callum looked at the set faces around him. ''I know of only one man wi' such a name and spirit, neighbors, if his forebears are any example. The young Prince Charles!''

Katrina's heart was thudding now. The man of whom Callum spoke was the descendant of that James I of England, their own Stuart king. The succession had gone through a stormy period. James had been succeeded by his son, Charles I, who was beheaded in 1649. The monarchy had been overthrown, and Oliver Cromwell had become lord protector; but when Cromwell died in 1658 his son abdicated from the position, and the monarchy was restored with the accession of Charles II in 1660. The Stuart line still existed with the succession of his younger brother, James II.

The names and numbers ran through Katrina's head in precise detail, the way they had been instilled in her mind in the schoolroom. She remembered particularly the importance of James II, as Hannah had drummed it into her.

''Of course, *they* call him James the Second,'' Hannah had said scathingly. ''To us, he was what he rightly was, James the Seventh of Scotland. But they didn't really want him to be their king so they invited William of Orange to England. James's only alternative was to flee the country.''

''So why didn't he come home to Scotland?'' Katrina remembered asking.

''Ah, dearie, they would have hounded him here. 'Tis too close. No, the only safe place was over the water to France, where they gave him protection. He was deposed then, naturally. The English were just waiting for their chance.''

''But he had a son,'' Katrina added. ''And *he* had a son.''

Hannah laughed. '' 'Tis pleased I am that you've taken it all in, lassie. But no more for today, or your head will be mazed with it all. Just one thing more, though. Ye recall what they called the followers of the exiled James the Seventh?''

''Jacobites.'' Katrina nodded. ''I never knew why, though.''

''Then I'll tell ye. It comes from the Latin for James, which is Jacobus. The son of James the Seventh in particular was recognized by the pope as the legitimate king of Great Britain when his father died. James the Eighth is the true king over the water as far as Scots patriots are concerned, but 'tis a sentiment to be whispered behind closed doors, even now.'' She had spoken these words in a reverent voice that made Katrina smile. But she wasn't smiling now. It was treason even to mention James VIII, and this nobleman, this Charles of whom Callum and Jamie were speaking with that strange note of expectation in their voices, was James VIII's son, the young Prince Charles. . . .

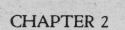

CHAPTER 2

It *was preposterous enough to be true. The supporters of the* Stuarts had stirred up rebellions in the past, the last one a mere thirty years before. The failure of it was still bitter in the hearts of the many Scots who still believed passionately in restoring the Scottish throne to a Scottish king. And who better to revive it than a new leader, a bonnie prince hardly older than Jamie? Katrina saw the warrior gleam in Jamie's eyes at that moment and guessed that it would be echoed a thousandfold all over the Highlands.

She felt her spirit quaver. In any rebellion there would be bloodshed, and she knew with a sixth sense that much Scottish blood would be spilled. It had always been so. She knew that Jamie would join the prince if he were needed, and if the male talk going on around her were to be believed, every able-bodied clansman would be needed. She would not have her Jamie any other way than ready to fight for his country . . . but perhaps because she was nearer to the schoolroom facts of recent history than the men here, she dared to question in her mind what the outcome of it all would be. There had been no successful uprising for the Stuarts so far.

But she dared not question it aloud. And she must not even think of defeat, as it would add a note of pessimism to the night's turn of events. James VIII had been called the "old pretender" in his bid to claim back the British throne. Now they had a "young pretender," and although his arrival in Scotland would lead the way to civil war, it would also stir many Scottish hearts to a patriotism that had merely been lying dormant until a new leader came to rouse it.

Jamie would rally for the prince and every red-blooded man would do the same. Katrina glanced toward her brother Hamish, as rapt in the tale of the young prince as the men, and at Iona, suddenly bored with the proceedings and fiddling with her hair. She looked toward her mother and saw that Mairi was pale but had a fierce light in her eyes.

"Mammie, your birthday seems to have been overlooked," Katrina said quickly, her voice oddly cracked and raw. She suddenly felt the need to bring back normality to this day that had changed so quickly. Mairi gave her daughter a slightly reproachful look.

"Not by me, my dearie. I'll not forget this birthday with such news! Mebbe 'tis the best birthday gift a loyal Scot could ever have."

Katrina felt a swift resentment, remembering the hours she had spent in stitching the cushion case for her mother. She smothered it, knowing she should be just as excited about the prince's arrival as anyone, yet conscious of strange forebodings and alarm that her mother seemed to be as besotted as any man. Was the whole country to be swept along in a fever of rebellion against the English? Somehow she knew that the pain and anguish would overtake the glory. It was as if she had been momentarily blessed or cursed with old Margret's second sight. She was young enough to be headlong in love and old enough to know that she could lose her love by an Englishman's hand. A shudder ran through her body even as her father and the Mackinnon men were congratulating themselves that at last they were getting the leadership to make a new attempt to beat the English bastards into recognition of the Stuart line.

This time, Mairi Fraser asserted her position as mistress of the house and scolded them severely for such language in front of the bairns.

"Their ears will soon rock to the sounds of victory, then!" Duncan roared out. "But come ye all, and we'll drink the health of my good woman, and of others!"

"Before we eat? 'Tis naught but folly and will spin your heads!" Mairi's protest was lost as Duncan shouted for a bowl of water to be brought to table and placed in the center of it. He poured the drams of whiskey himself, overgenerous for the occasion, and handed a goblet to each one. They all drank, first to Mairi's birthday, raising their goblets to shoulder height.

"To my Mairi, and God bless her for the fine wife she is to me." Duncan was exuberant and mellow. The whiskey stung Katrina's throat as she swallowed, and she saw Iona pull a face at her one sip of the diluted spirit. Then came the next toast, one as solemn as in any English home.

"The king!" Duncan declared.

Many an Englishman would have raised his eyebrows in disbelief at these fervent Catholic Scots supposedly drinking the health of their Protestant king, George II. But this was a ritual that occurred in many loyal Jacobite households. The bowl of water symbolized the English Channel that separated England from France, where the exiled James VIII now lived, and the king to whom loyal Scots raised their goblets was the one who still lived in their hearts. But tonight caution was thrown to the winds in Frashiel House as Duncan Fraser pledged a new and stirring legend.

"To the Stuart. To our new and bonnie lad, the hope of Scotland!"

Katrina drank as dutifully as the rest, but she felt a twist of dread inside her. It took but little to rouse the clans to any kind of action. The clan system was a tribal or feudal one, and a clan name was its owner's identity, a means of belonging. Some of the smaller clans or families would ally themselves to the larger ones, giving them their allegiance and having their support in times of trouble in return. Within each clan was its chief, its laird, who owned property and land, rented out to tenants or tacksmen, who in turn sublet plots to lowlier folk, the humblies. In times of war, too, the clan system had its own peculiar status roles. In battle, the more prominent clan members fought at the front lines, with lowlier men behind them in proportion to their class. It was a complicated yet simple code.

It was clear to Katrina that Hamish was fired with enthusiasm at the thought of a new rebellion and as eager to join as any man, but Mairi's adamant rebuke squashed any such idea at once. He was too young. But Katrina knew from the mutinous look in Hamish's eyes that there was not an end to it. He might be forced to stay behind if his father went to war, but he would not like it, and those still around him would get the rough side of his tongue! Katrina's heart gave an uneasy leap, knowing that her Jamie was not too young, nor her father too old, to fight for the cause. Callum would be unlikely to ride, for his leg pained him badly at times, however much he disguised the fact.

"Oh, can't we leave all this talk of fighting for the night?" she burst out as Duncan and Callum began discussing tactics that were used in the last rebellion, in 1715. Not so far from there, the old Mackenzie stronghold, Eilean Donnan Castle, had been blown up by an English man-o'-war when it was being used as a base for that Jacobite rebellion. Still a gaunt reminder, it had made Katrina shiver on the few occasions she had seen the ruins. There was still bitterness about it, and she could hear it now in the two men's voices.

"*Please!*" she pleaded. "It's still Mammie's birthday. Can we not have the feast and then sing and make music? If you all think so highly of the prince's coming, can't we rejoice for the night?"

"Are ye thinking o' wearing the yellow, Katrina?" Hamish jeered at her, still maddened by his mother's refusal to let him join the rebels, as the English would undoubtedly call the prince's proud new army.

Her eyes blazed at her young brother.

"I'm no coward, Hamish Fraser, and never would be if the need arose! I'd uphold the cause as staunchly as any man or woman proud of the Scottish name!"

"Well said, bonnie lass," Duncan said stoutly, and Katrina saw how easily she had fallen into her brother's innocent trap.

Her roots went too deep for her to be discounted if an army was called for, even though womenfolk didn't go to war in the physical sense that men did.

War! The very word made her heart throb sickeningly. Such a thing was alien to the expected course of her life. The future Katrina saw for herself was a rosy one, to marry Jamie and live in blissful contentment. But now, in the space of an hour, the security of that dream seemed to be slipping away from her. The fabric of their lives was changing.

"Katrina is right," Mairi said unexpectedly, as if seeing the shadows pass across her lovely daughter's face. "If the feast is not to be spoiled, let's eat and rejoice, and I'll not have it said that the Frasers forget to offer hospitality to their neighbors!"

Katrina darted her mother a grateful look. If this—this thing came to happen, then the two of them could be united in a way that she had hitherto never imagined. Both with their menfolk gone away to fight. . . .

She swallowed and forced herself to eat, since it was she who had insisted on following a normal pattern. The food was good, the bread still warm, the salmon fished from their own waters. It constantly amazed Katrina how even the humblies, those lowliest of men, had been known to complain at a constant diet of salmon, because it was so cheap and plentiful in Scottish waters! If they learned the art of cooking it the way Mairi Fraser did, poaching and spicing with herbs to her own recipe, they might not be so fussy! She smiled at Mairi with genuine warmth, complimenting her on her excellent fare.

At last the meal was finished and her mother's birthday gifts opened and enjoyed, and Katrina slid her hand into Jamie's under cover of the table. She felt warmed by the strength of his supple fingers as they closed around hers.

"Would ye go, Jamie? For the cause?" She could not help voicing the question. It was something that had to be put into words and acknowledged, in the same way she felt the need to hear him ask her to marry her.

And as she saw the swift anger in his eyes that she even needed to ask it, her heart sank. Still, she was too much a woman not to need the answer from his own mouth. She didn't want him to go. . . . The sudden burning shame of it overwhelmed her. As if once again old Margret had bestowed a moment of her gift on her, Katrina seemed to see a clouded vision of her Jamie. His face was gray and muddied, gaunt and fatigued beyond endurance. He was lost, changed from her laddie into a stranger. . . . She blinked away the terrifying images as she heard his strong young voice.

"Would I not!" he stated boldly. "What true loyalist would say nay to his prince!"

"Spoken like a true patriot, lad," Callum said to his son. "If my leg were not so hellishly stiff, I'd ride alongside ye, but it would be a folly. For me to march would be even more of a folly."

"Faither?" Katrina turned to Duncan. She could see by her father's face what his answer would be.

"Every able-bodied man would go," Duncan affirmed. " 'Tis what Scotland has been waiting for, lassie, though there will doubtless be those who choose to lose themselves in the glens rather than fight. It happens."

Callum affirmed this with a grim-faced nod. Clearly the two older men had no time for those dissenters. Katrina felt giddy with the rousing ayes that followed Duncan's comments. More whiskey was drunk, and the spilt drops lay glistening on the men's whiskers as eyes began to glaze.

Was she the only one here to see the fear in all this? Her mammie must feel the same way, but if she did, she was carefully avoiding Katrina's eyes now. They were all slightly mad as well as drunk! They were treating the news of the prince's arrival on the island of Eriskay as if it were the second coming of Christ! If it was blasphemous to think so, then so it was. She could hardly think straight, and not because of the spirits she had drunk, but because of the tumultuous feelings inside her. And while one part of her gloried with the rest for all that this news might mean for Scotland, another part of her was wracked with dread.

In deference to Mairi's birthday, they all retired to another room at last, where the tapestries softened the stone walls and the chairs were less functional and hard. Iona recited the poems she had been practising all week, and Hamish blew plaintive tunes on the bagpipes, his cheeks almost purple with the effort. They sang and made merry, and in most hearts there was a double celebration. When Mairi decided Iona had been up late enough, it was Katrina who said at once that she would take her sister to bed, and guiltily she knew that the reason was merely to be doing homely tasks instead of listening to the constant talk of rebellion against the English crown.

She settled her sister in the narrow bed. Iona was buttoned up in her nightgown, and the candle was left burning at the side of her bed until she fell asleep. Iona said fretfully that she couldn't sleep with all the talk downstairs and wanted Katrina to stay and tell her a story.

"What about?" Katrina said as patiently as she could, for Jamie was downstairs, and she wanted to be with him. But as she pushed the red-golden hair back from Iona's hot little forehead, she realized that the child was far from relaxed.

"Tell me about the kings," Iona said at once. "Hannah tries to tell me, and I don't understand. Will ye tell me, Katrina? Why do we like James over the water, and why don't we like George in England?"

Her voice was plaintive, putting the questions so naively, and Katrina knew she couldn't let the wee lassie worry her head over this all night without trying to explain it. She perched on the edge of the hard bed.

"Well, James is the man who should really be king, love. At least, we think so."

"Why don't *they* think so? And who doesn't think so?" She frowned, still not clear who *they* were.

"The English don't want a Catholic king, lassie." Katrina forestalled the next question. "You know the priest where we go to kirk on Sundays, don't you? Well, in England they don't have the same kind of kirks we do, and they're afraid that if a Catholic king rules them, he'll want to change their ways, and it's important to them to stay as they are. So they changed all the rules, and instead of letting our King James the Seventh be the king of England, too, they said he couldn't and he had to leave the country. After the reigns of William III and Queen Anne, they chose George to be their king— even though he came from Germany and couldn't speak many words of their language—because he was a Protestant."

"He sounds nasty," Iona pouted, and Katrina gave a short laugh.

"I don't know if he's nasty or not, but after our King James the Seventh died in France, a group of Jacobites in London tried to crown his son. They wanted him to be King James the Third of England and James the Eighth of Scotland. But there were too many people who didn't want this to happen, so they had to run away, and that's how our James the Eighth became an exile like his father. But lots of other people, as well as the Scots, know that James was the rightful king, and if you ask Father Macneil, he'll tell you that the pope in Rome believes it, too."

She saw that Iona's eyes were drooping, and she thankfully stopped talking. She had simplified the story for Iona's benefit, but in doing so she had made things clearer for herself. She rose from the bed softly to join the others downstairs.

"Will ye tell me about the prince tomorrow, Katrina?" Her sister's small voice followed her. "Ye make it sound much nicer than Hannah does."

Katrina smiled back at her.

"All right, tomorrow," she promised.

She hadn't intended to give a history lesson to Iona, but at least she had lulled the child off to sleep, and now she could sit beside Jamie. But she found that he had already asked permission for the two of them to take a stroll out-of-doors, and the request had been granted. It was the accepted way of things. The betrothed couple needed a certain amount of time alone to whisper their sweet love words.

They were scarcely out of earshot of the house when Katrina rounded fiercely on Jamie. "Ye didn't need to sound quite so eager to be away, Jamie! Is there naught here that would make ye reluctant to fight for the cause!"

He caught her to him, his eyes suddenly sparkling with laughter. All around them the sweet night scents of bracken and heather and earth were heady in their nostrils. They moved toward a well-known hollow between the house and Loch Shiel, where their embraces could be private and secluded in the soft pinky haze of the gloaming before the onset of darkness.

"Ye know full well there is, my sweet one," Jamie said, his voice as sensual as a caress. "And when we're wed . . . ."

"When will that be?" Katrina mourned. "Sometimes I

23

wonder if it will ever happen, and the bairns plague the life out of me at home, where I'm still treated as a bairn myself.''

Jamie laughed again. ''Hamish would'na thank ye for calling him a bairn now, when he thinks himself almost a man. But it pleases me that ye're as anxious for our wedding as I am, sweet dove.''

She felt his hand move around the front of her body to press lightly on her breast beneath the woollen shawl she wore. As always, her body responded quickly to his touch. For once, it almost angered Katrina. Becoming Jamie's wife was all-important to her, but she knew full well that a man could have other things on his mind besides the nuptials. It was as if the lust for warlike activities rivaled the desire for a woman.

And all this talk of a stranger arriving in Eriskay! The rumors had been spread about so often over the years—that one day there would be another uprising to restore King James to his rightful place, that the young Prince Charles was fast growing to manhood, and that surely he would be the one to take up the cause. . . .

Was this really the prince, this stranger of whom the fisherman spoke? Or was it all a charade?

''Ye seem distant from me, Katrina,'' Jamie said. They had reached the loch, still and beautiful in this most beautiful of glens, with the reflected images of sky and mountains in its glassy depths, together with the two figures standing close by its banks. The two figures Jamie would see merged into one.

''Come back, my dearie,'' he said softly, coaxing, his fingers trailing the length of her hair.

She stood mutely as he unfolded the long run of plaid cloth over his shoulder and laid it down on the soft grass of the hollow. Wrapped in such a cloth, the extension to the kilt, many a Highlander had survived a night on the hills, and after only a moment's hesitation Katrina sank down beside her man. It was only foolishness to feel such resentment for something that might never happen. Yet the gnawing dread still restrained her from melting into his arms the way she always did. . . .

''Jamie, I'm feared,'' she confessed hesitantly. ''There's glory to be had from an uprising, but there's bloodshed, too.

I—I find it hard to accept the news as easily as the menfolk. I fancied the Mackinnons were less surprised than we were. Did ye have prior knowledge, Jamie?''

He shrugged his powerful shoulders. ''Mebbe ye could call it prior knowledge. The signs were all there for those who looked for them, Katrina. Whispers as to the movements in France these past months have reached Jacobite ears easily enough. We have agents on both sides of the water between England and France, lass and 'twas well-known that Charles Stuart was planning to enlist French support for another landing in Scotland.''

''But they always talk of such things in whispers,'' Katrina said crossly. ''It's a dream, Jamie, and ye know it.''

''A dream that could become reality, dearie.'' His voice was edged with a keenness she couldn't miss, and a shiver ran through her. She twisted around to stare down at Jamie, lying full-length on the springy turf of the hollow. He had accused her of drifting away from him in spirit, but now it was he who had a strange light in his eyes.

''Why have ye never told me any of this?'' She spoke sharply.

''Would ye have listened? Your woman's head was aye filled with other things, and rightly so. I'm not blaming ye, Katrina, but ye've always managed to make your mind a blank when it came to understanding the ways of a man when honor was at stake. Ye've never had cause to be threatened in any way.''

''Ye make me sound as shallow as a newborn bairn!'' she said angrily, her eyes flashing. Jamie leaned toward her and kissed her lips, seeing the hurt in her.

''Not intentionally, hen.''

''Then tell me all ye know! I demand to know!'' She moved her head back from him. ''Don't treat me like a bairn, Jamie. I thought we shared everything.''

''Not yet, dearest. And ye'll know the need for careful speaking in Jacobite affairs as well as I do. We're governed by a Protestant king in London, and 'twould only need a careless word in the wrong ears for me and my faither to be clapped in prison, and I've no wish to languish there.''

''My ears are not the wrong ears, Jamie.'' She spoke with

sudden dignity. "I'm soon to be your wife. And I've no wish to be your widow! I've a right to know as much as ye do."

He chose his words carefully. The Jacobite agents in Scotland had been apprehensive about the latest news ever since the prince's promised French support had failed to materialize. Jamie made light of the whole affair to Katrina, knowing she was already agitated by the night's news.

"The prince had a French fleet ready to support him, Katrina, but they were forestalled by an English attacking fleet even before they left port, and the French dispersed. Despite pleas from Charles, the French government abandoned the idea of giving support to his cause, so Charles decided to set sail without their help, relying on Scots loyalists to support him when he got here—and those of the English who will rally as well. It's known that some clans are totally opposed to a new uprising and will have no part in it."

Katrina's eyes were wide as she listened.

"And ye knew all this? Ye knew he was sailing here, and ye did'na tell me?"

"There was no way of guessing if he would reach these shores. 'Twas best to say nothing. Don't censure me, lassie." The glint of anger was in his eyes, and she recognized that peculiar cloak of secrecy that kept men apart from their womenfolk in certain matters. And those who were staunch Jacobites in a country ruled by a king and government so opposed to Jacobite beliefs had grown used to keeping thoughts to themselves, even from their nearest and dearest ones. There was nothing new in that.

Katrina wanted her Jamie back. He was here, and so was she . . . and now it was she who wound her arms about his neck and nestled her soft cheek to his rough-textured one. And immediately he became her own Jamie again, all thoughts of wars and causes forgotten in the sweet joy of being together.

The nearness of Katrina never failed to stir Jamie's senses, and if tonight there was the added exhilaration in his veins by the news brought by old Dougal, he was wise enough to curb his thoughts from racing any further. He never doubted the truth of Dougal's words. The prince had come, and if the cause was begun, as soon it must be, then such delights as lying in a quiet glen with the lassie of his heart would be replaced by the fever of battle.

"Ye're so beautiful, my bonnie lass," he murmured against her mouth. "As fresh as a mountain burn and as fragrant as a summer blossom. Ye can twist my heart around your little finger, and I love ye for it, dearest one."

His tongue made a sensuous circle of her lips, its moistness leaving her mouth pleasurably cool and filling her with a wild tingling sensation. Her mouth was softly parted, and she felt the warm tip of Jamie's tongue teasing hers for a few seconds, then probing deeper and moving in little erotic movements as it sought the inner recesses of her mouth. As always, Katrina was aware of sudden leaping pulsations like miniature shock waves in the secret core of her being.

The sensations were as exquisite as ever; her breathing grew rapid, and a small groan of pleasure escaped her. An urgency of desire suffused her, and her arms wound more tightly around Jamie's neck, her fingers entwining in the thick coarse hair at his nape.

"I would have all of ye, Katrina mine," he said hoarsely, "here and now! Can ye honestly tell me ye feel any differently?"

How could she when every part of her ached to know him as intimately as he wished it? But they had made a vow to their family names. Until they were wed, she would remain pure. But truly there were times when it was hard to resist all that their own natures demanded.

"I want ye, Jamie." She spoke in a muffled voice against his cheek. "But ye promised—ye know ye did."

His mouth began a slow, tantalizing path downward, to where the swell of her breasts teased him with their milky softness above the neckline of her dress. He could hear her ragged breathing. He could see the flushed arousal on her cheeks and on her love-swollen mouth. He would not go too far . . . but just a little way farther . . . to assuage his raging need of her. . . .

"Ye've no need to fear, lassie. I'll respect ye as long as 'tis necessary, although it drives me near to madness to hold myself in check. But ye'll not deny me a little more of your tempting sweetness, will ye, Katrina?"

She made no protest as his fingers unfastened the bodice of her dress and his hands freed her breasts. His palms caressed them so gently it was as if the cool delicate touch of silk shivered across them. Katrina felt the waves of a mounting desire begin to course through her. It was time to call enough.

Her throat felt almost too thickened to say the words. She drew in her breath as Jamie's tongue circled first one erect nipple and then the other. She ached for more of his kisses, and when his mouth closed around each rosy peak in turn, her eyes closed and sheer ecstasy rippled through her.

"Do ye feel what ye do to me, lassie?" His voice whispered against her skin, and she felt the stiffened stalk of his manhood pressed against her thigh. At once her eyes flew open, and he gave a rueful smile at the brief panic in her eyes. "Will ye no' trust me, Katrina? I gave ye my promise."

And even though he felt as if it shortened his life by days to control his passion, he would not force himself upon her! But just this once, there was still more he needed . . . must have. . . . He fastened her bodice gently. Next minute she was conscious of his hand on her thigh. It was outside the linen of her dress, moving gently, inching its way toward her mound of Venus. Katrina realized she was holding her breath, and then she breathed so shallowly it seemed as if she might faint. At last she felt Jamie's palm caressing her fleshy softness.

Katrina's limbs relaxed a little, as if she were suddenly boneless, composed solely of a new physical sensation that completely enveloped her. She hardly noticed when Jamie's hand was no longer above the linen of her dress but beneath it, because the exquisite sensations went on . . . and the touch of his fingers was delicate, finely tuned, parting the soft tangle of hair protecting her moist pearl of desire.

As he moved one finger against it he was gentle, orbiting slowly and bringing her to a new peak of passion. He heard her give a small ragged gasp, and although every instinct urged him to forge inward to that lovely hidden source, he let his hand cover her for a moment more and then withdrew, adjusting her skirts and holding her close to him.

"Oh, Jamie, Jamie," Katrina said tremulously, her head on his shoulder. "Such feelings—so powerful they almost frighten me. Am I strange to feel that way? Is it bad?"

He gave a low laugh, exulting in the womanliness of her, anticipating the days and nights when she would share his bed for always. He rocked her in his arms, like a mother with a child, and even as he did so, the thought of Katrina nursing his bairns gave him a renewed dart of pleasure in his loins.

"There's naught wrong with ye, dearest." His mouth was as warm as honey on her cheek. " 'Tis merely the matching of a man's passion that ye feel, and rightly so. There's naught so wondrous in this world as the knowledge that a man can bring his woman to such a pitch. I long for the day ye'll be mine in every sense of the word, Katrina, and dinna ever think otherwise."

All this foolishness of needing him to go down on one knee to profess his intentions was but a childish fantasy. No woman was ever surer of her man than Katrina at that moment.

But they must not linger, or her mother would start to be anxious for her. There was a limit to how much freedom a young and bonnie daughter was allowed, even in these Highland regions where decorum was only necessary on high days and holidays and Sundays at the kirk.

As it was, Mairi Fraser looked keenly at her daughter when she and Jamie returned from their stroll; they had been overlong for a walk by the loch, and Katrina's face was more flushed than could rightly be attributed to the fresh evening breeze. Mairi must have words with her daughter, and soon. Betrothed she might be, but she was not wed yet, and Mairi wanted no shame brought on the house. There were still more than six months before Jamie would be of an age when the Mackinnon men married, and the two of them had best curb their natural impatience.

CHAPTER 3

The day after Mairi's birthday was not the best time to talk to a willful daughter. Mairi realized it as soon as she began. She felt less mild-tempered than usual after all the drinking and talking from the previous night. The bairns were crosspatches and their bickering would strain anyone's temper. Katrina had awakened with a throbbing head and had snapped first at Hamish a dozen times and then at Iona, until the child had flounced off in tears, calling her a hateful pig. Hamish had gone about hooting with laughter at the sight of her wee, angry figure. Iona's hair was as red as all the Frasers', and now her face was only a mite less fiery.

"Hannah could do with teaching ye some manners," Katrina scolded them both. Her temples ached, and she felt nauseated with the headache and angry at letting herself be so provoked. "I shall ask her to give ye both an extra hour in the schoolroom, for being so rude to your elders!"

"Ye're not my elders. Ye're just Katrina!" Iona stormed back at her. She hurled herself at her sister, thrashing her small arms against her in a childish tantrum. Katrina had to forcibly restrain her, and it was then that Mairi came to see what all the commotion was about.

"Will ye stop it at once, Katrina! She's only a wee thing! What are ye thinking of, to be so spiteful to the bairn?" Mairi's eyes flashed at once at her own interpretation of the scene. "Come here to your mammie, Iona."

Katrina raged as the child ran to her mother's arms, and it was the older sister who bore the brunt of the anger. No matter what was said or done, Iona would be petted and Katrina would be blamed. It was all so unfair . . . and once Iona was pampered to her mother's satisfaction, Mairi announced that she wished to speak to Katrina alone. From the steely look in her mother's eyes, Katrina knew it was to be nothing good.

Katrina had expected the house to be still simmering with last night's news, but she had seen nothing of her father all day. He had ridden off early to see what was afoot, and the rest of them had gone about the house like soreheads, each with his or her own feelings about the uncertain time ahead. The excited glow of last night seemed sadly lacking. She resolved to ask her mother more. Had she known about the expected arrival of Charles Stuart as well? Had it been a kind of conspiracy among men and their womenfolk, one that excluded her because she was still looked on as a child? The thought was as unwelcome as the coming confrontation with her mother. Katrina followed her silently into the small room Mairi called her sanctuary, where she did her sewing and had her respite away from the bairns. It was a woman's room, with Mairi's feminine touches in it—gifts from the children, wildflowers in a pot, a rag rug on the stone floor. A welcoming room, but not today.

"I want ye and Jamie to mind yourselves, Katrina." Mairi came directly to the point once they were alone and seated on the hard settle, and even the presence of the new cushion cover on one of the plump-filled pads couldn't soften her meaning.

Perversely, Katrina pretended not to understand, widening her eyes in innocence.

"Mind ourselves? In what way, Mammie? When we go walking, do ye mean? We've walked the glens often enough to know every inch of them. We'll no' be breaking our legs."

"Ye know full well what I mean, Katrina, so don't go all cow-eyed on me," Mairi said tartly. "Ye're near to being a woman now, and there's naught of the laddie in the way Jamie Mackinnon looks at ye sometimes."

"How else would he look at me?" Katrina said heatedly, uncomfortable at knowing the truth of it. "A man should'na look on his wife as if she's a block of wood, should he, Mammie?"

"Ye're not his wife yet, and that's my meaning. And if ye find it difficult to understand, ye're more of a simpleton than I took ye for. Is that what I'm to believe, Katrina?"

The quick temper flared at the words.

"I'm not simple. I understand a lot of things. And I'd understand more if ye all gave me the chance. But I'm shut out of things, aren't I?"

"You're behaving like a bairn," her mother said sharply. "And a wild one at that. Mebbe it would do ye good to get away from Jamie a wee while, my lass, and then I'd have less worries about ye. A spell apart may cool that hot passion."

"Ye would'na stop me seeing him! We're honorably betrothed, and Jamie's faither would have something to say if ye started making objections to our keeping company!" Katrina burst out, but her heart was jumping with fright. She could not bear the thought of being parted from Jamie. Her mother could have no notion of how high the passions had run between her and Jamie last night, but of course she would know the ways of a lad and a lassie, and the thought made Katrina squirm in her seat.

"I'd want nothing to change the good relationship we have with the Mackinnons, lamb. And I'd ask ye to remember the same. Be patient until the turn of the year when Jamie is of age. The two of ye must surely see the sense of it."

"So I do! But our private plans seem to have been overlooked since last night's news, don't they? Where will Jamie be at the turn of the year? And—and ye must know that sense is often lacking when it's feelings that are involved. I canna believe that ye've forgotten how it feels to be so deep in love that it hurts, Mammie. And to be parted from Jamie would be like—like tearing myself in two. Will it happen, Mammie? Did ye already know something of this arrival from France that ye all carefully kept from me as if I'm as much a child as my brother and sister?"

She couldn't help the hurt and resentment of it spilling out of her, even though she was still guarded enough to speak of Charles Stuart carefully. Even here, in her mother's sanctuary. But now the air was charged with a new tension as Katrina rushed on.

"Jamie seemed to know it all last night, Mammie! About the prince's plans for coming to Scotland and raising a new army. Jamie knew. Was I not to be trusted with knowing beforehand?"

Mairi took her daughter's tense hands between her own. Katrina was rigid with indignation. Mairi's slow voice was deliberate now. "Lass, we're a nation under foreign rule. The fewer who knew the movements of Charles Stuart the better. And yet so many must have known. There are spies and agents in every conflict, but we of the clans who have always supported the Jacobite cause had to keep closed mouths on it. I was only privileged to hear a little because I share your faither's bed. Matters of war are for men's ears, Katrina, and for men to settle."

"And it is for women to bear the price," Katrina said bitterly, with a wisdom growing by the hour. "Where is my faither, Mammie?"

Mairi hesitated and then sighed, seeing the direct look her daughter gave her. "Gone to see Father Macneil, lass, and then to find our neighbors. The men of these parts are loyalists, and our tacksmen will naturally follow your faither's lead."

Katrina listened with mounting panic. This was all alien talk. Yesterday all had been sunshine and lightness. Today there was talk of wars and partings . . . priests, whose vocation was to save souls, not discuss battles. And yet, why shouldn't priests be involved? If a war was as much a conflict between Catholic and Protestant as king against king, then why not a priest with a broadsword? Katrina's mouth was dry, seeing the small spark of ambition from an exiled king leap into the flames of bloodshed.

"Who will not follow?" she muttered, talking almost to herself. "We are all puppets in the hands of kings and governments, aren't we?" It was a new thought, one that had rarely touched Katrina's life, except in the learning of the schoolroom. Now, the feeling that her entire life was to be changed by a prince's ambition was at once terrifying and shaming. She resented it because of the effects it would have on her personally, and she was shamed by the thought; she should be valuing the greater glory of Scotland above herself.

"If ye've done wi' me, Mammie, can I leave ye?" She jumped to her feet, her voice tight and cracked. "My head throbs, and I've a wish to be out in the air. And I canna be doing with any more of Iona today. She plagues me, no matter what ye think."

The swift change of talk, to bring her world back to mundane, homely matters, was necessary to Katrina's peace of mind, but to her mother's ears it was merely the rebellious nature of her elder daughter showing itself once more. Mairi's own mouth was tight as she nodded.

"Mebbe 'tis best for ye to be by yourself awhile, to get the devil out of ye, Katrina," she said shortly.

The girl rose and left the room abruptly, and Mairi stood by the window for some minutes, watching her pick her way across the sunlit glen. Mairi thought keenly that if the house was to be turmoil in future days, perhaps Katrina's absence would give the rest of them a little harmony. Maybe a visit to her own sister Janet in the Lowlands would do the girl some good. . . . It was the seed of an idea in Mairi's head right then.

Katrina slowed her footsteps as she made her way through the glen. If she stamped and marched, it only made her head stab more painfully and did her temper no good. She must curb it and she knew it, to stop this surge of blood to her temples. She was too resentful of her mother to ask for a draught, and neither had Mairi offered it. Katrina would go to old Margret, who had so often soothed her ruffled temper in the past. And if only her head were not so full of things she wished to forget, the wine-fresh air might do its healing without the aid of potions.

But the old lessons learned in the schoolroom seemed to mill in and out of her head. When she had learned of the young prince born in a land across the sea, a child who was so important to Scotland, she had been charmed, wanting to know more, to hear every detail; and Hannah had been only too willing to provide every scrap of it. Now it all came rushing back to her in Hannah's clipped, precise chronological phrases. Bits of information gleaned from French and Scottish Jacobite agents over the years had produced a picture of the prince and his family. His father, the exiled James VIII, had married a Polish princess, Clementina Sobieski, in 1719. A year later, just before Christmas, they had a son, born in Rome and named Charles Edward Louis Philip Casimir. This was the child whom loyal Jacobites, in Scotland and in England, recognized as the rightful heir to the throne. Charles Stuart had come to Scotland now to seek justice for his father, and in turn for himself, for if James's cause was successful, then eventually Charles would also be king.

And this Charles . . . was educated in France and Italy, and said to be fluent in both languages as well as English, and with an ear for the Gaelic, too. Hannah had been moved by the idea of the prince over the water and thought he must be handsome, intelligent, and noble, as befitted the son of a king. For all her stuffy attention to detail in the lessons taught to the Fraser children, Hannah had an oddly romantic streak in her when it came to the royal Stuarts. She still remembered the old uprisings and had an unyielding sense of loyalty to them in her heart.

Katrina looked ahead, her attention caught by a sudden flash of scarlet, and in the distance near to the Blaineys' cottage she could see the bent figure of old Margret in her bright shawl as she worked at her fleece gathering. The scarlet was a frivolous color for one of Margret's years, but the sense of it was that Margret could more easily be seen in the heather if she should stumble or fall. There was no real need for her to work at this menial task at all, since Duncan Fraser had provided for her after years of faithful service, and old Angus was a loyal tacksman, but they chose to live in the hillside home, and Margret's fingers needed to be active with her gathering and spinning to stop them from becoming crippled.

Katrina paused a moment, struck by the fact that today there were no men to be seen about the glens or hills. Normally there would be shepherds, turf cutters, lads collecting bracken for thatching, lads in the burn taking home a family's supply of fish, even a brawny Highlander seeking to uproot a young rowan tree to plant near his cottage to combat witchcraft.

Today there were no swinging axes, no activity to stop and study, no good-days from neighbors. The glen was oddly silent, and there was a feeling borne on the air, as if the stillness were merely a waiting time. The underlying tension was almost tangible.

Was she becoming as addle-brained as old Margret? Katrina thought crossly, and then she chided herself. There was nothing daft about Margret, for all that she spoke in riddles at times. She strode ahead, seeing Margret straighten her bent back as her name was called. The canvas bag Margret carried was bulging with sheep rubbings, and Margret said thankfully that it was more than enough for the day. They would go back to the cottage and take a cool drink together.

"Was your mammie pleased with her cushion case, then?" The casual question made Katrina look at her almost blankly.

"Margret, have ye heard aught since yesterday? There's plenty talk."

"About the young Stuart, ye mean?" It was so odd for the name to be said in the open that Katrina knew there must be

35

substance to the tale. More than anything else, Margret's calm voice was telling her so. And suddenly Katrina was irritated by it. Did all the world know but her? There had been talk of a new uprising a year ago, but at that time Katrina had been sixteen and growing up, and she had other things to think about. It had all seemed so remote from her everyday life that she had effectively closed her mind to the hints, the rumors, the hopes. . . . Maybe she should have listened more, she thought now.

"It's true, then. And ye knew it all and never said a word to me! It will change things, Margret, and I don't want things to change."

"That's foolish talk, Katrina." Margret looked sideways at the beautiful profile of the girl beside her, which now clearly showed all her wilful determination in the upward tilt of her chin and the well-defined jaw. "Destiny always changes things, lassie. 'Tis destiny itself that canna be changed."

"That's daft talk, and I'm not sure I believe it! A person's own will is stronger than some unseen force plotting every move we make! Otherwise there's no sense getting out of bed each day. We may as well just lie there and let destiny do what it will with us."

"Katrina, your mammie would have plenty to say about such wild talk. And where's your loyalty, lassie? Why do ye look downcast for Scotland's hopes?"

"I'm not! But I'm loyal to my Jamie, too, and I'm feared that if he goes to fight for the prince, he'll be killed, and I'll never see him again, and I couldn't bear it, I couldn't!"

To her own horror, the tears streamed down her cheeks as the thought tore into her mind. She had put the fear into words, and if shame was attached to it, she couldn't help it. She felt the fierce heat in her cheeks as she knew the words to be treasonable against the Jacobite cause. But a cause that had barely begun . . . that had had no place in their lives until a short while past . . . It was difficult to readjust her thinking to all that lay ahead, and as the tears cooled her flushed face she felt Margret's arms around her.

"Hush now, my bairn, 'tis the most natural thing in the world for ye to feel that way, but your Jamie is made of tough

Highland stock, strong as the earth. His is the sort that survives, come what may."

"I wish I had your confidence," Katrina said thickly.

"Be as sure as your heart tells ye, lassie. Want him back enough, and he'll come back to ye."

"There's no doubting that I'll want him back, Margret!" They were nearing the cottage, and she heard herself give a strained laugh. "We're talking as if 'twere a foregone fact already, Margret. As if the parting were already certain."

"So it is, my lamb, so it is." Margret almost intoned the words, and now a shiver as cold as mountain air crawled over Katrina's skin. Whether or not she had the sight, old Margret's eyes held a bleakness at that moment, as if she were seeing something that Katrina could not see and refused to see. The shivering stayed with her until the two of them had entered the cottage, with its familiar smells of peat and baking and wool spinning.

"Where is Angus, Margret?" Katrina said abruptly. He should have been away in the hills, tending his sheep, but she had the uncanny feeling that he was not. Margret confirmed this after a moment's hesitation.

"Gone to find out what he can of the matter," she said, as if an obscure reference were all that was necessary. And so it was, for Katrina knew then why there were no kilted Highlanders dotting the hills and glens with the bright splashes of color from their plaids. They would be at their various clan meets called by the lairds; the tacksmen and the humblies . . . or gone by themselves to see what they could glean about the prince's arrival.

Margret was moving about the tiny cottage and bringing them both a cool drink. And still there was that burning sense of resentment in Katrina, that she had not been told and that she had been too blind to see.

"Did ye have some secret informer telling ye about the Stuart, Margret?" she said flatly.

"None but my own canny thoughts. And they tell me that as long as a Stuart draws breath he'll be ready to fight for his birthright. And as long as Scotland lives, there will be loyalists ready to follow him."

Katrina swallowed down her drink, the cool barley water

trickling down her dry throat, and then she rose to go. She was too restless to remain still anywhere for long. She told Margret she was going to find Jamie, and she knew she had better not stay long, for her mammie was already out of sorts with her.

She left Margret, feeling stifled by the cloying atmosphere of the cottage, feeling as out of step with herself as it was possible to be. And out of step with everyone else in her immediate circle, she thought wanly. That destiny, at which she had scoffed, was shaping their lives, imperiously overriding the mere wishes of a young woman in love as if she were of no more importance than a grain of sand on a beach. She felt that her life became puny and insignificant when measured against the greater pattern of things, which now included the arrival of Charles Edward Stuart from over the sea.

It was not often that Katrina's thoughts were so gloomy and introspective. For the first time in her life she was forced to think of deeper values. And she was not ready; she was far from ready. . . .

The Mackinnon house was nearer to Margret's cottage than her own, hidden in the folds and hollows of the glen, and she felt a comforting surge of relief as she saw Callum Mackinnon walking with his awkward gait toward her as she neared it. He kissed her soundly, thinking as always that his son would have a lovely young bride in due course, and that young Katrina would surely not be disappointed in her lusty husband. But she would be disappointed now, when he told her that Jamie was away from home.

She hardly needed to ask where he had gone. But ask it she must, declining to go inside the house if Jamie was not there. She had already tarried too long, and Mairi would be angry with her again.

"He was away at daybreak, lassie," Callum informed her. "I might have gone with him but for this accursed leg. He would have ridden to tell ye of his movements, then decided not to waste a moment but to inform ye of events when he returned."

"Then he will return?" Katrina said through lips that felt suddenly wooden. First her father, now Jamie. . . .

"Of course he will, lassie. If the story be true, and we've every reason to think it is, then there'll be much to do before an army is on the march! Once Jamie comes home, we'll be clearer as to what's to do. I promise ye he'll be with ye the minute he's able. Who would not, with such a bonnie lassie waiting?"

His teasing failed to charm her. Burning with frustration, she bade him good-bye abruptly and turned on her heel. Callum stared after her. He did not really sense her mood, but something had made him hold his tongue instead of relating his own and Jamie's talk in the early dawn of the morning.

"Find out all ye can, lad, and take my good wishes with ye. I'd be by your side—but ye'll do the work of two men if the cause requires it, and I've no doubt of that, Jamie."

"I promise it," Jamie vowed. "And I promise ye that the English bastards won't be unaware of a Mackinnon presence, Faither. Ye have my word on it. Callum Mackinnon's voice will be heard through me when the time comes."

It had been as solemn a vow as a sworn oath, and both men knew by the clasping of palm against powerful palm that Jamie would honor it. And if his son had to die for it, Callum thought as he watched Katrina Fraser walking away from him, then so be it. His loss and the lassie's would be immeasurable, but the pride and honor of Scotland must supersede all personal values.

As she walked, Katrina, too, had her own images of the future, and the disappointment she felt at not seeing Jamie that day was slightly tempered by a curiosity at Callum's words. An army could not be conjured up out of thin air, and however much the loyalist Jacobites had longed for a new uprising, they could hardly have been prepared to move at a moment's notice. Her thoughts shifted to the ancient clan system of rousing support.

In some cases, where the clan chiefs and the family members, the tacksmen or tenants, and those who allied themselves to a clan lived within sight and sound of each other, the rallying was merely a matter of word of mouth. What the chief decreed would be obeyed, for all his followers believed themselves to be descended from the same stock and looked to the chief for protection and punishment. He was the father figure, landlord, and judge. Where a clan was more scattered, the rallying could be made by beacons led through the glens, or more dramatically by the fiery cross sent over the land—two burning sticks tied with a strip of linen stained with blood. Passed from hand to hand by runners, it could travel many miles in a few hours, and a clan summoned by the cross dared not disobey its order.

Katrina shivered, remembering the tales told to her and her brother and sister, tales that had seemed legendary and a part of history. Now, the legends could be enacted in the Highlands for Charles Stuart's cause. The main body of their own Fraser clan lived away to the east, but there was hardly need to rouse them, for they were staunchly loyalist, and so were the Mackinnons. Others . . . For the first time Katrina wondered if all men would leave their homes so readily.

It was three days before Duncan Fraser came home again. In that time the household was filled with increasing tension, the younger children often banished to the schoolroom to stop their blathering. Even Katrina was glad to take refuge there from time to time. By now, Charles Stuart's name was spoken openly, and it seemed hard to realize that he had never set foot on his native shores before now.

"I wish Faither would let me go to war," Hamish frequently sulked. "I'm well able to hold a broadsword and fire a pistol."

Hannah's prim mouth became even tighter as she scolded him, the iron-gray of her hair tight in its coiled bun, her flat chest managing to heave just a little.

" 'Tis a fine thing to be loyal to your faither's beliefs, Hamish, but there's a time for learning and a time for warring. And your time has not come yet, laddie. God save ye from ever having to go to a war."

He glared at her. "That's women's talk," he said defiantly. "I wish Faither were here now. He'd not make me listen to it."

"That's enough, Hamish!" Hannah said coldly. "While ye're in the schoolroom, ye'll mind your manners and hold your tongue if ye've nothing more to say."

"He thinks he's a man already," Katrina said. "Mammie's thankful he's not old enough to join the prince. We'll need him here to defend us."

Hamish reddened, taking offense at the jesting.

"So I will, if the need arises. What will ye be doing the while your Jamie's away, anyway? Pulling sad faces and making us wish ye'd gone with him?"

"Katrina can't go with him. She's a lassie," Iona said suddenly, and then her small mouth began to tremble, and tears blurred her eyes at the sight of the three other faces in the schoolroom.

"I don't like your talk of fighting," Iona said shrilly. "I don't want to speak of it. It frightens me!"

Before any of them could comfort her the door had opened and Duncan stood there, hearing her small outburst and frowning at it. He had ridden hard to be back with his family as soon as possible, and this little scene was not to his liking. As soon as Iona saw him she hurled herself into his arms, where he swung her up in his great embrace at once.

"What's all this, my bairn? Who's frightening ye?"

"Hamish is cross because he can't go and fight, and Katrina's got the dumps because Jamie's going away," Iona sobbed. "And Hannah's cross as well."

"I'm not surprised, with the three of ye playacting," Duncan said mildly. "Just calm yourselves, because nobody's rushing off to fight this minute."

The question burned to be asked, but Katrina knew it had best wait until Iona at least was out of earshot. And knowing the two younger ones were still to be taught for another hour yet, she slipped down the stairs to join Mairi in the dining hall, where she was putting food on the table for Duncan's pleasure.

"Has Faither told you his news, Mammie?" she said at once, to be met with a shake of the head and the short reply that he would speak to them both when he had seen the bairns. Katrina was still somewhat out of favor with her mother; there was a new restraint between them. It was a relief when Duncan joined them and began to eat the cold beef Mairi had put ready for him with the warm-baked bread and soft crowdie cheese, swilled down with a long draught of ale.

"So will ye tell us, Duncan? For we're bursting to know," Mairi said finally, knowing that Katrina couldn't keep silent much longer, but that her man wouldn't be hurried when he had an empty belly to be filled.

"Ye'll know that what our neighbors told us was correct by now. Charles Stuart's ship landed on Eriskay in the Outer Hebrides, and he arrived with seven men and some arms and baggage. A fine start to an army," Duncan said grimly, "but 'twas his misfortune that the ship that sailed with him was sunk, along with many more supplies and men. Support for his cause was expected at once, and messages had been sent for clan chiefs or their representatives to visit him as soon as possible. And that's when he got his first shock, too."

"What kind of shock? He got the support, did he not?" Mairi said in disbelief.

Duncan shook his head. "Not from the Macleods of Skye, nor the MacDonalds of Boisdale, both of whom he had expected to rally for him. It was a sharp blow to his pride, but then he chose to leave the islands and make for the mainland, and now the ship, the *Du Teillay*, is anchored in Loch nan Uamh, on the coast of Arisaig. The prince awaits supporters and will make his decision on where to raise his father's standard."

"And ye've given your support?" Mairi said at once.

"That I have," Duncan said with quiet pride.

"And Jamie?" Katrina's voice was unnaturally low, listening to all this as if she were in a dream. Not wanting it to happen and knowing she should be following her family's lead. She should be as fervent a loyalist as they, and so far she was not. But that was a secret she tried to keep to herself.

"Jamie came to the ship with me and some others." Duncan nodded. "There was much dissent between some of the clan representatives who consider the prince's cause a foolhardy one. It seems that even his father did not know he had set sail from France until he was on his way. This was a secret undertaking, yet the Jacobite agents had word of his progress all the way and still hardly believed he would come so ill equipped."

"He would not be, had the other ship been saved," Mairi pointed out. "But ye've said what support the prince did'na get. What of those who will rally?"

Duncan shrugged. "Among the first of his visitors was the

young Cameron, Lochiel, who was strongly opposed to leading the clan Cameron for the prince. His brother had already tried to persuade him not even to meet the prince, but Lochiel had his way and after much argument seemed to have been completely won over by the force of the Stuart's personality. He is truly a man of charm and persuasion, and of striking looks. Lochiel was worried that the lack of support would mean the cause was doomed from the start, but the Stuart has a fine turn of speech, too. Not quite mocking, but bringing a man's pride to the fore.''

"In what way?'' Mairi said, and Duncan gave a chuckle, remembering.

"Why, while Lochiel was still blundering about whether to call out the Camerons or not, the prince said in a cool voice, 'With the few friends I have, I will erect the royal standard. Lochiel may stay at home.' To which Lochiel replied very quickly, 'No! I shall share the fate of my prince.' ''

"I hope those words are not prophetic,'' Katrina murmured.

Her father looked at her keenly. "I trust that they are if victory is to be his fate, lass.''

"And where is Jamie now?'' She had caught the annoyed look from her mother at her words and turned the conversation quickly to her personal anxiety.

"Not yet come home, dearie. He's riding the country hereabouts to find the mood of the Highlanders and has promised to be with ye as soon as he can. He knows ye'll understand, and he sends ye his love.''

Bright patches of color burned in Katrina's cheeks. She jumped up from her seat.

"No, I don't understand! I don't like this talk of war and causes any more than Iona does! I'm sick of it already, when it takes my Jamie away from me—''

"Katrina, that's enough!'' Duncan roared at her. "I'll not have my own bairn speak in such a way under my own roof! If ye canna keep a civil tongue in your head and stop acting the lovesick calf, then get out of my sight.''

"I will!'' she shouted back. "I wish I could be miles away from here, where I did'na have to hear the name of Charles Stuart!''

She ducked quickly as Duncan's arm came out to strike

her. He, who had never struck any of his children in anger, was suddenly incensed by this chit of a lassie who dared to defy him and bring shame to his house. He thanked God that his walls were thick and his neighbors scattered, so that they could not hear it.

"Ye'd better be away to your own room and look to your own thoughts, lass, for I'll have no such talk in my hearing," he thundered. "And there'll be no supper for ye. Mebbe a pang or two in your belly will make ye give mind to the gut pangs Scotland has for her own king instead of the German the English pay court to and expect us to do the same. Away with ye, before I give ye a thrashing!"

Katrina stormed out of the dining hall, crashing the door behind her. Yes, she knew all about the German King George who now ruled the English because of his feeble family links with the British monarchy! And yes, she could understand why the more avid Jacobites were affronted by the fact. But this Charles Edward, who had seemed as unreal a person as any other in a history lesson, was just as much a foreigner! Katrina knew she would get the promised thrashing if she dared to say so, for she recognized the light in her father's eyes that said this time he meant exactly what he said, and there would be no indulgences.

Were they all besotted by the prince's arrival? She threw off her clothes and climbed between the cold sheets, despite the early hour. Did they not see that the man was just as much a foreigner as the Hanoverian George, despite his father being the Scot that he was? Charles had been born in Rome and was therefore an Italian. She had the cold logical thoughts of a man at that moment, but it seemed it was the men of the Highlands who were swept up in the sudden lust for war and an ancient claim to a birthright. Maybe she should be, too . . . but it was still unreal to her. Maybe when she saw the man for the flesh-and-blood being that he was, she would understand this fervor. But not yet . . . not yet.

And even a long while later, when the shadows in her room had deepened and a servant had brought her some hot chocolate and a bite of bread and cheese on her mammie's orders after all, Katrina could not lose her resentment—against her father and his anger that had mortified her so, against even

Jamie for being so long away from her, and mostly against Charles Stuart, who had already caused these upsets and threatened to cause a great many more. She had no reason to thank the prince for being here. She was not even going to like him.

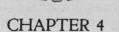

CHAPTER 4

Jamie came to Frashiel House several days later, but Katrina had already begun to feel she had lost him to the new fervor that seemed to infiltrate the glens. The Highlanders were quick to rouse, always ready to defend or attack, and Jamie had the same fierce ancestry. She ran to meet him the day she saw him riding toward the house on the sturdy little mare he favored. He slid from the mare's back and caught Katrina up in his arms at once, and she could tell from the horse's lather and his own body sweat that he had ridden a distance already that day.

"Jamie, Jamie, I've missed ye," she breathed at once, thinking of nothing else for the moment.

"And I you, my dearest one." He held her close, drinking in the sweetness of her, when he knew he stank of horses and seawater from the loch and God knew what else. But this was no time to be anxious for such things. "Is your faither home?"

"Aye," she replied. "And ye've come to tell us ye're leaving us, is that it?" She tried not to let the bitterness show in her voice, but he could read it in her eyes and hugged her to him again. Did she really think he would leave her side if not for something of such great importance! It was the first time in their lives they had met such a crisis as this, and Katrina must understand that a man's duty came above all things, even the great love of a woman.

"Not yet, but soon," he said steadily. He put his arm about her, spanning her small waist and squeezing her to him as they went inside the house together. How many more times would they walk like this, be together like this?

Duncan Fraser clasped Jamie's strong forearm in greeting, his face filled with anticipation, knowing Jamie could only bring one kind of news.

"The prince has called for the army to be assembled on the nineteenth day of August, a week from now," Jamie said. " 'Twill give sufficient time for the clans to rally and for leaders to be chosen among those already sworn to support him. It would be unwise to delay longer. The English would be alerted to his presence, if they are not already, and his ship will be sent back to France with the report of his successful landing and the hope that the French will then send more supplies and arms."

"The English will know by now!" Katrina burst out. "What of those spies and agents of whom ye once spoke?"

"Hush your tongue, Katrina," her father said coldly, not wanting this moment to be spoiled. "Ye've told us the date, Jamie, and what of the place?"

"Glenfinnan. Ye'll know of it. A good choice for an army to camp in that vast bay, and 'twill be a fine setting for the prince to raise his father's standard."

Katrina managed to bite her tongue from making the remark that Charles must have a fine sense of the dramatic to choose such a stunningly beautiful glen for his moment of glory. It was a most beautiful place, the meeting of two lochs surrounded by towering mountains. But of course Charles Stuart would not know the place. He was still a stranger to Scottish shores and would simply have been advised on it. She tried to be generous in her thoughts and not bitter.

"And from that moment, the cause will be recognized by all," Duncan commented. " 'Twill be a moment to be kept for the history books."

"Aye, but for now, history is ours for the making," Jamie said as solemnly.

Katrina listened to the two of them, wishing she were out with Mairi and the bairns and not an unwilling participant in the Stuart plans. With every word, it became more real; she was suddenly having to share Jamie with the prince, and she wanted all of him. She felt the need of Jamie's arms around her, reassuring her that there was still a time for lovers, in the midst of a world that was changing. As if he realized it, too, he told her he must go to inform his father, since he had ridden to Frashiel House first, but they could share half an hour together if she had a mind for it. A week ago he would not have needed to ask, nor would he have done so.

He left the horse tethered at the house, where Duncan's man saw to the rubbing down and feeding of the animal, and Jamie and Katrina walked the verdant glen as they had done a thousand times before, reaching their favorite hollow. For once, he seemed insensitive to her mood. If she was quieter than usual, he never noticed it, for he was too caught up in the great adventure that was about to begin. Jamie could think of it in no other terms. A lad of an age little more than his own, whether prince or not, was about to lead an army on an audacious mission, a bid for a crown, and it stirred Jamie's heart to be a part of it.

He was well aware of the growing excitement within him, different from the excitement that came from loving and wanting Katrina. This was pure male energy of a different kind, one that separated the sexes more fundamentally than shape or physical attributes, and it was a feeling new and heady to Jamie. Katrina sensed it without fully understanding it, knowing only that already he had gone to a place she couldn't reach.

But here, in their hollow, he pulled her to him with all the fervor she could wish, and for long moments she was lost in his kisses, forgetting everything but the warmth of being his love, his wanted one. She held him, wishing to hold this lovely moment close to her forever, to cherish every moment she shared with Jamie from now on. . . .

"Ye're cold, lassie. Let me warm ye."

He wrapped the length of his plaid around her, circling them both within its rough warmth. But she wasn't cold, not physically so, and she was not one to hold back her innermost feelings, especially from him.

"I'm feared for ye, Jamie. I don't know how I shall get through the days without ye if ye go."

"*If* I go?" He caught on the word and looked deeply into her eyes. "Would ye have me afraid to fight for the cause? Is it not your pride as well as mine to send me into battle with a smile and a kiss? Ye would'na have me disloyal and cowardly enough to stay behind because of a lassie's tears?"

She was helpless against such talk. She swallowed the lump in her throat as she shook her head.

"But I shall miss ye so. . . ."

"I'd expect ye to miss me, woman! What kind of betrothed would it be who did'na miss her man when he was absent? 'Twill be the same for me, and pray God the uprising will'na be a lengthy one, for I canna stay away from ye too long."

"Not even for your prince?" she whispered, knowing the answer and tormenting herself further by asking it.

"Aye, for the prince alone," Jamie acknowledged. "None other would take me from your side, henny, and well ye know it. And I canna tell how long it will be that the skirmish lasts, but ye'll hear of our victories soon enough. The air will crackle with news of them, and ye can spend the time planning our wedding with your mammie."

She felt his rough hand caress her body, moving gently to the front of her bodice. He wanted her as he had always wanted her, but the urgency of his need had lessened a little. Once, knowing her so pliant and near to tears, Jamie might have made more of the moment, but even as she swayed toward him she knew that it was too late. Her silent offer of surrender seemed not to affect him, and it made her even more resentful against the prince and his cause.

Jamie said that he must go to his father; they rose from the flattened grassy bed together, still clinging, and it was Jamie who loosened her arms from about his neck. They walked back to Frashiel House together, and then he was touching his lips to hers in one last sweet kiss and saying he would see her again soon. Before Glenfinnan. . . . Her world had started to crumble with the inclusion of those two words in her head. But after Glenfinnan?

There were many meetings of men and priests, and many avowals of loyalty in the days that followed. Some reports said that already certain individuals had begun to camp in the hills near Glenfinnan, where there was shelter at night from the bleak winds that blew through the glens. Others said that more clans had given word to the prince that they would rally behind him, notably the MacDonalds of Keppoch and Glencoe, with the Macleods still refusing to enlist their men, still calling the uprising foolhardy and reckless and too risky.

On the day of the 19th of August, the Fraser family and their tacksmen who were following Duncan's lead prepared to ride or walk to Glenfinnan, some thirty miles distant. The walkers were up before dawn and away, some in boots, many in bare feet, well used to the roughness of mountain and glen, their feet hardened to the toughness of hide.

Mairi Fraser and her three children rose early, too, to prepare for the day when Duncan would become part of Charles Stuart's army. Like most of the women that day, Katrina wore the Highland dress, the arisaid shawl over a simple dress and brooched up to her right shoulder with the Fraser pin, which left the floating portion of the garment gracefully gathered over her left arm. The women's garb made a spectacular addition to the peacock display of the men, with their ox-hide shields and their plaids and dirks, broadswords, and blue Highland bonnets. Small groups of similar families moved steadily toward Glenfinnan, and the Frasers and the Mackinnons met on the way.

For a while longer, they could all be together, and Katrina cherished the thought, knowing an undeniable feeling of pride at the way Jamie sat so tall and powerfully on his mare. With his red hair and strong physique, he was like a magnificent red deer that roamed the glens, she thought again, with a catch in her throat. He was everything she loved.

In the early morning of August the 19th, three boats moved silently along the loch in the direction of Glenfinnan. Charles Stuart scanned the horizon from one of the boats, his small group of supporters uneasily doing the same. The glen ahead looked more beautiful than his father had once described the Scottish glens to be, breathtakingly so in the virginal calm of the morning, the mist still lingering on the hills, the great mass of the mountains seeming to protect everything that lay below. It was beautiful . . . and it was also a silent, lonely place. For all his optimism and determination, Charles felt very much alone.

49

Behind him, on its way back to France now, was the ship that had brought him here, the *Du Teillay*. With him were his seven trusted men and others who were unquestionably loyal, a goodly supply of French money, a small amount of arms, and the baggage necessary for a prince. It seemed precious little, especially when ahead of him lay a land he did not know and a people he had yet to win over. The people were his, by right, but still ruled by the usurper of his father's kingdom. He had been schooled in those terms since babyhood, and all the years of his youth had been leading him to this day.

"We shall land at a spot a little way from Glenfinnan, sir," said the man at his elbow.

The prince nodded his agreement. "It seems abysmally silent," Charles observed. "Where are the crowds, the clansmen, the cheering? Do they not know the importance of this day?"

"I am certain that they do, sir. Be patient, I implore ye."

"Patient I am not," Charles said shortly.

"We have some way to go yet, sir, and the day is still early. The Highlands are vast, and some will take considerable time to get here. The bishop of Morar will be at the landing place to greet ye, I'm assured of that."

His words were met with a grunt of dismissal as Charles recalled the strong opposition he had received from some of the clan chiefs visiting him on the *Du Teillay*. To one of the MacDonalds who had advised him in no uncertain terms to go home, he had replied, "I am home, sir, and I will not return to the place from whence I came, for I know that my faithful Highlanders will stand by me!"

Fine words, but as Charles let his gaze roam over the beautiful mainland ahead of him, he found himself wondering what kind of home was this Scotland that did not appear too eager to greet its prince? Where were all the encampments he had envisaged? To be sure, he had been told of the numerous folds and pockets in the hills and glens where a man could hide for days without detection if need be, but he had expected his followers to be less inhibited on this day, completely overlooking the years of domination by the English government when even to mention the name of his father

James had been high treason. Charles was a mite put out and was not good at hiding his disappointment.

He had thought of wearing full Highland attire to greet his followers but had decided against it. That could come later. He was a fine figure now in a fawn-colored coat and knee breeches, a scarlet-laced waistcoat, and a yellow-bobbed hat. He had the good fortune to have the regal looks and bearing of a prince, which added to his presence, and he knew that he fully intended to capitalize on it when necessary. It had already stood him in good stead in swaying such a man as Donald Cameron of Lochiel to calling out the Cameron clan for the cause. Charles had been very taken with Lochiel and was pleased to have his support. But where was he now in this silent place?

The boats pulled alongside the mainland, and Charles stepped out onto the marshy ground, helped by his aides. Waiting as promised was the bishop of Morar. The bishop bowed low and greeted the prince warmly.

"Welcome, sir. If you will do me the honor to follow me, there is a place where you can rest until the clansmen come."

"They do not do me the honor of awaiting me?" Charles could not resist saying.

"Some are encamped in the hills, sir, but the morning is cold and your time of arrival uncertain."

"It has taken more than a cold wind to keep me from my people," he retorted with a small show of arrogance. "But no matter. Lead the way, my lord bishop."

The whole party walked the short distance to the narrow valley flanked by craggy mountains where Glenfinnan Bay opened out. A small hut was situated nearby, and it was to this place that the bishop led the prince. A humble resting place for a prospective future monarch, but Charles made no comment and went inside the hut to wait, out of the chill wind, his supporters keeping watch outside.

From time to time they reported the small groups of plaid-garbed clansmen appearing, as if they, too, awaited the next move. Charles became impatient as time passed—an hour, then two, then more. . . .

"I cannot believe Lochiel has failed me!" he exclaimed, stepping out of the mean hut time and again, clearly agitated now. "Nor those others who swore their loyalty. What keeps them, Bishop? How can they be so tardy, when so much depends on it?"

The men looked at each other uneasily, their glances shifting away as each wondered whether disaster was already near. Had King George's army been so alerted of the prince's movements that this place was a hideous trap after all? Were they, even now, surrounded and about to be slain?

As each fell silent, unnerved, a strange thin sound began to fill the air. Unearthly at first, the high wailing sound gradually developed into the skirl of the pipes and seemed to swell and echo throughout the glens and reverberate off the mountains. And with the sound, the watchers near the hut saw the first of a great company of Highlanders come over the brow of a hill, the plaid of their kilts swinging, blue bonnets on their heads. Their shields were before them, swords and dirks gleaming in the sunlight. In two long marching lines, the Camerons marched down to Glenfinnan, led by Donald Cameron of Lochiel. Heralded by the triumphant sound of the pipes, the first seven hundred men of Charles Stuart's army had arrived.

"Now is the time, Your Highness," one of Charles's men said in a husky voice, clearly affected by the sight of the Camerons and mightily relieved to see them. "Should we not now go to the spot to receive your Highlanders?"

Charles, too, felt vastly moved; Lochiel had not let him down. With the bishop of Morar, his own loyal friends, and those who had gathered in from the hills as if awaiting the signal that had come with the Camerons, he moved toward the spot chosen to unfurl his father's standard. Accompanying them was the old duke of Atholl, who was to read the proclamation. It had been written by Charles's father in December of 1743, when the uprising had been planned for 1744 and then abandoned, and it had been kept safely in the Prince's possession until now.

Duncan Fraser heard the skirling of the Cameron pipes in the distance as he and his family and the Mackinnon men neared Glenfinnan. Duncan held up his hand a moment, and the group halted. Then they, too, saw the great double column of men and heard the great swell of sound, and it was as if the mountains held it, rejoiced in it, and sent it back a thousandfold to stir the hearts and souls of all those it touched.

Katrina drew in her breath, never having seen so many marching men in one body in her life. To her it was an army already. And despite all her doubts and fears and reservations, the flicker of pride inside her was fast becoming a flame as she watched the proud progress of the Camerons.

They had passed camps where men were stirring, and the trickle of rebels—for that was what they would be called, as in those other uprisings—was becoming a steady stream of the determined, the curious, the fanatic.

"I never thought it would be like this," Katrina murmured to Jamie, as he rode alongside her. "I never thought there would be so many."

"Ye did'na have my faith, then." He smiled mockingly at her, though truth to tell Jamie had expected many more to be here at Glenfinnan. There had been the MacDonalds who had sworn their allegiance, and more . . . but he would not tell Katrina any of that. It was better that she thought the numbers so great, though if this was the strength of Charles Stuart's opposition to King George's army, then they would be crushed from the very beginning. . . .

"We had best move forward if we're to see or hear anything at all," Duncan said crisply. "The Camerons will break ranks as soon as they're into the glen, and the womenfolk will be wanting to see the prince."

"So do I!" Hamish said, still smarting that he was not to be enlisting his services with the men but not daring to go against his father's wishes. Iona was too dumbstruck to say anything and held tightly before her mother on the gentle mare that Mairi mounted.

"Will he wear a crown?" Iona asked suddenly, then went a fiery red as her brother hooted with laughter at her.

"Ye've been listening to Hannah's fairy tales again, ye ninny. He'll be wearing the kilt."

"That's where ye're wrong, laddie, and dinna be so quick to mock the bairn," his father chastised him as they rode nearer to the scene and the important group of men appeared, surrounding a simply clad young man with a vivid red waistcoat and yellow hat, tall and noble-looking, with an air of the dashing adventurer about him.

"There is your prince," Jamie whispered in Katrina's ear. "Does he not cut a fine figure? Do ye see now how he charms all those who see him?"

"I see it, but I don't hear it yet." She would not let herself be persuaded yet, either.

"Aye, well, I think ye'll like his way of speaking, then. He speaks the language well, but there's an accent to his voice that a lassie might find pleasing."

She gave a short laugh. "Well, ye've no need to feel jealousy on my account, Jamie Mackinnon! And well ye know it!"

All the same, Prince Charles was a very handsome young man, she was thinking, the more so as he stood so straight and alone. Even though he was surrounded by the group of dukes and a bishop and others, it struck Katrina that he was very much alone. And facing this fierce-looking mass of blue-bonneted, tangle-haired Highlanders, some with outlandish weapons, he could well be alarmed rather than pleased. If he was, he gave no inkling of it.

The pipes, and the uproar among the Highlanders and the spectators, dwindled away as the bishop called for silence and bade them all welcome on behalf of His Highness, Prince Charles Edward Stuart, the rightful heir to King James the Eighth's kingdom of Scotland and England, Ireland and their islands. A great roar of approval went up at that, a daring proclamation.

"I will now ask His Grace, the duke of Atholl, to raise the standard of His Royal Majesty, King James the Eighth, and to read the declaration on his behalf. His Grace, the duke of Atholl."

All who watched could not be unaffected by the solemnity of the simple ceremony, made all the more moving because as the old and frail duke held the royal standard and attempted to unfurl it, he needed help from the young prince. As the red-and-white silk of the royal standard fluttered in the breeze, a roar like thunder broke from the throats of those watching. While the bishop of Morar fought to make himself heard, to bless the standard, a great chant in the Gaelic tongue rose up from the Highlanders.

"Prionnsa Tearlach, righ nan Ghaidheil!"

Prince Charlie, king of the Gael . . . of all those who spoke the Gaelic tongue.

The old duke stepped forward when the chanting had stopped and read the lengthy and complicated declaration written by James for his people. Few could follow the pompous language. Read in the duke's slow, quavering voice, the speech took half an hour to deliver and told them little more than they already knew—that Charles Edward, James's dearly beloved son, was hereby appointed as regent on his behalf and entrusted with his kingdom.

At last the duke finished speaking, and almost as he did so more cheering rang out. Not merely with relief that he had finished, and that their prince was now going to address them at last, but from the arrival of a new influx of Highlanders—Keppoch, with the MacDonalds, and those from Glencoe and Glengarry, numbering about three hundred in all and swelling the size of the gathering considerably. With the individuals and the small family groups who would join with their clan allies, Charles had mustered about twelve hundred men at Glenfinnan. And now at last, he addressed them in simple words, without the flowery speech of which he was so fond, in stark and deliberate contrast to his father's words.

"My dear friends," he said in his lilting accent, "my friends and brothers in the cause, I bid you welcome, as you have bade me welcome by your presence here. I thank you from my heart, and on behalf of my father, your king.

"You all know why I have come. With my own money, I hired a small vessel. Ill supplied with money, arms, or friends, I arrived in Scotland attended by seven persons. I have now published the King my father's declaration and proclaim his title. The goodness of Almighty God has protected me thus far, and, I believe implicitly, will protect us all through the dangers to which we shall be exposed. Will you follow me to victory, to the ancient capital of this kingdom, and to the restoration of what is my father's birthright?"

The roar of approval interrupted his flow of words. Impassioned, warmed by their response, the prince gave them a last promise.

"I will not fail you, and if God is willing, we shall all be victorious in our endeavors to beat the oppressors of our country, for those who crush a nation for their religious beliefs are not worthy to live. Together, we will be the victors!"

The roar of applause that followed his words was deafening. Huzzas and shouts of joy rang out as blue bonnets were hurled into the air in a wild exuberance. However reluctant some of those present had been to rally—the MacDonalds and the tacksmen who had been persuaded in no uncertain manner by their chiefs—all were now swept on in a great surge of patriotic fervor. At that moment, the world was theirs for the conquering.

Once the ceremony was over, the bishop announced that the prince would retire and consider selecting his officers. The organization of the army into leaders and regiments would begin the following day, and those present must see to their own accommodation for the night. Since most were equipped with tents and cooking pots and a basic supply of food, and were used to fending for themselves from loch or glen on the natural foods that nature supplied, this presented no surprise or problem.

"Ye'd best be getting back home, my dearie," Duncan Fraser told his wife. "There's clearly no more for the women-folk here today. Take the bairns and make your way safely, with Callum to protect ye. When I discover what the orders are to be, I'll try to get back to ye before we march. If not, then keep safe, my dear one."

He clasped her in his arms, then the children. Iona was too overcome to be aware of all that was happening; Hamish was still incensed at not being a part of it; Katrina, like Mairi, had to hold back the tears at parting. For Katrina, however, it was a double parting: after her father's embrace, it was Jamie's strong arms that held her fast to him, and Jamie's kiss she sought. She touched his face, as if to imprint its memory on her mind, and as she did so his brooch scratched her hand, and a small spot of blood appeared there. He kissed it away, and she refused to think of the sight as an omen, thinking only that he took a small speck of her with him in the kiss.

"Try to see me before ye leave, Jamie," she said unsteadily. "And come back. Come home safe to me."

"I promise. Dinna fret yourself, my Katrina. Just think of me with love."

"Always, my dearie. Never doubt it." She was too filled with emotion to say more, not wanting him to see her weep. Her mammie's head was held high, sending her man to fight for the Stuart cause, and Katrina would be no less stoical. There was glory in the day after all, even for Katrina, who had been so reluctant to believe it. With a sudden wave of fervor, she knew that had she been a man she, too, would be riding alongside Jamie. Until that moment, she had never acknowledged the fact, never thought of anything but her own loss in seeing him go to war, never believed that she was capable of such depth of feeling. In that instant Katrina knew she was at one with every other loyalist at Glenfinnan.

For a moment she caught the look in her mother's eyes and knew that it matched her own. However much she had fought against it, there was a pride in sending a man into battle and knowing herself to be a woman who would share every danger with her man if the need arose.

There were many family groups of spectators like themselves straggling away from Glenfinnan now, women and children, and the old men who had seen other Jacobite uprisings and were maybe sorry they could take no part in this one. It was a small comfort for the Frasers to have Callum Mackinnon riding alongside them, and Mairi asked him to come back to the house to eat with them that evening. She knew that his pride would be bruised for having to side with the too young and the too old, when it was merely a stiffened leg that prevented him riding beside his son.

"I'd like that, Mairi," Callum said. "Your house is wi'out its man, and mine is wi'out its son. 'Tis fitting that we share the same table this night."

"The prince had a good turnout of men, did he not?" Mairi asked as conversationally as if she asked the time of day.

"He did that," Callum answered. "And let's pray to God the luck will be on his side, lassie."

Luck. They would need plenty of luck, Katrina thought. And plenty of planning, too. How did one organize an army? She could not guess at it, but long before she and her family had reached Frashiel House, Charles Stuart was already calling his men and his chiefs together, discussing their strategy and appointing leaders. As commander-in-chief, Charles needed generals, but few of those at Glenfinnan had had military training, except Keppoch. He had served in the French army, he informed the prince, and so, too, had one of Charles's companions on the *Du Teillay*, John William O'Sullivan, whom Charles appointed his quartermaster and adjutant-general.

The plan was to capture Edinburgh, the government-held capital, as the major prize for the present. Once Charles had Edinburgh, he would march into England. The plan was simple, the operation of it less straightforward than it sounded.

"We have plenty of agents and scouts to report back to us," Charles declared to his company that night. By then he was resplendent in full Highland attire, to his rebels' delight, and discussing tactics with them like the diplomat he was, drawing them into his every move, so that they felt a part of his cause from the outset. "How else do you think I chose this moment to arrive here, my friends, and with the knowledge that I have of the enemy's movements?"

"What movements, sir?" one Highlander asked boldly.

Charles smiled on him benignly. "Why, that the bulk of the English army is away fighting the French at this very moment, and that only the dregs are here in Scotland under the command of Sir John Cope, an incompetent if ever there was one. Our agents have seen to it that Cope believes there are large numbers of French soldiers landing on the coast near Inverness. Who will wager with me that the English army will be led in that direction? While we, my friends, will be marching right across the country below them and capturing Edinburgh under the English noses!"

The huzzas rose again. The Highlanders knew nothing of Edinburgh and cities, but all knew it to be the seat of kings and therefore the rightful possession of James, the prince's father. And with the Highlanders' suspicion of city dwellers, it would be an added delight to subdue their high and mighty compatriots.

"Sir, we need more men," Lochiel made himself heard. "We are but a small army as yet."

"A small army will move more quickly to begin with," Charles said swiftly. "So far we are not hampered with carts and wagons and cannons. Though these will come later, when we take what the enemy will provide! As for wagons and supplies, you'll all receive modest payment for the present. I would ask for volunteers for bakers and cooks and those who have carts at their disposal and can get them here within the next few days. Any physicians among you report to Quartermaster Sullivan with your names, and any priests are especially welcomed and invited to join their clan regiments with the immediate rank of captain."

"He has not been idle," Jamie Mackinnon commented to Duncan as the list of requirements went on amidst satisfied grunts. "Does he impress ye, Duncan?"

"Aye, he does, and he's impressing all here, by the looks of it, lad."

Commenting on this later, when most were encamped for the night and the night fires showed like a thousand glow-worms in the glen, Duncan gave his own opinion of the rally to the cause.

"I doubt he knows how fortunate he is, Jamie, that the Camerons came out behind Lochiel for him. Without their support, the gathering here would have been a poor showing. He'll have little idea of the loyalty given to their clans by the Highlanders. Loyalty to the cause is still unreal to many, but to defy their clan chief is more serious, as well ye know."

"Aye," Jamie said cynically. "Serious enough for the chiefs to order their homes to be burned and the cattle slaughtered if they disobey, if all my faither tells me of past uprisings is to be believed. And of tacksmen being dragged from their beds if they were unwilling."

"Why should ye not believe it?" Duncan grunted. "Why should not dependents obey their chief? They look to him for protection, and he has the right to demand their all in return. No, we've done enough blathering, Jamie. I'm weary of it, and we should get some rest."

Duncan turned away, and Jamie saw at once that the older man was of exactly the same mind as his own father. Clan chiefs were to be obeyed unquestioningly, and if your clan was of the Jacobite persuasion, then you came out for the cause. Not all were, preferring to sway with the wind behind whichever government was in power. But if you disobeyed your chief, then you suffered the consequences.

Jamie had been fervently willing, as had Duncan Fraser, but for the first time he wondered how many of those here had been coerced into leaving homes and families to cheer themselves hoarse for a stranger.

They were a tough breed, lawless and brave, but in military matters they were as children. Jamie felt his mouth twist wryly in the darkness. He could not have chosen a more apt word to think of all those here, however unwillingly he did so. The Gaelic word *clann* meant children, and so they were.

CHAPTER 5

I*t was a few days more before the prince's army was ready* to march. By then some wagons had been produced, offered or taken, and food supplies organized. They were meager rations—oatmeal, flour for the bread making, cheese, biscuits, and some meat. Water was plentiful in the clear burns, and the Highlanders were well used to surviving in the hills on berries and plants and wild birds and animals; they were quite ready to supplement their rations by fending for themselves without a second thought.

More men had joined them by then, persuaded by the new priest captains or by less genteel methods. Tales among the Highlanders were varied and colorful, and not always to be believed as each either gloried in his new status or bitterly resented the fact that he was here at all.

In those few days, Jamie had managed to snatch a couple of hours to ride home, informing his father of the army's future movements, outlined by the prince and the leaders. Jamie badly wanted to see Katrina but decided against a brief visit to Frashiel House. He could not bear to see Katrina's joy turn to tears again when he had to leave her. They had already said good-bye, and Duncan Fraser, too, had made his good-byes to his family and was impatient for the army to be on the move, resisting the temptation to go home for a little time.

Finally the army was assembled to Charles's satisfaction. Those with horses looked good enough, though most of the animals were poor thin creatures. The vast majority of the men were on foot and well used to the terrain, which was unpredictable and full of deep valleys and mountainous passes, beautiful glens and wild scenic wildernesses. No clansman knew every inch of it intimately, but none was afraid of it, either, finding the rugged peaks and hidden clefts both a challenge and often a sanctuary in bitter weather or in conflict.

The prince rode a good horse, brought to him by loyalist friends. He rode in the middle of his army, the wagons behind him and more foot soldiers at the rear. He bore his father's standard, and those chiefs already assembled bore their own. They marched or rode proudly, the pipers heralding their progress as they went, and the combined pipes of the clans made an ear-splitting cacophony of sound.

Jamie glanced back, thinking with a burst of pride that they did at least resemble an army. They were in good formation and a formidable sight with their ox-hide shields and their weapons, however old and unused of late. They would give the English something to remember, Jamie thought grimly. His own clan, mostly scattered among the islands off the west coast, had turned out a respectable number, and this, too, filled him with pride. He would be nowhere else on this day than riding to war for Charles Stuart.

Callum Mackinnon had taken his son's good wishes and the news of the prince's proposed march to Frashiel House and was listened to eagerly by the Fraser family. Katrina was piqued that Jamie had not found the time to visit her, and she had already started to irritate her mother by her red eyes and moping looks. She couldn't help it; she missed Jamie more than she had believed possible. He had always been part of her life and never far away. Now she couldn't reach him, couldn't touch him, and she felt as if half of her life were missing.

It didn't help her spirits either that the younger children kept teasing and baiting her about her tearful face and sharp tongue. She seemed to be always bickering with one or the other of them, and with her mother, too. Even on the day that Callum came to tell them all was well with their menfolk and to give them the army's movements, all Katrina could think of was that Jamie would be going farther and farther away from her. For the moment, at least, she seemed to have lost every spark of that sudden affinity with the cause she had felt at Glenfinnan. Now all she felt was gloom and irritation.

"For pity's sake, lassie, will ye stop your moping?" Mairi said to her when Callum had left them. "Ye look so down in the dumps ye'd think the battle was lost already! Have ye no pride in your country, and your Jamie?"

"Aye, I have pride, and I've feelings, too!" Katrina said passionately, as if her mother knew nothing about the kind of feelings she and Jamie shared.

"Then ye should put them to good use." Mairi was as tetchy as her daughter. "Occupy your time instead of wasting it, hen. The time will pass all the quicker for it, and time wasted can never return."

"I know it! Ye've told me so a thousand times." Her eyes blazed at her mother. "I don't want your lecturing."

"I'm thinking ye need it! Ye would'na speak so rashly if your faither were here, and I'll thank ye to keep a civil tongue in your head when ye speak to me. Now get out of my sight for a while, for ye make my head ache!"

Mairi's hands were clenched by her side as she spoke, finding the necessity to be both father and mother more than she liked. The house was filled with tension these days, and already it seemed that the familiar world they knew was all head-about-face. And Katrina's moods only added to it.

She watched the flouncing of her daughter's skirts as she marched toward the door, her face angry and flushed.

"I will. I'll go to the schoolroom, since that's where ye seem to think I'm still suited best!"

Why was she acting this way? Katrina asked herself in self-condemnation. She knew she was behaving badly, like one of the bairns in a tantrum, and she couldn't seem to stop herself. She rarely sought out the schoolroom, but today it was for her own needs that she did so.

Hannah looked up in surprise from teaching Iona her laborious lettering. "Well, lassie, this is a rare honor," she said caustically, and Katrina took a deep breath to stop herself from lashing back at the woman. She changed her scowl to a smile instead.

"I'm not done with the learning yet, Hannah." She dared the tutor to argue with that. "I want ye to show me where the prince's army will be marching. Ye have the map, and Callum Mackinnon has told us the route. Will ye point it out to me, Hannah, so I can be certain where Jamie has gone?"

Hannah couldn't resist a moment's crowing. "So at last something has fired a need for the learning, has it? Even if 'tis only to follow your laddie's progress."

"Is that so strange?" Katrina snapped. "Will ye show me or not? I can easily study the map for myself. I'm no dunderhead."

"That ye're not, but we'll make this a proper lesson for Iona's benefit, too. The bairn may as well learn something of her country's situation."

The tutor reached to a shelf and brought down the crackling parchment of the map, spreading it out on the big table. Katrina realized with a small stab of guilt that she was studying it with an interest she had rarely shown. But then, apart from the Highlands and the small corner of it in which she lived, what need had she for knowing about city dwellings and the Lowland south where her aunt and uncle and cousin lived? What need for anything other than their own glen and the small part of it where she and Jamie shared their lives?

But now all that was changed, and she quickly scanned the rugged shape of the west coast that Hannah was pointing out, with its dozens of inlets and craggy coastline. Out into the sea glittered the islands Skye and Mull, Tiree and Col; and away out into the far islands lay the long straggling isle of Eriskay, where the prince had landed a month ago at Moidart.

"Callum Mackinnon says the army will march to Perth and then to Edinburgh," Katrina said quickly. "How far is that, Hannah?"

"Ye learned all this in the schoolroom, Katrina," the woman rebuked her severely. "Have ye forgotten everything I taught ye?"

"Not everything, but I forget this, and 'tis important to me to know it now!"

"I want to know it, too," Iona said, leaving her lettering and coming to sit beside Katrina. "Is the army where my faither is, Katrina?"

"It is, lamb, and Hannah will show us where he's gone!" She hugged her small sister to her side, blessing her for once, and Hannah grunted and began a finger movement over the parchment map of Scotland.

"Ye'll see that Edinburgh is away over to the east of the country, then, on the other side from us here, and a bit to the south. It lies on the Firth of Forth, the wide inlet to the North Sea. Perth lies some miles north of Edinburgh, and to reach it the army will have to be heading generally southward and eastward, and crossing the mountainous regions. 'Tis fortunate he came in summer. I daresay 'twill take a week or more to reach Perth, depending on the stamina of the men."

"They'll not be short of that," Katrina muttered, tracing the imaginary route. There was no way of knowing exactly which way would be taken, but it was a small comfort to know the general direction that Jamie would go.

"And then Edinburgh," she murmured, her glance moving southward on the map to the old capital.

"Aye, then Edinburgh," Hannah said decisively. "That will be a great day for the cause when Charles Stuart proclaims his faither king."

"Will it happen, Hannah?" Katrina said swiftly, to be met with a scathing look.

"Don't dare to doubt it, Katrina. The failure of the cause is something none of us dare consider."

"Why won't Charles be king?" Iona said suddenly. "Charles is the prince."

"Because his father has the right to be king first, dearie," Hannah said patiently. "When King James dies, then Charles would be king, do ye see?"

"And to keep the kingdom of Scotland safe, James would need to conquer England, too," Katrina murmured, things becoming much clearer to her as well as she noted the narrowness of the land border with England and compared it to the wider contours of the Highland regions. If England was not claimed as well, as it should be by right, then the friction between the two nations would never end. Scotland had once ruled itself, but those days were long gone and seemed unlikely to come again. England was too strong. But England and Scotland ruled together, not by a German Protestant king but by a Catholic Stuart, would strengthen the alliances between Catholic France and Italy. . . .

"I see ye're beginning to think for yourself, Katrina. 'Tis a good and healthy sign," Hannah commented, seeing the girl's finger trace the various cities and towns between the two adjoining countries.

"So I am, but I don't always like what I think," she said.

She left the schoolroom, not wanting to stay any longer and let the disturbing thought enter her mind that it could be a long while before she saw Jamie again. A good week's march to Perth, to take the city that was presumably in the command of the English army. Then to Edinburgh, a city inhabited by Scots who would by now have been schooled in the ways of the English, having been so closely under their rule for so many years.

She was filled with apprehension, for beyond Edinburgh the road to England was long and fraught with dangers. The only small consolation was in remembering what Callum had passed on to them from Jamie's visit—that the English army in Scotland at the present time was relatively small, and that the stupid commander Cope had taken most of them off to Inverness, a considerable distance north of either Perth or Edinburgh!

Jamie had said that the air would crackle with the news of the army's victories, but in the days that followed there was no news at all. Word of mouth produced a network of rumors across the country, but it was not until the end of the first week in September that a real piece of news was brought to Frashiel House by a tacksman who had lost one arm in the

1715 uprising and so was not involved in this one except as a volunteer messenger. He slid awkwardly from the back of his scrawny horse and rapped on the door of the house.

"Mistress, I'm to tell ye that the rebels have taken Perth, and all is triumph there at this time. They are to march to Edinburgh and are filled with confidence. They stay at Perth a few days, gathering more men, for more are eager to join the prince now that he has gained a victory. He has more baggage and wagons and horses, and two important new leaders."

He paused for breath, and Mairi drew him inside the house at once, with a feeling of great joy in her heart.

"Ye'll take a dram, man, and sit ye down for a spell while ye tell me more. Did ye see it happen?"

The man shook his head as Mairi poured him his whiskey and handed it to him. He drained it gratefully, though he had been given so many drams that day from thankful Highlanders that his head had begun to swim. He held it steady.

"But the news is fact, mistress," he assured her. "And the duke of Perth, James Drummond, has joined the Stuart, and so has Lord George Murray. The prince has made them lieutenant-generals, and a fine pair they be. Drummond a quiet man, in the early thirties, well liked by the men and easygoing. The other, Lord George, about fifty years, a blunt, different kettle of trout, and often in conflict wi' the prince, they say, but a leader for all that, and 'tis what's needed. There was no great opposition when they took the city, and I'll wager they'll be a more confident army when they march on Edinburgh, wi' more men and arms, and two fine new generals."

His Highland pride, the vast quantities of whiskey he'd drunk that day, and the welcome he was receiving such as one of his means had never received before was making him blather on more than usual. When he stopped for breath, Mairi asked for more personal information.

"Have ye news of my husband, Duncan Fraser? Or of Jamie Mackinnon?" She held her breath, but the man was decisive.

"I know naught of them, mistress, nor any other. I only bring reports. Fraser, do y' say? The Frasers have come out for the prince from their stronghold under Simon Fraser of

Lovat, so your man will march behind his clan's standard. Now I must be away, and I thank ye for your hospitality.''

Mairi did not try to restrain him. She wished Katrina had been at home to hear the good news with her. It might restore the girl's good humor, which was sorely lacking these days. Something had to be done about Katrina, Mairi thought keenly. She behaved more like a wayward child than ever these days. That very morning they had had another to-do, and Mairi had barely resisted the temptation to thrash her daughter, whether she was almost a woman or not. Katrina had eventually gone storming off to visit her old nurse, who alone seemed to have the power to calm her. Mairi had shouted as much after her as Katrina went striding off, her chin in the air with defiance written all over her.

The power! Would that Margret had the power to stop the cause before it ended in bloodshed, Katrina had thought. Would that she had the power to bring her Jamie back to her. She felt swift remorse at the very thought. To encourage notions of witchcraft was evil enough, without the added treason of denying her country's right to its lawful monarch! But since Jamie had gone, her days had been empty, her nights often filled with weeping; and to be away from the house and her mother's constant censure was like feeling the clean air of the glens in her lungs.

Katrina took the well-trodden path over the grassy glen to Margret's small cottage. It was a haven she had sought more than once and would probably seek out again. But there was no escape here from talk of the uprising. Margret and old Angus, home for a bite and a jaw, were as full of the rebellion as everyone else.

''There's plenty rumors, o' course.'' Angus sucked hard on a clay pipe that had once been white and was now the color of damp earth. ''Some say they've already taken Edinburgh, but I doubt that. So long as there's no news that's bad, 'tis better to hear naught.''

''I don't think so!'' Katrina burst out. ''I wish I had news of Jamie. It's awful not knowing.''

Angus shrugged. ''Aye, well, there's no hurrying with news or rumors if there's naught to tell, lassie. For all we know, it mebbe all over already, and Jamie's on his way back to ye.''

Such talk only frustrated Katrina further. It was facile and worse than useless. She longed for real news of Jamie. She looked at the old woman pouring hot chocolate into a cup and handing it to her.

"When will he come home, Margret?" She asked it all in a rush. "I'm lonely without him. I miss him so—and Hamish and Iona plague me like thistles under my feet."

Her young voice cracked a little, and Angus stood up and reached for his shepherd's crook. Soft eyes and women's talk were not to his taste in the middle of the day, and he would rather be about his business. Sheep were preferable companions at such times, especially when women got that moist look about them, as Miss Katrina had now. Sheep were definitely less complicated creatures than women. . . .

"Now then, dearie," Margret said firmly when her man had gone from the cottage. "There's no use in crying over what canna be changed. Ye learned as much when ye were nobbut a wee one. Your Jamie will come home safe and sound, if 'tis God's will."

"But you can't be certain. I wish I knew it for certain!"

Passion and anxiety crisped her voice. Her hands were clammy as they clenched together on her lap. She had never put it into words before, this nameless dread she felt on Jamie's behalf. She needed to know what the future would bring. She had always thought she knew, when being married to Jamie had been the only goal ahead of her.

Margret's rough old hand covered Katrina's a moment, stilling the restless movements.

"I canna tell ye more than is in your own heart, Katrina. Ye must have faith. It's all any of us can do. I canna tell ye more than that."

Katrina felt an acute disappointment. Whatever revelations she had half hoped for were not forthcoming.

"Have faith! 'Tis a hard thing to do when I'm so feared for Jamie, Margret. I canna help it."

"Aye, and 'tis natural for ye to feel so," Margret said with gruff sympathy. "What lassie would see her lad go to war without feeling his loss so keenly? But the parting may do ye well, my lamb. 'Twill strengthen the bonds between ye."

"I thought you understood me, Margret! The bonds between Jamie and me can never be stronger. And I don't want to hear about other lassies feeling the same way for their menfolk. I'm not every other lassie. I'm *me*!'' She snatched her hands from Margret's grasp.

"And still the bairn, despite the womanly covering," Margret said tartly. "Your mammie would be sore displeased to hear ye going on so."

Katrina felt her face go warm. Her mammie was already out of sorts with her, and here she was, upsetting Margret as well, which had been far from her intention.

"I'm sorry, Margret," she mumbled. "I did'na mean to snap. Mammie wouldn't want to know it."

"Then none shall tell her," the old nurse promised. "Now, by the looks of ye, some fresh air will do ye far more good than idling your time in here wi' me, and I've my work to finish. Ye can walk wi' me awhile, if you care to, while I'm doing my fleece gathering. The breeze will mebbe cool your mood before ye see your mammie again."

Katrina waited while Margret pulled the scarlet shawl around her thin shoulders and slung her canvas bag about her body. It was an endless task that Margret did, but it clearly suited her to do it. They left the cottage and began to walk the hills, pausing time and again while Margret pulled at the caught tufts of sheep's wool from bracken and stone and stuffed them inside her bag.

As the old woman surmised, the walk cooled Katrina a mite, though the clean-scented air itself could normally do that. In the ruggedly beautiful corner of the Highlands, no hint of bloody battles intruded on the blue-and-golden afternoon. Hazed by distance, the mountains were age-old sentinels, old friends, symbolizing their protection of the glens and those who lived there. Some of the tension left Katrina, and by the time she and Margret parted company, she managed to talk with a hint of teasing in her voice.

"I'll come to see you again soon, Margret, and I'll try not to be so cross next time. Providing those wee burrs at home don't irritate me too much!"

"That's a fine way to speak of your brother and sister!" But Margret was teasing, too, relieved that the girl had lost some of that haunted look in her eyes from the worry over

Jamie. It did no good. Nothing would be changed for all the worry in the world from the women who waited at home. . . . Margret sighed, watching Katrina running light-footed now through the heather. The September breeze was balmy, and Katrina's long burnished hair caught the sunlight in a fiery blaze of color. Marget gave another sigh, this time of nostalgia at the nimble footsteps, and turned back to her fleece gathering.

If Katrina's intentions were good, they didn't last long. Hamish and Iona were arguing and in a vinegary mood. The two of them were outside in a break from their lessons, and Hamish was resenting the way Iona pecked at him like a troublesome chick.

"Ye're too young to go for a soldier, Hamish Fraser," the small girl chanted, dancing around him while he wondered if he dare lash out at her and risk her wailing to her mammie. "Faither says ye're still a laddie, and ye're to stay home wi' me and Mammie and Katrina."

"Hush yourself, ye stupid wean. Ye know naught about soldiers and fighting."

"I do! Hannah told me."

"What does she know? Hannah's no man to be a soldier. She only learns it from books, ye ninny!"

In frustration, Iona beat her small fists against his chest, where Hamish caught them and gave them a sharp twist, making the child cry out. The sight of them both, the boy red-faced with fury, the small girl just as red with frustration because Hamish already thought himself too old to play with her anymore, made Katrina's mouth start to twitch with laughter.

Mairi heard the commotion and Iona's sudden squeal, and she came to see her wee one being tormented by her older brother and Katrina apparently standing by, letting it happen, doing nothing to stop it. The sight of it, added to her elder daughter's newly calm face after the visit to old Margret, had an adverse effect on Mairi's previous good humor. She pulled the two younger bairns apart and went immediately to Katrina to shake her hard.

"Is this the way ye help me when your faither's no' here to

keep these two in order?" she stormed at Katrina. "Ye go off in a huff and come back all cow-eyed, letting the wee one be bullied."

"Iona was doing the bullying!" Katrina flared back. "Ye did'na see it all."

"I saw enough to know that ye were content to stand there laughing at the pair of them instead of trying to stop it," Mairi snapped, seeing the resentment come into her daughter's eyes.

"Hamish hurt me," Iona shouted. She rubbed her small wrists where he had gripped her.

"She hurt me first," Hamish shouted back. "She's a little vixen with her fists."

"How can ye be such a milksop, Hamish?" His mother rounded on him now. "Ye talk of being a soldier, and ye make such a fuss about a wee bairn's fists. I'm shamed for ye. And between ye, I'm right out of humor, when there was good news I had to tell ye, Katrina, from a visitor that came while ye were away wi' Margret."

Her heart leapt at her mother's words. "A visitor? Not Jamie? Oh, Mammie, tell me if it was Jamie."

Mairi felt a brief moment of sympathy with her daughter at the sudden glow that replaced the angry look in her lovely eyes. She wished for an instant that she could say the visitor had been Jamie, for didn't she feel every bit the same in her heart about Duncan?

"No, lass, it was'na Jamie," she said shortly, seeing the glow change to disappointment. "But it was a messenger from the prince's army, spreading the glad news that they have reached Perth as planned. They've done well, Katrina. Edinburgh may even be in Jacobite hands by now."

The dots on Hannah's map were suddenly more real in Katrina's mind. She could see the places in her head. She could feel the excitement and the surge of self-confidence the undisciplined Highlanders must feel at achieving a victory. Having conquered one city, they could conquer the world. There was no room in a Highlander's mind for doubting his fighting ability, nor in Katrina's at that moment.

"Mebbe 'twill not last too long, then, Mammie," she said hopefully, wanting Mairi to agree, to confirm, but in this she was disappointed. Mairi had seen other rebellions and could not be less than honest with her daughter.

"Dinna build up your hopes on that, Katrina. We have the news that the English army have gone north to Inverness and could put up little resistance with the numbers they had left at Perth, but we must not take them for idiots! They will soon try to put a stop to the prince's march through Scotland."

"Don't say it, Mammie." Katrina spoke fast, as if keeping the words unsaid would stop them from being fact. It was a child's way, and she knew it. With every day that passed, that childhood world was being forced away from her, that world in which rebellions and Stuart hopes were but legends in the history books.

Mairi recognized Katrina's strange longing. "Ye canna close your eyes to it, lass. A battle is not only fought by soldiers. We all become part of it in some way, even in the waiting."

Katrina felt her throat thicken, seeing the inevitability in the words, and Hamish saw his sister's sudden emotion and seized on it, not yet forgiving her for laughing at him and Iona.

"Mebbe Katrina should put on the blue bonnet and go for a soldier, if she canna even stand the waiting," he crowed. "Though I canna think Charles Stuart would want a weepy-eye to march behind his standard."

"At least I'd be full-grown and not a skinny undersized laddie!" she blazed back at him, knowing how Hamish hated to be reminded of the fact that he was not yet as tall as his sister. He glowered, his face a darkly furious red, and Iona clung to her mother's skirts as tempers flared.

"Stop it at once," Mairi snapped. "I'm weary of your pointless arguments and blathering that leads nowhere! Ye make my head ring."

"Katrina canna go for a soldier," Iona suddenly said. "She has the bumps on her chest like ye, Mammie. A soldier has to be a man, so Hannah says."

Hamish's hoots of derisive laughter at the child's simple logic made his mother smile also but did nothing to improve Katrina's temper. The bumps on her chest were the visible proof that she was past the age for such schoolroom nonsense as these two still indulged in, for all Hamish's swagger.

72

"And a boy needs to be a man before he can appreciate the difference," she said cuttingly.

"That will do, Katrina," Mairi said at once, not liking the way the talk was turning. "If ye've nought else to do but bait these two, then ye can take Iona indoors and help her with her sewing."

"I thought that was what Faither paid Hannah to do," she retorted, at which her mother rounded on her angrily.

"If ye think yourself so much the lady, then mebbe it would be a good idea to send ye down south to stay with your Aunt Janet awhile. They've softer ways there that would mebbe suit ye, miss!"

"Mebbe I should," Katrina snapped back. "For I canna seem to please anyone here!"

She almost snatched at Iona's hand and pulled her into the house, knowing she had best do as her mother asked and spend the time showing her sister the sewing stitches. But inside she still seethed. Was it all her fault? She felt constantly bruised by her mammie's remarks. She had never considered being away from her own glen in her life before, or wanted to visit her relatives in the gentler Lowlands of the country, but she almost felt the urge to go to her mother and say that she was ready to leave Frashiel House at once. She would go . . . anywhere but stay here, where it seemed she could do nothing right!

It was a foolish thought, of course. She had no wish to leave, when she and Jamie were on the brink of being wed— The thoughts stopped short. Everything was changed. . . .

"Are ye going to show me the stitches, Katrina?" Iona was saying, her small voice troubled. "Ye look so funny. Ye're not crying, are ye, Katrina? Did Hamish make ye angry when he laughed at ye?"

Katrina felt contrite at the way the poor wee bairn was caught up in the middle of the blathering. She gave her a quick hug as they went to fetch the linen that Iona was using with the colored wools.

"No, lassie, Hamish did'na make me angry, and I'm not crying, either," she said with an effort. "It's just that everything's topsy-turvy these days. Now, let's take a look at this sewing."

"All right," Iona said readily. She eyed her sister, seeing the way Katrina's chest still moved up and down with the heaviness of her breathing. "Anyway, I like the bumps on your chest, Katrina. When will I get them, too?"

Katrina began to laugh gently now, seeing the way the child was examining her own flat little chest.

"Not yet, darling," she told her. "But in about five years from now, when ye start to be a woman."

"Ye've been a woman a long time, then," the child said eventually, clearly working things out in her head.

"That I have, dove. I only wish it was as obvious to everyone," Katrina said wryly.

It was becoming clearer to Mairi that Katrina was feeling the frustration of being parted from Jamie more acutely than her mother had expected. Mairi had been caught up in the rush of loyalty like her man and had spared little enough thought for the way Katrina's ill temper came from the lovers' enforced parting. It was naturally so, when they were so close to being wed and had spent hardly a day apart in the whole of their lives before now. Mairi blamed herself for not having seen it before.

It was hard enough for any woman to bear being parted from her man, as she knew well enough. Mairi and her daughter were of the same passionate stock, and she should have given more consideration to her prickly daughter. It was not easy for Mairi to speak of personal things such as the feelings of a man for a woman, and the physical side of love. She blamed herself for this lack in her own character . . . that, and the fact that Katrina seemed too knowing already, whenever Mairi tried to broach such a subject in delicate terms!

Her sister Janet had always had an easier way of dealing with personal matters, Mairi thought suddenly. No doubt Janet would have had no such problems telling her own daughter, Helen, about the ways of a lad and a lassie! The idle thought that Katrina might benefit from a visit to the south was not such an unattractive one after all. But it was not a decision Mairi would ever take alone.

And that was where the notion ended. For without Duncan's

approval and support, Katrina would remain here and no doubt continue to stir up passions in the household. It was one more cross they all had to bear, but tolerance was badly needed on all sides from now on. Mairi would call the bairns together and try to make them understand that much at least. Tolerance must be the watchword from now on.

CHAPTER 6

Lord George Murray was well aware that Charles Stuart was not overfond of him. The fact that Lord George was a fervent loyalist did little to assuage the prince's unfounded suspicion of the man. Even though he was made a commander, and undoubtedly managed to swell the Stuart ranks by more roof burnings and evictions of his own tacksmen than many other clans, there was still a feeling of mistrust. Lord George bitterly resented it but chose to overlook it as far as possible. The prince needed him, he thought arrogantly, and so he did.

Charles had stayed at Blair Castle on his journey toward Perth, the home of the duke of Atholl, who was Lord George's kinsman. Here, and in the week the Jacobites remained in Perth after the easy capture of the city with no resistance from the few companies of English troops in the area, the Stuart army had grown to more than three thousand strong.

"Still not enough," Lord George told Charles bluntly in the authoritative manner that so irritated the prince. "We need more reinforcements, sir. We cannot hope to beat the English bastards, who are better trained, better equipped, and better fitted for war than we are, unless we have force of numbers."

"What do you suggest?" Charles was stung to say. "That I go out and burn cottages or shoot cattle to persuade the men to follow their prince?"

His sarcasm angered Lord George. "If our methods are too savage for you, sir, I must point out that they produce results where fine words sometimes fail. Urgency is our best weapon, and we must have more men, more supplies, and more money!"

"The French will send supplies and money," Charles said coldly. "Meanwhile, the people must pay for the glory that is to come. They cannot refuse to surrender a portion of their produce for their army, nor give up their unused carts to carry food for their clansmen. They must pledge some of their rent dues. There's no man disloyal enough to argue with his prince, and it will be little enough from each one."

"Each one has little enough, sir," Lord George retorted.

"You'll see to it, Lord George," Charles said. Lord Elcho, another strong supporter of the cause, had been listening quietly to the talk and now said quickly that there would be opposition, but that the prince's wishes would be seen to at once. There was little else to do. They needed the money for food and supplies, and the natural outcome of victory was for the victor to procure the spoils of war in whatever manner he chose.

The army began the march to Edinburgh, and orders were given for the pipes to be hushed and for the arrival to be in the early hours of the morning. Scouts had preceded the army and reported that there were only a few regiments of English dragoons in the city and its environs, awaiting the arrival of General Cope and his men, who were now marching southward from Inverness. This news cheered Charles and his commanders, for, still drunk with the ease of Perth's capture, they felt it could surely cause them little trouble to take the capital. And once Edinburgh was in their hands, James VIII could be proclaimed king of Scotland, as was his right.

The Jacobites met with a token resistance as they entered the city, on which they began a desultory firing. As if by a given signal, doors and windows of houses were thrown open, and panic-stricken townsfolk shrieked in terror, demanding that the English dragoons defend them from the barbarians.

"By God, we've come to a city of lunatics!" Duncan Fraser had to holler the words to make himself heard above the din. "Have they all been so Anglicized that they canna recognize their own Highlanders?"

"I'm thinking we're less welcome to them than the English," Jamie shouted back as he rode alongside him. "Will ye look at us, man? Who would'na be feared at the sight?"

He grinned, knowing the Highlanders presented a fearsome collection of men. They were brawny, heavyset in their Highland garb, and they had bushy, untamed hair. Their ox-hide shields were held before them, and weapons of every description adorned their bodies—swords and dirks, muskets and fowling pieces. A number of lowlier recruits carried scythe blades attached to pitchfork shafts.

The wagons rolled into the city, clattering on the cobbles now, with the food supplies and the larger arms and ammunition seized from those few English regiments at Perth. The prince was well protected in the midst of his clan chiefs, his generals, and his fierce Highland warriors, and the good citizens of Edinburgh wanted nothing to do with him. They had become used to English rule and their lives had not been unduly disturbed by it. They were not of such bloodthirsty disposition as the Highlanders and preferred the quieter life.

The citizens panicked, and in their panic and terror the invaders from the west seemed to be enemies, barbaric clansmen stampeding through their narrow, warrenlike maze of little streets. It was the fast-retreating English troops they shouted to for help, but help was not forthcoming.

Only the castle itself, high and impregnable on its granite rock above the city, remained in government hands, where the English retained command and could maintain a fine vantage point over the city. But for all that, the main objective in capturing Edinburgh was to establish Charles Stuart's presence in the ancient palace of Holyroodhouse, where kings before him had reigned and where he could proclaim his father once again as James VIII of Scotland.

"If every capture were as simple as this, then why in God's name has it taken so long for this new rebellion?" a clan chief was heard to mutter in Lord George's hearing. And immediately the man was reprimanded.

"Did ye never hear of the calm before the storm, man? Mebbe 'tis all too simple, and it cannot last this way. The struggle's not yet begun, and ye'd do well to remember it."

The clan chief glowered after him. Lord George, blunt as

ever, was adept at rousing resentment, for all his military expertise. But no blood had yet been spilled for the Stuart cause, and the Highlanders were becoming restless. This was not a battle. Was this all they had rallied for, this comparatively easy road to Edinburgh?

Orders were given to make camp. The day was still early, the sun not yet up, and to add to the Edinburgh citizens' growing fears, the rebels began to light their night fires in every open space. As if in defiance of the English, they even lighted them on the dark craggy slopes of Arthur's Seat right opposite the castle rock, the great ancient volcanic mass in Holyrood Park near the palace. This palace, once the home of Mary Queen of Scots, was the coveted birthright of the Stuarts.

The prince called his generals to decide on the next plan.

"We must send a summons to the lord provost, to call on the city to surrender," the lords advised him. "By the day's end, we must have ye installed in Holyroodhouse, sir."

The summons was dispatched immediately, and by the time scouts came running from the far corners of the city to say that Cope's ships had been sighted in the Firth of Forth, it was too late. Edinburgh had already been surrendered to Charles Stuart.

"The people will see their prince," Charles declared, when it was ascertained that the English ships stayed well away from port and seemed to be sailing slowly southward down the coast. "My father's proclamation must be made in regal style. You, Drummond, and Lord Elcho, shall ride by my side."

If this was a snub to Lord George Murray, he brushed it from his mind with his usual contempt. It took but a few hours after capturing the city and setting up camp for Charles to emerge from his quarters dressed in triumph. He had chosen carefully for this occasion and wore a tartan coat with red velvet breeches and knee boots. On his glinting golden hair he wore a blue velvet bonnet laced with gold and a white cockade. The star of St. Andrew gleamed on his chest. He was a prince in every sense of the word, in looks and stature, and despite the earlier aggression a good proportion of Edinburgh's population was drawn out to cheer him on his triumphal progress. Some had been forced out by the rebels at knife point and cheered all the more hoarsely at the memory.

Word was quickly spread that the procession was to make its way along the Royal Mile from Castle Hill to the gates of Holyroodhouse, the royal palace. At the city cross, the procession, heralded by a hundred pipers, gave way to the prince, and the cheering was hushed as he made to speak. Facing the crowds, his own rough Highlanders, the disgruntled or curious citizens of the city, the reluctant dignitaries obliged to watch and listen, and his own generals, Charles drew a deep breath. Now was not the time for simplicity but for an impassioned appeal to the people, spoken in the manner of their future king. He must be fair, and just, and truthful, and this Charles believed himself to be. If some of his speech seemed overdramatic to the simpler folk among them, then so be it.

"Citizens of Edinburgh, if my father has been represented to you as a tyrant, breathing out nothing but destruction to all who will not immediately embrace an odious religion, and your pulpits and clergy ring with the dreadful threats of popery, slavery, and tyranny, then listen only to the naked truth."

He paused, then spoke the simple words used at Glenfinnan.

"With my own money I hired a small vessel to reach these shores. Ill supplied with money, arms, or friends, I arrived in Scotland attended by seven persons. I published the king my father's declaration and proclaimed his title. . . ."

A scuffle in the crowd was immediately subdued as his voice became momentarily lost in the hubbub. Charles went on as if nothing had happened; his accent rendered much of the words and the sense of the speech unintelligible to the less educated, but the dignity of the man overcame the lack.

"That our family has suffered exile during these fifty-seven years everybody knows. Has the nation, during that period of time, been the more happy and flourishing for it? Have you found reason to love and cherish your governors as the fathers of the people? Has a family, upon whom a faction *unlawfully* bestowed the diadem of a rightful prince, retained a due sense of so great a trust and favor? . . . If I am answered in the affirmative, why has their government been so often railed at in all your public assemblies?"

Roars of agreement rang out at that. What had improved in the years of Stuart exile? Not the peasants' lot, nor roads, nor lower taxes, nor living standards. . . . From being one nation, Scotland was now even more divided: half the clans remained loyal Catholic Jacobites, others swayed in the wind for the Protestants, and townspeople were firmly under the Hanoverian thumb of George II, as much a distant figure from his throne in London as their exiled James.

"It is now time to conclude; and I shall do it with this reflection. Civil wars are ever attended with rancor and ill will. I, therefore, earnestly require it of my friends to give as little loose as possible to such passions. This will provide the most effectual means to prevent the same in the enemies of my royal cause. And this my declaration will vindicate to all posterity the nobleness of my undertaking and the generosity of my intentions."

The speech was delivered, and the prince stood down as the huzzas sounded, together with some rumbles of discontent. His own Highlanders bellowed out their pleasure, with half of them understanding only a fraction of what was said. This was what they had been roused for, and they would make their presence felt. They shouted themselves hoarse for Charles, their bonnie lad, the Bonnie Prince Charlie.

And Jamie Mackinnon wished fervently that his bonnie Katrina could be here to witness the acclaim given to their young prince, for surely her reluctant belief in the cause would be as strong as any man's here at this moment. Once the prince had finished speaking a fanfare sounded, and he heard the proclamation that the prince was here as regent for his father, King James VIII, His Noble Majesty, "King of Scotland, England, France, and Ireland." An expansive declaration, especially when the Union flag of England still fluttered within sight of them all, high over the castle ramparts at the far end of the Royal Mile.

The royal party rode in triumph through the gates of Holyroodhouse, but later that day Charles was told that Cope's army was disembarking at Dunbar, a little ways to the south along the coast.

"Is he, by God!" Charles exclaimed. "Then I suggest, Lord George, that we issue a summons demanding the surrender of all arms and ammunition in the city. If the enemy wants a fight, we'll give him one.''

He had already been agreeably surprised by the interior of the palace, which, though large and drafty, had an impressive royal portrait gallery depicting more than a hundred Scottish kings and queens, clearly a valuable collection. Leading from the gallery was the audience chamber, with its austere setting for business of state, and then the private apartments of Mary Queen of Scots, which Charles immediately decided to use for himself. The exterior of the palace was regal, in pale stone, with leaded turrets atop the round towers at each corner. It was a fitting royal home.

For now, though, he was more concerned with the news of Cope's progress than the pleasures of his new palace. They could wait until later. He gathered his generals in the audience chamber, seated himself before them, and got down to the business of war.

The crowds in the city took a long while to disperse that day, long after the prince and his retinue had vanished inside the palace. The Highlanders, let loose in a city for the first time in their lives, were in high spirits, undaunted by the resentment meted out to them by the populace. They were the conquerers of a city that had been strongly for the government, and they made their presence felt. They had lived on marching rations since leaving Glenfinnan, and here was the chance to have some sport, to find a change of diet, to seek out the town whores and the taverns. If they had little enough money to pay for their needs, they would take them anyway. They were the victors, and it went to their heads.

"What ails ye, Jamie Mackinnon?" one clansman hooted derisively as Jamie shook off the soft female arms in the smoke-filled tavern where he and a crowd of others had gone. "Is it your fancy to toy with wee laddies, rather than sniff a lassie's fair skin?"

His reply was a crashing blow between the eyes from Jamie's fist. What did these bastards know of the strong and faithful love between himself and Katrina! Jamie lunged at the man again, fury mingling with outrage as others about him laughed and jeered; then other hands were pulling him away, and he was tasting his own blood from a cut on his mouth.

"Get ye out of here, if ye can only fight and brawl!" the landlord was hollering at him, as if he were the culprit who had begun the fight. "Ye can have the hospitality o' the house, providing ye can pay for it, but I'll have no Highland violence in here."

Jamie was sorely tempted to holler back, but it suddenly seemed not worth the bother. Instead, he turned and stormed out into the night air. It was not the clean, cutting air of the glens but the smoke-filled fug of a city, close and reeking of smells alien to his senses—the filth that ran down the gutters, the rotting rubbish tossed out by taverns and coffeehouses, the paint and powder of the street women.

He strode off into the night, knowing that the thought of Katrina more than outweighed any brief temptation he might feel to seek out a pretty face and a pair of comforting arms. The thought of her was more potent a drug to his senses than the wildest night spent with any whore.

He walked and walked, through the narrow streets and into the open spaces, missing her with a sharp physical longing akin to pain, seeing her face in the yellow moon above and wondering if she looked at it, too, and thought of him. He seemed to hear the whisper of her voice in the sigh of the breeze and felt the pangs of homesickness, for the glens, for the mountains, for the wild free wilderness of home, and most of all for his lassie.

There was an ache in Jamie to be there, away from this part of Scotland that was as alien to him as the moon. It was all bustle, grand stone-built edifices and stinking hovels. It was duty that brought him here, and he would stay as long as his prince needed him, but he had needs, too, and they were all calling out for Katrina, his love. . . .

He was so deep in his own thoughts that he cannoned straight into something without noticing that it had shape and form. He had gone full circle and was back near his own part of the camp, the fires flickering, tents in haphazard clusters, the stringy horses munching on newly acquired hay from Edinburgh stables. A large hand suddenly gripped his arm, and involuntarily Jamie's hand went to the dirk at his waist.

"Are ye dreaming, Jamie?" Duncan Fraser's voice spoke with gruff amusement. "Would ye pass by your future kinsman without a word of greeting?"

Jamie would rather have seen Duncan Fraser at that moment than any other man. Duncan was a link with all he held most dear, and Jamie had almost blundered right past him as he'd meandered back to camp in the murk of the night.

"I'm glad to see ye, Duncan! And what thoughts do ye have on the pageantry in the city?"

"A fair day," Duncan grunted with dry understatement. "I'll wager our womenfolk will be wanting to know every detail, so ye'd best be remembering it, Jamie."

"Aye." Jamie's face relaxed into a smile. " 'Twould be good to sit and jaw awhile wi' neighbors again, and know the business for tomorrow."

" 'Tis not hard to guess on the business here, lad," Duncan retorted. " 'Tis certain the English ships have brought the army south from Inverness and will be meeting us in combat before many more suns have set."

Jamie shrugged. "The sooner the better. The waiting only makes a man itchy. We're here to fight, so let's fight and beat the bastards back to where they belong!"

"Well said, lad. Now I'm away to my rest, so good night to ye."

There was little else to do, since half the Highlanders were sporting in the city, and the rest had already had enough of celebrating and jawing and drinking, and were snoring loud enough to wake the dead. A great hum of noise seemed to throb through the tented town. Jamie crawled into his own tent and tried to shut it out of his mind.

The surrender of arms and ammunition in the city produced a good supply of muskets, powder, and ball, but little else.

"We know the enemy is near at hand," Charles told his leaders. "Do we wait for them to attack or go to meet them? I say the latter. Let them know that we mean to crush them."

His generals agreed at once.

"I will ride at the head of my army," Charles then announced, daring them to argue and tired of the protected position in the middle columns of his men.

"I oppose this, sir," Lord George said at once. " 'Tis the greatest folly."

"Since you oppose most suggestions I make, it is no surprise to me," Charles retorted coldly. "But you've heard my decision, and it stands."

The clash of personalities was becoming more evident, but there were more important matters to deal with. Scouts had reported that General Cope's army had taken up position near Prestonpans, a few miles to the east of Edinburgh, and the rebel leaders acknowledged that he had chosen well, with marshy ground behind his troops. If the Highlanders crossed that ground, they would be seen at once and cannoned down. If any reached the dry land where the English redcoats waited, they would meet the attack of an estimated two thousand trained soldiers.

"They have their training. We have our wits and our strength, and more than enough cunning to win the day," Charles said confidently. His chiefs were behind him: Keppoch and Lochiel, who had marched with him from Glenfinnan; Simon Lovat, the Fraser chief who had joined on the march; and more clans with their own leaders—the Robertsons, MacGregors, the MacLachlans, and others. . . .

"The prince is right," Duncan Fraser said to Jamie when the rebel army was ready to move camp and begin the march towards Prestonpans. "We also have our canny knowledge of the country and its weather, which should'na be discounted. We'll be ready to cut the redcoats down, laddie, whenever we get the word."

The word came at about three a.m. on a morning so dark and thick with mist that it was impossible to see more than a few feet in any direction. The English redcoats would be unused to mist and cold, crag and valley, the kind of weather and terrain that held no hazards for the clansmen.

A local man called Anderson had been enlisted to lead the rebel army silently toward the swamp in the early morning hours. Stealth and secrecy to begin with . . . and then the bloodcurdling screech of the pipes as each clan regiment swarmed toward the enemy. Under cover of the mist, with the prince at their head, the clansmen moved out from the camp in this, the first major encounter with the redcoats.

Jamie felt his blood flow hot and fast. Beneath him, his horse slithered a little on the soft ground, and he calmed her with murmured words. The group of kinsmen all around him, Mackinnons with grim faces and a warlike heritage, were as eager to be done with this battle as himself. Those on foot trod the rough and broken path carefully, light-footed for such brawny men, moving silently through the mist around the left flank of the English lines as their leaders had ordered. They were now on the flat stubble fields behind what Sir John Cope had considered his impregnable position. Jamie felt his breath sharpen in the cold air as the sky gradually lightened and the mist thinned.

A sudden movement ahead of them and an English voice challenged them, followed by a musket shot.

As if they had waited especially for this enemy signal, the rebel leaders shouted the orders to attack, and the air was suddenly and spectacularly rent by the sound of the clan pipers screeching out the battle marches and the Highlanders roaring their battle slogans as they surged forward. Ahead of them, in the thin daylight, the English lines were leaping to battle order, clearly terrorized by the sight of the blue-bonnetted, murderous clansmen bearing down on them, on foot or horseback, claymores swinging about their heads or broadswords gleaming aloft, muskets spitting out yellow fire in a wild and savage charge.

Jamie's ears were suddenly filled with screaming as he and his companions surged forward. There was no time for thinking, for a second glance. His eyes ached with the strain of staring through the thick fog of musket fire that replaced the mist with the acrid stench of gunpowder. There were other smells, too—rank smells of body sweat, sharpened by fear; the hot smell of blood freshly spilled. His mind seemed numbed to what he did. The only object was the nearest red-coated enemy . . . the only thought was for survival, to kill or be killed.

"Look out, laddie!" He heard a roar from behind him and turned quickly to see the redcoat almost on him, and without thinking he felt his own claymore sink into the redcoat's soft belly. Before he could even puke at the sensation, another of the enemy soldiers was hammering at his head, and he was defending himself again. The eyes of the first dying redcoat were still staring openly at him in a kind of hurt surprise.

He saw the flash of an English bayonet about to impale him and lashed sideways, defending himself with his shield. The next second the redcoat fell screaming, blood spurting from his neck in a red river as he dropped to the ground.

There was no time to listen for orders now. Jamie could hear nothing but the pounding of the blood in his own ears and the screams of the men mingled with the skirl of Highland pipes. English and Scots voices jumbled together, and God knew where Charles Stuart was.

There was no time to be sickened by men falling like packs of cards onto the dry dusty earth or by seeing it change to the color and texture of blood. It was survive or be slaughtered, and the clash of steel on steel, men's anguished screams, and flailing horses' hooves all became part of the bloody dawn morning.

"We've got the bastards! They're on the run!" The gasping shouts of triumph ran through the Highland camp. "Finish them, lads! Cut them down!"

Vaguely, Jamie was aware that the rebel generals were attempting to stop the wild slaughter now that it was clear the redcoats were on the run. But they would have found it easier to stop a stampede of wild animals. The Highlanders' blood was up, and in their frenzy they were ready to kill anything that moved.

The slashing went on, the skinny rebel horses stumbling, lurching over scattered bodies of dead and dying men as the surviving redcoats fled. The dragoons panicked, and those on foot ran in terror from the savage pursuit. The rebel attack had been a victory, lasting less than ten minutes.

"The prince is safe," was the cry. "He's sending to Edinburgh for surgeons."

It was a welcome piece of news on both counts. There was no help for the dead, but the sight of the wounded of both sides curdled Jamie's stomach as he picked his way carefully among them. Surgeons and priest captains were already at work, and through the yellow fog that still hazed the morning he heard the shouts of Lord George Murray and of Drummond, ordering the badly wounded Highlanders to be taken to a nearby country house that was to be turned into a hospital.

Jamie stumbled and nearly fell, after sliding off his horse's back, finding that his legs felt oddly boneless now that the danger was over. His red-rimmed eyes refused to look longer at all that was left of a lad little older than himself, his once proud English uniform dirtied, the red coat slashed, the boy's own blood bubbling and gushing over the white stockings from a fatal wound. Jamie was transfixed for a moment as he saw him, and then he tore his glance away. The laddie looked no more than a bairn in death, defenseless, vulnerable.

He convulsed without warning as the smell of blood nauseated him, vomiting wildly as he clawed on the ground, away from the body he had suddenly visualized as himself. No longer the enemy, but a laddie far from home, like himself . . . a laddie with a sweetheart waiting, like himself. . . .

"Jamie! Jamie! Is it you, laddie?" said a hoarse voice. "For God's sake, help me."

The sound of the voice close to him roused him from his momentary horror.

"Duncan Fraser!" Was that his own voice he heard? Jamie wondered for an instant. That thin reed of sound? But the recognition of Katrina's father among the human flesh strewn over the battlefield brought back a sliver of sanity to his mind.

Duncan lay beneath the heavy deadweight body of a redcoat. Kneeling quickly and hauling the body away, Jamie saw that Duncan's arm was hanging uselessly by his side, a deep gash having sliced it badly. The weakness from the loss of blood was apparent, and the man's face was gray.

"Ye'll need attention for the wound, Duncan," Jamie said swiftly, nausea replaced by the urgency required here. "Hold ye still, while I get help.'

He found a surgeon, already covered in blood and filth from men's wounds, who took one look at Duncan's arm and said he'd best get to Bankton House, now set up as a hospital, since there were no bandages to bind such wounds here. He pointed the direction, too far for Duncan to walk. Jamie could see the man was too weak to ride.

"There's wagons taking the injured," the surgeon said abruptly. "If ye've the stomach for it, I'd get your man on one."

Jamie knew immediately what the man meant as soon as he saw the wagon slowly drawn around the battlefield, for some of the groaning clansmen heaped inside it had appalling injuries. Somehow he got Duncan inside with the rest, and since the lad on the wagon horse seemed set to circle the field for the day, Jamie grasped at the lead horse's neck and took charge. The lad was too dazed to protest, and they made their way to the old house, now changed beyond recognition into an extension of the Prestonpans field. Jamie wondered if he would ever rid his nostrils of the smell of blood. It tainted the soul as well as the senses.

Duncan had to wait his turn to be tended. There were far worse injuries than his, and after the surgeon had finally salved the wound and strapped it tightly to his body, he wasted no words.

"Your fighting days are over, man," he told Duncan baldly. "Ye'd be more a hindrance than an asset to your clan now. Get back to your womenfolk and defend your own, is my advice to ye."

As Jamie heard this, he saw how the crudely barked words bit into Duncan's pride. But the surgeon was right. No man could fight with one arm, and Duncan's was useless now, though he was assured that it would heal in time. The surgeon was already turning to the next man lying on the floor and awaiting his attention.

"Can he travel?" Jamie said abruptly, seeing Duncan begin to quiver with rage, despite the pain his arm was undoubtedly giving him.

"Give him a day or two more." The surgeon shrugged. "If he's not dead from infection by then, then he should do."

"Ye bastard!" Duncan's roar was a feeble imitation of his usual one. "Ye've a fine twist o' the tongue!"

"I've no time for dressing up words, man," the surgeon whipped back at him. "I'm needed for dressing wounds, and if ye canna take the truth, then ye're no credit to your clan—"

"Rest awhile, Duncan," Jamie interrupted. Such a surge of temper could do Duncan no good. He needed to stay calm, though right now that seemed an impossibility. He almost dragged Duncan to a spare corner of the room and told him to stay there while he scouted for news. Lord George Murray was an approachable figure, especially now, when he was so concerned for the wounded and angered at the senseless slaughter by some of his Highlanders. Jamie went to him boldly.

"Can ye tell me our next moves, sir? I've a badly wounded neighbor who needs help to return home, and 'tis clear across the country. I could get him there and be back within the week, God willing. Do I have your say-so, sir?"

"Ye're not using the excuse for deserting, laddie?" the general said caustically, his eyes keen on Jamie's face and assessing correctly the swift anger his words provoked.

"That I'm not," Jamie snapped. "Duncan Fraser and myself were among the first at Glenfinnan, and I'd slay any man who called us cowards."

"Ye've made your point clear enough," Lord George said dryly. "Well, 'tis certain we need to reassess our position now. We've lost a good many men. So has the enemy, but the redcoats have far more reserves than our Highlanders. I doubt that we shall leave Edinburgh immediately. With victory a new incentive to those still reluctant to come out for the prince, I'd say 'tis to our advantage to recruit more men. And those poor devils here will need time to recover from their wounds, if they're to continue with us. Take your week, man, and I'll look for ye on your return."

Smarting a little, Jamie supposed he could hardly blame the general for the comment. There would probably be those rebels who had already had enough and would be deserting back to cottage and glen to lose themselves in the hills under cover of injury, however slight. That was not for Jamie, but he couldn't blame a trained soldier for being cynical enough to suspect it.

"I'm to escort ye home," Jamie told Duncan abruptly, and he saw the man bristle. "And before ye argue, how far do ye think ye'd get alone, wi' a useless arm? Ye're to stay where ye are, Duncan, and I'll get ye some food and find some horses. God knows what happened to yours, but I've my own still and will find another."

Jamie meant to wait a day or two, but he sensed that Duncan's temper would be bursting by then, his pride throbbing worse than his arm. Jamie left him glowering at Bankton House.

Before he returned a few hours later, it was known that the Bonnie Prince Charlie was taking up residence in Holyrood-house again now that the battle at Prestonpans had been won, and, as Lord George was insisting, the campaign for new recruits to the rebel army would be intensified while they remained in Edinburgh. Most of the prince's army had come from the Highlanders in the center and north of the country, but with the new persuasion from the priest captains appeal-ing to the finer sentiments of the people, and the harsher ones brought to bear by the clan chiefs, it was hoped that a bigger and stronger army would begin the march toward England. The battle today had left them badly depleted, although the rout had been a victory, and the capture of arms and ammuni-tion and carts from the enemy had made a useful addition to rebel supplies. Plunder was fair game in battle. . . .

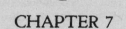

CHAPTER 7

News *of the victory at Prestonpans had spread like wildfire* across the country long before Jamie and Duncan arrived home. Their progress was slower than either wanted, because of the frequent stops when Duncan's arm pained him too much to ride and when he felt too weak to sit on the horse Jamie had acquired for him. An English redcoat's horse, left wandering in the field, he had told Duncan with satisfaction.

Shepherd and crofter, spinning wife and laird, all passed on the word that Bonnie Prince Charlie's army had won an important battle, and that the prince was now in Edinburgh, as he so rightly deserved to be.

"I'll wager the redcoats scurried like beetles when our laddies charged them," Callum Mackinnon, visiting his Fraser neighbors, said proudly. " 'Tis great news for the Stuart and for us all.''

Mairi and her family had been as elated as he to hear the news, and Katrina had sent up a prayer of relief. She still didn't know that Jamie was safe, but now that there had been a positive step toward victory for the cause, she refused to let pessimistic thoughts enter her head.

She glowed that morning as Callum related more snippets that had come to his ears through the network of messengers and rumors. He envied his son his lovely lassie, Callum thought momentarily, as wild and fresh as a wood nymph. For an instant he imagined the soft loop of the woman's garment she wore, the arisaid, gathered around her left forearm in the customary manner and cradling his Jamie's bairn. Callum prayed that he would see the day.

They were so skittish that morning, the three Fraser bairns and the winsome Mairi, that not until he left them to go stumping back over the glen to his own home did the faint shadow cross Callum's face. He was too old to believe that one successful skirmish meant total victory for the cause.

The capture of Edinburgh's palace and the victory at Prestonpans were indisputable facts, but that would not be enough for Charles Stuart. He would want the English throne as well, and ambition in a young man was as natural as breathing, in Callum's opinion. Why should the young pretender to the throne not have the desire to restore the Stuarts to British rule? Who could begrudge him that gleam of ambition and family pride? And though it meant that Highland families had to be separated from their loved ones, following the cause, that, too, would be borne with a national and wider pride. Separation was one of the penalties they paid.

It was barely a week later, as Mairi and her elder daughter sat together in the late evening, the bairns already in bed, when the sound of approaching riders put the Fraser menservants on their guard. Minutes later they were running in to their mistress .with the glad news that their laird was come home with the young Mackinnon.

Katrina leapt to her feet, hardly able to believe what she heard. All her prayers had been answered! Her Jamie was home . . . her father, too. Both women rushed to greet their men with cries of joy, only to stop short when they saw the gray pallor in Duncan's face and the way his left arm was bound tightly, still held stiffly in the sling of his plaid. But before Mairi could gasp out her anxiety, she was clasped tightly to her man by his strong right arm.

"Dinna fash, my woman," Duncan said roughly. "'Tis a deep gash I suffered, but as long as I have one good arm to hold ye, I have riches enough."

"I just thank God ye're home, dearest," Mairi said thickly, tears of relief shining on her lashes. "Does it pain ye much?"

His grimace said more than his words. "Somewhat. But I'm told the wound will heal in time, though the arm will never be much use to me, nor as flexible as I'd like. But 'tis a small price to pay, lassie."

"Aye, so it is." Mairi hugged him close, careful not to press against his left side, and her tears finally betrayed all her hidden feelings. Thankfulness spilled out of her, for her man and for Jamie, too, hugging the breath out of his own lassie. Then her practical side asserted itself. "But we should be feasting for your safe return to us, and instead there's naught but a warm welcome and a few drams and a leftover supper."

"A warm welcome's more than enough to fill our bellies this night, Mistress Fraser," Jamie assured her. "A crofter gave us cabbage soup and bread a while since, and I have all I need right here."

He hugged Katrina tight, and she was almost too choked with happiness to speak. Her Jamie was home, and it seemed like a miracle. Mairi called for whiskey to be brought, and the four of them drank to the prince, the cause, and to the safe and joyous return of their loved ones.

Later, sitting close to Jamie, Katrina listened as he and her father told their tales. Her hand was held tightly in his, and sometimes she felt its tremor and knew there was much that he had seen that did not get told.

"The redcoats hardly had time to load their muskets," Duncan grunted. "And those who tried to fix bayonets found them useless against our weapons. The dirk and broadsword found many marks that day, lass. They know the power of the clans now, by God. Our one charge was enough to send them all scattering like squealing mice."

"But one of their weapons found its mark," Mairi said, her voice edged as she gently touched her man's left arm, where the blood still caked his torn shirt and plaid. Tucked inside his rough sling was a dying sprig of yew, and a small smile curved her mouth.

"The old custom was followed, then?"

"Aye, dearie. We were able to find plenty of yew sprigs to signify our clan and passed them out to share the luck and ward off evil."

"The English would no doubt think our plant badge ritual akin to witchcraft," Jamie said dryly, "but I wore my sprig o' pine with the Mackinnons and roared into the battle wi' the Mackinnon slogan on my lips. There's many a redcoat whose last memory was the sound o' the Gaelic in his ears, and *Cuimhnich bas Ailpein* the last words he heard in his life."

Katrina shivered, and Mairi saw the movement and how pale her daughter had become.

"I think we've heard enough battle stories for now," she said quickly. "Can we hear something less harrowing? What of the arrival in Edinburgh? Was the prince welcomed?"

"Not by all, mistress!" Jamie grimaced. "If ye'd heard the roars of disapproval from the good citizens of the town, ye'd have thought we were the enemy! They've been under English rule too long there, but our bonnie lad has a way wi' him to stir many a heart, and a fine way wi' words, too, though I wager not many could follow all the gist of it. By the end of the speech, though, there were cheers and huzzas enough, and our own army made more than enough noise to cover the townspeople's din!"

Duncan laughed, remembering it.

"Aye, and many a lassie's head was turned by the sight of the prince in his velvet and lace. If the two of ye had seen him on that day, ye'd have thought we two some wild mountain men."

"That we never would," Mairi protested, but Katrina's eyes sparkled at the telling. She remembered seeing him, so alone in his cause at Glenfinnan, and hearing him speak. He had caught at her imagination, too, and she heard Jamie give a low chuckle and felt him tighten his arm about her waist as they sat together.

"Ye can see how it is wi' Katrina, mistress! The stars shine in her eyes at the mention of the Stuart. She's lost her heart to him like all the other lassies."

"I doubt that, Jamie," Duncan said. "But ye can be glad he's away from here, and ye're not! Now then, my wife and myself are off to our bed, and I've a wish to look in on my bairns besides. My greeting to your faither when ye get home, Jamie, and don't take all the night before ye leave."

His meaning wasn't lost on them, but neither really saw Katrina's parents leave the room together. They were alone now, with only the last embers of firelight to warm the room and the drifting scent of woodsmoke to envelop them. Jamie drew her to him, his embrace more urgent now, his kiss sweet and possessive. It brought her back to life, as if all her emotions had been frozen until now, locked away in that shell of her body until Jamie came home to release them. But now he was here and she was in his arms, and she swayed against him as if she would melt in the sheer joy of him.

He murmured against her mouth, kissing her lips, her eyes, her throat where a pulse throbbed like a wild bird seeking release from captivity. "How I've missed ye, my sweet, sweet lassie."

"And I you!" Katrina could hardly draw breath to tell him so as his hands spanned her waist and the soft curves of her hips as if to learn every part of her all over again. "Oh, Jamie, I've missed ye so much. Ye canna guess how much."

"I can guess," he said, his voice thick. "For I share the same feelings as ye, my love. It's hard for me to measure it in words."

Her eyes were large and lustrous in the firelight, her hair a fiery tumble over her shoulders. Jamie caught a handful of it in his palm, twisting its rich texture to his cheek.

"I canna measure it in words," she agreed in a soft whisper. "Only in feelings, Jamie. Only in the way I've ached for ye, and wanted ye—"

She stopped, knowing her feelings were running away with her. She was drunk with his nearness, and his ragged breathing told her his needs were finding renewed life this night, too. Yet when he spoke, it was in a strange, tightly controlled voice.

"A short while ago, my lassie, I'd have had no hesitation in taking my fill of ye tonight, certain that I could overcome your resistance, and God knows 'tis what I've ached for—"

He stopped abruptly, and an odd little chill ran through her, almost like a premonition. She understood his voice and moods well enough to know that all the love and the yearning were undoubtedly still there, but there was something else, too. Jamie had always been strong, and his few years' advantage of her had given him an added maturity, but it was more pronounced tonight. In the weeks he had been away, she recognized that he hadn't really grown away from her, but he had grown within himself. Maybe she was maturing, too, if she could see it and accept it. . . .

"Tell me what ails ye, Jamie," she said gently.

Her deep-hued eyes shone with an emotion she couldn't voice at that moment, and Jamie gathered her close to him again, not wanting to see their hurt as he said his piece in rough, staccato words.

"I'd make ye mine here and now, Katrina, but I could'na risk leaving a bairn in your belly, my sweet lassie. God knows when I shall return the next time."

"The next time!" She echoed his words with a little cry, all the ice closing in on her again. The battle was won . . . but there were more to be fought, and Jamie was only here for a wee while after all. How could she have let herself dream it was any different!

" 'Tis over for your father, lass but 'tis far from over for the cause and ye must have known that! Charles needs his clansmen, and ye would'na have me desert him! I must ride back tomorrow to see how things fare in Edinburgh. We needed many more men to start the push into England, and God willing, the support will be there after our victory at Prestonpans."

Katrina swallowed dryly. She could hear the pride in Jamie's voice. She could not hold him here while he had such a sense of duty, and neither would she. *Neither would she*, she thought to her own surprise. Even though it was her loss . . . and she was still woman enough to weep softly against his shoulder.

"So I am to lose ye again so soon?"

"Ay, my dear one," he said huskily. "There's no other way."

She felt his hands stroking her hair, and the moments of patriotic fervor she felt seemed to drain away from her as quickly as they came. She was not totally committed yet, as the brave fighting laddies were, she thought with a stab of guilt. She thought only of her own wishes, and in doing so she put an added strain on Jamie.

She drew a deep breath. She didn't need telling that he loved her and would choose to be with her if times were different. But times were not different. They were as they were, and Katrina realized with sudden illumination that it was for her sake that Jamie restrained himself tonight. And not only for the fear of leaving his seed in her that might produce a love child. There was another unspoken fear—that he might never return from his service to Charles Stuart. If that ever happened, she would truly be left with nothing. . . .

"I know ye must go, Jamie." She spoke quickly, before she lost her courage. "I'll not be the one to try to stop ye, even though it breaks my heart to say it. I have a loyalty, too, and be very sure that my heart goes with ye."

"Then I'm certain to return, to bring it safely home again," he pledged softly. His arms were holding her close, and he had never loved her more.

A week after Jamie had returned to Edinburgh, Iona ran bleating to her mother's skirts, red-faced and outraged, and Duncan was forced to chuckle at her little wildcat ways, which reminded him of his elder daughter. He had begun to feel more comfortable with his wounded arm now and was more content to deal with domestic matters in his own home, now that he was its master once more.

"Don't be laughing at her, Duncan!" Mairi reproved him, and he glanced at her in mild surprise. Was it wrong to tease one's own bairn now! But he saw the frown on his wife's face and refrained from comment, leaning back on the hard settle and glad of the fire's heat. The seasons had moved on, and summer was behind them. Mornings were cold and bleak, the glen taking on a new and savage beauty that was awesome and majestic. Clothed in dense mist, the mountains gradually emerged into the daylight like huge crouching monsters from another age. Guardians of the glen, Mairi called them.

"What's to do, then? Since when is it forbidden to smile at my own bairn?" he demanded to know now.

"We've had these tantrums aplenty while ye've been away," Mairi said tartly. "We've managed to keep them from your sight until now."

He sat up straighter. He didn't hold with tantrums from a child no bigger than a puffball. Iona saw his look directed at her and burst into her wild tirade.

"Katrina's always out of patience wi' me, Faither! She tugs my hair when she braids it, and when I shout, she gets crosser and tugs it more. My head hurts because of her, and then Hannah grumbles at me because I canna do my lessons for the hurt in my head—"

"Hush now, my wee one!" Mairi stopped the shrill little voice. Over Iona's head, she glanced at Duncan, her mouth compressed in a tight line. The look said there would be words between them later about all this. "Let me look at your braids."

They were noticeably too tight. The strands of red-gold hair were pulled out from the scalp at the nape of the child's neck and reddened from her squirming. Mairi loosened them at once and rebraided them.

"There now. And tell Katrina to leave your hair braiding to me in future, dearie." Mairi kissed the small flushed face.

"She'll not believe me, Mammie." Iona sulked.

"Then I'll tell her," Mairi said firmly. "I'll have no more of this squabbling between the two of ye. Away to your lessons now, and leave your faither and me to talk."

As soon as she had left the room, Duncan demanded to know how long this disharmony had been going on.

"How long do ye think?" Mairi asked. "Ever since Jamie went away and Katrina took on the wild ways even more than before. Her temper has been very sore, and it's been an uneasy house these past weeks, Duncan."

His eyes narrowed, detecting more than she said.

"Ye've given the matter some thought, I'll wager, Mairi, so ye'd best tell me what's on your mind. The lassie's too old for nursery teaching now, and she's a woman grown. Once she's wed to Jamie he can have the taming of her."

"So he can, but meanwhile she disrupts the household," Mairi said feelingly. "I canna handle her some days. She alternates between the foolishness of a bairn and the wisdom of a woman, and my head fair aches wi' never knowing which Katrina I'll see each morning! We all get the lash of her tongue at times, Iona and Hamish and me!"

"I canna see ye letting a bairn get the better of ye, dove."

"Nor I do, which means we end up blathering at each other like fishwives! I know she's worried for Jamie, and I try to allow for that, but if this situation goes on much longer . . ."

Duncan kept his face impassive. Who knew how long the rebellion might last? Even now, while the prince was still gathering reinforcements at Edinburgh, the English army would be doing the same. The clashes would go on; news pamphlets that came their way told of the frustration felt by the rebel army as it waited for the order to move toward the border. Leaders were restless, knowing the army must have more men to make the cause a viable proposition after the losses at Prestonpans and the reported strength of the English army. The prince was equally restless, obliged to entertain some of the Edinburgh society at Holyroodhouse in his new role as prince regent for his father, while his instincts told him this was not his prime purpose in being here. He had been schooled from birth to his destiny, and until the monarchy was in the rightful hands of the Stuarts, he was not fulfilling it.

But here and now, Duncan Fraser was more concerned with the effects Charles Stuart's cause was having on his daughter, Katrina. And if Mairi had some idea of how to handle her, then she had better out with it, and he bluntly told her so.

"I'd wish to see her more of a lady, Duncan. While old Margret had the handling of her, she seemed more agreeable, but as ye say, she's too old for Hannah's teachings, and 'tis hardly fair to closet her with the young ones all day." Mairi took a breath. "I want to send her to my sister's home for a while."

Duncan glowered, as she had expected. "Ye'd send the lass to the Lowlanders, lass? Ye know my opinion of your milksop sister! And ye'd see our fiery Katrina subdued in that way?"

"Be reasonable, Duncan," Mairi pleaded. "What ye've seen from Iona today is but a small part of it. She torments the life out of the bairns, and since Hamish thinks himself near to a man already, she hurts his pride. I tell ye, much as I've motherly feelings for the lass, I canna take much more of it!"

"And ye think your sister Janet will deal with her any better?" she said skeptically.

"Aye, I do! In a different environment, Katrina may well lose some of her wilfulness! Her cousin Helen will be a good influence, I've no doubt. And Janet was always the peaceable one of the family. I sometimes envy the calm of that household!"

He would have laughed out loud had he not seen that she was so serious. His Mairi, who had always thrived on verbal exchanges, envying her paler shadow of a sister! But he was quick to see she was genuinely distressed. It may not be such a bad idea, Duncan thought, letting it grow in his mind. The lassie could learn a few things in the gentler south of the country. And it would give her some interest other than fretting for Jamie Mackinnon's return!

He found her later that day, glaring at the piece of tapestry she was working and jabbing at some offending stitches with the points of her scissors. She was clearly in a bad humor, but by then Duncan had talked with Iona and Hamish and learned a little more about Katrina's tempers.

"Now then, lassie, I hear ye've been upsetting the bairns lately. 'Tis time ye had other things to do."

"So I have! I've this stupid tapestry that keeps puckering!" She flung it away from her, the scissors following, and she could have wept with annoyance. Nothing went the way she wanted it to these days. Her whole world had slipped sideways, and she was sliding with it, unable to recapture the laughing lassie who had run so often to meet her Jamie in the soft green glen.

Sometimes those days seemed so far away she could barely recall them, and that threw her into a more confused state of mind. Sometimes she found it hard to remember the roughness of Jamie's cheek against hers; to remember how it felt to breathe in the male scent of him and to know the strength of his love for her. Sometimes it frightened her to know she was unable to picture him clearly when she needed him most.

And no one seemed to understand how it felt to be seventeen and in love, and how could they? It was too private to share with anyone. Sometimes she felt as if she stood on the edge of a great precipice, the safe world of childhood behind her, the unknown world ahead. She longed for that other, more mature world, but without Jamie to share it with her, she was left in a void, and only by lashing out with caustic words did she feel any kind of release. Unfortunately, the relief didn't last long.

Duncan knew nothing of her inner torment, her fervent wish that she, too, could be as fanatical about Charles Stuart as everyone else. She wished for it because it would lessen her heartache on Jamie's account. And that, too, was a guilty thought. She should wish it for her country's sake, not her own. . . . Her father never guessed at her troubled mind; all he saw was the fury in her eyes as she threw her needlework across the room.

"Your mother and I have decided that ye'll go to your Aunt Janet's in Kirkcudbright for a while, Katrina," he said curtly, without dressing up the words. "For several months, I think."

She leapt from her window seat, her eyes blazing even more.

"Ye're sending me away, Faither? Ye canna! When Jamie comes home, I'll be far away, and we're to be wed after the turn of the year."

"Lassie, ye know as well as I do that Jamie will be with the prince as long as he needs him. It may be months before the struggle's over, and ye'd be better employed in your aunt's household. I'm told ye've not been treating your brother and sister fairly."

"They plague me. Ye know it, Faither."

"And ye're old enough to deal wi' that, too," he retorted. "My mind's made. A while away from home will be good for ye, and for your family. I'll send one of my men with a letter to your aunt requesting that she give ye hospitality, and I'll take ye there myself."

Katrina knew by her father's tone of voice that her argu-

ments would be futile. She was being banished. . . . The
drama of the word as it came into her head almost made her
smile, for in its wake came the thought that this visit south
might not be so bad at that. She and her mammie and the
bairns *had* been at each other's throats lately, and the parting
might do them all good! But it might be wise not to give in
too easily. They would not expect it of her!

"I suppose Mammie thinks I'll come back from Aunt
Janet's a lady, does she?" She put the sulks into her voice
and caught the glimmer of a smile from her father. He gave
her a quick hug with his one good arm.

"I'd not want ye to change too much, my lassie," he
murmured. "Ye've too much of your mammie's sparkle in
ye, and no doubt that's the reason the two of ye clash so often
now that ye're so near to being a woman. I'll promise ye one
thing, Katrina. Since ye'll be living nearer to the English
border in your aunt's house, I'll instruct the man, Alex, to
pass the word about that Jamie Mackinnon's betrothed is
staying in Kirkcudbright. There's always a chance he'll get
the message and find an hour to seek ye out if the army rests
in this area awhile."

Duncan knew it was a thin chance, but the thought of
Jamie finding a way to see Katrina was not impossible, and
more likely in the Lowlands than here. The Lowlands was a
link between the Highlands and the border with England, and
Katrina's quick thinking was telling her the same.

It would be the first time Katrina had traveled away from
home, though she remembered her aunt's family from their
one long-ago visit to Frashiel House. It would be a new
interest to occupy her mind, an adventure. . . . She tingled
inside at the sudden thought. The recent days had been so
dull, and here was something new, something positive.

Katrina realized that the dullness of her days here had been
the very trouble. Why hadn't she seen it before? The Jacobite
cause had made barely a ripple in her brother's and sister's
lives, but for her, everything had changed. Jamie had gone to
join the prince, but she was left kicking her heels, and it
wasn't her nature to be so lacking in spirit. The visit gave her
something of interest to do instead of moping so inanely.
Now that she finally admitted the waste of it, Katrina welcomed her father's edict.

"If I must go, then I must." She was still contrary enough not to let him think he had won. "Providing ye'll do as ye say and try to send word to Jamie, Faither."

"I've said so." He was clearly relieved not to have a storm of tears from his daughter. "We'll tell your mother together."

Katrina followed him from the room, not quite sure who was the victor here, but it didn't matter. Mairi looked at her warily, and at that Katrina lifted her chin, still not quite forgiving her for wanting to send her packing, and gave the expected retort as Duncan said he'd send the man Alex to the Lowland home as soon as Mairi had penned her letter to her sister.

"I doubt that I shall enjoy it there, Mammie," she told her defiantly. "I recall my cousin Helen being a weak little thing and calling me a roughneck when she was here to stay. She'll be as feeble as a mouse by now. Do ye think Aunt Janet may think me too bad an influence to stay there after all? Helen was her precious wee thing, wasn't she?"

"Ye'll mind your manners and be a credit to this house," Mairi told her at once. "Helen is only a year younger than yourself and will be a companion for ye."

"Mebbe," Katrina said noncommittally, though the thought had occurred to her, too. She had no young female companions her own age, and maybe Helen had a laddie, too. At once, Katrina hoped she didn't, for she had no wish to play the gooseberry, but Helen as a friend was a welcome thought after all.

In bed that night she still mulled over the idea with mixed feelings and was unable to sleep. Leaving home was the biggest adventure she had ever had. Indeed, what other had there been in her life? She couldn't ignore the stirrings of excitement at the thought, but she was a wee bit nervous, too. Aunt Janet and her family were strangers, for all that they were kin. She hardly remembered them, really, save for the tidbits she had told her mammie. Uncle Robert was a mite pompous, a farming man with a fine stock of cattle and fields of corn who had clearly thought his sister-in-law's children a lawless brood. Iona hadn't been born when they had visited, but Hamish had been a stubborn wee three-year-old, inclined to be bilious without warning. Katrina still remembered the moment the small Hamish had puked all over his uncle's fine new weskit and trews.

She smiled into the darkness. She would be miles nearer to wherever Jamie was right now if the prince had left Edinburgh yet. The border with England was not that far distant from her aunt's home, in an easterly direction. The prince would surely make for Carlisle on his march into England, the first major town over the border. Katrina quickly recalled the map she had studied in the schoolroom. Carlisle was not so far from Kirkcudbright. It was a poignant thought. So near. . . . Her restless thoughts moved on, unable to deny the bonnie prince his right to his kingdom. It was a man's destiny to fight for his birthright, and a woman's to wait and worry and feel helpless at her inadequacy.

Katrina's thoughts meandered on. There was still a fundamental need for a woman; not all the triumph of victory in battle could give a man what a woman could, in love and comfort. Old Margret had once said that a woman held the power of the universe in her body, and so she did. When the battles were over, it was to his mate that a man turned and neither then was superior, for each complemented the other, two halves of a perfect being.

The simple truth was oddly comforting to Katrina. In spirit if not in body, she and Jamie were already a part of each other. The good Lord would surely not deny them their lives together. Believing it with the simple logic of a child, Katrina finally slept.

The news of her impending departure produced a surprising bout of crying in Iona. She threw her little arms about Katrina's waist when she was told the next day.

"Dinna go, Katrina! I'll let ye braid my hair and never squeal, I promise!"

Katrina swung her up in her arms and kissed her soft cheek.

"It's for the best, dearie, but I'll miss ye, for all that ye get beneath my skin like a wee burr at times!" she said huskily. "Anyway, I'm not leaving yet. 'Twill take a week for Alex to take Mammie's letter to Aunt Janet's house and be back with her reply. Mebbe she'll not want me there!"

There was little doubt that Janet would offer hospitality to her niece, for the family ties were strong, even though the sisters rarely saw each other, and Mairi had told Katrina shortly that she'd refrain from mentioning that Katrina had been such a sorehead lately. Katrina bit her lips tightly at that, knowing that a snappy reply would only prove her mammie right.

There were other folk who needed to be told. Old Margret and Angus Blainey, who were old and dear friends, and Jamie's father. Katrina wrapped a warm shawl about her shoulders and did the telling to all of them in one afternoon.

"Ye mind and copy some of your fine lady aunt's gentle ways, dearie," Margret told her. "And your wee cousin will be a friend to ye."

"Dinna come home too changed, lassie," old Angus said from his corner seat by the peat fire, a thick blanket around his shoulders now as he prodded the sparking fire. Each winter he became more bent, but with the coming of every spring he rallied somehow, like a young sprig welcoming another year. She bent and kissed his wrinkled face.

"I won't," she said, a catch in her voice. "They will'na change me, Angus!"

A week later, visiting Jamie's father, Katrina's heart leapt as the man drew her close for a moment and then told her he had something for her.

"This very day I received a letter from Jamie, lassie, and the packet contained one for ye, too. Full o' the sweet-talk, I've no doubt! I'll leave ye alone to read it, while I get my man to serve us wi' some oaties."

Katrina hardly heard him, even though she was very fond of the oatcakes. All she heard was the sound of Jamie's voice in her head as she tore open the letter he had written to her. Seated in the wide stone window seat of the Mackinnon house, the panorama of the glen outside stretched before her, but that spectacle was also lost on her in the importance of this contact with Jamie.

"My dearie," he had written. "I've little time for writing, for we are in haste here. It seems our prince and his advisers realize we have tarried too long, although it was necessary in gathering more clansmen for the cause and for the wounded to recover. But now we must head toward England."

Katrina drew in her breath as she read the words, and her breath came fast as her eyes scanned the rest of the letter.

"Our spies tell us that the English have a fine new leader for their army, Katrina. 'Tis George's son himself, the duke of Cumberland. This duke is our own prince's relative, a sort of cousin, hen. But kin or no, they will be bitter enemies in the future, and by all accounts we can forget any fumblings from the redcoats now. Cumberland is a born soldier and will be marching his new army north by now. We're not afraid to meet him. But keep yourself calm, my dearie. Think of your own feelings for me and know that they're returned. Pray for me, and for the prince, dearest lassie.''

There was not so much of the sweet-talk, then! Katrina's throat was full as she finished reading, as if she recognized more clearly now that there was a part of Jamie's soul she couldn't reach. She could almost hear the pride in his words. And she had felt it, too. That fleeting moment at Glenfinnan, when the prince's eyes had seemed to look directly into hers, had produced a quick surge of patriotic fervor in her. She knew now, just as she had known then, that if she were a man she would fight for the Stuart cause, too, and die for it if need be.

If only this conflict between her fears for Jamie and her own deep-rooted loyalty didn't make her drift like a leaf in the wind in her feelings! One minute strong as a man, the next a softhearted woman who needed her Jamie at her side . . . She struggled with her own conscience. Would she really allow herself to be the weeping lassie who begged her man to come home because of her? She would not!

She heard Callum Mackinnon coming back to her, swallowed back the ache of emptiness inside her, and tucked Jamie's letter in the neck of her dress next to her heart like a talisman. If God willed it so, then Jamie's kiss would soon replace the rough edges of the paper against her skin. It was surely no disloyalty to hope for the day.

CHAPTER 8

It was time for Katrina to journey south. Her clothes were packed in boxes, and she was ready to leave in the traveling wagon with her father and Alex, the manservant. Any further delay might mean that the two men would be traveling back to Frashiel House in bad weather. The Highlands could be a vast white wilderness once winter got its grip on the country. Already a sprinkling of snow had come and gone, the portent of worse to come, and Duncan did not care to travel the length of the country in any needless hazards.

Mairi hugged her daughter tightly at the moment of parting.

"Enjoy the soft life awhile, dearie, and come home refreshed. Your aunt will welcome ye, and ye'll find a few birthday gifties at the bottom of your boxes."

"I'll miss ye, Mammie," Katrina said, the words tumbling out. "And the bairns, too!"

She hugged each one in turn, trying to recapture that feeling of adventure at her visit, but it eluded her for the moment. She tried to smile at her mother as she waved to her and the children, so that they would not guess at her churning feelings. It was hard to feel that sense of anticipation she had known, when every mile in the trundling wagon took her farther and farther away from her home. Even if Jamie were marching south with the prince's army, they might just as well be poles apart. Edinburgh was on the opposite side of the country. Although the army moved in the same general direction as herself, in a parallel way, Jamie was not even aware of it.

The journey took four days. They stopped at wayside inns to rest the horses and ease their aching limbs from the hard wood of the wagon and to rest during the nights. The rattling of the wagon wheels was muffled somewhat as they traveled from sleet to snow. There was no thought of turning back. Men and horses were used to peering through gray daylight and had both become sure-footed and immune to the cold. They wondered how the English redcoats would be faring in such weather.

"They'll be missing their soft beds more than our hardy Highlanders," Duncan grunted in satisfaction.

"Mebbe the prince is missing his, too!" Katrina said as they alighted thankfully at yet one more grim-looking inn, its roof insulated now by a snowy crown. This would be the last, she thought thankfully. They were on the final stretch before her aunt's home, and she felt bruised all over from the journey.

Duncan pushed open the door of the inn and saw at once that it was a bawdier place than he had expected. Katrina would cheerfully have slept in a cow barn at that moment. She was too weary to care if the revelers there were raucous or not, and after a minute's hesitation, Duncan said they would stay. Inside the smoke-filled room, there was a good stout inn wife smiling with her man to reassure the travelers.

"Have ye heard the ·news, strangers?" A merrymaker, bloated with whiskey and ale and blather, slapped Duncan on the back, his whiskers almost bristling with good cheer. "The Stuart has taken Carlisle, man!"

"What!" Duncan's eyes were as alight as the other's now. "How do ye come by this news, man? We've heard none of it. The prince still tarried in Edinburgh the last we heard."

"Aye, waiting for French aid and soldiers, they say." The next man to speak spat noisily onto the sawdust-strewn floor in an expressive gesture of his opinion. "The French ships arrived wi' guns and a dozen men, and there's the help o' your fine Frenchies."

"Our rebels be a match for the redcoats, and I'd fight any bastard here who says otherwise," the first one said, aggressive and fiery.

"Do ye know any details?" Duncan demanded, seeing there was little sense to be gotten from most of them and still wondering if it was all a pixie's tale.

" 'Tis true enough, stranger," the innkeeper said in a flatter voice, his eyes steadily watching Duncan's face. "The rebel army marched from Edinburgh in two columns, one led by the general, Drummond, the other by the prince and the Lord George Murray, who he's said to set such store by, despite their differences. The redcoats were muddled by means of our two divisions marching half a day apart and going by different routes, so they did'na know which border town they meant to take. Carlisle stood the siege for five days, and then it fell to the Stuart. And what I'm wanting to know, strangers, is how ye profess to know naught of the rout or the victory at Carlisle? If indeed it *be* a victory to ye three."

The innkeeper was suddenly close to them, a note of menace and suspicion in his voice. Until then, the revelers had been prancing around the inn, swinging the serving lassies in the air to their delighted squeals. The air got more and more rank, and Katrina was near to choking with it; when a leering southerner pushed his face close to hers with the offer of a dram, she drew back in disgust at the reek of him. The innkeeper was a deal more sober than his clientele, and at his voice the babble of talk eased off. Katrina felt a thrill of fear at the change in their manner.

Swiftly, she realized exactly what the innkeeper had implied. On this last halt before reaching her aunt's house, they were much nearer to the border with England than in their own remote Highlands. It would be easy for English spies to infiltrate here, dressed as Scotsmen, to take back news and the climate of the people. For all her family's standing in their own glen, these people here knew naught of them and might be thinking that very thing. As if Alex, the dour manservant, thought so at the same instant, it was he who shouted back angrily, outraged at this slur on his master and his daughter.

"This is Duncan Fraser of Frashiel House, and his daughter, dolt! They journey to the house of a kinsman, Bancroft of Kirkcudbright."

"I know of Bancroft," one of the revelers growled. "A farmer wi' a wife and—"

"Stay your talk, man. Let the strangers tell the details of his kin," the innkeeper ordered, and Katrina knew at once that she had surmised correctly. The query was a test, but her father replied immediately, the cold anger in him tempered by his own shrewd assessment of the situation.

"My wife Mairi is the sister of Janet Bancroft of Kirdcud-bright. She and her husband, Robert, have a daughter Helen, a year younger than my own here. They also had a son, Andrew, who died in infancy some years since."

"Aye, 'tis right enough." The innkeeper's neighbor nodded. "And I mind hearing Mistress Bancroft tell of Highland kin."

The innkeeper nodded in acceptance. "Then 'tis welcome ye are, and ye'll understand the caution. We've grown wary of strangers lately, for 'tis never known which be king's men, and this be a loyal house." His emphasis left no doubt as to where his loyalties lay.

Katrina was alarmed at the angry mutterings after his words. The feeling that this conflict was a true war was still unreal, despite her father's injury. As she looked about her, she realized that some of the faces in the inn were gaunt and haggard, and had probably seen and heard more things than she had dreamed of. Hard men, whose talk of victory was interlaced with gloating memories of other rebellions and other victories. She spoke to one man quickly, without heeding her father's displeasure at her consorting with such a scruff. But some of these might even have been involved in the siege at Carlisle. . . .

"Were ye there—at Carlisle? Do ye have personal knowledge of it?" she demanded.

The man wiped his hand on his straggly beard, seeing the comely young woman in the green traveling dress that hugged her shape, the hooded shawl thrown back from the bright tumbling hair, and the slender shoulders bared in the inn's heat.

"What will ye gi' me to tell ye, lassie?" he leered. "Such information be worth a kiss for an old rogue."

Katrina moved back as if he were something that had crawled out from a stone. He stank of body sweat and ale, a malodorous, nauseating mixture. She felt a quick fear and knew she had been rash to speak to him while her father and Alex were engaged in other talk.

109

"Ye weren't there! My own laddie's away fighting for the cause, but I'd not expect such as ye to risk life and limb when 'tis clear ye pay more attention to filling your belly."

"*Katrina!*" Duncan's thunderous voice was right behind her, but by then she had seen the tinge of respect in the other man's eyes, and his mouth broke into a black-toothed grin as he shrugged his massive shoulders.

"Let the lassie be, man. 'Tis a fine and spirited one ye've spawned. And she's not wrong. I was'na at Carlisle, nor would I want to be anywhere near the English bastards, though there's two in yonder back room who were. They've plenty o' fine tales to tell."

The compulsion to speak to anyone who might know of Jamie, to tell her how he fared, overcame Katrina then. She pushed her way through the merrymakers in the inn, with Duncan and Alex fast behind her. She knew her father would be angry, but she was suddenly driven on to seek information as if all the devils in hell were behind her. She felt Duncan's hand grip her arm before she reached the back room indicated to her.

"Will ye stop shaming us all!" Duncan hissed in her ear. "Have ye no thought that the men in there will be nobbut deserters? Is that whom ye wish to question?"

She hadn't even considered the possibility. It must be true . . . unless there were another reason. Unless they were injured and trying to get home, their usefulness in the prince's service over. . . . Katrina twisted away to push open the door of the room, the men still behind her. The moment she entered it, she stopped still, almost retching at the sight there, knowing at once that her thoughts had been the right ones. Duncan closed the door quickly, enclosing them with the two wretches there.

They sprawled on makeshift cots, filthy and ragged. One had his head roughly bandaged, and the stench of blood was so acrid it almost closed Katrina's nostrils. The other man moaned wildly, threshing with his one remaining arm while the other stump was raw and putrid and weeping. His eyes were wild, his voice thready, begging for water and for death.

A bowl of water stood on a table nearby. Trembling, Katrina picked it up and held it to the man's lips. He drank

110

deeply, spilling most of it, babbling incoherently. His arm knocked the bowl out of her hands, and she suddenly recoiled in horror as he clawed at her skirt with a bloodied hand. She couldn't move away, held by horror, and his glazed eyes seemed to pierce the void between himself and her.

"Is it my Sheilagh come to take me home?" The thin voice quavered at her, his pain almost tangible.

And before Katrina could struggle to find a reply or try to extricate herself from his grip, he suddenly vomited all over her, his grasp slackened, and he was dead. To her horror, she heard the sound of laughing coming from the other cot.

"Ye're a lucky bastard, Lachlan Muir," the wild voice croaked. "Gi' me your hand, lassie, for I'd follow my kinsman to eternity."

Bile rose into Katrina's mouth at the gist of his ramblings. She shook as if with the ague, and as she felt her father's hard slap across her face, she realized her own screaming was adding to the uproar in the room. The door flew open and closed again, the innkeeper coming to see what the din was about. The sight of him, still exuding the rough hospitality of a wayside hostelry when a man had just died in agony, changed her wild screaming to hysterical laughter that matched the rebel's. Her father slapped her again, a stinging slap that felt as if it bruised her bones.

"Don't, please don't, Faither," she whimpered. "I hurt!"

"Innkeeper, is there a place where we can sleep the night?" Duncan snapped urgently. "We'll need rooms and a lassie wi' hot water and towels and soap for my daughter's needs. We've money to pay, and I'll spare a little for the wretch here that's left. There's naught to do for the other, except bury him and inform his Sheilagh if ye can. Will ye see to it, man?"

"Aye, that I will." The innkeeper sprang to life as Duncan tossed some coins at him. Whether his wishes were carried out, Duncan neither knew nor cared, as long as he got Katrina away at once. He feared at the vague, distracted look in her eyes now, and she had to be gotten out of the obnoxious garments she wore with all speed.

"Send a girl upstairs immediately to a room where my daughter may rest," he ordered anew. "She is unwell and needs attention."

"My wife will be with ye directly," came the reply. "If ye'll follow me, I'll see to it."

He shouted for assistance as he took them by a back route up the stairs and into a small clean room. Katrina seemed unaware of her movements, as if she floated from one place to another, and Duncan was becoming more anxious at the sight of her and starting to censure himself for letting Mairi talk him into this visit. None of them had considered that in being nearer to the border with England, the girl would be so likely to hear tales of war, and certainly Duncan had never expected Katrina to be faced with such horrific evidence of the dangers that Jamie faced. In a single moment, she had become all too aware of it.

The inn wife came bustling into the room, her nose wrinkling at the filth reeking from Katrina's dress and skin. She had brought hot water, soap, and towels with her as ordered and clucked now like a mother hen.

"Leave the lassie to me, sir, and I'll soon have her tucked up and in bed and see to the cleaning of her clothes. This be woman's work, and if 'tis victuals ye be wanting later, I'll see to it when I've settled the lassie."

Duncan left her with a guilty thankfulness, and when he had gone the woman bade Katrina lift her arms while she removed the stinking garments. Katrina obeyed as if she had no will of her own, shivering on the edge of the narrow bed and oblivious to anything the woman did. She hardly noticed as the inn wife soaped a cloth and scrubbed at her body, rubbing it dry with a towel, nor did she notice the woman's envying looks at her milk-white skin and firm young curves.

"Lift your arms, dearie. Over your head wi' the nightgown, now," said the inn wife, alarmed at the girl's pallor.

She slid one of her own voluminous nightgowns over Katrina's head and pulled it over her body, pushing her gently until she lay in the bed, the blankets covering her. Katrina let her do what she would, as if she were watching it happen to someone else. It was only when the woman stuffed her offending clothes into a bucket and made to leave the room that her lips seemed able to form words.

"Jamie?" His name came out huskily, her eyes bewildered still, as if she expected to find him here.

"He'll be here soon, lassie. Try to sleep," the woman told her with rough sympathy. There was nothing else she could say.

Alone, Katrina stared at the blank ceiling with dry eyes. From her instinctive revulsion at the clinging hand of the dying man, she now felt nothing and seemed incapable of feeling. Momentarily, as the inn wife had prepared her for bed, she had imagined Jamie was with her. The touch of another skin against hers, the sensation of her body being studied, the awareness of being cared for . . . Into her scattered senses the image of Jamie had come and gone, and she couldn't hold on to it. Jamie . . . where was Jamie? She was alone in a great dark void, swirling her into nothingness. . . .

Had she slept or fallen into unconsciousness, driven there by her own demented thoughts? Katrina couldn't have said, but it seemed a long while later when her eyes slowly opened and she registered that she still lay in the hard bed in the inn, and that outside, the merest hint of daylight lightened the sky, heralding the start of a new day.

She felt different and tried to analyze the difference. Relief flooded her that she was even able to think, remembering with crystal clarity that dreadful sensation of being suspended in time, when everything about her had shape and movement, and she had nothing. What had prompted such a reaction?

Memory surged into her mind. There had been a ragged, filthy rebel clansman who had vomited and died, holding her hand in a death grip and gaining a crumb of comfort in believing she was his Sheilagh.

Katrina waited for the horror to sweep over her again, and it didn't come. Only the sadness and the pity, and the realization, after seeing death so close and for the first time in her life, that every moment spent on this earth was precious and not to be wasted. No one was immortal, not kings or princes.

The image of the man in the back room of the inn stayed with her, not in the nightmarish proportions she expected, but as a kind of symbol. Her mind struggled to understand, as if the image were trying to tell her something of which she was not yet fully aware. The man might have been Jamie, her speeding thoughts raced on, and some other woman might have held his hand, easing him from this life to the next, and he would call her his Katrina.

Yesterday's Katrina would have felt the sting of jealousy at the mere thought, but this new Katrina did not. What was happening to her? she wondered. It was as if she had never had lucid thoughts in her head until now. Her thoughts at this moment were clear and uncluttered. It was as if the dead man downstairs still held her, mutely begging her, as if she were his Sheilagh. Katrina began to understand why such a man needed to fight for what he believed in.

As if he were Jamie, telling her that their love was as worthless as the dust in the air if they couldn't share that deeper love, the loyalty her Jamie bore so proudly. A child learned it in the schoolroom, but learning it was not the same as living and breathing it. Katrina felt as if she stood outside herself for a moment, and as she did so she looked down on the eager, passionate girl-Katrina with the flame-colored hair and rebellious nature, and had the weird sensation of rebirth. The pangs were there, together with the joyous emergence of new life, as if she watched herself grow in stature and perception into a woman, a woman who knew in her soul that what Jamie gave to the cause, even if it were everything, was what she would give to it, too. She could almost imagine she felt the clasp of the dead man's hand releasing her, to stand alone and to stand strong.

She drew a deep shuddering breath, recognizing this moment as a turning point in her life. Why it should be so vitally important or how she knew it, she didn't try to understand. It was enough that she knew, that a great sense of calm was claiming her now, and she felt able to sleep, exhausted, as if she had come a very long way.

Duncan was relieved when he saw her come downstairs to the morning chill of the inn. The distracted look had left her eyes. In fact, she seemed more poised than he had ever seen her, and she assured him and the inn wife that she was quite well. She was paler than usual, but she spoke with a steady voice.

"I'm sorry I gave ye all a fright," she said with a small

smile. "I'm quite recovered and ready to travel on, Faither, and I thank ye, mistress, for your kindness."

"Ye're a brave lassie," the woman said. " 'Twas not the sight for a young one to see, but we'll talk no more of it. Can ye eat any food?"

"I'm ravenous!" Katrina said to her own surprise. But great emotion had always made her hungry, she remembered, and none of these here knew what an emotional, if not spiritual, experience she had gone through in the early hours.

The porridge that the inn wife made for them was thick and satisfying. She was a good woman. Sometime during the night she had seen that Katrina's boxes were taken to her bedroom so there were clean clothes for her to wear that day, and last night's stained garments had been scrubbed and hung steaming to dry in front of the fire and were now ready to be folded and packed. Duncan paid her well for her trouble and trusted that the coins he had given the innkeeper last night would find their rightful home.

He was proud of his lassie. He'd half expected tears and begging to be taken home this morning, but there was none of that. He had always known her to have a strong will, but there was a new dimension to her character now that he couldn't quite define, and he was too thankful for it to question it.

They were now on the last stretch of their journey. The landscape ahead of them was flatter than their own Highlands, less tortuous to unwary travelers. In summer, the Lowlands were lush green pastures, dotted with black cattle and glowing with golden cornfields. The land hereabouts was far richer than the coarse turf and bracken of the glens, but the recent snows had turned every field to a glittering white carpet as the sun brightened the morning.

Kirkcudbright itself was near to the sea, and the coast around it was well-known for smuggling haunts. The people were fishermen or farmers, and across the stretch of water called the Solway Forth was the western coast of England. Like her superstitious ancestors, Katrina strongly believed in omens, and it was surely no mere chance that her Bancroft relatives lived so near to the border with England, which Charles Stuart's army would have to cross.

"We're here." Duncan pointed out the granite farm building ahead of them, sprawling and welcoming with its spiral of smoke rising from the chimneys. The crow-stepped roof was snow-covered now, but as soon as the three travelers went inside they were met with a warm welcome. Katrina's Aunt Janet hugged her at once, exclaiming on how she had grown. Not surprising, since Katrina had been a wee bairn when they had last seen one another.

"And now ye're quite the young woman!" Janet exclaimed, holding Katrina at arm's length and studying her. "Though still with the wild tangle o' hair I mind seeing! Your cousin Helen has been looking forward to your visit, hen. She'll be down from her lessons directly to greet ye, and meanwhile ye'll all be anxious for a hot drink, I've no doubt."

She was older and grayer than Katrina had last seen her, of course, and a less robust version of Mairi. She wore a serviceable gray dress and apron, and with her graying hair, gray was the overall effect. But she had a kind heart and made every effort to bid her welcome.

It was a comfortable farmhouse with stone floors and solid heavy furniture as in their own Frashiel House, but with some frivolity about the wall hangings and tapestries, the little knickknacks everywhere, and the pots of winter greenery about the place. There was no evidence of battle glories, Katrina realized suddenly as she looked around with curious eyes, no shields and claymores decorating the walls, no pistols. Neither should there be, she thought. Such weapons were supposed to have been confiscated after the earlier uprisings, but some Highland homes had gradually brought them out from hiding places and displayed them fearlessly in the old manner as her father had done, in direct defiance of the English government's ruling. To a clansman of the Highlands, such a display was part of his own identity, like his plaid and his clan slogan in battle and the plant badge he wore.

The Lowlanders were almost a different race, Katrina thought with a start. They were nearer to their English neighbors, for one thing, and more quiet by nature than their Highland kin. She knew that was why Mairi Fraser had thought to send her here, in the hope that some of that gentleness would curb her wildness.

It might surprise Mairi to know that it would not now be necessary, Katrina thought dryly. All it had taken was the shock of a dead man's passing to jolt her into a new awareness of her own character. Her spirit was still there and would always be, she knew fiercely, but there was more understanding, too, and, she hoped, more tolerance.

The Bancroft family appeared all together by the time Janet had produced hot drinks and oatcakes for the travelers. By then, Katrina's boxes had been taken to a pretty room with a patchwork spread on the bed and rugs on the floor. Curtains hung at the casement windows and there was a distant view of the sea across the flat farmlands. Now, they drank gratefully in the comfortable farmhouse parlor, and Robert Bancroft, a big man with florid cheeks and a bulging stomach, puffed on his pipe near the fireplace and looked keenly at his niece. Helen sat shyly on the settle, pale-haired and paler-faced, only her eyes similar in color and shape to her cousin's. On Helen they appeared too big and lacking in confidence to be appealing.

" 'Tis welcome ye all are," Robert Bancroft said expansively. "Though I'm a mite surprised that Mairi sent the lassie south at such times as these, wi' armies on the move. But we're safe enough here, and the doings o' the Stuart does'na touch us overmuch."

Katrina heard her father give an expressive snort.

"They touched us, man," he growled, pointing to his lame arm.

"Aye, ye were always a fiercer set o' folk than we." Robert wouldn't be drawn into an argument and spoke amicably. "And foolish, mebbe, to join the rebels at your age!"

"Would ye have me show myself for a coward?" Duncan replied angrily. "There's loyalists near twice my age rallying for the cause."

"Now, let's have no family feuding between the pair of ye," Janet broke in. " 'Tis well-known that ye're on opposite sides o' the fence, so let's leave it at that."

"Not opposite, lass," her husband said. " 'Tis just that we've cooler heads, being so near to the border, and not so hasty to follow a futile cause."

"Futile!" Duncan roared his disapproval this time. "When

we've heard news that the prince has marched on Carlisle and taken it? Would ye call that futile to be already over the border and into England?''

''And mebbe we know more than ye, Fraser,'' Robert snapped. His feathers were ruffled now, despite his efforts to be hospitable. His wife's kin were of a different breed, and he and Duncan Fraser had rarely seen eye to eye for very long. ''Your Stuart still awaits French help in vain, and 'tis said that some of his supporters are against the march into England and have begun deserting. 'Tis a long hard cold road back to the Highlands, and some have had enough.''

''Ye would'na say that if ye'd seen them rallying at Glenfinnan, Uncle Robert!'' Katrina spoke up, hating to hear his words and seeing them as a slur on lads such as Jamie.

''Be quiet, lassie, and hear what your uncle has to say. What else do ye know, man?'' Duncan snapped.

Robert shrugged. ''Rumor has it that Lord George Murray was so weary of the Stuart's constant mistrust of him that he resigned his commission of power and said he'd remain in the cause as a volunteer, whereupon other officers demanded that the man remain as general. The prince was obliged to listen, and Murray still wields the power he had. Squabbles among the leaders does'na help the morale o' the men.''

''They should be in the best of spirits! Taking Carlisle!''

Robert smiled sourly. ''They expected English support, and I doubt they'll get much of it. When they see the fierce savages swarming among them, they'll not want to be tarred wi' the same brush! They'll not have seen such wild men before, Duncan, and I wager they'll not want to be counted among them.''

''Then 'tis poor loyalists they are, and the prince is better off wi'out them,'' Duncan retorted.

But he was uneasy as his sister-in-law insisted that they speak of other things or both girls would be frightened out of their wits. Duncan doubted that Katrina would be unnerved by such talk, though the wan-faced Helen looked disturbed enough. What alarmed him more was the fact that the reputed Jacobite supporters over the border had not come out for the prince once the march into England had begun.

''Would ye like to see the schoolroom, Katrina?'' Helen

asked in the small silence, obviously making an effort to be friendly.

"Yes, go along, lassies, away from this talk of fighting," Janet said at once, with no notion of how Katrina had been hanging on every word her uncle said. As she hesitated, wondering if she dare ask for more, her father forestalled her.

"Do as your aunt bids ye at all times, Katrina, and be no bother to her. Alex and me will leave here once we've rested awhile, to beat the weather."

"Faither, ye'll not forget your promise!" Katrina turned back quickly, her eyes wide. "Ye'll see about the message for Jamie."

"Alex will seek out a likely person to run the message," Duncan said shortly. "Mebbe your uncle will know of someone. 'Tis certain that communication between here and England is a commonplace thing." He just managed to keep the words from being an insult.

"Is Jamie your laddie?" Helen asked her shyly as Katrina followed her up the stairs to the schoolroom. Katrina nodded.

"We're to be wed at the turn of the year," she said, and for the first time the words failed to give her the expected glow. The prospect of marriage to Jamie seemed farther away than it had ever been, and this cousin, who seemed so much younger than herself, hardly seemed the person to understand how the despair of it filled her at that moment. Helen was pretty and gentle but still very much a child at sixteen. How would she have reacted if she had been in the clutches of a dying clansman?

Helen opened a door, and inside were tables and chairs. The schoolroom pattern of Frashiel House was repeated here, with maps and pictures on the walls, and books and papers spread about. Mairi and her sister were of the same opinion that a child needed to be schooled, and it was as evident here as in Katrina's own home. The only difference was the large-boned woman with angular looks and the flat accent of a Yorkshirewoman. Katrina felt a distinct shock. An Englishwoman! She reminded herself that Scotland was still technically under English rule, despite the prince's claims to Edinburgh, and in this corner of the country, nothing had changed.

Jean Saunders

"So this is Katrina," Miss Brierley said, her gaze taking in the untidiness of the girl's hair and the womanly appearance of her compared with Helen. "I trust you'll enjoy joining your cousin for lessons."

"Lessons!" Katrina burst out, still too taken aback by the tutor to heed her words. "I've done wi' the schoolroom! I'm almost eighteen years old and to be wed to Jamie Mackinnon!"

"You're not wed yet, miss!" the woman flared back, seeing the mutinous look in Katrina's eyes. "And from the tone of your voice, I see there's work to be done in turning you into a lady!"

A lady! Jamie Mackinnon wouldn't want to find a prim-faced lady in place of his bonnie free-spirited Katrina! He wouldn't want a stiff-neck replacing the lassie whose tumbling hair he loved to rake with his fingers and to whom he was pledged. Jamie wouldn't want her changed, and nor would she be changed. She rebelled at the idea of it, even more so because it was an English tutor who belittled her so!

"Miss Brierley is very knowledgeable, Katrina," Helen said nervously. "I'm sure ye'll enjoy the lessons. She makes them interesting."

"Does she fill ye with pride at having a German king on the English throne?" Katrina suddenly blazed. "A king who can barely speak the language o' the people he rules?"

The tutor's face burned hotly; she was unused to such opposition. "Such talk is treasonable, miss," she snapped. "I'll not have it in my schoolroom. I had hoped you would be a girl of sense, but it's clear to me that you've had your head filled with the same wild nonsense of all your Highland folk."

Katrina gasped with fury. "*Nonsense!* Is that what ye call the defense of a man's birthright?!"

Miss Brierley's voice was as cold and unimaginative as herself. "How long must your so-called loyalists continue with this farce? To enlist the help of the French is only to antagonize our government more, with religions and politics always at such odds between us. Your so-called Bonnie Prince Charlie is an *Italian*, girl! He speaks with an Italian accent and is no more a Scot than George the Second is an Englishman! But you can't fight a government and a people's wishes

120

forever. We want no papist king on the British throne, and there's an end to it. Will your prince abandon his religion for the throne, any more than his father or grandfather?'' she finished sarcastically.

Katrina saw at once that there was no compromise here. Were these the politics Helen's tutor was instilling in her? And was her Aunt Janet content to let it happen? Appalled, she realized that it must be so. Her Lowland kin were so Anglicized that they saw no disloyalty in turning a blind eye to the new Jacobite rebellion. They did nothing to oppose it, but neither did they offer any help. They took no sides, and to Katrina's mind such lack of action was as cowardly as deserting the cause. With every hour that passed, it seemed that she was moving ever more steadfastly toward its support. She had chosen her side.

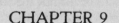

CHAPTER 9

"I'm sorry ye don't feel easy wi' Miss Brierley, Katrina,'' Helen said unhappily a week or so later. "I know she ruffles ye, but she does'na mean to, I'm sure. She has her beliefs and is sad at the waste of life on both sides of the struggle!''

They were out walking, as they liked to do for a spell each day when the weather was less inclement. A favorite walk took them through the narrow streets of the town, away from the farmlands, and out to the shore. If Katrina's thoughts often strayed across that cold stretch of water to England and Jamie, she knew better than to talk about it in front of the tutor. And Helen's words were a poor understatement of how Miss Brierley managed to rouse Katrina's anger. She suspected the woman did it deliberately. Maybe she even liked to see the glint of battle in Katrina's eyes, to make a change from the more gentle responses of Helen. What ever the reason, the clash of wills and temperament permeated every lesson.

One exchange in particular still rankled Katrina. Before returning home, Duncan Fraser did as he had promised and arranged for a reliable lad to be sent to the border with a message for Jamie that would be passed by word of mouth in the hope of reaching him. When she learned about it, Miss Brierley had had something to say.

"You'll be fortunate to get any message through, miss! Do you think folk have nowt better to do than pass messages for chits of girls following soldiers?"

"I'm not following him! I'm his betrothed and am anxious for his safety!" Katrina hated her insensitive attitude. Miss Brierley gave a sniff.

"Your prince should have thought of that when he stayed so long in Edinburgh. Six weeks to recruit more men and wait for the French ships that never came! Or not in the way he expected. Any man of sense would have given up then, instead of holding court and acting the dandy."

"Would ye expect a prince to sit twiddling his thumbs in a tent when his place is in the royal palace?" Katrina retorted.

"And what's happened to his recruits now?" the tutor went on relentlessly. "There's deserters all over, tired of the ambitions of a foreigner and wanting their homes. Tired of marching in deep snow with little food to fill them, by all accounts. And we don't want them in England! They're like savages in appearance and behaviour."

This was too much like an attack on Jamie for Katrina to allow. "And what o' the rumor that the German 'king has packed his baggage ready for a flight back to where he came from, since the Stuart army has gone so deep into England? Does that sound like defeat?"

"I don't care to argue with you, Katrina," the woman said dismissively. "Do you think the English people actually welcome your upstart prince? I received a letter from my sister in London recently, telling me the actors at the Drury Lane Theatre have been singing a new song called 'God Save the King.' I trust you'll have heard of the theater," she added, guessing that Katrina wouldn't have. "Does that sound as if your Stuart prince is their champion?"

Katrina bit her lip now, remembering the tutor's moment of pleasure, and caught sight of Helen's troubled face. In the time Katrina had been at the farm, she had become fonder of her cousin than she had expected to, for all that she was too docile at times and let Miss Brierley reduce her to silence with her cutting remarks. Her aunt and uncle, too, were kind in their ways. Aunt Janet, at least, had a little sympathy for Katrina's fretting over Jamie.

She hugged Helen's arm now as they neared the harbor of the town, dominated by the gaunt granite mass of the ancient McLellan's Castle.

"I'll try not to antagonize Miss Brierley for your sake, Helen," Katrina said wryly. "But 'tis a promise I'll find hard to keep, for she riles me so."

"And what do we have here, lads?" A strange voice stopped her in midsentence, and Katrina felt a shiver of fear run through her as Helen clutched at her arm. They had walked to a sheltered spot away from the open sea where the wind blew in strongly. She heard Helen's quick breathing as they encountered three men now circling around them.

They wore tattered kilts and were draped in filthy blankets, and Katrina knew instinctively that these must be some of the remnants of the rebel army . . . deserters. Who else would look so desperate and haggard, red-rimmed eyes telling their own tale of exhaustion? Their appearance matched that of the two wretches Katrina had seen in the inn on the way south. As Helen clasped her hands together and held them to her mouth to stop from crying out, one of the men laughed hoarsely.

"Aye, say a prayer for me, lassie—or for yourself. 'Tis a while since we've seen a pair o' bonnie lassies."

Katrina seized on the man's words, seeing that Helen was now dumb with fright. With luck she could turn the men's moods from the sudden lechery she saw gleaming in their eyes and rouse a little patriotism in them.

"We'll pray for ye and hope that my own laddie returns from the cause as safely as ye three. Mebbe ye know of him—Jamie Mackinnon?"

She prayed that if they did, he would not be in the sorry state of these three. Stinking, and so gaunt they looked near to starving. . . . She managed not to shudder and shrink away from them as Helen was doing. She hugged Helen's arm to hers, trying to instil some of her own courage into her cousin.

She stared at them unblinkingly, while fear raced through her. Deserters would be shunned in all directions, and none would be willing to harbor them. They could do herself and Helen physical harm, take them hostage, demand food and money for their safe return. . . . Her bold stare seemed to deter them from whatever their intention and each looked at the other a moment and then shook his head.

"If there be a hundred Jamie Mackinnons, we've not heard o' him." The spokesman growled. His brawnier companion spoke up, a gleam in his eye.

"Mebbe we could help ye forget him, lassie."

"Ye could not," Katrina said coldly. "And if ye've a lassie at home waiting for ye, get back to her before ye disgrace yourself further. Where is your home?"

Her father would flay her alive if he knew she was making so bold with these ragtags, and her cousin was near to swooning with the nearness of them. But Duncan Fraser was many miles away, and Katrina stood her ground as she turned the questioning on the men.

"Away by Loch Lomond."

"Ye've plenty miles to go, then, and we'll not hinder ye," Katrina said pointedly. "I'll not forget to pray for ye."

They stood, hands on hips, weighing up this lassie with the flame-colored hair who seemed so unafraid. Their road back from England had been littered with whey-faced English girls who ran screaming at their approach, when all they had wanted was a crust or a drink or a moment of comfort. Little wonder they had been obliged to steal and kill, when it was either that or starve to death. They were dispirited to the point of bestiality, shields and weapons long discarded save for the faithful dirks that had served them well.

"Aye, we'd best not delay too long, Cameron," the third man grunted. "Leave the lassies be, and let's be finding our own firesides."

They hitched their blankets around them more tightly and slouched away. As they did so, Helen sagged against her cousin, her face white as the snow.

"Ye were so brave, Katrina," she whispered. "I'm ashamed that I did'na stand up to them the way ye did. I was so afeared."

Katrina's smile was a little one-sided. "No more than I, cousin! But I'd have died rather than let them see it. They're scum, deserting their clansmen. Don't they know they make it harder for the rest to carry on? 'Tis they who should be shamed, Helen!"

She felt the muscles twitching in her face and neck, and Helen's small hand curled around hers.

"Do ye miss your Jamie, Katrina?" she asked hesitantly. "I've not had a laddie o' my own, so I don't know how ye feel."

Miss him? A sudden wave of anguish swept over Katrina at her cousin's embarrassed words. She felt years older than gentle Helen at that moment, knowing the love of Jamie Mackinnon, and missing him so much . . . so much. . . .

"Aye, I miss him," she said in a choked voice. "But I'd see him dead rather than turn and run like a coward, like those others, Helen. He's pledged to me, but he's pledged to the prince's cause, too, and one day this bitter conflict will end. Then my Jamie will come home to me, and he'll be all mine."

Helen's face went pinker at the impassioned words, and Katrina knew it took more than years to turn a girl into a woman. Helen was still a child, while she . . . Ever since that night of revelation at the inn when the poor rebel soldier had died clinging to her, Katrina had known herself to be as committed to the cause as Jamie, and she had learned that maturity came with experience. Katrina was aware of this new dimension in herself; it lifted her. She smiled at her cousin now and spoke more lightly.

"We'd best get back to the farm, or your mammie will be anxious, Helen. We've been away too long already, and my feet are near frozen."

Her words were timely. They had walked farther than usual, and Janet was anxious for them, and in a bad mood, having heard from Miss Brierley that Katrina had flounced out of the schoolroom before finishing the lesson set for her and had taken Helen with her. It was not the first time Miss

Brierley had reported Katrina's behavior, and her aunt looked at her with annoyance.

"I'm sorry to chastise ye, Katrina. Ye're my sister's bairn, and I'm fond of ye, but I canna have ye disrupting my household! I've sympathy with ye, and I know your Highland ways make ye more passionate for the cause than ours do here. We do not get so fired up wi' passions, lass, and we don't like them in this house. I canna see why Miss Brierley's remarks that she hopes the fighting will end soon should upset ye so much! I'd have thought ye wanted it, too, with your Jamie away in the thick of it!"

"Ye don't understand, Aunt!" Katrina burst out. "It was the way she said it. Crowing over it, as if she wanted our army to be pushed back."

"Well, why should she not? She's an Englishwoman, lamb. She wants peace for her country, as we all do," Janet said keenly.

"Why do you let her stay? Why not have a Scottish tutor for Helen? It would seem more . . . more . . ." She floundered, seeing her aunt's face darken and hearing Helen's gasp.

"Loyal?" Janet whipped out. "Is that the word you were about to say, lassie? I'll thank ye to leave the running of my house to me, and for all my fondness for ye, I'll not stand for such upsets here."

"I wish I wasn't here! I wish I was back home where I don't have to mind my tongue every time I speak!" Katrina was pushed to say. She knew she was being ungrateful to her hospitable kin but she was unable to stop herself. It was nearing her birthday, and her aunt was planning a special tea, and there would be gifties from the Bancrofts as well as those her mammie had packed in her boxes . . . and the tension of spending the day so differently from every other birthday of her life and the worry she felt for Jamie was making her as tense as a spring. But she knew she had gone too far from the flash in her aunt's eyes.

"Mebbe ye'd best spend an hour or two alone in your room, hen, away from these folk ye seem to despise. Mebbe some time alone will make ye reflect, and consider your apology to me!"

She watched the girl stalk from the room with head held

proudly and gave a small sigh, half wishing that Helen had some of Katrina's spirit.

The fourth of December was bitterly cold as the grave-faced group of leaders and advisers gathered around their prince, gaunt and anxious in the candlelight. The prince's headquarters at Derby, where the rebel army had finally halted after the push south into England, was at Exeter House. There was more comfort here than for the rebels quartered in English houses that were forced to take them in, or in tents in ragged groups in and around the city. Here at Exeter House, Lord George Murray opened the debate in his customary blunt manner. It was the second bitter altercation that day, and tempers were more than frayed.

"Sir, there's little doubt from our scouts that there are now three English armies in the vicinity. It would be madness to go on. Cumberland's army is a force to be reckoned with, Wade has another, and 'tis said they are rousing a third to defend London from a rebel attack. The position is hopeless, sir. They are thirty thousand strong against our five thousand."

"So you want us to turn and run like frightened rabbits, do you?" Charles snapped at him. "Is that your loyalty to me? You betray me with every word."

Murray's face was dark with anger.

"I'd slay any other man who called me traitor," he said furiously. " 'Tis no time for blind stupidity! Our men have done all they could for the cause. They're starving and ragged and weary to the bone, sir. They've marched into England on the constant promise of Jacobite supporters in England joining them or of a French landing with troops and arms. Neither has come. Instead, they're constantly met with abuse and jeering and doors slammed in their faces."

Drummond, Lord Elcho, Lochiel, Lovat . . . they and all the others growled their assent. It was sheer madness to attempt to go further. The government army was too strong for them, and they had done all they could. Now was the time to retreat.

Charles thumped the table with his hand until the candle-lights danced. "I can't believe we've come so far for you all to act so feeble now. A mere hundred or so miles from

London, and you want me to give the orders to retreat? Are these my fine countrymen? Is this what I risked my life for, to see you cowering before my bastard of an English cousin, William Cumberland?''

"Have ye heard o' his reputation, sir?" Even the gentle Lochiel was roused to snap back. "Will ye no trust in your own generals to advise ye?"

"From now on, I'll listen to no advice!" Charles shouted. "Do you know what you ask of me, to abandon my father's dream?"

"And his own," a voice muttered under cover of the babble of raised voices.

"We're hopelessly outnumbered, sir," Lord Elcho tried to shout down the others in a bid to sway the prince's folly. "Cumberland is ruthless, and your clansmen will be slaughtered if we delay much longer. Is that part of your dream, too?"

"Aye," came the rumbles of agreement. "There's those that have already deserted, rather than be the tools of ambition, however noble the cause. They've sickness among them, dysentery and fevers, and what use will such men be to ye compared wi' a strong new English army? See sense, sir, before 'tis too late!"

Charles felt bitterly resentful of these hard-faced men who faced him. Knowing their words were brutally true did nothing to ease his temper or the deep sense of betrayal he felt. He had come here with such ideals and fine hopes, and now he felt himself betrayed by all—the generals, the so-called English Jacobites who had failed to rally, the French promises, his own clansmen. Until now, his army had been on poor-enough rations, biscuits and bread, and a cupful of oatmeal mixed with water to make the hideous porridge they enjoyed but which was so distasteful to him. So far, they had taken what they needed—barracks to house as many as they could, horses, wagons. They had fared moderately as the invaders, and all that would be changed if Cumberland had them on the run. It was a prospect Charles's pride wouldn't let him face, but these bastard generals of his were forcing him to face it. Other Jacobite uprisings had failed over the years, and his had been the one he'd hoped so desperately would succeed. Finally, after many hours of arguing, he gave in with a bad grace. The generals could hardly expect anything else, but he was not a man for surrendering, and his cause had been too dear to his heart for too long.

"Very well, but in future I shall be accountable to no one but my father," he told them coldly. "Until the day I die, I'll remember how you betrayed your king this day, and I shall not demoralize my brave clansmen even more by the call to retreat. You'll tell them we march to attack in a new direction, or that we go to meet the French reinforcements."

He spoke more wildly, and the generals knew that few would believe him. But for the moment, it was enough that they had gotten his grudging agreement to the retreat from Derby, and they allowed the false orders to be given.

Charles still didn't really believe that his cause was in ruins. He delayed departure another two days while he readied himself for the straggling march back through villages filled with angry townspeople who knew as well as the sullen clansmen what was happening. In their mood of battered pride, clansmen began looting from these jeering English, who threw rotting vegetables at them as they passed and openly spat at them.

Jamie marched with the rest, smarting with the indignity, lending his horse to a clansman suffering with the dysentery and too weak to stagger, let alone march. They were right to retreat, for that could only be the reason for this order, Jamie knew, but that didn't take away the stinging shame of it.

"Do ye want a turn on your horse, laddie?" The kinsman's voice came weakly to him through the mist of snow blinding them on their way north again. Through Manchester and toward Carlisle, and the towns where Charles had read his father's proclamation so proudly on the march south. Manchester, which had received him with bonfires and cheers, being of a more Jacobite persuasion than the rest, now despised the ragged remnants of his army. . . .

"Save your breath, man," Jamie said harshly to his kinsman, knowing from the glazed look of him that the horse would be beneath himself again soon enough. If the cold and snow didn't get the Highlanders, then the exhaustion, lack of food and warmth, and the sickness did.

Each English town they passed through seemed grayer than the last, and each night of the march Jamie crawled into his tent and curled himself in his long plaid. Reassured by the touch of his dirk by his side, and the warmth of the wool, he slept uneasily.

But the strain of the past weeks had changed Jamie, physically and mentally. Sights he had seen and the hardships he had endured had hardened him. His powerful body was still strong, but sometimes it seemed he lived on a knife edge, the atmosphere in some of the close quarters with other clansmen was fetid and cloying, and the hawking and rasping of his companions was enough to make the strongest man retch. Some had died from the poor conditions and disease, rather than by an English sword, but Jamie promised grimly that none of it was going to happen to him. Not while he had strength in his body and a home and lassie to return to in the Highlands.

A garbled message had reached him that Katrina was staying with her Lowland kin in Kirdcudbright. He could not be sure how genuine it was, and he would as soon trust a fox as trust a deserter to take a message back to her. If it were humanly possible, he would go there himself. In the two weeks it took to reach the border and cross the swollen river Esk, the idea grew stronger in him. The army crossed the river holding on to each other's collars, and on the farther bank the pipers played and the men began to dance reels in the realization that they were on Scottish soil again. Fires were lighted, and the dancing and the fires brought cheer and comfort to them.

There seemed little pursuit as yet, though Cumberland's army was known to be advancing behind them. Jamie thought hard and long before deciding he could ride through the night to try and contact Katrina and be back with the rebels before any damage was done. They would rest here awhile in their makeshift camp, so, telling the kinsman nearest him he was going to scout about the place, he slid on his horse's back and was swallowed up in the night.

Katrina lay on her bed, staring at the ceiling. It had been another blistering day of arguments with Miss Brierley, and she had gone to bed early because of it, her head aching. The woman seemed determined to ram her English history down Katrina's throat, and her ears still rang with it.

"I really believe you're unaware of the Act of Settlement passed by Parliament in 1701," the woman drawled in her flat monotone. "You like to appear so clever, miss, yet you think your savage Highlanders and your Italian prince can uproot our laws."

"*English* laws," Katrina snapped.

"Since England and Scotland come under the same rule, such sarcasm is unnecessary, Katrina! The Act of Settlement states specifically that no Catholic king can rule the country, and since your precious James, your bonnie prince's grandfather, would not convert his religion, there was an end to it. A Protestant successor to the throne had to be found to keep the country the way Parliament decreed it."

"So ye imported a German!" Katrina burst out. "Was that so much better than an Italian?"

Miss Brierley's eyes flashed with impatience. "I know you're not as stupid as you sometimes choose to appear, girl. England will never suffer papist rule. The thought of such a thing is against everything we believe in. And your Charles Edward's father really set the cat among the pigeons when he married his Polish princess. Not only a Catholic, but the goddaughter of the pope! England's identity would have been swallowed up in popery if he had been allowed access to the throne."

"So you let Scotland lose her identity instead!"

Miss Brierley looked at her with open dislike.

"You forget yourself, Katrina. You had best look to your history books for the rest of the day and give me a full outline of the events of monarchy that interest you so passionately."

She had done none of it. She had come to bed early, still seething over the tutor's unfairness and thinking she might be quite happy here with her Lowland kin were it not for Miss Brierley. She lay in the darkness, still brooding, and it was a long while before she slept.

She awoke with a start, her heart pounding, not sure of the reason. She twisted quickly to face the window as a sound came to her from its direction. She stifled a scream as a dark shape clambered over the wide sill and moved toward her bed. As she leapt up in the bed a hand was clamped over her mouth and a familiar voice spoke urgently in her ear.

"Don't cry out, Katrina. 'Tis me, Jamie. Be still a moment and just let me hold ye."

Her breath came in ragged gasps as she came fully to her senses to find herself in Jamie's arms. It was unbelievable. She swayed dizzily, her voice incoherent.

"Oh, Jamie, is it really you? I've dreamed of ye so often. . . . Am I still dreaming?"

He held her so tightly she could hardly breathe, but it hardly mattered, for he breathed new life into her by his presence. He rocked her to him, his need for her sweeping aside all his weariness for the moment. He had not let himself think how much he needed her. There was no time for such sweet thoughts in the struggle for a kingdom. But here and now, for this brief time, as he kissed her soft lips and tasted their honeyed warmth, all the male desire in him came to the fore. He could feel her tears on his cheeks, and they were his tears, too, mingling together in shared joy.

"How did ye get here, Jamie?" he heard her whisper in a muffled voice against his shoulder. "I've longed so for this moment, to see ye again, to love ye." She could hardly speak for the thickness of her throat.

"I rode like the devil, lass." He spoke with harsh urgency, knowing he could stay but a short while and not yet wanting to break the spell by telling her so. "I was'na sure if your message was a true one, but I took a chance and roused a household nearby to direct me here. Then I climbed the wall and peered in the bedrooms until I found ye. Have ye seen the large woman sleeping in her curling rags?"

Katrina felt the laughter bubble up inside at the image of Miss Brierley. It seemed so long since she had laughed. It felt like a lifetime. But if he was here, then what was happening? She knew of the retreat; such news had reached them quickly enough, but Jamie was surely not . . . not . . . She searched his face in the gloom and would not shame him by asking the traitorous question. Jamie would never desert his prince. Then he must go back . . . he didn't need to tell her.

"How long can ye stay, dearest?" she asked huskily.

"An hour, mebbe more," he said gently, loving her more for not weeping and begging him. She was different, his Katrina, though in what way he was too exhausted to define. "I'm fair to dropping wi' sleep, lassie, and I canna keep my eyes open. Wake me in a wee while, my dearie, and just lie here beside me."

He lay back, still holding her, and in seconds he was asleep. Katrina knew they had found each other again, only to be parted so soon. The cause was not done with yet. She lay beside him, cherished by his arms and uncaring that he smelled of horses and sweat and the odd stink of river water. It was enough that he was here, and she still marveled at his presence while her turbulent thoughts raced on in crazy, staccato form. At last, when he breathed more heavily, she slid out of his embrace, a flicker of resolve growing stronger by the minute.

Accustomed as Jamie was to catnapping in half alertness for redcoat patrols, he became gradually aware that she was no longer close to him, and his eyes opened at once. He could not have said how long he had slept, but now he saw the candlelight by the window, and in its warm glow Katrina sat by a small table. Her long tangled hair fell forward over her shoulders, the soft light turning it to the color of fire. She sat graceful and taut, the well-remembered tilt to her chin. Jamie felt a half smile tug at his mouth, for how often she had tilted it defiantly at him!

He didn't feel like laughing now. He had ridden miles to be with her, and he ached for her, wanted her, and cursed himself for the promise made long ago not to take her fully until they were blessed in wedlock.

As if drawn by his gaze, Katrina turned slowly toward him, her breath catching as she saw that he was awake.

"Why do ye stay so far away, bonnie lass?" He spoke soft as a caress. "Come to where ye belong."

He held out his arms, and Katrina moved into them in one fluid movement, hardly knowing how she crossed the room. She sensed at once that his tiredness had gone, and now was the time for saying all that had filled her mind while he'd slept . . . but it was almost impossible to speak when his mouth was possessing hers, his hands seeking her body, the

133

beat of his heart at one with hers. . . . She felt the tingling scratch of his whiskers against the soft flesh of her breasts and trembled at his touch.

"Did ye wonder what I did by the window, Jamie?" she said huskily. His voice was muffled against her skin.

"I only knew ye should be here, dearest, in my arms, where I've wanted ye so often."

She could feel the heat of his hand through the cotton fabric of her nightgown and stayed it with her own as it reached her thigh. Every sinew of his body told her of his needs, his longing to make her his in this brief respite from the nightmare of retreat.

"Do ye want me badly, Jamie?" She felt herself color as she asked the question. He pulled her to him more fiercely, sending a sweet thrill through her.

"Have ye forgotten the way I want ye, Katrina mine, in the months we've been apart? The way I've *always* wanted ye?"

Her breath came quickly as the glint of desire deepened in his eyes. "I'd remind ye of your promise, Jamie." Her voice was faint, for oh, she wanted him, too. "Ye always said ye'd never take me by force, that ye'd wait until we were wed."

He gave a low, vehement oath. He leaned over her, drinking in the sight of her lovely face and the deep, passion-filled eyes, and cursed himself anew for ever making such a promise, when it must shorten his life by hours each time he held himself in check with such sweet agony.

"Ye've been wi' your Lowland kin too long, then, and taken to the soft talk," he said harshly. "Ye've been too long wi'out your man, and I'd not have thought ye such a tease."

"I don't tease ye, Jamie."

"What do ye call it, when I long to have ye here and now and thought ye were offering it! Ye've not been sweet-talked by some Lowland farmer while I've been away, have ye? Is that it?"

Katrina sat up at once, bright spots of color in her cheeks as the hot temper filled her at his words. She slipped out of his embrace, her voice shaking with suppressed rage.

"Ye insult me, Jamie Mackinnon, when ye should know me to be as true to ye as I trust ye've been to me! Ye speak right in one respect, though. I've been here too long, and the large woman with the curling rags is one o' my reasons for saying so. A very big reason!''

She moved across to the table, to hand him the letter she had been trying to compose, thrusting it under his nose and holding the candle close so that he could read it.

"What's this? A note of good-bye in case I came looking for ye, hen?'' Misery sharpened his voice. He scanned the letter, his head jerking up once he had done so.

"That's right, my doubting laddie,'' Katrina said, her voice shaking. "Not a note of good-bye for you, but for my Aunt Janet! I canna stay here one more day, Jamie, for the English tutor is against all that we believe in. She treats me like a bairn, and belittles the cause, and tries to ram English politics down my throat. She even tries to put me against ye, Jamie, by telling of the women who take to the wagons and follow the Stuart's army.''

"Aye, and I'd not have my lassie one o' them,'' Jamie said angrily, seeing where her thoughts were leading. "Light-skirts, most of them, and your mammie wouldn't want ye knowing them.''

She pushed thoughts of her mammie aside, for Mairi wouldn't approve of any of this, not Jamie coming here in the dead of night, or herself in her nightgown with her arms pressed tight around him now in passionate persuasion.

"Not your lassie, Jamie, your *wife*!'' She said what had been simmering in her mind as she'd watched him sleep. Her voice was intense with passion and urgency. "Take me with ye, Jamie. In a few weeks from now, we'd have been wed at home in our own kirk. Nothing is as we'd planned it, but we can still be together.''

'' 'Tis madness! Have ye any idea of what ye're saying, Katrina? The army is in retreat, and God knows the outcome of it all. The redcoats pursue us, and more blood will be spilled before 'tis over.''

"I want to be your wife, Jamie!'' She couldn't stop the trembling in her voice. "Wherever ye go, I want the right to be with ye, to give ye comfort. I canna bear to lose ye again now that I've found ye, and ye would'na be so cruel as to leave me again with the tyrant of an Englishwoman.''

"And what of your kin? Are they not kind to ye?''

She knew he was wavering. She knew it by the way he held her close. She spoke breathlessly now.

"Aye, they've been kind, Jamie, and my cousin has been a friend, but ye are more than that to me and always have been. Would ye not serve your prince more vigorously if we were wed, Jamie? We could be away from here and be at an inn where an innkeeper could make the marriage binding before witnesses. I've heard it's so, Jamie."

She had thought it all out, and her words came swiftly. Tremulously, she took his hand and pressed it against her yielding softness. She hid her burning face against his shoulder as she heard his ragged breathing.

"A woman's longings are no less passionate than a man's, Jamie," she whispered, "though 'tis not seemly to speak of them so freely. I love ye, Jamie, as I've always loved ye, and I want to be your wife, to share your life, and I want it *now*!"

"Ye're a seductive little witch, my lassie," he said hoarsely, "and ye'll know how I'm torn to know what's best to do. I should'na take ye into danger."

"Then I'll follow ye," she said defiantly. "I'll be one of the light-skirts in the wagons, and ye'll have the disgrace of having Katrina Fraser ask for ye at every camp! I won't stay here one more day and listen to the blasphemies. So will ye take me and give me the protection o' my own man? My *husband*?"

She held her breath now as his eyes glittered down into hers. Something in her words had caught him up short.

"So ye think strongly enough o' the cause to leave the comforts of your aunt's home, do ye, lassie?" At her nod, he began to smile and to let a note of teasing creep into his voice. "I never thought to have a blackmailing wife, but I'd not stand for my lusty kinsmen ogling ye, so I suppose there's no help for it. I must give in to ye."

Her arms were tight around his neck then, her spirit soaring. His mouth on hers was a pledge for the future, the kiss a passionate sealing of the love between them. In those moments, Katrina felt that strange sense of emergence once more, as she had done when the rebel soldier died and she committed herself to Charles Stuart's cause. This was a new and different kind of emergence, an exultant avowal of her life to

Jamie's keeping. It was at once a humbling and an exhilarating sensation. They had always been destined to belong together. Now there was to be no more waiting.

Jamie removed her clinging arms from about his neck and bade her finish her note to her aunt; there was no time for delay. And she was not allowed to forget that Jamie must rejoin the prince's army as soon as possible.

"I hardly know what to write!" She had tried earlier and not gotten very far.

"Tell them the truth. Ye owe them that, lass. Say that ye've gone wi' Jamie Mackinnon to be wed, and we'll be traveling wi' the Stuart prince's army. And ask them to inform your parents and beg their understanding."

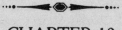

CHAPTER 10

It *was still difficult to write the letter and not sound as if she* were uncaring and rushing off into the night without proper thought. Katrina spent as long as she dared on it, knowing the truth of Jamie's advice, and that her kinfolk had the right to know of their movements. Gone to be wed to Jamie Mackinnon. . . . The words sent a shivering glow through her. Now he would be her husband, with all the word implied. She scribbled her name at the foot of the letter, remembering to thank her Aunt Janet warmly for her care these past months.

"Leave it by your pillow, now," Jamie instructed, seeing the way her hands shook a little. He looked deeply into her eyes. " 'Tis not too late to change your mind."

"I've not changed my mind about loving ye, Jamie, or about the wish to be by your side whatever comes," she said steadily.

"Then pack a few garments, quickly, and we'll be on our

way. I left the horse chewing on your uncle's fine hay in the barn." Jamie grinned. "She'll be too full to carry us both if we leave her too long. One carrying bag only, now."

"Ye'd wish me to look like a scarecrow on my wedding day!" The words shivered through her senses again as she made haste. "A woman needs certain things for traveling, Jamie, and Mammie would'na like me to resemble one of the eloping English brides who come over the border to be wed in haste!"

She teased him back but bit her lip at the mention of her mother. Mairi Fraser would not like any of this, and the action of running off to marry Jamie would merely confirm Mairi's opinion of Katrina as her wayward daughter. As if he read her thoughts, Jamie put his arm around her as she finished her scant packing.

"I think your mammie will understand our need, dearest," he said gently, "but ye must listen to me, Katrina. I'm a wee bit dazed by all that's happened here so fast, but I'll not forget my purpose. Charles Stuart's cause may shine less brightly than before, but there's plenty who still believe in it and will follow him to the end. Ye understand me, lassie?"

She nodded steadily. "I'd not have ye any other way, Jamie."

"There's more," he added grimly. "I'll not risk putting my wife in danger, nor let ye ride wi' the light-skirts. Ye'll travel close by, but when I decide on it, ye'll remain in cottage or farm where there's safe shelter for ye. I'll have your word on it, Katrina."

Seeing his seriousness, she could only promise in a tense voice. There would be many partings as he described, but once the words were said over them, they would be a part of each other, and none could take that away. She wrapped the thick woollen shawl around her heavy traveling dress and gave him a quick nod of readiness. They opened the door silently and crept through the sleeping house and into the cold night air. But Katrina never felt the cold. The excitement of their venture fired her blood and warmed her like a fever. The entire plan was dangerous, foolhardy, yet so simple it seemed to her it must have been preordained.

Jamie lifted her onto the horse, now sated with Robert

Bancroft's hay, and trotted the animal away from the farm until he felt it safe to mount behind her and speed away into the night. The snow muffled the hoofbeats, and a soft fresh fall began to drift down, covering their tracks.

"I'd get as far away as possible before we find an accommodating inn, my dearie," Jamie said in her ear. "The usual village for eloping English couples is Gretna, just this side o' the border, but we'll go a wee bit farther north than that, in case your uncle sees fit to come storming after us!"

"I won't even think of that!" she cried in alarm.

"No more do I, love," Jamie said caustically. Nor would he think too deeply of the outcry at their two homes when the news was sent there by Robert Bancroft. Betrothed they may be, but they would need to stand firm together when the time came for them to face their families,

Katrina, too, would only think of this night, and no further. And if it wasn't for the bumping of Jamie's body against hers as the horse slithered now and then on the uneven ground, she might have thought it was all a dream.

Several hours later they reached a small village north of the border, all in darkness as befitted a God-fearing community in the predawn hours. They located an inn quickly enough, and Katrina felt the tremors run through her again as Jamie lifted her from the horse. His arm stayed firmly around her as he rapped on the inn door. A candlelight flickered upstairs, and then the door was carefully opened to reveal a bewhiskered face beneath a nightcap.

"What's to do?" the voice belonging to the face bellowed at them. "Do ye know the time? If 'tis whiskey ye're wanting, come back in daylight."

" 'Tis not whiskey, landlord," Jamie spoke quickly. "Would ye turn away a loyal supporter of Charles Stuart who wants to wed his lassie this night?"

Katrina drew in her breath, knowing Jamie risked much by declaring himself this way. The village was not so far from the border, and they had no way of knowing which side the innkeeper favored. To her wild relief, she heard him give a guffaw of laughter, and then a woman appeared behind him, her face ghostly in the candlelight, with a frilled nightcap to match her man's.

The woman touched the man's arm. "See to it, man, for folks so set on it will likely hammer at the door until ye do. I'll waken the bairns for witnesses."

She was gone before the man could argue. As the innkeeper bade them come inside with a poor enough grace, Jamie whispered in her ear.

"Dinna think ye'll rule me the same way as that one, dearie!"

She squeezed his hand, knowing that a woman's wiles were cannier than a man's at times and not needing to say the words. She had gotten her own way in this, and it was enough. They were told to come inside, and the inn was warm still, the embers of a fire still smoldering in the stone fireplace, the close odors of ale and men still lingering. But Katrina heeded none of it once they were assembled near the glowing embers, herself and Jamie, the innkeeper and his wife, and their two coltish children barely roused from sleep with shawls hastily thrown around their nightclothes.

There was a lump in Katrina's throat as she waited for the small ceremony to begin. It was not the way she had imagined it, without benefit of kirk or solemn words, yet it would be nonetheless binding in the eyes of the law. She pushed the thought away. All that mattered was that she and Jamie would be together from now on.

She felt his hand reach for hers and hold it tightly. She looked up at him quickly, saw the love in his face, and was warmed by it. She gave him a tremulous smile in return, and the innkeeper produced a piece of paper and a quill pen and cleared his throat.

"I'd have your names, and then ye'll have this paper to prove to any concerned folk that the declaration was made fair and proper this night," he grunted. The man took an age in scrawling the names, saying the bairns would add their scratches to the rest when the words had been said. He looked sternly at the betrothed couple.

"Do ye, Jamie Mackinnon and Katrina Fraser, wish to live together as man and wife for the rest o' your natural lives, and declare it before these witnesses?"

"That we do," Jamie said in a strong voice. "For all time."

"Yes," Katrina whispered, for despite the hustle of it all, this was still her wedding day, and from the way the innkeeper's wife glanced her way with a small smile, she guessed the woman knew the way of her thoughts.

"Then so ye be," the innkeeper declared, putting his name to the paper with an indecipherable flourish and thrusting the paper at his children. Once they had scrawled their names they scurried back to bed, grumbling at being disturbed in the night.

Jamie pulled his wife to him and sealed the marriage with a kiss, while the innkeeper's wife spoke quietly to her man. She heard the innkeeper's voice next.

"My good woman thinks that if ye're wanting a bed for the night, ye may be more comfortable away from the inn. We've little room at present, but there's a wee cottage a mile from here if ye've a mind for it. 'Tis empty, but dry enough if ye light a fire, and I doubt that the rats will disturb ye. There'll be other things to occupy ye both."

"McLaughlin, spare the lassie's blushes," the woman chided.

"Thank ye, mistress," Jamie said. "We've money to pay, so if ye could supply us wi' matches and candles, food and milk, we'd be obliged to ye, and then we'll be on our way."

"Aye, ye'll want to be alone, and rightly so," she replied. "'Twill take but a minute to get the things ye want, and my man will direct ye to the cottage."

By the time they reached it, Katrina was even more convinced that this must all be a dream. The first pale heather-colored streaks of the dawn sky let them pick out the contours of the landscape, the soft hills to the north, the flatter terrain of the Lowlands still surrounding the area here. In a hollow, the snug stone cottage awaited them. The horse tethered in the small outhouse, Jamie pushed open the cottage door cautiously, but it was empty and silent. Nothing scuttled or slithered away at their approach, to Katrina's relief. At the hearth were bundles of dry wood and blocks of peat, and Jamie set about lighting a fire to cheer the place. At once, the drab interior took on a cozier look.

"Are ye hungry, Jamie?" Katrina asked, suddenly nervous. His large frame seemed to fill the tiny cottage as he rose from the fire, his cheeks glowing from the quick heat. And glowing with something else, too, as he moved toward her and took her in his arms.

"Aye, I'm hungry, dearie," he said softly. "But not for food. I'm hungry for my wife. The food can wait."

The cottage had only one room for eating and sleeping, and a tiny corner for cooking. Along one wall was a bed with a solid-looking mattress, which she eyed dubiously. Jamie caught the glance and let her go as he pushed the sticks of furniture from the middle of the room and placed the old mattress on the floor alongside the fire, his own plaid spread over it. The room was softly lit by the firelight, and now Jamie reached for his wife's hand.

"Lie here wi' me, Katrina, and let me take my fill of ye, as I've wanted to do for so long," he said huskily. "Ye'll not be shamed by the light? I promise ye the belonging will be as pleasurable as I can make it for ye, my darling one."

The belonging. . . . Such a simple word to convey the union of a man and woman the way God intended! Katrina looked into the face of her beloved, and the flickers of fear died away as a matching desire deep within her leaped to match Jamie's. No, she wouldn't be shamed by the light. The belonging was wanted and needed; she, too, wanted to see, to touch. . . .

He gently pushed aside the traveling shawl from her shoulders and began to untie the fastenings of her dress. Katrina's fingers moved toward him, loosening his shirt, pushing her hands inside it against the dark mat of hair on his chest. She traced his rib cage and the flat male nipples exploringly. She had rarely touched him like this before, with this new sense of belonging. The beautiful word still held her as if by magic, its meaning unique in these first hours of being man and wife.

She heard Jamie draw in his breath at her touch and remembered instantly that time when he had groaned at her to stop being cruel to him. She had misunderstood him then, but in a new wisdom, Katrina knew he wouldn't accuse her of being cruel ever again. For now there would be no holding back, no aching unfulfillment.

His hands trailed over her throat, her shoulders, and Katrina knew an urgency, wanting him to touch her breasts as the wool dress was removed from them, the slight roughness of the fabric giving way to a delicious coolness that was warmed sensuously by the fire's heat. As long as she lived, she would remember the scent of the wood fire and the look in Jamie's eyes as he slowly removed her garments. As if he would savor every moment, his touch lingered on each new portion of her flesh that was revealed to him. His fingertips, then his lips. . . .

Katrina still stood, a golden statue in the firelight, the flames glinting red through the tangle of her hair. She felt Jamie's lips brush her nipples, circling, teasing, nipping, then move lower while his hands curved her hips and buttocks, arching her toward him. Her eyes flickered as she felt the warm teasing tongue divide and part her woman's gift, and then it was she who gasped a little at the fire running through her veins.

"Jamie, my knees will'na hold me up much longer," she whispered in a trembling voice as the sweet torture continued. He gave a low laugh against her moist flesh.

"Good, for I'm impatient to have ye beneath me, my lovely," he whispered back in a way that sent excitement searing through her. He laid her down gently, pausing just a moment more to drink his fill of her lovely naked body, then he removed the last of his clothes quickly. The sight of him, magnificently male, the hard bone of his manhood circled at its base by the dark body hair, stimulated all her feminine responses. Her gaze moved over him slowly, the way he had watched her, with sensual awareness, exploring with unembarrassed wonder.

"Pleasure me, Katrina, before I make ye part of me," Jamie said softly.

Hesitantly, she moved her fingers to stroke the taut skin, hearing his ragged breath again as she did so. Tentatively, Katrina grazed her thumb along the erect smoothness, guided by instinct and by Jamie's low-throated reactions to her touch. Soft as a butterfly's wings, she continued the feather-light stroking, until he groaned in mock pain.

"Kiss me the way I kissed ye, Katrina mine," he said hoarsely, suffused in such intense pleasure now he could scarcely speak at the delights so long desired. Her eyes were a deep wild sea-green with passion as she looked into his, and his mouth smiled down at her. "Ye know well what I mean, lassie."

A tingle of playfulness made her lean toward him a moment, touching her mouth to his.

"Like this, Jamie?" She breathed against his skin, her mouth moving down to his throat. "Or this? Or this?" She tugged at each male nipple in turn with her lips and then let her kisses trail farther, her cheeks tickling on the rough hair of his chest, to the finer line of it that ran to his navel, over the flat hard belly and beyond.

This time his gasp of pleasure was more audible as she reached his aroused manhood, kissing gently, and then more surely as the contact pleasured her, too, in a way Katrina had never before imagined. Jamie did not allow it for very long. By now his longing for her was at its peak, and suddenly she was pinioned beneath him on the plaid-covered mattress. The fire blazing at their sides was no less than their own blaze of passion now.

The weight of him was a welcome pressure on her body as his hands cupped her breasts. He sank his face between their softness for a moment, tasting each one. Katrina's arms were around his powerful shoulders, her nails grooving his back in delicious tingles, pulling him to her as she arched upward. Jamie's hands slid down the curving length of her, letting them glide beneath her buttocks and raise her toward him, his knees gradually edging her own apart.

"Don't be afraid, dearest," he murmured now. " 'Twill be but a little pain for a lifetime's pleasure."

He was still murmuring to her when she felt the first hot sweet piercing of the maidenhead. She was so aroused with love and Jamie's infinite patience that it was as he said, no more than a prelude to the rhythmic symphony of his loving.

Joined at last in love, in tumultuous passion, Katrina became unaware of her surroundings, conscious only of the intense feelings gathering in her body, as if all her senses battled with one another to experience the most sensation, sight, sound, touch, smell. All were concentrated in one magical, glorious soaring of spirit.

Delighting in her responses, Jamie prolonged the pleasure,

sometimes thrusting deep and slow, sometimes forging into her with all the vigor of lusty young manhood. At last the moment arrived when he could hold back no longer. Then it seemed to Katrina that heaven and earth merged together. She cried out, clinging to him, the deep rippling waves of fulfillment pulsating through her body as Jamie shuddered against her, releasing his life-giving seed.

Bodies glistening, they lay very close for a long time afterward without speaking, reluctant to break apart, to break the spell, to be two separate people once more. The fusion of minds and bodies had been so perfect it brought the salty tears trembling to her lashes. Understanding without the need for words, Jamie kissed away the tears, folding her in his arms, his lassie, his wife. . . .

"Now we belong," he said, and locked in each other's arms, they slept.

It was midday before a discreet knocking on the cottage door brought them back to reality. Katrina heard the innkeeper's voice calling to Jamie, and a cold feeling ran over her. She knew their time here would be brief, a mere interlude in their lives. But so soon . . . so soon. . . . She didn't restrain Jamie as he wrapped himself in a blanket to let the innkeeper in from the cold, and she stayed snugly inside the plaid coverlet. She, too, had pledged herself to Charles Stuart's cause, and if this was the summons for them to go, then she'd not hamper Jamie. He had asked McLaughlin to let him know the moment he heard any news of value, and now the man averted his eyes from the marriage bed after acknowledging the pretty lassie lying there.

"Do ye have some information, man?" Jamie said at once.

"Aye, of sorts. My own laddie was away on errands early this morning, and heard reports that the Stuart army is making good progress toward Stirling. The bonnie prince has caused a fuss in Glasgow, demanding coats and shirts, shoes and bonnets for his men, and large sums of money to pay them. Wi' such a force swarming o'er the town, they have little choice but to do as he asks."

" 'Twill be welcome for the men to have clean clothes and money," Jamie retorted, remembering the state of some, and of himself. "I thank ye, landlord, and we'll be on our way directly."

Katrina caught her breath. The glint of battle was back in Jamie's eyes, and the time for loving was over.

"I wish ye both well, and a good long life," the innkeeper said before he left them. At once, Jamie threw off the blanket and began to dress. His eyes blazed now with a different passion. She had known it would happen, but she couldn't help feeling a thrill of anxiety. He seemed not to notice as she, too, reached for her dress and put it on with shaking hands. It was not that he loved her any less, and she knew it. But his vigor had shifted away from her now, and his need was to be away from here, their brief heaven, and to return to the side of his prince.

"Hurry, dearest," his voice came to her. "I'd not have it said that Jamie Mackinnon had deserted like some of the scum o' the army."

"None who knew ye would dare to say it!" she retorted. Soon she straightened her shoulders and told him quietly that she was ready.

Jamie caught her to him with a fierce possessiveness, raking his fingers through her hair. He cupped her face, looking deeply into her eyes, reassured by all he saw there. He nodded.

"I'm proud of my woman, Mistress Mackinnon. Given the chance, I'll make ye proud of your man."

"I could'na be prouder than I am right now," she said huskily, never letting him know by a pulse beat how the woman's fear in her tightened her stomach at thoughts of the future.

They glanced back at the tiny cottage as they moved to the door, and Katrina knew that in each of them the sweet images of the wedding night were there for all eternity. Nothing could take that from them, and if they never had one more day together, they had had everything.

Outside it was cold, and as Katrina sat on the horse, she was glad of Jamie's protective body before her to take the worst of the weather as the snow continued to fall. If fate—and Charles Stuart—had not intervened, the first days of their marriage would have been so very different, and the idyllic beginning at the Lowland cottage would be continuing.

She knew that they rode into danger and hardened her heart against the fears, resolving not to let Jamie have any reason to be ashamed of her. She made the silent vow as they rode northward through the mist-white morning and knew it to be as potent as their marriage vow.

"Where do we go, Jamie?" she said through cold lips.

He had to shout back the words to make her hear.

"If the innkeeper's words were true, then 'tis Stirling we make for now. Unless we hear different on the way, 'tis where we'll find our men."

It could have been on the other side of the world to Katrina. Stirling was a town somewhere to the north of Glasgow, with a castle standing on a sheer crag. She recalled learning of it in her lessons of Scotland's history. The towns having the romantic castles had always been the ones to appeal to her—Edinburgh; Glamis, where Charles Stuart's father had once lodged briefly in the uprising of 1715; Douane; Stirling; and a host of others—lovely, medieval, romantic castles.

How unromantic would they be now, under siege from a desperate Jacobite army wanting to reclaim them from their English enemies! Katrina shivered at the thought and snuggled more closely into Jamie's broad back. The horse took them over rough country, the lower grasslands giving way to more hilly terrain as they journeyed, with welcome pockets of shelter among them, both from the weather and the chance of being halted by redcoats. They saw none, and Katrina felt a gladness in her when Jamie commented once that maybe he looked less conspicuous with his lassie riding with him. They were merely two travelers moving from one place to another.

She was glad, too, when they were resting the horse a short while, and he guessed at her feelings of guilt at the way she had left her Aunt Janet's house. Now that the excitement of the flight was over, and she felt fulfilled as Jamie's wife, Katrina couldn't help feeling a pang of remorse.

"Mammie and Faither will be displeased when they hear how we fled the farm," Katrina fretted.

Jamie tipped her chin up, forcing her to look in his eyes. "Does it displease ye to know ye're wed to me now, then? Or that from now on I'll champion ye and fight your battles for ye? Does that not compensate for the anger ye leave behind, that will lessen as days go by?''

She gave him a small smile, and he drew her close, speaking softly in her ear.

''But 'tis good for me to see ye caring so much about your mammie and faither's feelings. 'Tis good to know my wife is a woman grown with deeper feelings than the wayward lassie who I sometimes suspected thought of little else but her own wishes!''

He was teasing her, but she recognized the thread of truth in what he said. These months had changed her, as they had changed Jamie. Once she would have flared at him and demanded to know what he meant by accusing her of being self-centered; but now she could stand back a little and see, with a faint sadness for that other Katrina.

''I'd be selfish now, and suggest we've traveled nearly far enough this day,'' she said huskily instead. ''Do we have to go much farther, Jamie? The light's fading, and I'm cold.''

He had a tattered scrap of a map that he had been following. They had covered enough distance for one day, and even if they neared Stirling, the army's camp would presumably be spread about in tents and all available hostels and cottage beds. It might not be so easy to settle Katrina safely if they arrived very late at night. He folded the map.

''We'll stop at the first inn we come to, then. We've tarried here long enough and the mare's rested by now.''

They climbed on its back, and a mile or so farther on they saw the welcome lights of an inn sheltered in a hollow of the glen. Jamie tied the horse at a rough shelter to one side of it, and Katrina felt a growing anxiety as they went inside.

The usual fog and smoke and strong smells of ale and bodies met their noses, together with the suspicious eyes of those inside. Now, Jamie made no secret of their purpose in making for Stirling. The innkeeper and his wife looked genial enough, but a bedraggled old man in the corner of the inn spat noisily at their approach.

''Ye'd be better employed in keeping each other warm, if ye be fresh wed, than chasing after the dregs o' your bonnie prince's army!'' He cackled.

Katrina felt her face go hot at the inference, but Jamie bristled at once.

"Mebbe 'tis such traitorous thoughts that stop the army from being victorious. Every able-bodied man should be proud to follow the Stuart, man, and I'd fight any here who said different."

To Katrina's horror, the man held up the stump of one arm and wagged it in front of them. It had been previously hidden by the rags about him.

"Would ye see the thanks I got for following this one's faither thirty years ago, laddie? Do ye think this cause will be ending any differently from the rest? My relic is my reward for trying to stop my croft burning down when the redcoats suspected me o' Jacobite leanings. When this skirmish is over and lost in the same way, ye'll want to mind yourself, laddie, or ye'll mebbe unable to hold your lassie, same as me."

"That's enough o' that talk, McGrant," the innkeeper grunted, clearly used to his mitherings. "Ye'll be upsetting the lassie."

"Aye, well, I'll hold my whist for the price of a dram in my good hand for an old campaigner," the old rogue said amicably.

"See to it, landlord." Jamie threw some coins on the tabletop, suddenly seeing the sheer horror in Katrina's face at the old man's ramblings. He felt he could almost read her thoughts. This was what war could do to a once proud man, and this was the ghost of a struggle long past. Even here, so near to where the prince's army was reputed to have gained a new victory at Stirling, they thought this new cause already doomed.

She felt suddenly nauseated in the cloying atmosphere. Were all the young men who weren't killed to end up maimed and bitter like this wretch? The swift memory of the young man who had died clinging to her skirt and begging for his Sheilagh filled her mind. She was shamed to think she had ever forgotten him; but now, in a split second, she relived every horrific moment.

"What ails ye, lassie?" Jamie said urgently. "Don't let the man frighten ye. We'll buy food and drink, and ye'll be revived, I promise ye. There'll be a bed for us here, too."

Katrina nodded without speaking, and Jamie saw to it. She felt obliged to eat the pies and drink the hot chocolate the inn wife brought. The older woman felt sympathy for the beautiful girl with the pallid face. She told them a room would be made ready for them at once. Her son's room, she added wistfully.

Hours later, it seemed, when the inn was quiet and they had been asleep in each other's arms, Katrina was suddenly, frighteningly awake. There were new noises below, new voices, in accents she didn't recognize, and the sounds of whinnying horses vied with men's shouting and catcalling.

"What is it?" she whispered hoarsely into Jamie's shoulder, then gave a strangled cry as a deafening shot rang out, followed by another and then another. She felt Jamie leap out of bed, wrapping his plaid around him and reaching at once for his dirk. Her throat tightened with fear.

"Ye'll not know the voices, lassie," he said harshly. "But I'll wager they're redcoats."

She gasped. She had thought of this inn as a refuge. Words trembled on her lips. *Dinna leave me, Jamie!* She bit them back before they were said, biting so hard she tasted her own blood. Was this how she was going to react when danger threatened? But this was not how she had imagined it to be—Jamie being but one rebel among a drunken patrol of Englishmen, by the sound of them. She slid out of bed and pulled her shawl around her as Jamie opened the door a crack. She peered over his shoulder to see what happened below.

By now the redcoats had roused the innkeeper and his wife, demanding food and ale. The louts had already fired at the ale barrels and burst them, and the acrid smell filled the air as the innkeeper tried to shout for order.

"Order! 'Tain't order we want but good red meat and ale to wash away the dust of traveling, you cow-turd." The raucous jeers went up. "If we don't get them in double-quick time, we'll put some shots in the nags outside, and your woman can stew them for us. What say you, mates?"

More jeers and laughter accompanied his words, and Katrina felt her heart pound. Their own mare was outside. Without her, their journey would take ten times longer. As the innkeeper argued, another shot rang out to burst another barrel, and a spurt of golden liquid stained the sawdust floor.

"There'll be naught left in the barrels if ye fire them all!" the innkeeper shouted back in a fury. "Have ye no sense?"

He was rewarded by the butt end of a weapon on the side of his head. Katrina heard the sickening thud and the shrill scream from the inn wife. He was clearly not badly hurt, for his angry voice told the redcoats to get on and take what they wanted and then get out of here and leave them in peace.

"Hear that, boys?" came the taunting reply. "Did we spoil something upstairs, mebbe? How many more of you are there in this godforsaken hole? What's upstairs? Any wenches for some skirt-hungry soldiers?"

Katrina suddenly clung to Jamie's side, hearing the inn wife speak quickly. Too quickly, maybe. . . .

"There's only my son and his wife. They'll be sleeping as usual, the useless lazy pair. We don't cater for other needs here."

Through the crack in the door, Katrina saw several of the redcoats glance upward, their faces grimed from traveling, swaying somewhat already in their drunken state. Fear sent trickles of perspiration running down her spine.

"Is that so, missus? Well, I'm thinking that's something we should find out for ourselves, eh, mates? Just in case you're hiding a fine daughter or two up there, or one o' the bastard bonnie Charlie's rebel lads! Either will do for a bit o' sport."

Katrina listened with eyes dilating and her bones seeming to turn to water. She hardly felt Jamie close the door quickly and grip her arms, pushing her across the room and back toward the bed. She was bundled beneath the covers so fast she could barely think, and within seconds Jamie was there, too, wrapping his strong arms around her and hiding her from view.

"Follow the inn wife's lead," he whispered savagely. "Much as I'd wish to run every one o' the bastards through, I've no wish for us both to be slaughtered, and 'tis useless to try and fight off a dozen of them. Stay as still and silent as ye can, Katrina, and if ever there was a need for prayers, say them now."

CHAPTER 11

She hardly dared breathe as she burrowed beneath the covers. Seconds later the bedroom door was kicked open, and she could smell the raw stench of soldiers too long on the march without access to washing or cleanliness. Even through the bedcovers she could smell them, or maybe it was her own fear that she smelled. It shuddered through her as she heard one of the redcoats lurch toward the bed.

"What have we here, mates? A pair of simpletons dead to the world from their coupling!"

Katrina felt the ripples of fury run through her man's body and dug her fingernails more deeply into his flesh, willing him not to heed the taunts, guessing how dearly he'd wish to throw back the bedcovers and run the hated redcoat through. But with a dozen more of them lurching about the inn, it would be sheer madness and would probably mean slaughter for them both, and for the innkeeper and his wife, too.

She felt the redcoat's hand grasp the bedcover and graze her skin as it did so. It was callused, roughened by days and nights exposed to wind and weather. Through her half-shuttered eyes, she saw the man's leering face. She felt the tension in Jamie and wondered how long he could remain so still and passive, and in the pretense of sleep.

"Leave 'em be, Jake!" another English voice snarled. "You wouldn't think much of being hauled off your own woman. Be satisfied with food and ale and let's be on our way. Leave them to their rutting, if you ain't knocked all the rise out of the dolt."

Katrina's cheeks burned with rage and humiliation as the first one sniggered. She held on to Jamie with rigid fingers and thankfully heard the redcoats clattering back down the stairs to join the others as the innkeeper bawled at them to come and eat the victuals or be gone. The first redcoat's voice drifted back up the stairs, ripe with innuendo.

"From the glimpse I got of the wench's white shoulder and red hair, 'twon't be long afore he gets the rise back in him again, and in her, too, mates!"

Katrina wilted against Jamie's body. He whispered to her to keep silent a while longer, until at last they heard the sounds of movement outside the inn and the clatter of horses going into the distance. Minutes later, there was a tap on the door, and the inn wife called to them softly. Jamie bade her come in. She looked remarkably calm in the light of the candle she held.

"I'm sorry for the inconvenience to ye both, and I trust ye'll sleep easy now. Good night to ye."

She left them, and for a minute Katrina didn't know whether to laugh or cry at the incongruous remark said so sincerely. And then it dawned on her that this was probably no isolated occurrence to the inn wife, and that this was how it could be for her and Jamie from now on, while they traveled in the wake of the prince's army.

Tonight was the first time she had actually seen the enemy they called the redcoats. The struggle they called the Jacobite Rebellion was no longer a distant, hazy affair for her parents to fret over, for her Uncle Robert to call a futile aim. It was here, in the bedroom she and Jamie shared, made doubly vivid by the savage obscenities Jamie was mouthing in his impotence at being too outnumbered to attempt a fight.

"Jamie, it does no good," she whispered, laying a tremulous finger against his lips to stay the words. "Let's just be thankful we're safe to fight another day, dearest. Let's try to sleep, so that we're fresh enough to ride on in the morning."

He breathed heavily, knowing she was right and unwilling to accept the fact that he had lain so rigidly while the murderous redcoats mocked him and his bride. But brooding on it did no good at all, and it took his lassie to make him see it. Besides, he'd not want to frighten her further by telling her this was only the beginning.

He wrapped her in his arms once more, warming her cold flesh.

"Aye, we'll sleep, then," he said grimly. "And I'd suggest that ye stay here with this kindly inn wife, save that the inn seems ill protected from cutthroats like those we've seen."

"I'll not stay," she said instantly, all thoughts of obeying vanishing from her mind. "I'm coming with ye, Jamie!"

"Ye'll stay in farm or croft when I tell ye to." His dark eyes glinted in the darkness, but she was glad enough to turn his thoughts away from the fright of the redcoats' appearance.

It was a long while before Katrina slept. Every creak of the old inn had her nerves jumping, and her nimble mind would not be stilled. She thought of the few deserters she had seen on the harbor at Kirdcudbright; the poor wretches at the inn where the one had died clutching her hand; her own menfolk coming home from a battle, with her father wounded; and the one-armed man in this very inn, waving his horror of a stump at her . . . and she compared them with this first glimpse of the redcoats of the English army.

The one force so bedraggled, pushed into retreat from their proud surge into England. The other, if all accounts were true, rallying ever more men, to be instantly replaced the minute one fell, and seemingly as indestructible as her brother Hamish's toy soldiers. The imagery of it wouldn't leave her mind. As each toy soldier toppled over, it was instantly righted again.

For quavering moments in the dark stillness of the night, while Jamie breathed deeply beside her, Katrina could wish that her history lessons had not been quite so comprehensive. It would be a comfort not to know that in every other Jacobite uprising the English had always come out the victors, and that the Highlanders in particular had borne the brunt of the victorious army's triumph, in the burning of crofts in routing out the rebels, and in all the killing and maiming and plundering. She shivered with more than the cold of the night and tried to close her mind against the unwanted images.

Jamie was decisive next morning, his voice brooking no arguments from her as he said they must be ready to move on. He had already been downstairs and spoken with the innkeeper, and now he reported his words to Katrina as she dressed.

"The redcoats are everywhere, then. 'Tis a miracle we've encountered none before this. The innkeeper calls them a plague of locusts that travel in small patrols even when scattered from their army. Naturally so, since they'll be sore afraid o' the Highlanders," he added with a growling pride. "If I'd not been so outnumbered last night, I'd have given them a taste."

His hands clenched, and Katrina didn't need telling how the episode had wounded his male pride. As if she sensed his brooding thoughts, she turned to him and spoke quietly, her shawl around her head and shoulders, covering her hair. She had told him she could not eat so early in the day, that the inn wife had given them pies and oatcakes to take with them, and that the horse had been fed and watered while they'd slept.

"I'm ready, Jamie. If we're to make for Stirling, we should make haste and leave, and not put the folks here into more danger because of us."

They left the inn with nerves more alert now than when they arrived, eyes aching from the effort of trying to see through driving sleet and snow, keeping themselves covered up with wool and plaid. Accustomed as they were to the icy conditions of northern winters more rugged than this, it still chilled them to the bone to be traveling constantly, day after day. It would have been easy journeying, but for the threat of the redcoats ever near and the times when they had to lie low for hours on end when the vivid color of the enemy jackets suddenly appeared against the snowy ground.

"At least they let us know of their presence," Jamie said sarcastically as the two of them crouched low in the lee of some thornbushes and watched a straggling patrol of redcoats go by. "None can miss the hated sight of their jackets."

They waited until the group was well out of sight, then stood and flexed their aching muscles. Katrina gave a sudden gasp as she turned her head. Right behind them were two men in Highland plaid, unkempt and filthy. In front of them they prodded some sorry-looking cattle, at which they growled constantly for being stupid English beasts. Deserters. . . . Katrina felt as though her heart had leapt to her throat at the barbaric appearance of the men.

"Ye did well to keep out o' sight, neighbors," one jeered

at Jamie and Katrina. "Ye'll have tired o' the game, too, laddie, and looking for other sport."

"No, ye bastards, don't class me wi' yourselves!" Jamie rounded on them angrily. "Ye shame your clans if ye're running from the redcoats, as I suspect."

"Och, we have a loyalist still thinking our bonnie prince can win, Ogilvy!" The taunts went on. "The sooner he gets back to France the easier we'll all rest in our beds, and any man still fool enough to follow a lost cause should take to the boats wi' him."

"No cause is lost until every loyalist lays down his weapons," Jamie snarled.

"Ye'd do better to lay down wi' your wench, laddie. Ye'll be little use to her if yon Charlie sends her home a corpse in a box. She'll be needing a live stiff, no' a dead one!"

"I'd thank ye not to insult my wife," Jamie snapped.

"Wife, is it? A hasty tyin' o' the knot, I'll wager. Then ye're twice the fool I took ye for, fighting a lost cause and tyin' the knot while ye're still wet behind the ears."

Jamie moved toward the leering ruffian and Katrina let out a scream as she saw the man's companion pull the dirk from his stocking top and draw back his arm to aim it. But Jamie was quicker, and his own dirk whistled through the air to strike cleanly into the man's heart. He fell in a heap on the white ground, the blood staining the snow in a spreading pool about him.

Terrified sobs constricted Katrina's throat. She couldn't speak or even breathe properly. She could only stare in horror at the crumpled thing that seconds before had been a man and accept that it had been Jamie's dirk that had killed him. Ogilvy had backed away, all the fight in him gone as Jamie bent swiftly to retrieve his dirk and wipe it clean on the dead man's plaid. Ogilvy turned and scrambled away over boulders and hollows, beating at the English cattle in a fury, not wanting to share his companion's fate.

Jamie turned sharply to Katrina, hearing the ragged breath in her throat. He bent to cover the dead man with his own plaid and told her to remount the horse.

"Th-that man . . ." she stuttered through chattering teeth. "One minute he was alive, taunting, and the next . . ."

"That's what war is, lass. It was his life or mine. Ye'd best understand that this is how it has to be." His voice was grim, without emotion.

"He was'na the enemy, Jamie. He was a Highlander!" she whispered, staring at the granite-faced man who was her husband.

"He was a deserter. He'd turned his back on the cause and deserved to die if he'd stand back and see all that we've fought for trodden into the dust after swearing his allegiance."

Katrina felt a shiver of shock at his cold callousness. This was a new Jamie, one she didn't know. She was learning very quickly that war changed people. It had changed her, too, whether she was willing to admit it or not.

She turned to climb onto the horse, her whole body shaking.

"No one deserves to die, Jamie. I canna believe this is you talking."

He didn't touch her. "Katrina, I swore to follow the prince, and to defend his cause with every breath in my body, and so did *he*, with his face in the ground. Do ye think he wouldn't have aimed for my heart just now? Would ye rather it had been me lying there? And what do ye think would have become of my wife wi'out me to protect ye from women-starved scum? Had ye thought of that?"

"No," she said through lips suddenly wooden. She hadn't thought of that . . . and she didn't want to think of it. None of it. She felt near to tears, and she had vowed not to cry. She tried to be as hard as Jamie, but it was far from her nature, and the words came out wobbly. "It—it just seems a terrible waste of a life, Jamie."

He climbed on the horse behind her, and his arms around her were still tense. "All war is a waste of life. 'Tis a fact we must learn to accept, dearie."

"Should we leave the man like this?" she asked tentatively.

"There's naught else to do. The snow's too hard-packed to bury him, and the horse can't carry three. War makes practical men, Katrina, and the important thing now is to get ye settled safely, for ye hamper me now. Once I find lodgings for ye, I'll be moving toward Stirling, and I'd thank ye not to argue wi' me."

She knew better than that right now. Jamie was as hard and

unyielding as the winter ground beneath their feet. But the thought of a warm fire indoors and a hot meal was more inviting than all else at that moment. The trauma of the last encounter with the deserters had reminded Katrina that for all her resolve, she still had a woman's heart and could grieve for the unknown woman whose man would not be returning to her. The man Jamie had killed. . . .

But she knew he was right about her added weight on the horse hampering their progress, and much good it would do Jamie if the horse went lame; Katrina would not want the blame of it to rest with her. At last they saw a farmhouse, a curl of gray smoke rising straight from the chimney. As they approached, a swarthy-looking farmer appeared, his manner suspicious, until Jamie told him the circumstances of their being there.

"Aye, we'll keep the lassie safe for ye, and welcome," he grunted then. "My wife will be glad o' a bit of women's talk. And we've a lad of our own away wi' the prince. Hamish Blair. If ye meet up wi' him at all, tell him his family is well."

"I'll do that," Jamie said gravely, as though such an eventuality was likely among a few thousand men. They followed the farmer inside, and a red-faced woman welcomed them both.

Katrina felt cheered at once. It was far different from home, or even from Aunt Janet's farm. This one was frugal in appearance, but with the warm baking smells of bread and fish, and in that respect it felt like home. She turned to say as much to Jamie, thinking they could have a small respite here, but she saw with a shock that he was already questioning the farmer on other matters.

"Can ye tell me exactly where we are, man? I'd be on my way once I've rested a wee while, and I'd be glad of a hot bite o' food if your good woman would be so kind."

"I'd not let ye go wi'out it, lad," she said at once, with a sympathetic glance toward Katrina's pale face. Were they to part so soon, then? She had expected him to stay this one night at least. It was already dusk . . . and she knew that Jamie thought it safer to have the cover of darkness when a man traveled alone. With the stars for guidance, a man could track his quarry with animal stealth, and the thought of it curdled her blood, knowing it could well be Jamie who was tracked.

"Ye're but a dozen miles or so from Falkirk, Mackinnon," Farmer Blair told him. "Our lad, Hamish, was here a short while back, and ye'll know that Falkirk and Stirling are close enough together to make each of importance to the Stuart, and within reach of Edinburgh."

"Edinburgh?" Jamie said sharply. The farmer gave a low oath.

"Did ye think that the government army would allow the city to stay in Jacobite hands once the rebel army had marched toward England, Mackinnon? The redcoats are in control again there, and our Hamish says that one of the prince's goals will be to take the English barracks at Ruthven."

Jamie scanned his map and nodded. " 'Twould seem a sensible move. Our army heads in a direct northern line and seems set to aim for Inverness. Mebbe the prince thinks to gather more clansmen there. I thank ye, man, and would be glad to see the army move north. 'Tis a fair guess that the English army will muster at Edinburgh, thinking it such a prize, but more Highlanders will be within calling of Inverness."

He hoped he sounded more confident than he felt. It was still retreat, a word he didn't like. But he'd not risk distressing Katrina still more by admitting as much.

"I have a brother called Hamish," he heard her telling Mistress Blair now. "He's too young to fight, though he sorely envied my Jamie."

"They're all too young to fight, lass," the woman said quietly, and Katrina knew the two of them were united in their unspoken fears. The woman took Katrina to a clean room and left her there while she went to prepare some hot food for them both. Jamie followed her upstairs a moment later and caught her in his arms. He held her tightly, so tightly it felt as if he would crush her bones. She almost welcomed the pain and willed it to stay with her after he'd gone.

"Your own heart must tell ye how much I love ye, Katrina," he murmured against the cool skin of her cheek. "And ye know well enough that there's none but Charles Stuart who'd take me from your side.''

"I do know it, Jamie. Loyalty before love," she said tremulously, knowing it had to be.

"Dearest, we both know I've stayed too long from the prince's side already. I'm not blaming your sweet self, for God knows 'tis hard for a man to leave his woman, but leave ye I must. I'll return for ye when I can."

"Take all care, Jamie." She resisted the urge to beg him to stay a little longer, for it was evident that the news of the army's movements had fired him anew. One last sweet kiss in the privacy of this room where Katrina would once again sleep alone, and then they went to eat the good food the farmer's wife was setting out on the table for them. Fresh-caught fish baked to a succulent crispness, hot bread dipped in a nourishing onion soup, a parcel of bread and crowdie cheese for Jamie to take with him, and then he was gone. Katrina tried not to let the instant loneliness envelop her as the sound of the hoofbeats faded into the distance, and she stifled the tears that threatened as she closed the farmhouse door behind him.

"So ye've decided to have done wi' the white feather, have ye, Jamie Mackinnon?" a clansman growled in the darkness as Jamie rode stealthily toward the Jacobite camp now at Bannockburn, between Falkirk and Stirling. A gray pall of smoke had heralded the cooking fires, and it was an easy matter then to find his way to his own Mackinnon clan tents.

"I'm no white feather," Jamie snarled back. "And I'd run through the next man to say so."

"That ye won't," grunted another. "We've enemies enough wi'out fighting among ourselves. We're glad to see ye back, though ye've missed the small victory at Stirling."

"Ye'd call it small?" his companion snorted. "Any victory's preferable to a defeat, man."

"I heard of it." Jamie nodded. "The town fell to us without much opposition, I heard, but the castle withstood the siege and remains under English control."

"They're welcome to it," the first clansman jeered. " 'Tis more important to take the Ruthven barracks and take the enemy's arms and ammunition, but what we say has no effect on prince or generals. They play a game o' their own wi' their arguments over which plan to follow."

"Does the prince stay in Bannockburn?" Jamie asked.

"Oh, aye," the second said. "But not here wi' the likes of us, lad. He's charmed us all into spending the winter in the freezing mire instead o' by our own hearths, while he's now cozy at Bannockburn House wi' one Sir Hugh bloody Paterson and his bonnie niece."

"Hold your tongue, man," another voice snapped. "Would ye have your prince bedding down wi' the likes of scurvy clods like yourself? Dinna begrudge him his soft bed. He knows what he's about, and 'tis best that he and Murray keep well apart."

"Where's Murray's section?" Jamie asked quickly.

"Already at Falkirk, and 'tis my bet we take the town first before pushing on to Ruthven. I'll take wagers on it."

"Take them in the morning, man. My head fair aches wi' your guessing games," he was told sharply. "And ye'll do well to find a place to put your head as well, Jamie Mackinnon, and be fresh for what's to come."

Jamie was only too glad to do as his clansman suggested, and he curled himself inside his plaid in the close warmth of the tent alongside the rest of the brawny Mackinnons there. It had been a long hard ride over the slippery tracks and rough slopes to reach here, and he ached in every part of his body. It was even good to rest among these evil-smelling companions rather than next to the soft warmth of his wife, and those were comparisons at which he closed his mind deliberately. It was already well past the turn of the year. His own birthday had come and gone without noticing. He was officially free to wed Katrina Fraser, according to his family's tradition, but he doubted his or Katrina's kin would be overpleased at the way they had conducted themselves. Jamie knew that once this Jacobite reckoning was over, they would have their own reckoning.

Lord George Murray was pondering on which way the reckoning was to go next and anticipating the prince's opposition to his plan. The prince was partial to holding frequent councils of war, at which tempers usually flared, and now that scouts had reported the rapid advance of the English redcoats, there was no time to mince matters.

"I question the wisdom of having our men quartered over such a wide area in small detachments, sir," Lord George said frequently. "We'd present a more impressive force if we were massed together."

"We need to show ourselves in as many areas as possible," Charles argued vehemently. "If we're a smaller force than the redcoats, then for God's sake, man, let's make them believe we're invincible with enough reinforcements to rout them!"

Lord George thought it a feeble hope. The English had as many spies and scouts as themselves and would know of the grouped clan regiments and their positions. The shorter the distance between the two armies, the more likely the redcoats were to pick off a section of rebels, then another, and another.

Persuaded that a mass force was the better aim for the moment, the prince called a council of war after reviewing his troops on a plain several miles southeast of Bannockburn. For two days they had massed here, and the English army failed to attack, though the main body of it, under the harsh leadership of Lieutenant-General Hawley, was known to be in the vicinity. He was rumored to have erected gallows in Edinburgh in preparation for dealing with rebel prisoners.

On January 17th, the Highlanders massed for the third time on the plain, grumbling at being roused from their quarters at Bannockburn for another day's fruitless waiting. By midday, Lord George put it bluntly to the prince.

"I say we attack now, sir. We've the advantage of the high ground around Falkirk if we move small detachments to left and right and let Drummond's regiment and the cavalry take the main road from Bannockburn to Falkirk to divert the enemies' attention. If ye'll agree to it, sir, ye should leave your standard flying over Plein Muir here, to confuse the redcoats."

The prince nodded. "It's a sound plan, Murray. Outline it further, and we'll put it into operation as quickly as possible. The men are tired of this cat and mouse game, and so am I."

"I propose to lead one column headed by the three clan Donald regiments, sir, and suggest that ye take the other with the Atholl brigade. The main body of Drummond's men can cover the center position.''

"Is it agreed to be a good plan?" Charles demanded of his officers. There were ayes from generals and clan chiefs and the orders to proceed were given. Led by the prince and the officers, the regiments began to move southward toward Falkirk, strategically important for the rebels to hold, from its nearness to Edinburgh and to the Firth of Forth, should the elusive French troops ever come. Murray was totally convinced that they never would, while Prince Charles was equally certain they would.

The battlefield was a contrast to that of Prestonpans. Jamie Mackinnon was in the center section of the rebel army's approach, and as the three sections of the Highlanders began to close up and merge, they covered the entire face of the hillside of folds and gulleys and ridges. The snowy moorland scrub of the slope was transformed by a moving sea of varying shades of plaid.

"By God, man, if this storm breaks, we're in for an uncomfortable wetting," the man next to him grunted, eyeing the storm-filled sky. "The sooner we fire these bastards and get back to the comfort o' camp, the better I'll be pleased."

"Ye've been away from home a long while if ye can call the camp a comfort," Jamie growled. "But I follow your meaning, Blaikie."

The rain suddenly lashed down on them in torrents, blown by a ferocious wind. Almost at the same time, the English army, gathered below, began to toil up the hillside, swarming toward the Highlanders as if believing the weight of numbers would discount the disadvantage of position.

"They'll have their muskets soaked," Blaikie jeered in Jamie's ear. "They'll be no challenge."

"Don't underestimate them," Jamie snapped. " 'Tis a fool that does so. Why in God's name don't we get the order to attack? 'Tis what we came for!"

It was near four in the afternoon before Murray raised his musket as the signal to fire. The light was starting to fade, and by now the redcoats were almost upon them as a sudden blast of firing split the English lines with a deafening roar. Their front lines were the dragoons, and at the Highlanders' intense vollying, the horses panicked, hooves flailing in the air and blood spurting from torn carcases as they fell. The redcoats had no chance against the onslaught. Already tired from the toil up the hill, those that could turned and fled as the roars of the Highlanders and the wail of the pipes behind them filled the air and merged with the yellow acrid stench of powder.

"Get the bastards!" The Highlanders roared out the battle cries now, crawling on their bellies until they were within range of the enemy, then rising like phoenixes to stab the hated redcoats with their dirks, thrusting again and again, using pistols where possible, but with little space to wield swords. They gave little attention to battle orders now, if any were heard above the pandemonium of howling wind and lashing rain, horses' heaving agonies and mens' screams. The Highlanders clambered over bodies without noticing them.

Then there was a great burst of firing from the enemy side, as English reinforcements took the place of those fleeing. Blinded and deafened, some Highlanders fell immediately, while others seemed too dazed with shock to do more than keep on pursuing mindlessly. But the rebel strategy proved good, and inch by inch the redcoats were pushed back. Although the Stuart army was in total disorder now, the bulk of them were still advancing, able to fire pistols and strike terror with dirk and sword. Hawley's redcoats had had enough. The prince's army entered Falkirk from both ends of the town. Lochiel and Keppoch, Lord George Murray, Drummond and his troops, marched in triumph, to find most of the enemy already gone. Soon afterward, the prince himself arrived and declared Falkirk for his father.

"The bastards tried to fire their tents so we shouldn't take them," Blaikie snarled to Jamie. "But they fled too fast to do much damage. We're to take what's left."

There were wagons as well as tents, kettledrums, small arms, baggage and clothing, and food and drink besides. The rebels were the victors and enjoyed the fact for the night, despite the appalling weather. And while the Highlanders feasted and made merry, the prince and the generals argued over the merits of the day in the prince's quarters in the town.

"I don't question the men's bravery," Murray was roused

to say. "But as soldiers they shamed their clans. They don't know the meaning of discipline."

"Ye're too hard on them, Murray," Lochiel said. "They did all that was asked o' them, and we've done what we came for. Must ye always want more?"

"I want the best."

"Then mebbe ye should have brought in more cavalry and not insisted on fighting on foot yourself," Drummond retorted.

"The bloody horses got in the way."

"We're just wasting time in these recriminations," Charles broke into the arguments. "Do we stay here or march on Edinburgh once more, or go south again to London?"

An outburst followed his words. To attempt to go south to London again was beyond most of their credulity. There were one or two as reckless and blindly optimistic as the prince who voiced their approval of the suggestion, but they were quickly shouted down.

"We stay here to rest the men and settle our claim on the town," Murray snapped. "There must also be a force at Stirling, but since the clan chiefs and myself have made an assessment of the depleted state of our troops, sir, we beg to give ye an ultimatum."

Charles's eyes glinted angrily. "I take no ultimatums, Lord Murray. I'll have your suggestions and act on them as I choose!"

"Sir, I beg ye to listen." Murray held his temper with a great effort. "The farther back we retreat the more deserters we encourage."

"Then we push back into England," Charles said immediately.

"*No*, sir!" Forgetting whom he addressed, Murray roared out the words. "If ye'll listen, I'll outline the plan your generals think fit to follow." *Most* of them, he added beneath his breath, knowing there had been as much dissent about this as about everything else. He saw the elegant lift of the prince's eyebrow, and guessed that His Highness was digesting the fact that Murray's suggestion had already been discussed without him. Murray plunged on without waiting for further comment.

"We think it best for an immediate retreat to the Highlands, sir. By the spring, our army could be strengthened a hundred-fold by new recruitings, and we could usefully spend the time in revitalizing those still loyal to us now, who are badly in need of proper food and nourishment.''

"And you think this retreat to the Highlands makes sense, do you?'' Charles said in genuine astonishment. "When our men are nearer to their own homes, do you really think they'll remain loyal and not desert all the more?''

Lochiel spoke up. "Sir, there are useful government forts to be taken between here and Inverness, the barracks at Ruthven being the most obvious, as ye know. We don't propose to set the men in aimless flight, but with a purpose to keep up morale. Small victories will be sweet, sir, and will give your French allies more time to send us fresh troops.''

Charles looked at him sourly. Fond as he was of the man dubbed the Gentle Lochiel, he saw the words as a kind of blackmail—or a carrot dangled beneath his nose. . . .

"You're certain that another retreat would have that effect, are you?'' he said sarcastically. "You don't think it would lower the men's morale even more and let the enemy crow over us? You don't think the French will choose to see my cause as futile, once they know of our movements?''

"I'm sure Your Highness will send messages so they'll know the sense o' the moves,'' Murray said glibly. There was a complete deadlock between them, and finally Charles gave way, again with a bad grace, for without the support of his generals he could do little. The clans were too strongly supportive of their chiefs, both in heritage and fear of repri-sals on cottage and holding. He had learned that well enough.

"Then we'll strengthen our positions here,'' he rapped out. "I'd have it known that Charles Stuart commands Falkirk and Stirling, and let the men enjoy the facilities the towns offer for the time being. I trust you'll advise me when I may move again, Lord George?''

Murray ignored the heavy sarcasm, merely relieved that the arguments were over—for the moment, at least. Battling with the redcoats was a struggle he understood. These verbal battles with the prince were something he could well do without.

CHAPTER 12

The Stuart army was to remain in the area of Falkirk and Stirling and the camp at Bannockburn for twelve days. When the news rippled through the camps, the men welcomed it and rejoiced in the amenities the towns offered. Forces were positioned to watch for enemy movements, but by now the scouts reported that the redcoats were solidly entrenched at Edinburgh, where they awaited the arrival of their new leader, the duke of Cumberland. Now, with time to waste in drinking and merrymaking and wenching, and some to take the chance to desert, the Highlanders made the most of their leaders' decision.

There was only one thought on Jamie Mackinnon's mind. The next move was to march to Ruthven barracks and capture the English stock of arms and ammunition and supplies. Ruthven was still a good distance north, and beyond it lay Inverness, the town that was Charles's eventual goal.

Jamie's mind was made up. He couldn't possibly get Katrina to Inverness, but he could take her some way there and see her safely settled in a new lodging. She would be safer there than stranded in an isolated farmhouse where frustrated English soldiers might swoop for food or wenching. There was payment for the troops now, under the prince's confiscation plans, and he foresaw no difficulty. He spoke of his plan to Blaikie before he approached his clan chief.

"So when someone asks after me, Blaikie, ye'll tell them I've not done as some o' the others, man. Tell them I've not deserted," he said fiercely. Blaikie nodded his wild head.

"Aye, lad. No one seeing Jamie Mackinnon wi' a dirk in his hand and bawling his battle slogan would take ye for a deserter. I'll mind and tell them."

167

Jean Saunders

This time Jamie had no compunction about taking one of the captured English wagons and a fresher horse than his own to ride back for Katrina. If he encountered any pockets of the enemy on the way, he'd merely profess to be a farmer riding with an empty wagon to pick up his family supplies of grain. Clan pride was necessarily subdued when it came to dealing with the enemy, and any devious methods were preferable to being the target of an English musket.

Katrina heard the clattering of wagon wheels on the snow-packed ground in front of the farmhouse. Hardly believing her eyes, she dropped the piece of linen she was mending for Mistress Blair and leapt to her feet with a cry. The next second, Jamie was inside the farmhouse, clasping her to him and smothering her face with kisses. It all happened so fast, Katrina wondered if she were dreaming, except that this was surely no dream, this flesh-and-blood Jamie here in her arms, who was hardly letting her breathe. . . .

"Thank God ye're safe, my dearest! We heard o' the victory."

"Aye, 'twas a fierce one, but soon won, lassie," he said huskily, wanting to think of it no more for the present, wanting just to hold her close and breathe in the warm scent of her hair from the firelight, and feel the softness of her against him.

"Oh, Jamie, Jamie, I was feared for ye," she whispered as he rocked her to him.

"I'd no' expect ye to be otherwise, dearie," he retorted, his pleasure in seeing her sharpening his words. He had become adept at closing his mind to all other needs but those of the Stuart while he marched behind him, but now, for a few sweet moments, he could allow other needs to be revived and glory in them.

"And ye've come for me now, Jamie?" Katrina lifted her head expectantly, her eyes glowing like rich jewels. "Ye'll take me with ye now, in the wagon?"

"Ye'd best agree to it, lad, for your lassie's sore fretted over ye," said a dry voice behind Katrina's head, and Jamie realized the farmer's wife sat there by the fireside, and he hadn't even noticed her. How could he, when he was so fired

168

up inside at his lassie's welcome? He kept his arms around her still as he acknowledged the woman's presence.

"Aye, Mistress Blair, I've come for her, and 'tis my wish that I'd find another lodging as homely as your own."

He felt Katrina's arms tighten around his neck.

"Why not the wagons that follow the marching?" she demanded. "They're not all light-skirts, we're told, and I'd be as close to ye as possible, Jamie. Some o' the women are wed to the clansmen."

"And most are not," he growled, his face darkening.

"They still give comfort in the bonnie prince's service, Jamie," Mistress Blair put in, seeing the sudden clash of wills between the two. "There's many ways o' fighting wars, and dinna discount a lassie's part in it!"

Jamie said nothing for a minute, and then he grunted again.

"I'll mebbe think on your words when I've rested awhile, mistress. And when ye've offered me some of your good soup, if ye've a mind to it."

Mistress Blair rose, laughing, to pat Jamie on the shoulder for luck. "Och, but ye've as much o' the canny charm as they say of the bonnie prince, Jamie Mackinnon, and 'tis welcome ye are to be bringing a breath of fresh air into the house. If ye've the sense to it, ye'll take the lassie wi' ye in the army wagons, for I'll wager she'll not be corrupted by any loose women. More likely she'll convert them to the virtues of wifehood, if the fretting for ye is anything to go by!"

Ignoring Katrina's blushes, she paused a minute longer before leaving them. Her eyes searched Jamie's face.

"Tell me, did ye hear aught of our Hamish? A lad as tall as yourself, though not so brawny-built. . . ."

Jamie shook his head gently. He'd not heard of him, and he could only answer truthfully that among the few thousand men involved at Falkirk and Stirling, it was impossible to know more than a few names, even among the clans, which were a maze of names and allegiances in themselves.

The woman nodded, accepting his word, and went to the kitchen for the food. And Katrina was caught to Jamie's chest once more, as if he could never let her go. When she finally caught her breath, she spoke hesitantly but with the undercurrent of determination he knew so well.

"Do as Mistress Blair says, Jamie. Take me wi' the wagons. I'd be a part of the cause. I want to be with ye, Jamie. I want to see for myself, to share everything with ye."

"The stench o' men's fear and the filth o' the traveling being part o' the sharing."

"But we'd be together, Jamie! If it means as much to ye as it does to me."

He held her tightly. "Ye know it does. But 'tis not the way I'd want us to be together, with my wife sharing dangers and following in the light-skirts' wagon."

"I do want to go, Jamie. I want it more than anything," she said quietly as Mistress Blair came back to the room with the soup and bread and bade them eat. Farmer Blair came to join them soon after, anxious-faced at the unknown wagon outside, until he saw Jamie, and then he insisted that they all drink a dram or two of whiskey together.

"Not too many, or I'll be in no fit state to drive the horse back in a straight line," Jamie began, when Katrina caught at his hand.

"Ye're not leaving so soon? Jamie, there's no need, if ye say there's a resting time at Falkirk for the army. If I'm to travel wi' the wagons, then ye can bide here a night or two before we go back. 'Tis so, Jamie!"

She heard Farmer Blair give a rumbling laugh.

"I'm thinking ye've married a witch, lad, for if a woman o' mine looked at me wi' eyes half as wheedling, I'd be denying her nothing at all! So ye've a mind to be a wagon wife, have ye, lassie?"

"Do ye see aught bad in it, Farmer Blair?" Katrina appealed to him now. "I've heard tell o' the good the women can do, wi' mending and preparing food and washing the clothes and giving herb drinks and helping wi' the wounded—"

"All right!" Jamie broke in. "Mebbe ye're best kept where I can see ye after all! Ye'll travel wi' the wagons," he said grudgingly, and he was rewarded by a kiss of such sweetness he knew he would be hard put to refuse her anything. It had always been so between them and always would be. And it would be good to rest here a night or two. There was

170

time, and he had no wish to join in with the revelers in Falkirk when he could hold his own sweet wife in his arms. The longer he thought of it, the more attractive the notion became. By the time the four of them retired for the night, he could almost think it had been his own idea to stay here with his wife and take her to travel with the wagons toward Ruthven . . . and since the outcome would be the same, it didn't matter a jot to him who had thought of it. All that mattered here and now was that he and his Katrina could warm each other all through the night, renewing the marriage vows so recently made, relearning the joys of belonging, of loving.

They left the Blair farm after two nights, continuing the roles of farmer and his wife in the wagon, now filled with food from Mistress Blair, a change of clothing for Jamie, and hay for the horse, which was placed over everything else in case they were challenged by an English patrol. Jamie had felt revitalized both by his wife and the good basic cooking they had enjoyed, and by the welcome scrub down and washing of his dirt-encrusted clothes. He felt ready to conquer the world, and it was their good fortune that they encountered no enemy patrols on the journey back to Bannockburn where Jamie's regiment camped.

Now he was to make certain Katrina was known to be his wife and not one of the women who followed the soldiers. He made that perfectly clear to all, including the light-skirts themselves as he took her about the wagons. Katrina hushed him.

"Can't ye see ye'll make them hate me if ye go on like this?" she hissed. "If I'm to ride wi' them, don't make me out to be so much above them, love, or my life will be made a misery! Some o' them are wives, ye said. And the rest . . . well, they're still women, and there must be many a Highlander here who's glad of it!"

He had to see the sense in her words, and Katrina smiled at the women, some as young as herself, some raddled, others with the undoubted look of wives about them—with high-buttoned dress and scraped-back hair, and an air of usefulness about them as they stitched or mended their men's tattered plaids and shirts. The light-skirts were tolerant of any newcomer, while the wives welcomed Katrina into their midst. She especially warmed to one not much older than herself, called Fiona Patterson.

"They tell us we move out soon, Katrina," the girl told her when Jamie had seen her settled and had gone to find news of his companions. "We go to Ruthven barracks, and we're a small town o' wagons then, when the men go off to war."

"Does it frighten ye?" Katrina asked, hearing the girl speak of matters so new to her.

Fiona shrugged. She was fair-haired and pretty, and spoke as Katrina would have spoken. "If it does, I'd rather be here wi' my Andy than fretting away at home. I pretend he's away at the shepherding, and then 'tis no' so bad. Ye'll get used to it quick enough."

"She'll have to," said an older wife. "And pray to God this is the last time we're called on to follow our men, lassie. 'Tis the third time for me, and I'd as soon the Stuarts settled their kingdom one way or another!"

Katrina didn't care for the woman's talk. "Do ye stay wi' your man at night?" she asked Fiona delicately, and the girl laughed mischievously.

"Have ye recently wed? I guessed it when I saw ye, Katrina. Aye, we stay wi' our men, except when 'tis obvious that we can't, when they're away fighting the redcoats! Some take their lassies to lodgings in town or village, some to tents, and those"—she jerked her head toward the light-skirts—"they're no' so fussy where they sleep, if ye take my meaning!"

She did, and she felt too tired to talk anymore. They had come a long way that day, and it was a relief to be in the comparative safety of the camp here, north of Falkirk and in easy reach of Stirling, protected on all sides by the wide-spread army. Night fires were already burning, and Jamie came for her in a little while, to say they would go to a nearby village to an inn for a few nights before the army was ready to move. Katrina felt relieved at the thought, for as a newlywed she felt embarrassed at so many rough Highlanders and women with knowing eyes about her. And she had best get such prissy notions right out of her head, she told herself severely, for she was as much a part of the raggle-taggle company now as any of them.

The rebel army marched out of their camps on February 4th, after more wrangling and argument among the leaders. Token forces were left behind, and Lord George Murray took one division of men toward the coastal road to Inverness, while the prince and most of the Highland clan regiments took the Highland route for the attack on the English-held barracks.

Katrina was to learn just how shaken her bones could be as the wagons trundled over rough tracks, ravines, and hillsides, the prince's standard fluttering proudly ahead, the clan standards spread out behind as the Highlanders marched or rode their stringy horses in as reasonable a formation as was possible. The wind moaned bitterly through the mountain passes, and their progress was often halted by rain or sleet blinding them so that it was impossible to do other than huddle in plaids and against horses, in tents and wagons, and wait for the storm to pass. Katrina was glad of the women's company then, and she tried not to think too longingly of her mammie's cooking as she chewed on a dry biscuit or the dregs of soup twice cooked, or of a cozy bed as she lay on the hard boards of the wagon and tried to sleep. Although Fiona Patterson had said they stayed with their men when they could, this particular journey was too long and hazardous for such intimacies. They crossed mountains and held their breath at ravines far below them, and lost more than one to the icy waters below as a man's hold on horse or wagon was lost.

But at last, weary to the bone, the march was halted, and the order was given to make camp. Ruthven barracks was now within attacking distance, and Charles ordered his men to rest and prepare. The barracks were well fortified, but the plan was to attack by surprise. In the dimly lit, hastily erected tents, the prince's orders were passed through the Highlanders' ranks. Clasped in Jamie's arms, Katrina swallowed back the fear that gripped her. Away in front of them was the enemy, and she was sending her man into battle.

"Come back safe, Jamie," she said huskily. "Do what ye must do."

A minute more, and he was gone, her prayers going with him. She felt Fiona's hand gripping hers as they watched the army move out stealthily under cover of darkness.

"Ye're so brave, Katrina," the other girl said, her voice wavering. "I canna stop the tears."

"I swore I'd not let Jamie see my tears, but they're here inside me, as sharp as yours," Katrina told her, voice tight, for even now she wouldn't cry. Not while Jamie rode proudly behind the Mackinnon standard and went to fight for the Stuart. She turned fierce eyes onto Fiona, the only way to hold in the tears. "Ye'd do better to keep them in check, too, lassie, for an army's made up of strong men and stronger women! We may well need to be strong at the end of a battle."

The other girl twisted away from her, not wanting to hear and choosing to close her mind to the ravages of war. Katrina couldn't blame her. Each had to face the war in her own way. Hers was to give Jamie all her strength to add to his, even when she was alone. It was a deep instinctive feeling, one she hadn't known she possessed until it was required of her.

Jamie's thoughts were far from such noble sentiments as he crouched in the darkness, along with his companions, breathing in the cold damp night air.

"By God, how much longer must we wait here? I'm near to taking root in the ground," Blaikie snarled in Jamie's ear.

Before Jamie could answer, the signal to attack was given, the prince's standard raised aloft, the wail of the pipes and the Gaelic war cries of the clans bursting into life in a single moment—the sounds that must surely have brought terror to the redcoats inside the barracks as the Highland army rushed upon them.

Jamie's ears were suddenly ringing with the night-splitting noise. The voice tore from his chest as he, too, roared his slogan and prayed that he wouldn't be blinded by the sudden answering burst of musket fire before he had the chance to slash his sword on some of the English bastards.

The redcoats were suddenly everywhere as the Highlanders swarmed through the gates, but they were taken too much by surprise to put up a real defense. Not expecting an attack, they had bedded down for the night, leaving only a token force in the supposed safety of the barracks. Even as they rushed out into the night firing wildly into the darkness, they still struggled to fasten breeches and cursed vehemently at being forced to fight in this godforsaken wilderness.

A great clash of steel against his shield brought Jamie staggering to his knees as he met the enemy full on. The stench of the yellow powder-filled air dried his throat and made his eyes stream so that he could hardly see. For a moment his blood seemed to congeal in a great knot of fear as a red-coated soldier loomed above him, his pistol aimed straight at his heart.

Hardly thinking what he did, Jamie rolled sideways and down, his arms flailing out to catch at the redcoat's legs as the shot exploded all around him—but not into his body. There was no piercing agony to follow the sound that was sheer pain in itself, only the deafening rocking in his head that almost made him vomit with the excruciating tremors of it.

He fumbled for the dirk at his waist, still clinging to the enemy soldier as if in some hideous embrace. He was slipping, sliding, losing his grip on the man, knowing that once he did so he would be dead. He reached high against the redcoat's chest, plunged in his dirk, and dragged it down the length of the soft body, shouting at the same time, shouting as if to shut out the noise that came from the thing he was still holding that had once been a man. In the violent confusion and uproar, the redcoat's screams dwindled to a nauseating gurgling, then stopped.

Jamie felt the hot spurting blood and guts wash over his hands from the man's wound, and smelled the sickly stench of it. He retched furiously, hackingly, and added his own vomit to the filth beneath him. There was a wild unmanly sobbing in his chest. He felt it burn, knew the pain and the shame of it, yet he seemed momentarily lost in a crazed agony of his own. He couldn't think. There was a sudden overwhelming desire to sprawl across the body of the redcoat and be out of it all.

"Mackinnons, fight! Mackinnons! Mackinnons!"

Dimly, he recognized real voices through the surging blood in his ears. Explosions all around him seemed to have stupefied his brain and his senses, but now he heard other clan names called in triumph, rallying them for the cause. The cause. . . . God help him, he was here for a purpose, the cause!

"Do ye want help, laddie?" a Highland voice rasped close to his ear, and Jamie hauled himself up from the sticky mess beneath him.

"By Christ, but ye stink worse than a goat's arse," another roared out, leaping past Jamie into the attack.

He shook his head to clear it; the night sky seemed to spin around him. Faces of clansmen floated without shape or form as he struggled to feel the comforting chill of his dirk in his grasp again. There was death all around him, but his mind refused to see the grotesque images as men of either side, redcoats or clansmen. He forced his red-rimmed eyes to see through the haze of yellow-black darkness.

"We've got them!" Suddenly it was the prince's voice that seemed close, hoarse and ragged like his own, but with victory uplifting it. "They're on the run, my brave lads, so let's finish them. Those that surrender to be locked in their own jails, and those that don't."

"Run the bastards through and save us the trouble o' taking prisoners!" roared the clansmen, still too swept up with the success of the night to heed him. The scene was of total confusion. One minute the prince was among them, the next he was gone. Faces came and went. Jamie couldn't have said how long the battle lasted, minutes or hours. He felt as if his mind as well as his ears had been blasted and shocked with noise. But as he stumbled about the body-strewn barracks, he realized that the horrendous sounds all around were becoming gradually muted. The screams were lessening, sometimes lingering as a ghastly moaning and then fading. The priest captains knelt by dying bodies, intoning words meant to bring comfort to the dying, to men who cared only for release from their agonies.

The air hung with the pall of smoke like a funeral pyre. Some clansmen, with more stomach for it than he, were slapping each other's backs and laughing at the victory, already plundering the bodies of comrades and redcoats. Any pride Jamie had in the victory seemed to vanish in a curl of shame in his gut.

Somewhere nearby a piper was playing a sad lament over a dead kinsman. The plaintive sound of it made the hairs on the back of Jamie's neck tighten, and a cold sweat trickled uncomfortably down his spine. The sadness of it could have been for him, or for any one of the laughing, jeering rebels.

He stumbled over bodies still warm in death. He felt a sudden longing for the clean Highlands and home, for the glen and for Katrina. . . . Her name surged into his mind and out again. It was an affront to be thinking of a woman when he still grieved for dead comrades. War was not the time to think of the soft embraces of a woman, or maybe it was. Without her there would be nothing.

He felt a hard clasp on his shoulder and looked into Andy Patterson's black-grimed face. Two of the women would be getting their men back, then, this time.

"How do ye fare, Jamie?" the boy said in a cracked voice. "Ye look wild-eyed. We've orders to rest. The barracks will be under our command now, and we push on to Moy, and then to Inverness."

"Moy?" Jamie tried to collect his thoughts. It was a name he knew, but for the moment he couldn't think why. He was still too muddled in his mind.

"There's a place called Moy Hall," Andy Patterson grunted. "I daresay the Stuart will be resting there awhile. There's always plenty of good resting places if ye've a title and a victory behind ye."

"Moy Hall . . . I know of it."

"Well, if ye're thinking of visiting, ye'd best get some o' the muck off yourself, for there's few who'd offer ye welcome tonight, Jamie! Not even your lassie!"

Jamie lurched away from Andy Patterson, needing space as he had never needed it before, away from the claustrophobic atmosphere of the barracks and the shame of the plundering. He needed to rid himself of the redcoat's memory and the clinging particles of the man who still daubed his plaid.

Outside the barracks, a distance away, groups of clansmen were stumbling toward horses and wagons to make their way back to camp and tell of the victory, to celebrate with a dram or take a bit of food. Jamie staggered toward the small encampment as if drunk, his legs seeming to go whichever way they chose with no conscious direction from him. He searched for his horse and fell across her back, digging his heels into her flanks. Ahead of him, across the Spey valley, lay the wide silver ribbon of the river Spey, its gleaming waters contributing so much to the whiskey making, and the abundance of salmon and fat brown trout that added to the useful position of Ruthven barracks.

Jamie cared nothing for that right now. He was far from ready to eat or drink. He slid from the horse's back, scrabbling about in the snowy ground for a footing. He needed a fire. Furze bushes grew spikily nearby, and after some effort he coaxed them with some bracken into a small blaze near the water's edge and bade the horse stay still. He eyed the rough blanket on the mare's back with something like relief, never knowing the real need of it until now.

He moved toward the river, caring nothing for the fact that it would be near suicidal for a man of less than average strength to sink himself in those freezing waters, again and again, to rid himself of the stink and the shame, to cleanse himself in the only way possible. The splintering cold of the water closed over his head, and he came up gasping and spluttering, and blaspheming at his own need and the certainty that he was stronger than most.

Must be, he thought savagely, for he had no intention of freezing or drowning. As his head became clearer with the sting of the water, he climbed out, shivering as if with the ague, to snatch at the mare's blanket and scrub himself furiously with its prickly warmth until his skin was red but tolerably dry. He heaped more furze and bracken onto his fire, wrapped himself in the blanket, and crouched in front of the blaze to warm himself through. His plaid was cleansed of the filth that had stained it, washed away by the river water, and he'd take it proudly for drying and wearing again. He'd not be called a coward, even by himself, for fearing to wear a once bloodstained plaid.

As he shivered before the fire, rubbing his body frequently with the blanket, Jamie's eyes hardened with a new resolve. It could so easily have been he, lying with his guts ripped out in the tangle of bodies at Ruthven barracks, instead of the English redcoat. It could so easily have been Katrina who mourned him, instead of some unknown Englishwoman whose man would not be returning.

And if it had been Jamie . . . what, then, of Katrina? A wagon wife, but no longer a wife. There were kinsmen who would protect her, but plenty more clansmen who would not. Left alone, in the company of the wives and the greater numbers of light-skirts, God knows what would have happened to her.

It must not go on. There would be other battles, not all as successful as this one. Katrina had had her way this time . . . as she usually did, Jamie thought grimly, but in this he would prove his strength. His wife must remain in a safe place once the army moved on from Ruthven. A spark of memory surged into his mind.

"There's a place called Moy Hall," Andy Patterson had said.

"Moy Hall. I know of it." Jamie repeated his own words aloud, without being aware that he did so.

He had rarely left his Highland home before now, but one rare visit had been to Moy Hall, years back, before his father's leg had been so troublesome. Moy Hall was the home of the laird of Mackintosh, and the present laird served King George's army. The tale had run swiftly through the Stuart army that once the laird had gone to fight for the English, his spirited young wife, a staunch loyalist, had roused the Mackintosh clan for the prince. The tale was too well told for it to be anything but true. Jamie did not know the lady. He and his father had known the dowager Lady Mackintosh, who now lived elsewhere. But the Lady Anne would surely give sanctuary to the wife of Jamie Mackinnon at Moy Hall, on the strength of an earlier acquaintance—especially since they were loyalists all.

The thoughts spilled through his head as his mind and spirit recovered. The refuge of Prince Charles was of less concern to him right then than seeing that Katrina was safe.

His new resolve strengthened him, until at last he threw snow to douse his fire and roused his mare, bundling up the sodden heap of his plaid, squeezing out as much water as he could, and placing it on the mare's back behind him. Wrapped in the blanket, his shield and dirk were still a familiar comfort as he turned the mare and began to ride in the direction of the rebel camp.

Its fires were hidden behind ridges and hollows, but over the barracks the cloud of yellow-gray smoke still hung as silent witness to the night's savagery. At some time, Jamie's sword had been wrenched away from him. He mourned it briefly, but it was of no matter. In the next skirmish, or the next, he would retrieve another. Plunder wasn't plunder when it was a means of survival, and the dead needed no swords to defend themselves.

As he neared the rebel camp, Jamie saw that there was great activity there. Food and drink were being meted out from the meager supplies, horses fed and watered from the wagons. The surgeons did what they could for the wounded, aided by those women who could face the tasks asked of them. The priests intoned their pious words and tales were bandied about to any who would listen, tales of bravery and cowardice, and above all, of the victory over the bastard redcoats.

"Jamie! Oh, Jamie, I've been asking everywhere for ye! Andy Patterson said ye were so wild-eyed at the barracks he was afeared for ye and thought ye must have blundered off like a good many others." The soft voice blathered on in his ears.

He stared down at Katrina, her own skirt bloodied by the seeping wound of a clansman as she tried to stem it with a cloth. She had been too busy to rush to his arms, to heed the incongruity of his appearance wrapped in a blanket. He felt a wild desire to laugh. Was this really his bonnie lassie, taking on such tasks so unblinkingly? She showed a strength now that he hadn't expected as she crouched among men who were dying, with torn limbs and glazed eyes. She grew in stature in front of him as she told him briefly that he'd best find more suitable clothing to wear before he froze to death and then went back to her ministerings.

He turned abruptly, to find the supply wagons. For the moment, Katrina didn't need him. He knew a swelling pride for her, for who she was—Jamie Mackinnon's wife, who must be given no cause for being shamed by her husband . . . and nor would she, he vowed. Together they were strong, and Katrina had been the one to see it all along.

CHAPTER 13

"So ye've a mind to take your wife to Moy Hall, Jamie?" the Mackinnon chief asked him keenly. " 'Tis not yet decided if the prince goes there."

"But we go to Inverness, and 'tis not out o' the way. And I'd be willing to act as scout. I could bring back any news of the enemy, if any be in the vicinity."

The chief nodded thoughtfully. "It could be useful. Ye could follow the ruse of the farmer and his wife and take the wagon ye brought." He rubbed his nose. "Ye're known at Moy Hall, ye say?"

"My faither and myself went there some years back. I've not met the Lady Anne, but 'tis my hope that she'll offer hospitality to Katrina."

The chief guffawed. "Ye can be certain of it, laddie. A spritely lady, by all accounts, and mebbe glad of your own lassie's company while her man's away on the other side o' the fence. I'd not be in her shoes when he returns."

"Then 'tis settled?" Jamie was impatient to have his agreement. Already several days had passed since the taking of the barracks, and he preferred Katrina to be safe in the protection of Lady Mackintosh.

"Aye, Jamie. But ye'll do as ye suggested. Act as scout, and if need be, ye'll ride back here with any warnings."

He went to tell Katrina and admired her stoicism anew as she listened to the new plans. No longer did she argue nor did she mourn the loss of her new friendship with Fiona Patterson. She had learned that friendships must be brief, and although there would be comfort at the end of their journey to Moy, they still had to reach there. And who knew how many small

181

pockets of redcoats may have fled in that direction from Ruthven? It was an anxiety Jamie kept to himself.

They left at dawn the next morning. By now Jamie's own plaid was dried, and the colors refreshed by their wetting, and his shield and provisions lay in the wagon beneath the hay. Katrina was well wrapped, a shawl covering her red hair. He glanced at her as the wagon trundled out of the camp, the thin mist covering the snowy ground in a shroud, and smiled briefly.

"We'll be seasoned travelers soon, eh, lass?"

"We will that." She nodded. "How far to Moy, Jamie?" She spoke lightly, but her eyes strained in the dawn gloom, trying not to show how her nerves jangled.

"Twenty miles or so," he answered. "If we meet no obstacles, we'll be there by nightfall, my dearie. 'Twill be good to sleep in a proper bed again."

He tried to sound cheerful, too, but the question on all the clansmen's lips these past two days was ominously in his mind: Where did they go from here? To Moy? To Inverness? To the very north of the country and the islands? They had just taken the English barracks and scored a small victory, yet after the first wild elation, none had felt like rejoicing. They still retreated. . . . It was an inescapable fact, one that wiped the smiles of victory from the clansmen's faces very fast. Where from here? Where were the French ships with new troops that never came? Where the support of so-called English Jacobites who had never materialized south of Manchester?

He concentrated on guiding the horse through the slippery tracks and tried to still the uneasy questions in his mind. Katrina was silent beside him, and for a moment he felt she was remote from him. They touched from shoulder to thigh in the clattering wagon, and yet he felt as far from her in spirit as when he'd fought at Prestonpans or Ruthven and hadn't been able to picture her face. It wasn't a feeling he liked. He caught at her hand and held it in his large palm, feeling her warm fingers curl around his.

"There's a scent of springtime in the air, Jamie," she said with a false cheerfulness. "Did ye ever see the snow peaks so beautiful except in our own mountains and glen?"

"I never did," he answered gravely.

The sun had risen, tinting the distant mountains in shades of silver and gold, and gradually the wreaths of mist dispersed. They chose the route carefully, traveling in the lee of ridge or hillside where possible, stopping alongside tumbling burns to drink and stretch their limbs. When spring came, all this would surely be over, one way or another, Jamie thought, and he still dared not guess at the outcome. The prince's own high optimism, which rarely wavered, seemed sorely lacking in many of his Highlanders by now.

A wayside inn provided them with a warm fire and a meal when they were roughly halfway on their journey, and it was already growing dark by the time they arrived at the gates of Moy Hall, having seen no sign of redcoats at all. At the inn, their careful questions had revealed nothing but rumors. Some said a large army was in the area; others said it was all talk, and there'd been no burnings or rapings, so they could safely assume the English were thinking better of braving the wild country and staying put in the gentler climes of Edinburgh. Jamie had to be satisfied with that, to Katrina's relief. Scouting could be a hazardous task, but with no real evidence there was no reason for them to turn back and report to the army.

They were challenged at Moy Hall and told to enter when they'd established their identities. If it hadn't all been so earnest and serious, Katrina might have thought it one of the games her brother Hamish and wee sister Iona used to play. She stepped stiffly down from the wagon as a man came to take it and the horse to the stables, and she walked with Jamie to the old stone residence, harsh and unwelcoming in appearance.

Inside, there was all the welcome Katrina could have wished for. The hall was very grand, with tapestries lining the walls and portraits of past lairds and their ladies, mementoes of heroic deeds in the crossed claymores and weaponry displayed; it was an odd mixture of a family home and an austere stone-built fortress. Katrina found it hard to understand how the laird here could be away fighting for the English, while his wife remained loyal to the cause. Such a conflict within a marriage was unthinkable to her.

A young and beautiful dark-haired lady came toward them

with hands outstretched. She smiled with genuine pleasure, her eyes glowing in the light of the candelabra.

"You're both welcome here. You'll know that my husband is away on business of his own, but we need not trouble ourselves with that! You'll be hungry and cold after your ride, so you'll do me the honor of sharing my meal?"

"I'd ask more than that, my lady," Jamie replied. "My wife, Katrina, has been traveling with us, and I'd beg for your hospitality awhile. I go shortly to Edinburgh, but I wish my wife to remain in safe hands."

"And so she shall. I'll be glad of your company, Katrina," Lady Anne said warmly. "If you wish to rest a wee while before dinner, then you may, while I have words with Jamie here."

She pulled a cord in the wall and a young servant girl appeared. Lady Anne ordered the girl to take Mistress Mackinnon to a guest room. There was no surprise shown; strangers arriving unannounced in the night were no longer surprising. The girl showed Katrina to a room upstairs and left her there. For a moment Katrina stood still, hardly able to appreciate that she was in a real home again, where there would be properly cooked food and genteel conversation. It seemed so long since the day . . .

She caught sight of herself in the looking glass and gasped. What a ragamuffin she looked to enter the house of a lady! She glanced around the pleasantly furnished room with its four-poster bed and heavy curtains, and saw with pleasure the washstand with its water jug and bowl, the towels placed ready. At the same moment, there was a tap on the door, and the servant girl appeared again, a large kettle in her hand and a few garments over her arm. She gave a quick bob.

"My lady says ye may find something to your fit and choosing, mistress, and begs that ye be not offended by the offer."

She was gone before Katrina could thank her, the kettle placed on the washstand, steaming with hot water, the clothes dropped on the bed. Katrina moved to them quickly, her eyes lighting up with pleasure at the soft blues and greens of the gown and the heather-colored shawl. There were garments for Jamie, too, a fresh-laundered kilt and jacket, a shirt and thick

plaid hose. The lady was thoughtful, and Katrina cared not
who the clothes belonged to. It would be so good to wash
away the grime of traveling and feel feminine again. It would
be good to have Jamie look at her as though she were a
woman, a wife. . . . She caught her breath, her eyes straying
to the big bed, her cheeks already flushing at thoughts of
being wrapped in his arms there . . . wrapped in love.

"You'll know of me, I think, Jamie Mackinnon," the
Lady Anne said, her eyes sparkling. "I fear my reputation
has gone before me!"

Jamie smiled, wishing he could join Katrina wherever she
was now and tidy himself before sitting on the edge of the
lady's fine chair in his crumpled clothes, but she seemed not
to notice.

"Your name was mentioned once or twice, my lady," he
commented. "Though ye need have no fears as to your
reputation, if all we heard was true."

Her laughter pealed out. "Oh, 'twas true all right, Jamie!
If you mean did I turn turtle on my husband's wishes the
minute his back was turned and rouse the clan for the prince,
then you heard the truth of it! I merely did what my heart
dictated, and what the loyal Mackintosh clan wanted. They
needed a leader, and I gave them one!"

"Even to riding at the head o' the clan, ma'am?" Jamie
dredged up the tales told around campfires and frugal meals.

"That, too." The lady smiled. "I gave each of my loyal
clansmen a white cockade to wear in his bonnet and wore a
man's blue bonnet myself, with my plaid riding habit. There's
little that a woman can do in time of war, but this was a
moment for me!"

"And they dubbed ye Colonel Anne!" Jamie said dryly.
"A masculine title for a comely lady, if ye'll pardon the
familiarity, ma'am!"

"Of course! But not an unexpected title for the cousin of
Lord George Murray, I think! Now tell me, Jamie, on that
subject. How fares my cousin George? Do he and the prince
clash at every turn as I've heard?"

Jamie shrugged. "There have been disagreements," he
said cautiously. "The prince is obstinate in thinking the cause

can still be won, while most of the chiefs are resigned to failure. And now that the duke of Cumberland has a reputed English army of great numbers, fresh and eager and hot on our trail . . .''

"Aye, so I believe." Lady Anne's eyes were serious now. "I fear there must be a reckoning soon."

She paused as Katrina appeared, garbed in the blue-and-green dress, her hair pulled and tugged into a more tamed cascade by a wide-toothed comb. Lady Anne rose at once and bade her welcome by the fire.

"How lovely you are, Mistress Mackinnon! But I refuse to call you so, even though I guess that you've not held the title overlong! Katrina, isn't it? You and I will have some women's talk while your man makes himself presentable for dinner."

She rang for the servant to show Jamie to the bedroom, but he lingered long enough to let his admiration of Katrina's changed appearance warm her heart. Her spirits lifted. The war suddenly seemed far away, part of another time. . . .

When Jamie had gone, the lady looked at her sympathetically.

"You're very young, Katrina."

"I'm eighteen years, ma'am, and was betrothed to Jamie from the cradle," she said swiftly, lest Lady Anne thought their marriage a hasty tying of the knot.

"And you couldn't bear to be left at home without him?" the lady hazarded.

Katrina's brows furrowed a little. It had been that way at first, but then so many events had shaped her thoughts—the rebel soldier dying at the inn, the emergence of her own loyal feelings to the cause, the new determination that while she was by Jamie's side she could give him moral support and physical comfort. It was all those things, but attempting to tell it was no easy matter, and her words sounded clumsy to her own ears. Even so, the lady seemed to understand.

"Aye, we all have to do what we feel is right, Katrina. We don't truly become adult until we make our own choices. . . . But we'll put such complexities aside for tonight and enjoy each other's company. You'll not have sampled much good food on your journeys, I daresay, so you'll relish a meal of Mackintosh hospitality. There's roast beef and Spey salmon, and as fine a cellar of wine as you could wish for, with

whiskey, too, of course! You'll grace my table, Katrina,''
she said freely, bringing the warm color to Katrina's face at
her kindness.

Across the dinner table from Jamie, she could hardly keep
her eyes off him. Refreshed, clean, and tidy, and in the
borrowed clothes of the house, he was her own bonnie lad
again, the Jamie with whom she had run wild and free in the
glen at home, in what seemed like another age, another time.
They ate and drank well, and retired early. Understanding
their weariness and the need to be alone, the lady bade them
goodnight and a good night's sleep. But the tiredness was
secondary.

Once inside the bedroom, Jamie caught his wife in his
arms.

"I was'na thinking of sleeping, my lassie. I was thinking
more o' warming ye with my love. 'Tis few chances we'll
have to share a bed in such a house. Fit for a king—and
fitting for my wife and me to reaffirm the vows we made. I
love ye, Mistress Mackinnon.'' His voice was husky-rough
with passion.

She tilted her face to meet his kiss. "No more than I love
ye, Jamie,'' she whispered. "So much, that I could'na begin
to find the words.''

"Then don't try, dearie. We've no need for words between
us.'' Suddenly he bent to lift her in his arms and carry her to
the bed, all the love and tenderness he'd had to subdue for so
long glowing in his eyes. There was a time for war, and a
time for love . . . and when the fine new clothes lay discarded on the floor about them, and the bed curtains were
drawn around them, Jamie took his wife in his arms, covering
her with himself as if he would protect her from all ills. The
belonging was as sweetly exquisite as the first time, each
giving and receiving, loving and beloved. They finally slept
exhausted, still bathed in the afterglow of fulfillment, still
entwined, still part of each other.

They slept deeply until daylight penetrated the thick curtains.
Jamie removed his arm gently from around Katrina's body
and massaged it carefully into life again. Her eyes opened

sleepily as recollection slowly came to her, and she smiled into Jamie's eyes.

"Did ye sleep well?" she said softly. He laughed, the old teasing look on his face as he bent to touch her mouth with his, parting it gently with his lips and speaking against them.

"If I never sleep again, 'twould be worth it," he said. "Does that answer ye well enough?"

He straightened as she stretched languorously in the bed, saying that they'd best be dressed and make their faces shown downstairs, or the lady might be suspicious of them. Katrina laughed now, a soft, contented sound.

"I think not, Jamie. She's a canny lady, and knows well enough that we've not been wed long. But ye're right, and I feel so fine today, I've no wish to lie abed."

They could hear sounds of activity outside and below. Tidied and refreshed, they left the bedroom and descended the staircase together. The lady came to greet them from the dining room.

"Good morning. I don't need to ask if you slept, for I'm sure Jamie would have been out of bed in a trice at the arrival of visitors during the night, had he heard them."

"Visitors?" His voice was alert at once. The lady smiled.

"There's no need for alarm. Come and have some breakfast, both of you."

They followed her into the large dining room, and Katrina's heart seemed to stop for a minute and then rush crazily on. Seated at the table was a man of whom she had caught only the briefest glimpses on the journey from Bannockburn to Ruthven. Her sharpest recollection of him was at Glenfinnan, when she'd seen him unfurl his father's standard. Now, still slim and elegant, though not attired quite so regally as then, Charles Stuart rose at their approach, and Katrina prayed that he'd not hear the pounding of her heart.

"Your Highness, may I present my young guests?" Lady Anne said coolly. "Jamie Mackinnon, your loyal clansman, and his wife, Mistress Katrina Mackinnon."

She was flustered, unsure how to greet the prince, and gave a quick bob as Jamie inclined his head.

"Ah, yes. Your face is familiar to me, Mackinnon," the

prince said at once. "But not that of your lovely wife. I'm charmed to meet you, Mistress Katrina."

He took her hand in his as he spoke and touched it lightly to his lips in the continental manner. Katrina felt the blood rushing in her ears as the full force of his magnetism struck her. It was said that he could charm the birds from the trees. He was not called their bonnie Prince Charlie without reason, Katrina thought in confusion, and hoped that she murmured a suitable reply.

"Come now, before this good food gets cold," Lady Anne said brusquely, seeing the girl so nonplussed. "Jamie, I daresay you're acquainted with our other guests."

Until now, Katrina had hardly noticed anyone else, save for a blur of plaid at the table. Now, as Jamie acknowledged them, she saw that there were officers of the MacDonald clan with the prince and heard him say that a small guard was with him on his way to Inverness.

"Then the army follows, sir?" Jamie said at once.

"Inverness is our objective." Charles nodded. "I expect Lord Murray to join us there from the coastal march, and then we will assess our position and our resources. I'm sure that more of our loyal Highlanders will rally there when they see that we're of a fair strength already."

Katrina didn't miss the glance that passed among the officers; she had the uneasy feeling that they were not as certain as the prince. She let the male talk wash over her and concentrated on the breakfast fare, though she felt all fingers and thumbs. Taking breakfast with a prince was something she had never considered. It would be something to tell their grandchildren, she thought, with a rush of warmth to her face.

Once the meal was over, the officers resumed their duties in the grounds, and the prince, Lady Anne, Jamie, and Katrina retired to a more comfortable room. As scout for the journey, Jamie was entitled to the privilege of reporting to the prince in person on this occasion. He was asked at once what signs of the enemy he had seen on his way from Ruthven.

"None, sir. We came by a devious route, of course, but I'm assured that no redcoats were in the area at that time. Their uniforms stand out so obviously against the snow, I'm sure they would have been spotted."

"Good. But we must not underestimate them. They'll move quickly under my cousin."

"Your cousin, sir!" Katrina spoke the words before she could stop them, and he smiled across the room at her as she stopped in embarrassment.

"I fear the relationship among the royal houses of Europe is as complex as your own clan system, Katrina. Yes, William Duke of Cumberland is my cousin of sorts, though neither of us is keen to recognize the fact, nor do we have any warm regard for one another. When Queen Anne died in 1714 and the Act of Settlement was brought about to exclude Roman Catholics from the throne of Great Britain, the government preferred her second cousin, George of Hanover, to the rightful Stuart successor, my father, James. You'll probably know as much from your history lessons, and I won't bore you with more to spin your pretty head," he concluded smilingly, but Katrina guessed that his reason was more because he wished to hear further news from Jamie than to flatter her.

"Do you know of the country around Inverness, Jamie?"

He shrugged. "I know there are moors to the south of it, and that the town is one of good heart for the cause. The moors would hardly hide an army of redcoats, and between them and the town is a wide river, the Ness."

"I've a useful scout in you, Jamie," Charles stated. "But we'll not count the roosters until we have Inverness safely in our hands. Murray's regiments must be almost there, and God willing, we'll take the castle and the town with little fuss."

Charles might be pushed far back into Scotland, but in spirit he was far from beaten. Katrina admired his cheerfulness and optimism, and she was encouraged enough to question him further.

"Ye'll forgive me, sir, but I'm ignorant of kingship! If—when—your father is restored as King James, then what . . . what . . ." Her voice trailed off as she floundered.

"Katrina, ye forget yourself," Jamie said angrily, but the prince stayed his words.

"Your wife is understandably curious, Jamie, and since Lady Anne tells me your home is on the far west coast near to where my ship landed, I can understand that the affairs of kings and governments seem very remote to Katrina. And you wonder what role I am to play when my father is king?'' He spoke calmly, daring anyone to question the likelihood, even now. ''We think the country has been put to tyranny by the rule of protestant kings and governments. The monarchy has become but a pawn in government hands and can hardly be said to flourish under a German king and a ruthless band of advisers. To restore the Stuart house and Catholic rule is to open the door to our European neighbors, instead of being at constant war with them. France, Italy, Spain . . . all would favor a Catholic restoration.''

''But they do not send help,'' Katrina blurted out, at which Charles looked at her sorrowfully.

''I cannot deny that I am sadly disappointed on that score,'' he admitted. ''If only help had come . . . but it's a waste of time to fret over what cannot be changed, and I still live in hopes that a French fleet will be with us at Inverness.'' He saw her give a little shiver and spread his elegant hands. ''But since we have such an excellent hostess and food and warmth, let's not worry ourselves unduly. We will speak of other things.''

And when Charles made the gentle suggestion, it was as good as a command. Although the undercurrents of anxiety were never far from their minds, the day passed pleasantly, and Katrina gradually became aware that the hall was well protected by small local groups of clansmen and villagers, who reported to the well-respected Lady Anne from time to time. Charles was evidently to remain at Moy until Inverness was safely in Jacobite hands, since no skirmish was expected there, and the news was awaited hourly.

It hadn't come by two days hence, in which time the small company at Moy Hall grew alternately alarmed and merry. Determined to make his stay as comfortable as possible, Lady Anne encouraged dancing and singing, with the officers joining them, and the occasional diversions of fishing in nearby waters allayed some of the strain of waiting and watching. On the second night after Katrina had met the prince, she awoke in the pitch blackness as bloodcurdling noises throbbed and wailed in the night. She clutched at Jamie, almost too fearful to draw breath. Had the redcoats learned of Charles's whereabouts and come for him? Were they all to be murdered in their beds?

"Jamie . . . Jamie!" She gave a small scream in her throat, for what she had thought was his shoulder was no more than the heap of bedclothes where he had lain. She trembled all over, sliding quickly from the bed and pulling the plaid dress over her head. She had no wish to be seen naked by the redcoats. She shuddered at the thought and crept to the bedroom door, opening it a fraction.

She listened and sensed the air of activity—softly speeding feet across stone floors and faint quick whispers in flickering candlelight. She moved outside the room hesitantly, and a hand touched her arm, making her heart jump with fright. She turned quickly to see Lady Anne holding a candle, a shawl around her nightclothes and a rosy tinge to her cheeks, as though she had lately come indoors from the cold night air.

"What's happening?" Katrina said fearfully. "Where's Jamie? Is the enemy here?"

The lady calmed her at once. "No, not here, Katrina. But nearby, and being diverted this very minute, we pray, by our ruse."

"What ruse?" Katrina's voice was shrill. Where was Jamie . . . and the prince? She bit hard on her trembling lips.

"Will you listen?" Lady Anne said quickly, seeing that the girl was too fearful to be fobbed off with untruths. "Your clansman, Donald Fraser, a local blacksmith, came here a while back and raised the alarm that a large government army was in the area. He and some others have posted themselves on the road in the hope of creating a diversion. They shout and beat the drums and wail the clan slogans, rousing imaginary regiments of Highlanders to create the illusion of a large force awaiting the redcoats. It's a ruse well thought out, Katrina, and we must pray that the redcoats will think themselves outnumbered and retreat."

"And Jamie goes with them?" The question was answered in the lady's eyes. "Then so do I, ma'am! God may protect them, but he'll not mind a wee bit extra help."

"No! 'Tis men's work, Katrina," Lady Anne said vigorously. "Though I might feel the same way as you, had I not more important duties—"

192

"Ye canna stop me! I'll go, with or without your blessing! The more noise the better, I'm thinking. Is there a gong I can beat to add my noise to the rest?"

Lady Anne saw at once that there was no hope of stopping her. She nodded. "But you'll take one of the menservants with you. Jamie would wish it." She spoke rapidly, but Katrina was already running back inside the bedroom to wind her shawl about her head and drag her boots over her feet. She heard Lady Anne call for someone called Eian to escort Mistress Mackinnon, and minutes later the two of them were equipped with gongs and hammers and speeding away from Moy Hall into the blackness.

There was no need for pointing the way, for the noise of the shouting was deafening. The musket fire from the blacksmith and his companions seemed to come from all directions. Pipes screeched into the night, and even as Katrina ran, panting, she and the manservant added their own cacophony of sound to all the rest.

"Shout your noise as well, mistress!" Eian hollered back at her as she gasped at the sawing pain in her side from the exertion. She hardly took time to breathe, let alone shout. But the thought that Jamie was somewhere ahead of her and that her voice might tip the balance of survival or death spurred her on. Behind Eian, Katrina shouted until she was hoarse, the sound of her own gong blasting in her ears.

The night was an explosion of noise. She hurt with the intensity of it, and her ribcage seemed to throb with a sickening beat to the gong's hammering. It vibrated through her body, but she never dared stop. How many others contributed to the rout she didn't know and couldn't guess. It seemed like hundreds, but she guessed that it couldn't be. It was so few against God knew how many redcoats . . . waiting, gauging, preparing to attack.

"Katrina, for God's sake, why aren't ye safe in bed!" Jamie's savage, roaring voice penetrated her senses. He held a musket, and without waiting for an answer he blasted it off into the sky once more, his voice blazing out the Mackinnon slogan. The noise of it rocked her mind and blurred her reason. She coughed in the dense dry smoke, hardly able to swallow, to feel.

The smoke and the appalling din seemed to permeate her very bones and stifle her lungs. Even so, there was a wild, primitive exhilaration inside, knowing she was a part of Jamie's war in however small a way. She was adding her own slender weight to the battle, and it overcame the fear. Far stronger was the need to survive, to win.

How long she and Eian assisted, or how far they had come from Moy Hall, Katrina could no longer have said. It was but a moment, it was all eternity. Time ceased to have meaning. She shrieked alongside Jamie, her eyes no longer flinching at the thunderclaps of gongs or the sudden blastings of musket fire and the leaping redness of the explosions, no longer the lady, the wife, but one of a desperate rebel band defending their rights and their prince.

She was filthy, her dress torn, her shawl lost somewhere, her arms aching so badly they felt near to being pulled from their sockets. Still she banged the gong and would do so until she dropped. It was a nightmare, but one that brought its own weird satisfaction. Through eyes that felt unbearably gritty and raw-rimmed, she became gradually aware that the noises were dwindling away and the answering enemy fire was no longer a threat. Other arms were holding her, powerful hands were shaking her.

"Leave me!" she screamed. "Would ye deny me the right to save my prince?"

"Katrina, dearest, it's all over!" Jamie's voice came swimming into her senses. His face loomed backward and forward in front of her as she became oddly weightless, and then she realized he had scooped her up in his arms. A moment's panic gripped her as she felt the gong and hammer taken from her blistered hands. They had become so much a part of her that she fought and scratched to retrieve them, then found herself beating against Jamie's broad hard chest instead. He pressed her close to him, so that she heard the deep vibration of his voice from within him, as if it came from a long long distance away.

"Calm yourself, my brave one. 'Tis finished. The redcoats were fooled by it and are on the retreat. We'll get back to Moy Hall with all haste and get ye into a warm bath and a

194

clean set o' garments. Ye'll need to sleep the day 'round, my darling.''

Sleep . . . did ever a word sound more beautiful to her ears? She had been rudely awakened from sleep. She heard the hoarseness in Jamie's voice now and couldn't guess whether it came from emotion on her account or the strain on his larynx from the night's work. And then she gave up fighting or guessing as the sudden relaxing of her taut body made her loll insensibly against him.

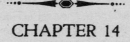

CHAPTER 14

Later, Katrina couldn't have said how she got back to Moy Hall. She was unaware of hands helping her, gently bathing her, dressing her in clean nightclothes and laying her carefully between the bedcovers. It was all dreamlike.

Jamie sat by his wife's bedside, waiting for her to awaken from her long sleep. She looked like a fragile flower, he thought, her face pale and small within the confining four-poster. The long lashes drooped against the pearly cheek, and the only vivid splash of color was the long curling mass of her hair spread about her with the sheen of red silk.

On impulse, he leaned forward and touched her lips with his, careful to avoid her poor blistered hands, which lay upturned above the bedclothes like two small shells.

"Jamie." The whispered voice spoke his name, and her eyelids fluttered open, as if his touch had been a magical thing. She winced as she would have reached out for him, and his hands were gentle on her shoulders, pushing her back against the pillow.

"Hush now, my dearie, and try not to move. I should be angry with ye for being so reckless last night, but I'm too thankful to see ye restored to me again to scold ye."

"Last night—how long have I been here?" She turned her head a little. Wasn't it night now? The shadows were lengthening across the room, the moon patterning the white mountains through the window with its light.

Jamie's voice was rough, and she knew at once that it hid his concern for her. She couldn't see his face properly as he nestled close to her for a moment.

"All this day and into the night, my dearie. Ye're a lazy layabed."

"But I never sleep so long!" she cried in genuine astonishment.

"Aye, well, this time ye were aided by a sleeping draught that Lady Anne's physician thought necessary," he said grimly.

Memory rushed back at her so fast her head rocked with it. For a few minutes she hadn't been able to think where she was. Outside, the mountains were their own, the glen stretched green and verdant, the loch still and beautiful, the tumbling waterfall gurgling incessantly.

Now, she remembered everything and would have clutched at Jamie if her palms didn't feel so sore and stiff. She swallowed back the ache of longing for things past, and now she was fully awake and searching Jamie's face.

"The redcoats—they were fooled, Jamie? And the prince? What of the prince?"

"Hush, now." He soothed her. "All is in order, and we'll not be troubled by the redcoats again, I wager. However large a force they were, our noise fooled them into thinking they met a matching army, and they turned tail readily enough. And the prince is safely away and must be in Inverness by now. 'Tis where I must go, too, Katrina."

"And what must I do, Jamie?"

"I think ye know. I want ye to remain here with Lady Anne until 'tis safe for ye to be with me again. Ye'll do as I say now, Katrina."

She didn't feel like protesting. She was still light-headed, and her hands felt raw and uncomfortable. She nodded slowly, not wanting to feel her head swim again.

"I'll do as ye say," she repeated. "I see the sense of it, and I'll pray for ye, Jamie, and I'll pray, too, that we'll not be parted for too long." Her voice broke a little, for she longed desperately to keep him here. But duty had to come first. Gently he told her that he must leave now, at once, and that he had only lingered to make sure that she was well again. So soon? Katrina bit back the tremulous words, knowing she must appear strong even though her head felt like wool.

"Then go in safety, dearest," she murmured against the warm texture of his skin as he bent to kiss her again, gathering her to his chest for a long moment and matching his heartbeat to hers. And then he was gone, leaving her alone in the four-poster where they had loved and whispered and dreamed.

Lady Anne was a sympathetic hostess, glad of the company of a girl but five years younger than herself. They shared many hours together once Katrina had recovered, and assured her that her hands were not badly hurt, merely reddened and slightly blistered. The surroundings at Moy Hall were grander than Frashiel House, but there was the same warm feeling of a home about it, and in the days following Jamie's departure, Katrina found in Lady Anne an easy person to confide about her love for Jamie, her home, and the sometimes overwhelming need to see her family again.

"I miss my mother," Katrina told her wanly one morning. "I never realized how happy we all were. It's a sad thing that ye never see it until it's past—even the bairns plaguing my life, and Mammie scolding me and calling me her wayward one." She felt her face tinge with colour. "I think that it's all a part of love, isn't it, ma'am?"

"I think your mother would be proud to hear you say so, Katrina. She sent away a child, but she'll receive back a woman."

"And ye don't think she'll mourn too much the loss of the child?"

Lady Anne patted her shoulder. "Enough of this moping! You seem determined to be in the doldrums today, and I prefer sunny looks. We've enough to be cheerful about, haven't we? Inverness is now in Stuart hands, and let's be thankful for that."

"I am thankful!" Katrina cried fervently. "And I promise

to cheer up. Could we take a walk about? The air's so fresh and clean today, and I know I can smell the spring.''

Lady Anne laughed with quick affection. "You share our bonnie prince's sense of optimism, Katrina—most of the time, anyway! Yes, we'll take a turn outside. It will clear our heads from the stuffiness of the fire.''

Katrina determined not to be such a dullard. The sky was less gray today, almost blue in places, like a patchwork quilt between the clouds, and here and there small clumps of snowdrops had pushed their way through the hard-packed ground; they were the heralds of spring. Katrina loved her Highland home in all its moods, in all seasons, but the merging of winter into spring was the loveliest to her, with that feeling of life renewed, reborn.

"I think we had best go inside the house, Katrina," Lady Anne said suddenly. "We've been outside long enough, and there are riders coming this way. Until we're certain who they are, it's unwise for us to linger.''

They went quickly toward the house, and Katrina felt her stomach lurch as they went. For a while it had almost been possible to forget that they still lived with danger, that they were still caught up in a conflict that seemed to have no ending and no clear direction. The two women stayed well inside the long windows, watching the riders approach. They would have been challenged at the gate, so presumably the guards were satisfied with their identities. One of Lady Anne's men came with them.

The riders looked disheveled and flushed as if from overindulgence in the whiskey as much as from their ride. It was borne out in the unsteady gait as they slid from their horses and moved toward the house. They were shown into the room where the two women waited, Lady Anne's man hovering behind them as a safeguard.

The two looked anything but part of the army Katrina had seen rallying for the prince on that far-off day at Glenfinnan, when every man had seemed to stand two inches taller as he swore to follow the cause. For a moment the tattered men seemed struck dumb by the vision of the two young women before them, both slender and beautiful, one with glossy dark hair, the other with an abundance of hair the color of fire.

"Say your piece," Lady Anne's man barked from behind the men, nudging them into action.

" 'Tis the young lassie we've come for, lady," one of them growled, slurring the words. "We bring a message."

"From Jamie?" Katrina blurted out, hope flaring inside her. It was more than a week since he had gone to Inverness, a week of agonizing anxiety. She felt Lady Anne's hand on her wrist.

"Be careful. It may be a trick," she breathed. "Let me deal with this, Katrina."

It was almost unbearable to stand silently and not demand to know what these louts knew of Jamie. Was he well, or injured, or worse? Her throat dried up, but Lady Anne, accustomed to such encounters as these, was more cautious and on her guard. She questioned the men minutely about things that seemingly had no bearing but clearly did so from the nods the lady gave at their answers.

After several minutes the first man drew out a crumpled piece of paper from inside his shirt and handed it to Katrina. She took it, trying to hide her distaste. It smelled of its recent hiding place, rank and malodorous. But the hand that had penned her name on the paper was undoubtedly Jamie's. She opened it quickly and felt a rush of relief.

"Then 'tis true that Charles Stuart has successfully taken the town and the castle at Inverness? We heard so but we were not completely sure."

"It's true, mistress." The second man was a mite less aggressive than the first. "The town surrendered several days since. There's been some rejoicing and some fighting in small pockets o' men. Some o' the citizens oppose all the trouble the Stuart brings wi' him, and there's still the few redcoats who try to make a stand. But the main body o' the English army has retreated to the moors to the south o' the town over the river now. I've nae doubt they'll be making their way to England. They canna stand the Highland weather, the softnecks."

Katrina was absorbed in Jamie's note, and Lady Anne spoke sharply.

"How do you know the note is genuine? Who gave it to you?"

"Jamie Mackinnon, o' course," the first man said.

Katrina handed the note to Lady Anne, who held it as though it were a poisonous insect and scanned it quickly.

"And you two are to be entrusted to take Mistress Mackinnon to Inverness to join her husband! What proof do we have that you will do as the note says?"

The brawnier man glowered at her. "None, lady, save the word o' the Stuart's men. And the fact that Mackinnon chose his messengers wi' care, so he told us."

"With care?" Lady Anne tried not to let her sceptical gaze sweep over the swaying pair.

"Aye, lady." The other grimaced at her. "Yon Mackinnon would have none but a Fraser and a Bancroft deliver the message."

Relief flooded through Katrina, turning at once to Lady Anne.

"The note is genuine, ma'am. 'Tis Jamie's way of telling me so. Fraser is my family name, and Bancroft that of my Uncle Robert. I'm sure all is well."

Lady Anne nodded, satisfied but still keen that Eian should accompany Katrina to Inverness along with these ruffians, so he would be able to assure the lady that Katrina had arrived there safely.

Since the night of the rout, when Katrina had shrieked her noise like a hoyden beside him, Eian had been her silent champion. She knew he wouldn't refuse the task of escorting her to Inverness, and Katrina suddenly felt the blood sing in her veins. Escorting her to Jamie . . . they would be together again.

"Would you take these two to the kitchens and see that they have food and hot drinks?" Lady Anne ordered the manservant.

Once they had gone, the lady took Katrina's hands in hers with real affection. Not for worlds would she diminish the glow on the girl's lovely face, but she'd be doing less than her duty if she didn't warn her of the dangers.

"I beg you to take care, Katrina. There will be redcoats everywhere, and I fear they're not done with us yet. The battles continue, large and small, and you are young and beautiful and very vulnerable."

"Wi' three strong Highlanders to protect me, ma'am!" she retorted lightly, but she knew Lady Anne spoke wisely. There was no sense in reckless behavior, and she promised to hide the telltale femininity of her long hair inside a dark shawl. She would be glad of its warmth, for it was decided that they would travel that night.

Late February was still bitterly cold at night, and never would spring be more welcome, Katrina thought longingly once more. But Inverness was little more than seven miles from Moy, and once there she would be with Jamie. The thought was heady, exciting. For a moment she could think of nothing else. She was a woman in love with her man, and soon they were to be together. She clasped her hands tightly, exulting in the joy of it.

When darkness fell, Katrina and Eian were ready. Lady Anne hugged her quickly, told her to take all care, and promised that her prayers would go with her. Katrina turned away, her eyes moist. So many brief friendships. So many hurried farewells. She pushed down the well of tears in her throat, moved out into the night, and mounted the docile mare Eian held ready for her.

Then the four of them trotted silently away from Moy in the direction of Inverness. Katrina tried to make her mind a blank against the raucous banter of the two rebels. The distance was not far, but time and again the men paused to listen and wait, for fear of a band of redcoats suddenly appearing out of the darkness. Once when Eian snapped at them for their rough tavern talk in front of Mistress Mackinnon, they turned on him with sullen eyes.

"Mebbe if young Mackinnon had'na been canny enough to pay us half the fee before we left Inverness wi' the promise o' the rest to come, we'd be leaving ye to escort the finnicky lassie," one jeered, making Katrina's cheeks burn with anger.

"And mebbe she's no' so finnicky as ye think!" she whipped back, before Eian could reply. "I promise ye Jamie Mackinnon's wife is made of stern stuff, like any true Highland lassie. And if ye two want to carry on wi' your boasting and preening, then I'll listen or close my ears as I choose!"

The two looked at each other uncertainly, and whatever

their thoughts, they desisted from the tavern talk from that moment.

At last the dark mass of Inverness town came into sight. Katrina felt a stirring of excitement. She had never been to a town of such importance in her life before.

"What is the town like?" she asked the man Fraser as they neared it and the gray mass ahead took on the shapes of buildings, with smoke curling from chimneys into the night sky.

"Like any other," he grunted.

"But I don't know any other, so what is this one like!"

"It's got four main streets, mistress." Bancroft was a bit more agreeable. "Three of them meet at the cross where the daily market business goes on. 'Tis a dirty town, and the comings and goings o' ships and sailors don't help."

"The houses are pleasin' enough," Fraser retorted. "They shine in the sun wi' their red sandstone walls and stepped gables, and many have the occupants' initials carved into the walls, which may bode ill for them if the redcoats ever take possession o' them! Aye, the town itself's no' such a bad place if ye can pinch your nose to its reekings. Ye'll mebbe enjoy the hagglings at the market cross, if ye care for such things. There's no' much else to do."

"But your man lodges outside the town, mistress, and that's where we take ye to," Bancroft told her. " 'Tis a poor place, though not such a hovel as most. The worst be wi'out windows and are faced wi' turf. The scum o' the town live there, using the river for their body washing and scrubbing clothes and cleanin' o' vegetables."

Katrina listened, appalled. This was where Jamie waited for her? Eian broke in, his voice harsh.

"Are ye sure this is where ye're to take Mistress Mackinnon? I canna believe her husband means her to be lodged so poorly."

Fraser shrugged. " 'Tis where we take the lassie, man. If Mackinnon's made other arrangements by now, we know naught of it."

Katrina prayed fervently that he had. The hovels sounded far worse and more spartan than even old Margret Blainey's cottage in the glen. Her nerves were taut as they neared the hotchpotch of poor dwelling places, with the cutting remark from Fraser that a body should be glad enough to find shelter anywhere at all in this town right now. Apart from half the rebel army seeking lodgings in preference to the frugalities of the camps, Inverness seemed to be bursting with soldiers and sailors, lawyers from the cities keeping their eye on Highland estates, spectators from the villages curious to see any battle sport, army scouts constantly coming and going, and couriers with dispatches near and far.

"Is it such a wild town?" Katrina asked, all this alarming her. Fraser snorted, his voice heavy with sarcasm.

"Nay, lassie! There's a fine courthouse and gaol to deal wi' villains! There's a tollbooth and plenty kirks, even though half the kirkyards be overrun wi' cattle more often than not."

"I think ye've explained enough about Inverness," Eian said shortly. "How much farther to the house?"

The rebels stopped their horses and pointed a little ways ahead. Through the gloom, they spied a huddle of cottages with a thin layer of snow covering their thatch. Other cottages stretched away from these, interlinked by dark alleyways. The men slid from their horses, motioning Katrina and Eian to do the same as they approached the last cottage. Her heart beat fast. Now that they stopped, all seemed quiet, as if this were a ghost town. Yet the rebels said the town was crowded with people and strangers. She swallowed back her fears, yet jumped when Bancroft touched her arm. He pointed ahead and told her that was where her man had lodged of late.

She gripped Eian's arm, suddenly fearful. Who knew what might be inside the hovel, for hovel it was now that she saw it properly. Eian's presence comforted her, and he spoke harshly to the men.

"Ye'll go in ahead of us. If there's aught amiss, ye'll meet it first. And dinna fear, lassie, I'll not leave your side until your man is beside ye. My lady would'na wish it."

Heart pounding, she waited until the men pushed open the door and called out cautiously to someone inside. A gray-faced old man eventually appeared, grumbling in the darkness, his face lit grotesquely by the candle he held.

"Be this the lassie?" He peered at Katrina. "Come ye inside. Your man's on the night watch and should be here

203

directly. He's to take ye to lodgings in the town, since he does'na think my place holds room for the three o' us.''

Katrina could only feel a swooning thankfulness at his words. She had to forcibly stop herself from turning and fleeing from the unbelievable filth that seemed to emanate from the very walls and the old wretch himself. She would feel herself alive with lice and vermin if she ever had to lay her head down here.

''We'll wait,'' Eian said, clearly as appalled as Katrina.

Her only grain of comfort was from the man's words. It was obvious that he knew Jamie, and that he had lodged here. But no longer, Katrina thought in wild relief. Nights spent in the freezing mountains would be infinitely preferable to this.

''We've done our task and delivered ye, mistress,'' Fraser said abruptly. ''We'll finish our business with Mackinnon at a later date. I doubt he'll think to run wi' the rest of our fee, and we'll find him on the watch.''

''Thank you,'' Katrina said as they left the hovel. She was more than grateful for Eian's company. They gave no thought to sitting down, and the old man seemed at a loss to know how to deal with the visitors. Then, within minutes of their arrival, the door opened again and Jamie came inside, bringing the cold air with him, and sweeping her into his arms.

''Thank God,'' he said harshly. ''I met the messengers a wee way back and was told ye were here safely, love. My thanks to ye, Eian. I've a due to pay old Ferguson here, and then we'll move to our new lodgings.''

''Does your man want your bed the night?'' Ferguson suddenly croaked, looking at Eian, who answered immediately.

''I do not! I'm away back to my lady! Ye'll keep the horse, mistress, and may God be with ye.''

On impulse, Katrina kissed his cheek. ''And with ye, Eian. Go in safety.''

She rode close behind Jamie, the sight of his powerful back and shoulders a reassurance as they crossed the river and went up the hill toward the denser areas of the town—not toward the finer main streets and red sandstone houses Fraser had described, but through more alleyways until they entered a small courtyard and stopped in front of a narrow house among a dozen others. Jamie helped her down and tied the horses to a post set in the cobbles.

He held her hand tightly as they entered the narrow house, certainly a mite cleaner than old Ferguson's hovel, Katrina saw with relief. Jamie called out to someone called Mistress Denny, and a wizened old woman appeared, the candlelight sheltered in her cupped hand.

"Come ye in and shut out the cold, laddie, and 'tis welcome ye both are. If ye'll poke the fire to fan the flames a wee bit, I'll find ye some bread and cheese, for I've no wish to be cooking at this hour."

"I want no food, mistress," Katrina said swiftly. "Thank you, but 'tis not necessary. I'd like to sleep."

"Aye, a bed is all we need," Jamie said now. "There's time for eating when we've rested, and we'll not keep ye from your bed, Mistress Denny."

The woman grunted and led the way up the twisting stairs, pointing out the room where Jamie's belongings were scattered. Then they closed the door behind them and forgot everything but the joy of being together. Outside the house the night was bitter, but inside their room there was love to warm it and the pleasure of belonging.

"I would have found ye a palace if I could, my dearie," Jamie said huskily as he caressed the fiery glow of her hair and trailed his hands over the remembered shape of her body.

Katrina stilled his words with a soft kiss. She felt his fingers against her breast, sweet and warm.

"It matters not to me where we stay, Jamie. I would sleep with ye beneath the stars if ye asked it of me."

He gave a short laugh, delighting in the warmth of her and the love that flamed between them.

"Dinna prophecy such things, dearest! Ye have a habit of it, and your omens are uncannily near to reality at times."

"Like old Margret Blainey's, ye mean?" And suddenly she felt a sharpness between her breasts, as if Jamie's words had started up unwanted images inside, churning her stomach and forcing her to speak out as he demanded to know what ailed her.

"I have a strange feeling, Jamie. A coldness that will'na go away. As if—as if everything we have ever done has somehow led us to this place. Yet not this place, but near to it. I feel a portent of sadness all around here, as if gathering stormclouds hover above me and I'll never see the sunlight again. It's—it's a feeling of death, Jamie, and it frightens me. Oh, warm me, Jamie. Make the feeling go away.''

He caught her to him at once, the strength of his body near to crushing hers, as if he would submerge all her fears by his own life force.

''Ye need fear naught while I hold ye, my darling one,'' he said roughly. ''Nor think of death, for we two are only just beginning our lives together. We have all the time in the world, my sweet. We have forever.''

He folded her close to his heart and felt the soft relaxing of her body as he murmured words of love. He had felt it safe to send for her, and she had come to him, and not even their sworn loyalty to Charles Stuart could spoil this sweet reunion. These hours belonged to no one but themselves.

When daylight came, Katrina could chide herself for her feeling of ill omen, for the day was bright and sunny, and she was with Jamie again. He warned her strictly not to go out after dark if he was away on army business, nor to venture down the dark alleyways or around the harbor. Remembering the waterfront at Kirkcudbright, Katrina promised him.

For the present, it seemed that neither army was anxious to wage another major battle, and it was a time of comparative calm while more Highlanders were forced or cajoled into joining the rebels, to replace those who had fallen or deserted, or merely to swell the ranks against the reputed force of Cumberland's redcoats.

She struck up an odd friendship with Mistress Denny. There were days and nights when Jamie was away from the house, and the two women sat before the sweet fug of the peat fire and talked of the way the town had changed with the coming of soldiers and sailors and the attendant swell of business for the bakers and pie makers, the ale houses, and the lodging houses like Mistress Denny's own. War brought good news and prosperity to some, she would cackle from time to time. And sometimes there were small victories to celebrate, too, sufficient to send a brief flare of hope to Jacobite supporters.

There was a greater hope when Fort Augustus fell to rebel besiegers in March, only to be dashed when its twin fort, Fort William, withstood another siege and remained firmly in the hold of the redcoats. It was a seesaw game, Katrina said tightly.

"If it wasn't so serious to say so, 'tis more like the games my brother Hamish used to play wi' his tin soldiers," she said bitterly. "Except that these soldiers are our clansmen, bleeding and dying, and the game they play is to the death!"

"Aye," Mistress Denny agreed. "And in the marketplace today 'tis all agog wi' news that Blair Castle is firmly in the hands o' the redcoats again, lassie, and withstood the fiercest siege the rebels could wage. 'Tis becoming a desperate matter, I'm thinking."

Such days were filled with anxiety and gloom, yet there were other days when she and Jamie donned fresh clothes and walked about the streets of the town, and it could almost have been part of another age as they went in the coffeehouses and met others like themselves, even one brief meeting with Fiona and Andy Patterson, who had come into town from the camp outside. The two girls had fallen on each other's necks with cries of delight. Such small things cheered the days.

Never could Katrina forget that she shared in Jamie's role as loyalist to the Stuart, defender of his person. Nor did Fiona, even though such noble words were unspoken. They shared that bond, and it was only occasionally that Katrina felt as if she stood back from herself a little, watching these new people that she and Jamie had become.

War had changed them both, as it had changed everyone it touched. She wondered sometimes if it had changed anything at home, if the war had touched their parents' lives, apart from the loss of their two young rebels. Sometimes the ache to hear news of them was unbearable.

"Do ye think they'll have forgiven us, Jamie?" she asked him one evening when they sat with Mistress Denny in front of the aromatic fire, pungent and thickening the air. The old woman knew their background now, and they spoke freely of it with her.

207

"I'm certain of it, love," he reassured her. "They'll be as welcoming to see us home again as we'll be happy to be there. I have no doubt of it."

"Even my wee brother and sister?" she said wryly. "They'll be ruling the roost by now, and I'll be in disgrace."

"Ye've overlooked something, my dearie. When we go home, it won't be as two runaways, nor hanging our heads in shame. Ye're Jamie Mackinnon's wife, lassie, and after we've paid our respects to your family at Frashiel House, ye'll take your rightful place wi' me and my faither!"

It sounded like a distant dream, and in all the strangeness of her life lately, she had forgotten that most important fact. Frashiel House was no longer her home in the strict sense of the word, for she would be expected to live with the Mackinnons. How could she have forgotten it!

"I'm sorry," she said contritely. "But sometimes I fret over my mammie's anxiety for me. And I pray, too, that Aunt Janet was'na too scathing in her letter about us, Jamie."

"Even if she was, I'm sure your mammie will be reassured to know ye're with me, hen. 'Tis what was planned, and our kinfolk will'na begrudge us these extra days together."

"We've not had so many of them, have we? Married near to three months, and half of that spent apart!"

"We're not apart now!" Jamie squeezed her shoulder, and Mistress Denny cackled and rose stiffly to her feet, saying she was away to her bed and advising them to do the same, for the hour was late.

Still they lingered awhile in front of the fire, and Jamie's arm was warm about her as she nestled her face against the rough cloth of his plaid, lost in thought. Rarely had she felt so contented as in moments like these, Katrina thought dreamily. Doing nothing—and yet doing everything, for being here in Jamie's embrace made her feel complete.

She couldn't read the thoughts that ran so differently through Jamie's mind, and he was glad to know it. But since early April now, while the rebel army had waged their small battles, gained or lost, the duke of Cumberland's army had reached a point south of Inverness and was assembling there. The rumors that there must soon be a confrontation between them grew stronger each day, and most clansmen were impatient for it to begin. They had delayed too long in the recruitment of more men and the arrival of French troops that never came.

Their assets in arms and ammunition were considerable now, and they had upwards of five thousand men. Whether the redcoats had more was difficult to determine, with wild tales circulating everywhere. What was solid fact, and a bitter blow, was that the Jacobite ship, the *Prince Charles*—a ship that would have brought more money and supplies—had run aground and was lost. Busy as the Inverness bakeries and food suppliers were, they simply could not cope with the thousands of extra mouths to feed. Many of the rebels had become dispirited and angry at the lack of food and facilities, and those that hadn't resources of their own were ragged and near to starving. Others had simply taken the chance to desert when they could, out of sheer physical exhaustion.

Jamie tried to think positively as the thoughts skimmed through his head. There were many more like himself, young, vigorous, ready to defend the cause to the death . . . though praying grimly that it wouldn't come to that—especially when his bonnie Katrina lay so warm and pliant against him. He was almost loath to move away from this languorous atmosphere in the cozy little parlor where they relaxed in such harmony together.

His eyes were drawn to the windowsill, where Katrina had placed a stone pot containing several long-stemmed buttercups plucked from the hard-packed soil that morning—to brighten the house, she had told Mistress Denny. Now she turned to Jamie with a soft catch in her voice.

"Buttercups, Jamie. Spring must surely be on its way, even in this dismal month. Nearly halfway gone already, and still as miserable as winter. What lovely wildflowers will be blooming in our glen right now! It will be good to be home again and see a real spring, with the mountains and the burns so sparkling fresh, to smell the sweet young grass."

Jamie could almost smell its fragrance now as he recalled her words. Mid-April. Springtime. A wave of longing for home swept over him, too. He had the same feelings. Women weren't unique in their desires and their emotions, but a man needed to control them more.

And once all this conflict was over, whatever it held . . .

then there must surely be time for love and all the good things in life that he wanted to share with his Katrina. She stirred against him, and he told her gently that they had best be away to their bed. As he put his arm around her and they moved drowsily toward the staircase, a small moaning breeze rattled the stone pot on the windowsill that held the buttercups, and some of the petals fell.

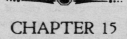

CHAPTER 15

The prince surveyed his generals with a glowering face. He lodged now at Culloden House, just south of Inverness, and was again at loggerheads with Lord George Murray, arguing as to the best time for the attack on the English. It was Murray who had been instrumental in choosing the piece of ground best suited for the rebel army attack, and the prince, on other advice, had opposed it.

"A wide-open moor for a battlefield is the height of madness, sir!" Murray raged.

"We've tried all else!" Charles whipped back. "Hill and ridge and plain. What matters is that we attack, man! If they see us, we shall also see them."

"And they'll blast us to bits wi' their cannon fire," Murray shouted. "Our weapons are puny against cannon."

"Are you for me or against me, sir?" Charles fixed him with an unblinking stare.

Murray changed tactics. "Do ye know how quickly the enemy advances, sir? They are already at Nairn."

"Then we'll surprise them by marching at dusk. We're but eight miles from Nairn."

"Even so, we'd not reach them before daylight."

"We march," the prince ordered finally. "Tomorrow is the duke of Cumberland's birthday. I wager he and most of his army will be in a mood for merrymaking. It will be a good day to present him with a Stuart victory."

The rebel army, roused from their quarters at an hour when most had assumed the day's activities to be over, were disgruntled, disbelieving, and too hungry to contemplate a night marching to a distant, sleet-cold moor. The meager rations had dwindled to a biscuit a day, apart from what they could forage for themselves, and few of the brawny Highlanders felt able to do justice to dirk and broadsword on that.

It proved a disastrous march, some regiments floundering in bogs and losing their way, the marching lines disintegrating into unruly brawling. Lord George led the first column, Drummond led the second, with the prince and his company of French troops in the rear. Most officers who had supported the prince's plan for attacking hard and fast under cover of darkness were now strongly against it. It was doomed before it began, and long before the rebels reached their target the distant sound of enemy drums could be heard on the wind, signaling that their aim of surprise was a failure.

Riding forward to see what was happening, Charles encountered the retreat of the second column, men and horses and gun wagons in total confusion.

"What's happening here?" the prince shouted in fury.

" 'Tis Lord George's orders, sir," he was informed. "He turned his men back a good while since, for 'tis hopeless to go on. Most of the men are thigh deep in the quagmire and refuse to go further."

"Is this my brave army?" Charles roared. "Are my orders to be disobeyed at the first sign of danger?"

"Sir, 'tis the wildest folly to go on with half an army."

"And wilder still to lower the men's morale by leading them all night into battle and then retreating!" But there was no help for it. His own division was already turning back, weary and hungry at the thought of another futile march. Charles rode among the various regiments as best he could on the marshy ground.

"We'll rest awhile men, and my orders are to send my officers and trusted men into Inverness directly to obtain food. If we have no money to buy, I will order the inhabitants to send food on peril of the town being burnt. We fight for them, and they must share in the cost.''

He rose among the men, encouraging, rousing them, seemingly tireless, still thinking there was no road he couldn't conquer. He ordered that cattle should be slaughtered in readiness for the victory feast he confidently expected. Once the battle was won, there would be time for merrymaking.

Jamie Mackinnon rode into the town of Inverness to collect what food he could on the prince's orders. He and the officers and others on horses splayed out in all directions to rouse the townsfolk and issue the prince's command under threat of having their town burned around them. Jamie rode directly to the cottage where Katrina was barely awake, to beg of Mistress Denny her small supplies of bread and meal and vegetables before moving on to other dwelling places. There was little time to snatch a kiss from his wife or to tell rapidly of the previous night's disaster. He reeled it off in harsh tones as if to minimize the seriousness of it all.

''Aye, 'tis not a good day for soldiering,'' Mistress Denny grunted, hearing the moan of the northeast wind and shivering at the sight of the flurries of sleet through the window. Katrina felt wild hysteria at the words. As if any day were a good one for a meeting with the enemy . . .

''I canna stay, now.'' He had the parcel of food ready and caught her to his chest. ''Pray for us all.''

As she had prayed so many times before . . . She felt his mouth on hers, cold from the freezing air outside, and pushed down her fear. She sent him bravely, but it cost her much to do so. When he had gone, she stood for a long moment, as if transfixed and numb. Her eyes caught the stone jug on the windowsill as she peered out. As if needing to occupy her hands, she scooped up the scattered petals and tossed them out the window to be caught on the swirling wind. A choking prayer went up from the depths of her soul as she watched the progress of the dancing golden spirals.

Keep him safe . . . keep Jamie and all of them safe . . . all those who still rallied behind their prince in search of a dream. . . .

* * *

The army was exhausted but had little time to be so. A few hours after it had straggled back in retreat, it became obvious that Cumberland was going to allow them no time to recover. At Culloden House, Charles was informed by a cavalry patrol that Cumberland was already on the march with his formidable army, and the sounds of kettledrums were carried on the wind. They could be as little as four miles away.

"Are they, by God!" Charles leaped to his feet, rousing the officers who still felt desperate for sleep, had eaten little if anything all night, and drank only cups of hot chocolate to sustain them. "On your feet, my brave ones, and assemble your clans. We march to meet the enemy. There's no time for new battle procedures. We march, and do what we can, and may God go with all of us."

Already near to dropping with fatigue, the Jacobite army was reassembled. There was little time if any to distribute the food brought from Inverness, and fighting broke out among the clansmen as they began the weary march back toward the moor. Tempers were near the bursting point.

"Have ye naught better to do than break each other's heads?" Jamie shouted at one pair, whose wrangling and clashing of shields had caused his horse to rear and kick beneath him. "We've enough to do wi'out the likes of ye behaving like fishwives." He slid from the horse's back to calm it.

His answer was a cuff about the head from one of the men. He felt the warm trickle of blood above his temple, and it incensed him to know it came from one of his own kin. He dragged a finger across the blood and thrust it in the attacker's face.

"Are ye all born stupid?" he snarled. " 'Tis the enemy's blood ye should be spilling, not your brother's!"

"The laddie's right," roared the second man, rounding on the first, his kilt flying in anger. "Save your brawn for the English bastards, man."

The three glowered at one another while Jamie pressed the length of his plaid to his split head to stem the flow.

"Just keep out o' my way in future," he growled, "or ye'll see whether I've any brawn left in me or not!"

He remounted his horse, twisting it away from the two, and

moving toward the assembling troops. The long marching finally began, flanked by those who still had mounts to ride, the gun wagons, and the officers. Jamie counted himself fortunate to have a horse still beneath him. Many had been stolen or had bolted or, some suspected, had been slaughtered for meat. He prized his horse above all things, save Katrina.

The march was as uncomfortable as the previous night's. Squelchy underfoot, the open moor was a desolate place, with the great gray masses of the mountains to the south of them. In his heart Jamie, too, questioned the wisdom of this march, but with the enemy steadily advancing toward them, it was either that or retreat, and he had had enough of retreat.

But he had dire thoughts about the outcome of this battle. The scouts had reported that the rebels were outnumbered two to one by the redcoats, and whether or not the enemy had been celebrating the duke's birthday, it was certain that if they were half-drunk, they would be fighting drunk. And the Jacobite army would arrive at the battlefield desperate with fatigue, hungry, ill equipped compared with the reported cannon and artillery of the English. Like lambs going to the bloody slaughter, Jamie thought with a sudden savage oath.

"Rest . . . rest . . . rest. . . ." The word passed along the straggling columns until it reached the rear, and the exhausted Highlanders slumped onto the damp soft ground, easing their aching muscles.

The prince, the officers, and the clan chiefs rode back among them, encouraging, cajoling, cursing the prone figures, grimed with dirt and weariness, hair wild and lank, looking less like an army than a flock of untidy sheep. And they were none too pleased at being forced to march so soon after the abortive attack of the night before, with scarcely hours between one march and the next.

"Give us a good square meal in our bellies, and mebbe we'd feel better equipped to fight for ye!" one clansman bellowed after the prince. Charles turned his gray horse's head to stare levelly at the man.

"I'd give you the clothes from my back if I thought it would help the cause, man. I weep for your plight."

"No more than we do, Your Bonnie Highness!" another jeered, too weary to care how he spoke. "Do ye think ye have the charmed life, mebbe, to last out so long against the English? If so, mebbe ye'll gi' me a touch o' your hand, to pass the luck on to me."

The prince leaned forward and gripped the outstretched hand before moving on.

"Aye, well he may weep," a less vociferous Highlander muttered. "Like his father before him. God knows how he stays cheerful when he's so near defeat."

"Ye don't help matters wi' that kind of talk," Jamie snapped at him. Another with ample girth, sprawled out alongside, jeered at him.

"Does the man think he's God Almighty? What good will it do to a simpleton like yon clansman, thinking he's magic touched by the prince's hand? We need food and warmth before we all die o' cold and starvation."

"Ye'll not die of anything, by the looks of ye," Jamie retorted. "Ye've fat enough to warm ye and to feed your vitals for weeks yet. And there's no sense blaming the Stuart for the weather."

" 'Tis not just the weather, laddie," the hugely built man snapped back. " 'Tis everything. The whole foolhardy bastard cause that's doomed to failure like every other, and we're all doomed with it! I've kinsmen who rallied behind this one's faither and died for it in the fifteenth uprising, and I'll wager here and now that history has us marked down for the same fate."

"History is what's past, ye fool," Jamie snorted.

"Tell me I'm wrong in five years from now. Or five days!" he growled. "If ye're still alive to tell me aught, and I'm still capable o' listening. I tell ye he's done for us."

"Rest over . . . rest over . . . rest over," came the echoing call like rippling waves through the columns of men, and Jamie was glad to haul himself away from the aggressive one with his ominous predictions that found an unwilling echo in himself. He didn't want to believe it and refused to believe it, but his staunch belief in a final Jacobite victory was being stretched to its limits. The dream was fast becoming a nightmare, and who knew what this next great confrontation might bring?

*   *   *

They seemed to have been marching forever. The once bright colors of the plaids were filthy and torn. Shields and weapons seemed to drag them down, as finally they camped in readiness for the attack. It was Jamie's misfortune to find himself once more beside the rank-smelling man with the huge girth, still blathering on at the futility of the day.

"Why do ye stay then?" Jamie swore at him. "Ye've only to join the ranks o' deserters to be rid o' the trouble. What's to prevent ye, man?"

The other suddenly bent down and dragged up a fistful of sodden earth that oozed between his fingers. The look in his eyes was as fierce as the wild mountains as he spat the words out at Jamie.

"This! *This*, laddie! 'Tis mine. 'Tis ours. And 'tis *his*! And there's none who will dare to say that John Joyner Innes deserted his prince! So shut your noise and leave me to get on wi' my blathering!"

He stumped away across the squelching mud. The old fool was as loyal as any man here and had his own way of dealing with his fear by bellowing to any man who would listen. Jamie was suddenly shamed by his anger toward the man. And suddenly he felt a raw fear spiking his gut, for away in front of them was a bright-scarlet gash on the horizon—the emergence of the English army out of the cold sleety morning. Jamie felt fear clutch at his inside so badly it nearly turned his bowels to water.

And here was their prince still encouraging them to fight, still arguing with his generals over which flank to take, still insisting that from now on the orders would come from him and him alone . . . not the same charismatic prince who had ridden so triumphantly through the streets of Edinburgh in velvet and lace, but still dignified for all that, in his mismatched tartan jacket, trews, and tunic.

"By Christ, will ye look at them!" Jamie's bulky adversary lumbered near. "They'll mow us down like emmets beneath their feet. We're nae match for them."

"Save your blathering," Jamie said. "Ye'll fight, same as the rest of us, and try telling me different!"

"Aye, and more fool me," he grunted. "And when all this

is over, remember that John Joyner went into battle still cursing, laddie.''

"I'll not need to remember it. Ye'll be telling me so yourself over a dram."

He turned away from the sidelong glance of the man, not wanting to see such a naked premonition in a man's eyes; not wanting to acknowledge by every report brought to the rebels, that the redcoats were better fed, better armed, better disciplined.

As the morning went on, it seemed to the cold and hungry Highlanders that both sides were reluctant to start the actual fighting. On their side, it was again a clash of wills between Charles and the generals. Again and again the prince sent orders for Murray's men to begin firing from the right of the field, and the orders were ignored until Murray thought the time ripe. Drummond's command was to the left of the field and was more eager to attack. Finally Murray's men began to surge forward. Any action was preferable to none in the freezing sleety cold.

There was a shrieking of pipes from the Highlanders, matching in noise the vibrant beating of the enemy drums. As the rebels watched and waited, it seemed they were faced by scarlet waves of redcoats behind a bristling hedge of steel, their bayonets fixed. Each section of the enemy was grouped in three lines of soldiers, first line kneeling, second and third standing close behind. To the Highlanders, it was like an inpenetrable red wall, and opposing that wall was a mass of savage, starving, and undisciplined men, weary with a war that seemed endless, going nowhere, achieving nothing . . . but the desperate men found a strange courage within them.

The sudden roar into action at one o'clock split the tense, heavy atmopshere of the day. As if set off by a spring, the massed clansmen leapt to their feet and charged wildly toward the English lines. Firing pistols indiscriminately, shields guarding their bodies, they surged forward. The prince was in their midst.

The clansmen were met by red-misted blasts of cannon fire and the murderous effects of grapeshot scattering through the Highland ranks like hailstones. They seared through flesh and splintered bones.

The armies were now less than five hundred yards apart, and in an instant of time red was the new horror color of the morning. Red blazing fury, red uniforms, red Highland blood seeping and gushing from torn limbs, ripped bodies, gaping flesh. The red-stained moorland that had once been virginal and clean, was now forever desecrated in the morass of screaming, twisted, falling bodies as the noise and stench of battle enveloped it.

Behind the Jacobite surge still soared the raucous skirl of the pipes as the clans thrust forward. Before them lay death and mutilation, somewhere amidst the dense yellow-gray smoke that choked their throats and gritted their eyes. Those who had lost swords or had none wielded axes and dirks; those with pistols aimed as best they could, with the roaring of their own field artillery supporting them.

But they were no match for the swarming redcoats in their precisionlike advance. Few of the clansmen reached farther than the first line of the English force before they were battered and slaughtered by the second line and then the third, and then by the next wave of the seemingly inexhaustible redcoats.

The duke of Cumberland had trained them well. There was no mercy shown to the rebel upstarts, and he wanted the head of Charles Stuart.

"Watch out, man!" a voice screamed out right next to Jamie, as a gleaming bayonet pierced the air alongside him. Deflected by the voice, maybe, the redcoat's aim slid past Jamie's head by a whisker, and instead of striking him it sliced right through the rebel's face, leaving him screaming in agony as half his face fell away, and he dropped to the ground.

Jamie moved with savage swiftness, firing his pistol between the redcoat's eyes as the gleam of the bayonet rose to attack him next, its tip still bloody. The soldier's spattered head shot all over Jamie, blinding him for a moment, and he had to force the vomit down at the hot gushing taste of it.

There was no time to vomit. No time to think or breathe or know fear. No past or future, only the slashing, exploding struggle against an enemy proving infinitely stronger.

Each time a bayonet crashed against his shield he thought

he was doomed. He had lost all sense of place, of time. At some stage his horse had buckled beneath him and gone galloping away in terror, and he slithered about on the marshy moor like all the rest. Each time a redcoat came within eye contact, he could sense the same desperate need to be the victor, the one to live.

God knew how many he had killed or maimed. He was past caring. It would go down in his record in heaven or hell for this day. He suddenly heard the roaring voice of John Joyner Innes nearby, cursing and blaspheming into battle. The sheer sight of him, kilt swirling, his huge girth, murder in his face, was enough to make an entire company quail. But not this army. Not Cumberland's men.

"Get the bastards, John Joyner!" Jamie heard himself screaming. Cannon fire was exploding all around him, rocking his senses and making wool of his brains. An arm, severed from its owner, touched his face as it was blown to the ground. He trod on it without noticing the soft dead flesh or the oozing blood. He was crazed.

"I'll save a few for ye, laddie!" John Joyner bellowed back at him, and then the bellowing dwindled to a horrific gurgling as the spattering of grapeshot caught him full in the wide expanse of his belly, and blood spurted out as if from a flour sprinkler. He dropped like a boulder, and Jamie knelt without thought behind the great mound of his body to fire straight up into the next leaping redcoat's heart.

The soldier fell soundlessly, right over the dead body of John Joyner, and toppled onto Jamie. Then he knew sheer horror as blood suddenly gushed from the soldier's mouth and the great hole in his red jacket. What was uniform and what was blood, or were they all one and the same? The wildness of the thoughts sped in and out of his mind as though they went through a sieve. He pushed with all his strength to get the body away from him, but there was always another, and another. . . .

He was surrounded by dead bodies, or bits of bodies, arms, hands, ragged remnants of limbs. He retched, despite his own efforts to keep sane. He was becoming disoriented, not knowing which way his lines were moving. He had lost his clansmen and scrabbled in a sea of blood. Panic tore at him.

"Mackinnons! Mackinnons! . . . Mackintoshes! Mackintoshes! . . . Camerons! Camerons! . . . Retreat and scatter! Retreat and scatter!"

From all around him he seemed to hear the various clan slogans, some roaring in a final attempt to rouse their men, others feeble and declaring the inevitable. In no wild stretch of imagination could it ever compare with the triumphant roars at Prestonpans or Falkirk. Through the mist of cloying powder smoke and the rancid, acid smells all around, Jamie suddenly saw some of his own clan and stumbled toward them. It must be near the end. The Jacobites were stricken, broken, and of the prince there was no sign. God preserve him, Jamie thought fervently, for after this, Cumberland would surely show no mercy.

Jamie himself felt less than human. He was covered in muck and smelled worse than horse dung, and his mind reeled at sights such as he had never seen before. Yet still he fought on whenever a brief surge of the enemy came near, even in retreat, along with those who hadn't already fled. Even now, Cumberland had one last 'trick. The dragoons, held in reserve until the final triumph, now charged through the beaten rebels, fresh and alert, where the clansmen were all but done for. It was over.

"Retreat. Retreat. Retreat and scatter!"

The commands were more urgent now, and all who were able obeyed the hoarse words. Some preferred to be taken prisoner, to be immediately shot on the orders of the English duke. From that moment, every man had to look to his own safety, and Jamie was no less anxious than any man to stay alive. Someone shouted in his face that Charles had had his horse shot from under him but had gotten away safe. Jamie hardly heeded the words at that moment. Self-preservation had a sweetness all its own.

There was precious little shelter around Culloden moor: some huts, scattered farms, dips and hollows in the marshy ground. Behind one of the huts, Jamie crouched to listen in case he was pursued, having already witnessed some of the redcoats in their vicious triumphs, stabbing clansmen already dead, taking what little they had, mutilating the bodies. A burning anger gripped him. It wouldn't happen to him, even if he had to use all his cunning to survive. But survive he would.

The fleeing rebels would head east, south, or west, he reasoned as well as his swimming senses would allow, not north to Inverness where the English army would shortly march to take the town once more. And with the turncoat mood of the townsfolk, the rebels would once again be spat upon and the redcoats cheered. He supposed he couldn't blame them if it came to a choice between that and rotting in jail for their pains.

But he must go to Inverness, Jamie thought with increasing alarm. Katrina would not be safe there. The duke's men would start searching for Charles Stuart, and he was spurred on by a new fear now, leaving the shelter of the hut and racing on in the direction of Inverness, his heart a great sawing pain in his chest. His shield was long gone, and he had only his pistol and dirk with which to defend himself if the need arose, but thank God it did not.

A sudden whinnying brought him sharply to a halt, and he dropped to the ground in silence. It could be an enemy. . . . The coldness of his pistol grip in his hand reassured him, and he made himself think more coherently. *He must survive.* He didn't altogether welcome the clarity of thinking, for with it came all the rushing horror of the battlefield, a horror that had lasted barely forty minutes, he guessed, but that would leave scars on his soul that would never be erased. He would almost prefer the numbing emptiness of the simpleton he'd thought himself to be when the two dead bodies, John Joyner's and the spewing redcoat's, had seemed to want to possess him. Now, he thought such numbing detachment a blessing.

The horse's whinnying came nearer. He had somehow dropped into a hollow and inched his head upward to see who was about to leap on him. At any second he expected to be looking into the barrel of an English musket and to know the sick instant of fear before his brains were blown out. Instead, he felt the hard wet push of a horse's nose against his head and heard the restless pawing of the frightened hooves.

Through eyes suddenly blurring, Jamie grabbed at the animal, blessing his luck now at this runaway that sought his companionship. It must have been tied to a stake in the ground and may have belonged to a farmer. Jamie didn't care. All he saw was a faster means of reaching Inverness, and he scrambled to his feet, still clinging to the animal's flanks. The stake the horse had pulled free trailed behind him, but in doing so, the rope was being pulled tighter around his neck and was near to strangling him.

"Hold still, my beauty," Jamie croaked, the voice not sounding like his own. "Ye're the proof that a guardian angel's still watching over me this day."

Quickly he freed the rope from the animal's neck, soothing it and hearing the rasping breathing calm a little. In seconds he had climbed on the horse's back and was digging his heels in, urging him on toward Inverness. The animal responded at once, and Jamie found to his own horror that as he clung to the unkempt mane, wild sobs were wrenching out of him.

It lasted but a few minutes, but it shamed him to his core. He threshed against the horse's mane, clutching at the wild hair and blaspheming at the bastard Cumberland who had reduced him to a shivering wreck of a man. For however short a time, he had felt real, unimagined terror, and just as quickly it was turning to hate. Those moments had unmanned him, and that was something he could never forgive.

CHAPTER 16

"Jamie!"

Katrina gasped out his name in shock and horror as he staggered through the door. He had ridden through back alleys and streets that all seemed to look the same. His mind was so muddled and distracted he had begun to wonder if he would ever find the house again. Finally he had, and had tethered the foaming horse out of sight, knowing they would need it again later.

Mistress Denny came hurrying out of her parlor at the small commotion of Jamie's return. Without thinking, she clapped her hand to her mouth and nose at the sight and smell of him. Katrina, too, was hardly able to resist putting her apron to her face, and though she ran to clutch at his arms in wild relief, he hardly blamed her for wanting to keep her distance.

No one in her right senses would want to throw herself into the arms of such a creature. He had ridden hard, pressing himself flat over the horse's back as if he were a corpse whenever he heard the distant sound of firing, or the suspected rasp of English voices. It had been a harrowing ride, knowing that the redcoats would be uncaring about taking prisoners, and that any stray rebel would be shot on sight.

Away to the south of the town, a great pall of smoke rose in the sky from the direction of Culloden moor, and until he had ridden well away from it, he had not dared to rest. Now, in the light of the lodging house, he could see that he was caked in mud, and in blood that was not his own.

" 'Tis all done, then," Mistress Denny said swiftly, seeing the varying degrees of shock on the faces of the other two. "News travels fast, laddie, and by the looks of ye, ye're one of the lucky ones to survive."

Jamie gave a harsh laugh. "Ye call this lucky? Wi' men's blood and guts seeping into me?"

He seemed to read her soul. Inverness was a town forced to take sides, or to take no side at all. She had sheltered them, believing in the cause . . . but now that the cause was in tatters, she would want to live her life as peacefully as possible. There were many like her, and who could blame them?

"Heat the water, Katrina." Mistress Denny took charge. "There's some already warming, and your man is in need of a scrubbing."

"There's no time," Jamie said curtly. "We must get away quickly."

"Ye'll travel nowhere in such a state," the woman retorted, seeing the way he swayed on his feet. "Ye're half-dead wi' fatigue, and ye fill my house wi' your evil stink, so ye'll do as I say."

"Mistress Denny's right, Jamie. You look . . . terrible."

She meant that he looked exhausted, but he took her words as a slight on himself. He spoke caustically, eyes flashing dangerously.

"Aye, well, mebbe I've a right to look so. Battling for a lost cause never produced the scent of roses on a man."

" 'Tis truly lost, then?" Katrina whispered, ignoring the stinging hurt she felt at his curtness.

"Aye, 'tis lost!" He was suddenly shouting, hating the sound of his own words, hating the failure of it all, his country's and his own. "The bastards were too strong for us, blasting into us wi' their cannon before our men could gather their wits. They were blasting us even before we had received any commands. The bastard redcoats reduced the battle to a bloody massacre."

He was stopped by a wild slap across his cheek with all the force that Katrina could muster as she heard the sudden crazing of his voice. Her eyes blazed with fury as she tried to bring him to reality from that fearsome world into which he seemed to have retreated, filled with memories that sickened and shamed him.

"Would ye act this way before Mistress Denny, Jamie, and shame me by such talk? 'Tis not my husband I'm listening to, but a savage! I don't know you, Jamie! I'll do as I'm bid and stoke the fire beneath the water pot, for wi' such rough talk, 'tis no more than a servant that ye make me feel."

His hand gripped her wrist, holding it in a clasp of iron. His face bore the new marks of her hand among the grime. His eyes were still filled with that demented look, and she felt very afraid. Afraid of her Jamie. . . . Just as swiftly his expression changed, as if he noted the fear in her, and the hand gripping her wrist slid down to grip her fingers instead. He fought to stay calm on this day—this day that was the destruction of all their hopes. He knew it in his gut, his soul. His bones ached to know it.

"Aye, a scrubbing's mebbe what I need to get away the surface muck," he growled. "Nothing will scrub away all that's gone on this day."

They weren't listening to him. Instead they moved about the lodging house now that there was an activity to be done and were clearly glad to have something to do. They didn't know how to react to this new, hard Jamie, who seemed so remote from them. He didn't blame them for that, either, when he didn't know himself anymore. He watched Katrina doing Mistress Denny's bidding, and he hardly knew her. He felt a panic at that thought. Trying for an instant to recapture the memory of those other two who had shared so much of life in their own glen.

They didn't exist any longer. They seemed of a different age, another time, when to run had meant laughter and gaiety and sweet loving in the capture, not the fearful eluding of the king's men . . . and those were the thoughts that superseded all others now. Maybe Katrina was still the same, and only he was different, seemingly frozen inside and never to be the same man again. He felt an impotent rage.

Dear God, the feeling must surely pass, he thought savagely. The hell of impotency, in mind and body, was something that every man believed only happened to others, not to himself. Not to Jamie Mackinnon, virile laird of all he surveyed in the land about Mackinnon House, with a wife lovely enough to make other men envy his good fortune.

"Ye'll need clean clothes, Jamie." Mistress Denny spoke to him as if he were her own son. "Ye can have your scrubbing here in the warm, and I'll keep out of your way while Katrina attends to ye. The rags ye're wearing must be burnt, and I'll see to it."

"Aye, mistress." He avoided her eyes, knowing exactly what she meant. If the soldiers began searching every house for Charles Stuart, they must not find soiled garments that had clearly belonged to a rebel. They mustn't find young man's clothing here at all, since Mistress Denny had long been a widow. Neither could he roam about naked. He couldn't think sensibly. Thank God the old woman was thinking for him as she and Katrina hauled down the large bathing bowl from the hook in the yard and brought it into the warm stuffy parlor.

"I have a box o' my man's clothes," Mistress Denny said. "I'll bring ye a shirt and trews and jacket, and a blanket to top it all, for ye'll find it cold to be traveling."

Katrina began to feel that the two of them were passing

secret messages between them by the very blandness of her words. Mistress Denny would have seen all this before, of course, during the other Jacobite rebellion of the old pretender, Charles's father, in 1715 . . . another failure to win the throne for its rightful successor. She bit her lips hard.

"Where will we go, Jamie?" she said, her voice thick.

He lifted the heavy water pot from the fire and tipped it into the bathing bowl. Katrina added some softening soap to it as he stopped pouring and eyed her blankly for a moment. It was as if the question were incomprehensible to him.

"Go? Where would we go?"

A surge of longing swept over her as she smelled the sudden sharpness of the softening soap in the water, and pungent though it was, it was almost reminiscent of the sweet young grass in the glens and the tangy scent of bracken.

"Will we go home?" she asked passionately, praying that he was only teasing her, making her wait. Then she heard his harsh laugh.

"We go where I'm ordered, lassie." He spoke as if her wishes were of no importance. "Where the prince decrees it."

"Jamie, it's over!" she said tremulously now. "You *know* it's over. Ye said as much."

"We've not yet disbanded, except for those who deserted of their own free will, and I've no' done that, Katrina! No man will say it of Jamie Mackinnon!" His eyes seemed to burn with a strange intensity.

The Stuart cause had done this to them, Katrina thought with a rare bitterness. It had divided lovers, and husbands and wives, in ways more far-reaching than merely physical partings. She and Jamie had once been like two sides of the same coin. Now she couldn't reach him.

"I'll away and fetch the garments." Mistress Denny's voice broke the brittle silence. "Then I'll leave ye with your man, Katrina. He'll smell sweeter in a wee while."

"I hope so," Katrina replied with a crooked smile. "I'd not wish to be close to him in this state!"

It was meant to be teasing, but there was no answering smile on Jamie's face. She went cold inside, for it seemed as if Jamie had no more thoughts of their closeness than declaring himself a king's man. He was so remote, detached, except when he was angered. And how quickly he could be roused to anger now! He had gone away her strong, loving Jamie and had come back a stranger.

Katrina's heart ached to see him like this, so closed up within himself, not allowing her to share his pain. The sight of him, naked, easing his tired limbs into the bath, moved her with a poignant sadness. He seemed more vulnerable than she had ever known him, and it grieved her to know it.

"Shall I scrub ye, Jamie?" Her voice was a husk of sound.

Once, she needn't have asked. The bathing would have been a frolic, a sweet prelude to loving. Now, seeing his fine broad shoulders half-bowed, as if he carried so many cares on them, she was deeply afraid for him, for his sanity. He gave that strange unlaughing laugh again and handed her the washcloth.

"Ye'd better, lass, for I've no interest in doing for myself. Scrub all the memories away if ye can, though I doubt that an army would have the elbowing to accomplish that! Ye can try to scour my mind of poor brave fools like John Joyner Innes, who's just as dead as the redcoat lying beside him and will be just as quickly forgotten, except by those who were there. Those who saw, and felt, and *knew*—"

"Stop it, Jamie!" Katrina snapped the words at him, rubbing the washcloth hard against his back with furious movements until the skin was reddened and glowing. "Ye çan't bring them back, so where's the sense in reliving every moment and torturing yourself anew?"

"And who's to mourn them if we don't? Tell me that! Only those who were there, those who are left, can mourn for them. If I was one of them, lying with half my guts blown away, or with arms and legs scattered about Culloden moor, would ye not want someone to remember me?"

Tears scalded her face as he spoke.

"Ye know full well there's someone who would always remember ye, Jamie! But I canna bear to hear ye speak this way! Please—just for my sake—try to put it to the back of your mind, just for a while."

She finished scrubbing his back and worked around to the front of him, over his powerful shoulders, across the hair-roughened chest, and then downward. Her burnished hair swung across his face as she worked. He lay against the back of the bathing bowl as if she scrubbed a rag doll, unaware of her, as if some devil had taken possession of him.

"Will ye stand, Jamie?" she asked huskily. "I would scrub the grime from your legs."

He obeyed, childlike. She refused to let him see how deeply she was affected by his apathy. He swung from violence to apparent numbness in the blinking of an eye. She rubbed at the dirt-encrusted knees while Jamie stood as motionless as a statue.

Then she felt the lightest touch of his fingers on her hair, and she was holding her breath as if she sensed that the soft stroking of it was rekindling the flame of his awareness. The movements of the washcloth slowed as she looked upward into his face. With wild thankfulness she saw that some of the gray pallor in his face had gone, and there was a more lucid gaze in his eyes at last, replacing the anguish.

Suddenly Jamie pulled her to her feet and into his arms, holding her in a savage embrace. The dampness of his body seeped through her clothes, but she cared nothing for that. She was in Jamie's arms where she belonged, and his mouth was seeking hers once more.

He held her so tightly she could scarcely breathe, but she knew at once that though he held her, wanting her comfort, this was no sexual arousal. His need was for the sanity of her presence, her love, needing her to be as she had always been.

"Dinna begrudge me their ghosts, my dearie," he said, a world of sadness in his voice. "For us two, there's all the time in the world. For those that lie broken on Culloden moor, time has no more meaning."

"I'm sorry, Jamie. I'm sorry." Her voice was muffled against his shoulder. There were no rules to say how a woman should behave when her man came home from war, no way of knowing whether he would want sympathy or silence or forgetfulness in her arms. She was not sure if it was herself or Jamie who shuddered just then, but she pulled slightly away from him.

"Ye'll catch cold. I'll dry ye, Jamie."

"I'll do it myself, now," he said roughly. "I'll dress in the

228

garments Mistress Denny brought, and then I must take an hour to rest, for I'm desperate for sleep. If ye'll ask her to prepare some food for when I waken, we must be ready to leave then. 'Twill be dangerous to stay any longer than we need.''

She turned away from him, knowing that their brief closeness was over.

''I'll tell her. But if we're to travel, then I'll lie beside ye for a while, Jamie. I've had little sleep, too. I've been too feared for ye to sleep.'' Her voice caught a little. ''I'll just lie with ye, Jamie, just to rest and be your comfort.''

She gave him the towel and went to inform Mistress Denny of their plans, what little she knew of them. Her words had been true. She had not slept since Jamie had left for the abortive attack on Nairn, and just to rest beside him had become more precious to her than a jewel in a crown. How quickly the priorities of life changed, Katrina thought.

Jamie had already gone upstairs when she returned to the parlor. Mistress Denny had told her to leave the bathing water, and a lad would help her empty it later. Katrina followed Jamie to their small room. He looked young and vulnerable sprawled out on the bed, already asleep, clad in the unfamiliar dun-colored trews instead of the proudly worn plaid that was now waiting to be burnt.

Quickly, Katrina changed out of her damp dress into a darker, less conspicuous one, so that she would be ready for traveling when they awoke.

Jamie stirred as she slid carefully onto the bed beside him. For a moment she studied his face, knowing and loving every line of it. In sleep he was less hardened by war, less aggressive and more the man she loved. How often she had listened to his heartbeats like this; only then, in their own glen, they had quickened with passion for her. How often his desire had awakened an answering flame inside her! The child-Katrina had so longed to be all that he wanted of her then. Gently she put her arms around him now, drawing him close to the warmth of her body and careful not to awaken him.

Katrina gradually became aware of the slow heaving of Jamie's shoulders against her. He had wept as he'd fled from the battlefield and had vowed to himself then that never again in his waking hours would he weep unmanly tears. But sleeping, he wept for all the young men who had died on Culloden moor in that sleet-driven hell. He wept in his sleep and never knew that he did so.

Katrina made a vow, too, that she would never tell him. This much she could do for him. In her silent, womanly way, now she was the strong one, the comforter. Holding him, she felt moved and comforted by the knowledge. The room they shared was mean and cold, but they were wrapped in love and never felt the chill.

Muffled voices awakened Katrina with a start. Jamie was already moving cautiously toward the door, opening it a crack and then wider as he saw Mistress Denny outside. Two men were with her, shadowy in the dusk but, from the tone of Jamie's voice as he bade them come in, apparently Stuart men. Katrina's heart had leapt with fear the instant she'd awakened and it still thudded unevenly.

"What news do ye bring?" Jamie asked.

The men glanced at Katrina, and Jamie told them rapidly that this was Mistress Mackinnon, and they could speak out. He knew both men, whom he addressed as Moffat and Gordon.

"The move is to Ruthven barracks, Mackinnon. We're to make a last rally for the cause there. So all who still believe in it . . ."

Moffat left the question in the air, and Jamie growled his assent, as if daring the man to question his loyalty.

"There's been a flurry of excitement among the redcoats," the swarthy Gordon said with a sadistic leer.

"Shut your noise, man," Moffat warned, looking toward Katrina.

Jamie was keen-eyed at once. "What's afoot? Why do ye look so shifty? The prince . . ."

"Safely away, we're told," Moffat said quickly. "But since this dolt has begun to tell ye, ye may as well know, Mackinnon, though we two are still reeling from the shock of it, seeing as 'twas quite near to us that it happened—"

"Get on wi' it, man," Jamie snapped. From the cautious way the men were looking her way, Katrina knew it wasn't to be a pleasant tale.

"Ye'll have heard o' the rebel laddie wi' the great likeness to the prince's looks, Jamie," Moffat went on. " 'Twas uncanny to be fighting alongside him and hear him shout in the Gaelic when he resembled the other so much—and even worse when he was slain so near to the two of us . . ."

"Go on, man," Jamie said brutally, seeing Katrina blanch but needing to know what this was all about.

"We heard his call as he lay dying, and plenty redcoats heard it, too, Mackinnon. Our man declared that the redcoats had killed their prince. The words threw them all into confusion. Wi' a price on the Stuart's head of thirty thousand pounds, they needed to be sure it was the Stuart who was slain."

The man, Gordon, who had spoken, glanced at Katrina again, hesitating. "Mebbe the lassie should'na hear it all."

Katrina moved toward Jamie, her chin high.

"I'm no' moving from this room," she stated flatly. "Ye may speak freely, and I'll no' swoon in front of ye!"

She resisted the urge to slide her hand in Jamie's as she spoke, wanting to appear strong and praying that she spoke truly. It was Moffat's voice that took up the telling then, quickly and brutally.

"The redcoats cut off the man's head and have sent it to London for identifying. Until they can be sure the dead man is Charles Stuart, the search for him is slowed down a mite."

The taste of bile rose swiftly to Katrina's throat as she listened to the harsh words in horrified fascination, the coldness with which they were said sharpening their impact on her. It was like the tale of John the Baptist's head being delivered to Herod on a platter, she thought wildly. She forced down the nausea, realizing with growing hysteria that Jamie was still conversing with these carriers of horror. It was as if such tales were almost commonplace, and it was even more appalling to her to sense the fact.

"But 'tis certain the prince got away?" Jamie queried.

"Aye," Gordon grunted. " 'Tis assumed he's making for Ruthven barracks, which is where we go now for the rally. Much of our army is scattered, and God knows what size the force will be, but 'tis sensible to make for one place where there's food and supplies. There's no estimating how many fell at Culloden. Some guess at more than a thousand, though 'tis hard to tell and to make a real count, wi' the tangle of arms and legs and bits o' bodies strewn over the moor.''

A choking sound escaped from Katrina's throat despite all her efforts not to show any emotion. But she couldn't stop the trembling in her legs, or the sudden swaying of her body against Jamie. It wasn't even so much the horrific imagery the men's tale brought to her mind, as it was the thought that they might have been talking about her own husband.

''We've heard enough,'' Jamie said shortly. ''I thank ye for bringing the news, and 'tis Ruthven barracks that we will make for within the hour.''

Gordon spoke warningly. ''Take care, Mackinnon. The search for the prince may be less frantic at present, but every rebel is a target now. Cumberland is making his presence felt very forcibly and shows no mercy to those who harbor them.''

''Then the sooner we get away from Mistress Denny's house the better,'' Jamie went on. ''I'd not want to put the good woman at risk. My thanks to ye both.''

The woman had been listening all this time, and Katrina couldn't blame her for the small expression of relief that crossed her face. This was her home, and she would want to continue living in it, no matter what faction was in control of the town.

The danger was only just beginning, Katrina realized, yet Jamie was calmly talking about food. The very idea of it made her want to retch, and she told him so through shaking lips. He held her hands tightly, and she knew that the energy in him was indeed restored.

''Ye must eat, Katrina,'' he ordered. ''Good food inside ye before we travel is common sense. Unless ye want me to leave ye here.''

''No! I'll not be left behind again, Jamie. This time I go with ye. Those men spoke of a last rally. Don't they know, as well as we both know, that it's hopeless?''

''Mebbe, but we go to Ruthven.'' His voice was hard, daring her to argue. ''And before we go, we get some food in our bellies.''

She didn't think she could force a mouthful down, but somehow she did, knowing that Jamie spoke sense. They had no way of knowing what lay ahead. If the redcoats were seeking out every rebel who ever swore allegiance to Charles Stuart, then they must watch every step they took.

When the time came to leave the lodging house, they each had a bundle of food and clothes. Most of Jamie's money had been left with Katrina for safekeeping, and they paid Mistress Denny their dues as Katrina hugged the old woman. She had grown fond of her after all, and Mistress Denny's eyes, too, were moist as they slipped out into the night.

Jamie led her to where the horse was tethered and helped her onto the animal's back. They moved quietly along the cobbled alley onto the rutted tracks and away down the hill from the town of Inverness. She clung to Jamie's back, his body shielding her from the wind and weather, and the only thought she allowed into her head at that moment was that at last they were together.

"We'll travel by night and stay hidden in the daylight, hen," he told her. "There's plenty rough country to travel, over mountain passes, before we reach the Spey valley and the barracks. 'Twill often be more sense to walk the horse than to ride him. Do ye have the strength for it?"

She hugged his body to her. "I've the strength," she told him, praying that she did. "How far a journey is it?"

"Upward of thirty miles, mebbe," he said, "though with detours for the easier tracks, it could well be far more than that. The only comfort I can give ye, lassie, is that the redcoats will be too busy wi' their spoils after their victory to come chasing us too soon. Cumberland will be making his presence felt in Inverness and taking the town."

They took direction by the stars and the gleaming water of the river Ness and the small lochs to the south of the great Loch Ness. They spoke little as they went, often holding their breath as they paused to listen at any unusual noise coming out of the darkness toward them. Sometimes they heard other voices similar to their own and guessed that they were not the only rebels making this hazardous journey. That, too, gave them a small comfort. Not that any joined them. It was each one for himself.

"Do ye think the redcoats will try to recapture the barracks, Jamie?" Katrina said as they walked the horse through a craggy pass. She tried not to notice the yawning chasm that plunged alongside them. Her heart pounded with fear, but she tried not to let her head swim. One stumbling step, and she could be over the edge.

"My guess is that they won't—at least not right away," he commented. "They'll be too busy with the feasting and merry-making at Inverness. And they'll not want to make too many moves until they hear from London if it really was Charles Stuart that was slaughtered."

Katrina shuddered, remembering the horror of the rebel's fate. Once the English discovered their mistake, it was certain that no attempt would be spared to hunt down the prince.

"Can we rest soon?" she asked, switching her thoughts away as quickly as she could and seeing to her relief that they were descending from this particularly dizzy ridge. "We seem to have been traveling a long time, Jamie."

" 'Tis not yet dawn," he said briefly, and then, as he heard her indrawn breath of weariness, he relented. "We'll go on until we find shelter that's less exposed than these slopes, my dearie. Mebbe a derelict croft."

"There!" Katrina's eyes made out a gray shape in the gloom of the predawn even as he made the suggestion. It was no more than a tumbledown shack, probably left empty by a shepherd, but it was as welcome to her as a palace.

The croft was in the cleft of the mountains and unlikely to be spotted. All the same, Jamie entered it cautiously, and when he was satisfied it was deserted, Katrina followed him inside.

"We had best bring the horse inside, too, if we're not to find ourselves wi' a dead beast on our hands, or one that's wandered off," he said. "Besides, I'd as soon have the animal within sight than have him give our position away to prying eyes."

There was barely room for them all in the one-room croft, but Katrina was thankful for the shelter. "Can we light a fire?" she asked Jamie. " 'Tis so cold here, and no one would take it as odd if a wisp of smoke appeared from a crofter's cottage. They'd hardly notice it among the thin pall of mist in the mountains, Jamie. Any that saw it would think it no more than the morning mist."

"Aye, ye're probably right," Jamie grunted. "And we'll

neither of us fare well if our fingers and toes are numb with the cold. I'll see what I can do, hen.''

The day was gradually lightening, and there were twigs and peat and bits of moss in the fire grate. It took some effort, but a small fire was soon blazing to cheer them. They ate the food Mistress Denny had given them, sparing some for the next day. Their muscles ached from the strain of the journey so far, and Katrina was almost dropping with sleep and exhaustion. The warmth of the fire made her even drowsier, and she sank down onto the rough matting, rolled herself in the blanket Mistress Denny had given her, and closed her eyes. Just for a little while. . . .

It was hours later when she came to her senses again. The horse stood sleepily beside her, and Jamie peered through the window opening into the gray daylight.

"Jamie, is aught wrong?" she whispered through cracked, dry lips. He turned swiftly, his voice reassuring.

"I'm just keeping watch, lass. There's nothing in this wilderness but ourselves, so if ye want to sleep a wee bit longer . . .''

She felt a gnawing in her stomach. It was food she felt the lack of now, not sleep. The biscuits and meat Mistress Denny had provided seemed to dry her throat and make her long for cool drinks.

"Could we search outside the croft for herbs or roots? Old Margret told me of some that could be used to make a broth.''

"And mebbe end up killing ourselves from poisoning! Better not to risk it, now. There's a burn nearby, and there may be fish in it. If ye'll pile more sticks on the fire, I'll see what I can find.''

Jamie went outside while she prodded the fire into life again. He took the horse for some exercise, and Katrina was glad to rid the croft of the animal scent for a while. A short time later, Jamie came back in triumph with a small speckled fish. It made a poor enough meal, roasted over the fire, but it tasted like ambrosia to them both.

They were descending toward the Spey valley, and the going began to get easier. The second day they spent in comparative comfort in a cave among the lower hills, and before the next night was over, Jamie stopped the horse and pointed ahead through the gloom to where a gray shape rose into the sky.

"We've reached the barracks, Katrina. Say a prayer of thankfulness."

He urged the horse on with renewed vigor. Never had Katrina been more thankful to see a place. She ached in every part of her, and much as she loved Jamie there had been an uncanny sense of loneliness among the silent mountains; she welcomed the thought of noise and people again. She wondered about the women she had met before when she had traveled with the wife wagons, and she was especially eager to find her friend Fiona Patterson and her young husband Andy. It would be good to see them again.

CHAPTER 17

I*t was like a small town inside the barracks, overpopulated* and bristling with angry clansmen. Lord George Murray's troops had been led to expect ample food at Ruthven, but supplies had not arrived, and the bags of meal sent to feed the army at Culloden from Inverness had also fallen into enemy hands before they could be brought to Ruthven. If it hadn't been for the resourcefulness of the clansmen in finding meager food supplies, there would have been a revolt among the men before Jamie and Katrina even arrived. As it was, there was much fighting and discontent and uncertainty. Charles Stuart still had not arrived among them, leading many to wonder as to his movements. Had he fled rather than joined this last rally for the cause? Or had he been captured, or slain?

"There's no way o' telling," a clansman growled when Jamie demanded to know what details there were. "Every arrival here is questioned, but none has seen the prince. 'Tis as if he's been spirited away.''

"Aye, mebbe on one o' them fine French ships he was always telling us about," slurred another. "Ye're welcome, Jamie Mackinnon. One more rebel here is one more to stand and fight against the bastard Cumberland."

It was evident to Jamie and Katrina that much of the spirit had gone out of the rebellion. After Culloden, it was hardly unexpected, but if the prince had been here, Jamie suspected, the mood would be very different. In victory or defeat, the presence of Charles Stuart was a vital asset to the morale of his followers.

"Ye did well to come here dressed like that, Mackinnon," said a man wearing the Cameron plaid. "They've banned the wearing o' the kilt, and a man wearing it will be shot on sight."

"Who's banned it?" Jamie demanded to know.

The clansman spat noisily onto the ground. "The bastard Cumberland, man. Who else but our fine and dandy butcher of a victor? Did ye know that's his new nickname? Butcher Cumberland! The name says all."

"Aye, and there's a ban on the Gaelic tongue. Is the butcher a fool? Does he no' have the sense to know that there's many in the Highlands who know no other tongue? He objects to the use o' the pipes as well, calling them the screeching o' cats. There'll be another uprising before he knows it, if he tries to put such rules into force."

Katrina's heart lurched, listening to the uproar among the men. To condemn the very heart of the clansmen, the wearing of the kilt, the Gaelic tongue, the playing of the pipes . . . They may as well cut out every man's heart here and now, for they stole his very soul in forbidding his uniqueness. She gave a great shudder, for if the cause were truly lost, then the redcoats could enforce any law they chose.

Her dry throat suddenly watered as it registered a strange smell, one that she hadn't encountered for a while. There was meat cooking somewhere. A woman caught her eye and came slouching toward them.

"If ye want food, 'tis yonder." She jerked her head toward the rear of the yard. "Some redcoat bastards stole some sheep and slaughtered them, but our men stole them back, so enjoy it while ye can if ye're hungry. 'Tis all the tastier for being the redcoats' leavings.''

She moved away. Katrina hated her on sight. She was as hard and tough as any rebel. Was this what happened to a woman constantly in the company of lawless men? She was suddenly too ravenous to care for long and begged Jamie to come with her to get some meat. It was tough old mutton, but it was hot and roasted, and it tasted so good.

"Katrina, is it really you!" She heard a woman's voice cry out her name and whirled around to see Fiona Patterson hacking off the portions of mutton to hand around. Katrina's heart leapt with relief at seeing a familiar face, and then she gasped at the sight of Andy Patterson alongside her, the left side of his face livid and raw, one ear shot away and a blankness on his handsome face.

"Oh—Andy!" Katrina heard herself croak as she clutched at his arm in swift sympathy. He hardly seemed to know her, and as she looked mutely at Fiona, the other girl went on calmly handing out portions of mutton.

"He takes a while to know who's speaking to him, Katrina. 'Tis the shock, so they say. But he's alive, and that counts for a lot, so we're no' complaining. And your man is well, I see.''

She might have been inquiring at an afternoon tea party, and Katrina felt like weeping at the sight of her taut young figure and that of Andy, bewildered and with the helpless stance of a bairn. Once Fiona had found another helper to take her place at the carving, Katrina watched her lead her husband to a place where he could sit and lean against a post. A great lump filled Katrina's throat at the sight of them. Jamie left her with the Pattersons while he went to report his presence to his officers.

Katrina felt her eyes start to fill with tears as Fiona put the piece of meat between her husband's lips and instructed him to chew. She repeated the order four times before Andy's lips began to move, and then Fiona praised him as if he had performed a miracle.

"I'm so sorry," Katrina whispered to her. "So sorry."

"We manage. It won't always be like this, Katrina. We're

no' so bad as some. When we've rested awhile we'll make our way home. There's no more fighting for Andy, and we've the promise of a wagon to share with several others who are worse off than he is.'' Fiona had a new dignity about her.

"Home!" The word seemed to be torn from Katrina's lips. She missed it so, especially here in this alien place, not knowing what they did here or what tomorrow would bring. But still she knew that as long as Charles Stuart needed Jamie he would remain, and so would she.

There was only one more day to wait before Lord George Murray assembled his followers with a message from the prince. The first rumblings of unease grew into a great confusion of anger and lamentation as Lord George read out the last royal command.

"Prince Charles commands that every man should now seek his own safety the best way he can.'' Murray's voice was devoid of expression, and all who could remember past bitterness between him and the prince could only marvel at his self-control.

But few were wasting time in considering officers' moods. The orders had been given. They were clearly stated, and they said what each in his heart had known and prayed against. The cause was over, and even this last rally had come to nothing. Charles had already fled, and if they were to save themselves, they must do the same. Every man for himself. . . .

The last order the officers gave was for the barracks to be burned to the ground to prevent the English from taking them and claiming this final bitter victory.

Katrina hardly believed how swiftly the order was put into action. Long before the clansmen had begun scattering in all directions, fleeing back to homes and hiding places, a fierce tongue of flame soared skyward, followed by great shooting sparks and explosions that lighted the heavens. Any redcoats near must have wondered if a new battle already raged. In the choking, smoke-filled pandemonium, Katrina was filled with anxiety on Fiona's account. How would she and Andy fare?

"Their own clan will see to them, now,'' Jamie said harshly. "There's no time for good-byes. The Stuart is now a fugitive, and that makes fugitives of us all. We'll take what we can and go.''

It was what everyone else was doing—fighting over food and blankets, and barely having the time for it, with the great leaping flames all around them. Fear throbbed like a living thing in Katrina's mind, and that one word drummed into her head. Fugitive . . . fugitive . . . fugitive. . . .

"Our one hope is to get back home with all speed, Katrina. The redcoats will surely follow.'' He didn't try to mellow his words. "They'll seek out every man who may harbor the prince. Have ye the strength for the journey so soon, then, when we thought we were safe here?''

She swallowed down the fear. "The thought of home gives me strength,'' she said quickly.

He caught her hand, and they ran as wildly as the rest, searching now for a horse—any horse—only to find that those that hadn't already been claimed had stampeded in panic, tearing away from the posts that held them, eyes rolling, mouths foaming. Jamie cursed loudly at the discovery.

"I would'na worry for myself,'' he growled. " 'Tis probably for the best that we travel on foot. We'd be less conspicuous.''

Katrina's eyes flashed. "Then don't worry on my account, Jamie! I'm no milksop, and I go where my man goes. Besides . . .'' Her voice faltered a fraction. "The longing to be home will spur me on.''

His grip on her hand tightened. They were jostled on all sides as men fled, accompanied by the sounds of women screaming and clansmen shouting and cursing, and the crackle of the fire beginning to override all else. They must move quickly, and the small bundle of belongings they had gathered up had to see them through the journey—bits of food and a blanket each, which they used to shield their faces from the furnace heat as they fled. The fire was ripping through the barracks with frightening speed, sending showering splinters of wood all around them.

They pushed their way through the hordes of rebels, hardly able to breathe as the smoke took their breaths and dried their throats. Gasping and stumbling, they forced their way to where the air would be cleaner and fresher, beckoning them toward the west, and home. They raced as fast as they could away from the barracks, their breathing a sawing pain, until at last they collapsed, filthy, smoke-grimed, with hearts pumping erratically and chests heaving. But they were alive, and they were together.

How long they stayed hidden in the bracken-filled hollow, watching the remnants of a dream disintegrate, was hard to judge. It was clear that they must not stay too long, but they both needed to recover their strength a little. Katrina wasn't aware of the great weariness overcoming her or of leaning against Jamie's comforting shoulder. But she must have slept, and when she awoke it was dark, and he was nudging her, wanting to move on.

"We'll head west by the stars again, and with luck we'll find shelter by daylight. A farm or a deserted barn."

He saw the sudden glint of tears on her lashes, which she tried to hide. But she had to say what was in her heart.

" 'Tis a sad ending to it all, Jamie. I ache to know what's happened to the prince. Will he be safely away?"

"He'll never be betrayed, that much I promise ye." Jamie spoke with fierce certainty. "There's no Highlander alive who would sell his heritage for thirty thousand pounds!"

She nodded slowly. There was a pride in their race that couldn't be dominated by the banning of the kilt or the playing of the pipes, however demeaning those things seemed. There would be plenty who would defy the English bans and would probably die for it. A rebel who rallied to an unknown prince because of the loyalty of generations before him was always a rebel. His spirit was not so easily quenched.

Katrina could not bear to think that these last months had all been for nothing. And the thought of that elegant, noble prince now a fugitive stirred her to an even fiercer loyalty in wishing that she could do something to help him . . . anything.

"Are ye dreaming, dearie?" Jamie said abruptly when she remained silent for so long. "We've no time for it. We must move cautiously, and if ye see any redcoats before I do, drop like a stone without saying a word. If ye see me do so, then ye'll do likewise without question. Ye'll obey me in this, Katrina."

Just for a moment, as he spoke with unconscious arrogance, she glimpsed the old Jamie, laird of the glen. She nodded, trying not to betray the lurch of fear as his words penetrated.

"I'll not scream or swoon or resort to women's tears," she told him, and prayed that she could live up to the words. She had ample time to put them to the test during the next ten days. It took that long to walk the dangerous miles home, traveling by night and hiding by day.

Jamie had expected to be offered shelter at farms or cottages by accommodating clansmen. But it became obvious that the fear of harboring rebels was as strong as the fear of the redcoats.

"I hope Charles Stuart fares better than we two," Jamie said grimly as a door was slammed in their faces at one point. The woman there was awaiting the return of her own man and afraid to let strangers in.

"I canna blame her, Jamie. She only wants what we want. To resume a normal life again, and she wants her home intact when her man returns to it, not burnt to the ground by the redcoats because it's a rebel hiding place."

Her voice shook as she spoke. They had already seen the sudden flaring from a thatch roof and guessed at its reason. They had seen fear on the faces of those who waited anxiously for their men and had decided not to look for lodgings unless the place was deserted. Mostly they slept in what shelter they could find outdoors, sometimes covering themselves with bracken to remain hidden.

Always the threat of discovery was like a silent companion. The distinctive uniforms of the redcoats became more evident as they began their relentless search for the prince—sometimes in groups of three or four, sometimes seemingly a whole army swarming through bracken and glen and mountain slopes. Their bayonets gleamed in the pale sunlight, viciously stabbing at anything that moved. Once they came very near to where Jamie and Katrina lay hidden in the bracken, and although she never uttered a sound, she was terrified that the enemy must surely hear the drumming of her heart.

She felt the earth vibrate beneath the redcoats' boots. She heard the raucous blasphemies they shouted as they stabbed at the bracken and cursed the Stuart upstart who had brought them to this godforsaken country. She closed her eyes tightly, wondering if the next stab of a bayonet would pierce her flesh.

Would she be able to keep silent then? Katrina wondered in a blind panic. Would there be any sense if she did, when the soldier would extract his bayonet and find its tip stained red with her blood?

Her chest ached with the effort of holding her breath. Her heart would surely burst with the strain of it . . . and then at last Jamie was squeezing her shoulder and whispering that they were safe. The redcoats had gone. This time they were safe.

Jamie was rubbing her lifeless hands between his own. Seconds before she had felt so tense that she'd thought she would snap in two if he touched her. Now she was a leaf in the wind, weightless, a mass of jelly. She forced down an overpowering feeling of nausea and fixed her eyes firmly on Jamie's face as he peered anxiously down at her. A few fronds of bracken clung to his hair, like devil's horns. She felt a wild urge to laugh but dared not. There may yet be other redcoats. She squeezed the hands that held hers and gave a small nod.

"I'm well, Jamie," she said as levelly as possible, considering the way her stomach still churned. He leaned forward and kissed her briefly.

"I've such a pride in ye, Mistress Mackinnon," he told her huskily. "There's no lassie on earth that I'd exchange for my own."

She felt her throat thicken, knowing that their feelings for each other were still strong, even though they seemed so often smothered in the new passions that devoured them—the passion for the cause and the need to survive. Then Katrina almost lost that hard-won control of minutes ago as the scent of burning, all too familiar now, stung her nostrils. Drifts of gray smoke moved relentlessly toward them.

"The bastards are firing the bracken," Jamie swore in low throbbing fury. "We must move quickly, now. The wind is sending the fire this way, and it will spread quickly enough, for all that there's a dampness in the earth. They'll not be content with a few flames. Quickly, Katrina!"

They rose stealthily, bent double as they ran. Katrina blessed the fact that Jamie wore the dun-colored trews Mistress Denny had given him—not because of the hated decree banning the kilt and the plaid, but because it made him less conspicuous as they fled. Even the choking smoke that followed their tracks helped them make their escape from redcoat pursuers. They ran until they reached some higher ground among the hills, and when they looked back Katrina gasped in horror at the scene of devastation that met their eyes.

Not only was the bracken burning; far behind them a cottage blazed furiously, and the bleating of frightened sheep as they blundered about in terror with their wool ablaze was pitiful. There was distant shouting in the Gaelic tongue, a burst of musket fire, then silence.

"English bastards!" Jamie ground out the words in savage fury. "They would quench our very spirit if they could. They'd lay waste the Highlands in their need to prove themselves the victors. They know little of us, Katrina. Such butchery as this will only charge our determination to get the bonnie prince back to France."

" 'Tis his only chance, then?" She spoke through shivering lips, forcing herself to ask, to take her eyes away from the scene below . . . the scene that made the very question superfluous.

"Aye, lassie," Jamie said grimly. "There's no safety here for him now, nor for any of us! Pray God that the French ships come for him in time."

"Then all this will have been in vain." She could not bear to look any longer at the burning cottage that had once been home to a family. A sudden bitterness at the futility of it all blinded her loyalty for a moment. She felt Jamie's fingers dig into her shoulders, and his eyes burned into hers now as fierce as any fire.

"Dinna say that, Katrina. No cause was ever in vain when it had right on its side. So long as ye believe that Charles Stuart is Scotland's rightful heir, then ye'll not say those words again. Those who died would rise in their graves to deny it. One day I'll tell ye of one of them, with a love so proud and fierce of the very earth—" He stopped, suddenly bereft at the memory of John Joyner Innes, whom he had known so briefly yet who had made such a deep impression on him.

He took her hand and motioned her to run, crouching, with him, until they reached the shelter of an overhang of rock, almost a small cave entrance. It was chill and dank, but it gave them shelter, and they were both exhausted and hungry. The food they had brought with them was long gone, and they ate what they could forage—roots, berries, the occasional fish. Sometimes they were lucky enough to milk a wild goat, but more often than not the hunger pangs gnawed at their bellies. The Highlands could be protective in their sheltering and cruel in their harshness. Would this journey ever end?

Mairi Fraser walked in the glen with her small daughter, Iona. The child had begged her mother to take her gathering wildflowers for the table, and Mairi had agreed, thinking there was gloom enough in the Highlands lately without denying a child her innocent pleasures. Mairi's heart had been heavy ever since the day she had received the contrite yet oddly dignified letter from her elder daughter, Katrina, accompanied by the furious tirade from her sister, Janet, washing her hands of the ungrateful chit and wanting to assure Mairi that she had done her very best for Katrina.

Mairi had sensed the anxiety in her sister's words and had admitted to worrying herself if Katrina had been made fully welcome in the Bancroft house. It was so different from their own. Neither could she rid herself of the feeling of guilt at sending Katrina away. And nothing could lessen the longing to see her daughter again—and Jamie, too. Nothing could stop her mother's wish to welcome her daughter back to the fold, nothing could take away the unspoken anguish of wondering if she would ever see her again.

Long gone was the anger she had felt on hearing that her daughter had taken matters into her own hands and run off to marry Jamie Mackinnon. Mairi was nothing if not practical, and if the deed was done, there was an end to it. More urgent a worry was the thought of Jamie being wounded or killed and Katrina being at the mercy of the redcoats. It was a thought that rarely left her.

Reports of all the Jacobite victories and defeats had quickly reached the west coast, but of Jamie and Katrina there was no news, save for a garbled message that Katrina had been safely at Moy Hall for a time. What was certain was that the cause was finished—the heartbreak of it as searing as in the other uprisings for the Stuarts—and that Charles Stuart was now a fugitive. That much could not be disputed, nor the grim tales that Callum Mackinnon and Duncan Fraser discussed, tales that filled both men with a burning rage.

"Would the bastards relinquish their own native speech on the whim of a victorious duke, the way they expect us to do?" Callum's face was purple with the boiling fury of it. "They insult us, strip us naked in taking our identity away from us."

"Aye, but 'twill not last forever," Duncan growled back, his eyes glinting. "Do they think the sound o' the bagpipes will be silenced forever, any more than our own Gaelic tongue?"

"But ye'll obey the new rules, Duncan," Mairi said fearfully. " 'Tis as hateful to me as to anyone, but what use will any of us be to Scotland if we're cut down because we object? So long as the clans live, we still have a voice, even if 'tis not our own Gaelic voice."

"Your lassie speaks sense, man," Callum was forced to say. "It twists my gut to say it, but if there's to be a future of any sort for our bairns, we have to submit."

"I'll submit on the surface, but my heart will never deny the Stuarts their right." Duncan's voice was vibrant with the anger and frustration of knowing the victors made the new rules. He still wore his cravat tucked into a buttonhole of his shirt, denoting a Jacobite supporter, and to Mairi's dismay he suddenly wrenched the cravat free. "Mebbe such symbols as these had best be done away with, too, since we're to obey the tyrants, though 'twill make no difference to my beliefs."

Hamish had been watching and listening, and his face had grown redder at the talk. Already fourteen and getting taller by the day, he clenched his hands together and growled in his young-old squeaky voice.

"If the English duke comes around here looking for trouble, then he'll be sure to find it."

"And ye'd do well to stop that kind of blather." Duncan rounded on his son at once, as if seeing the way the old men's talk could affect the young ones to their own dangerous rebellion. "Ye'd best get used to wearing the trews, laddie, as we'd all better do." He was the more aggressive, knowing he spoke against his own feelings, and he hated himself for doing so. But he had to protect his own, and mebbe Mairi had shown more sense than he had.

"They'll not come here, Faither." Hamish was still not prepared to be cowed. "We're too far west."

"Use your head, laddie," Callum put in tersely. "The Stuart landed on the west coast from France. 'Tis certain he'll take the same route back. Aye, they'll come searching," he went on with a note of certainty in his voice. "And since 'tis known that our army has scattered, pray to God that your sister and my son return home before the redcoats start probing. If they don't, then 'tis best that we all spin the same tale. Katrina is still away visiting her aunt, and Callum Mackinnon will swallow his pride and swear that his laddie fell at Culloden!"

Iona, clinging to her mother's skirts all this time, turned frightened and indignant eyes on Callum.

"Those are lies! Mammie says 'tis sinning to tell lies."

"Grownups can tell lies," Hamish said loftily. "It's not called lies when grownups tell them, so we'll just have to pretend that we're grownups and do as we're told."

Mairi had felt a rush of pain at his words. Poor bairns, to be so initiated into the art of growing up. And she wondered briefly just how she was going to untangle Hamish's youthful arrogant thinking and ensure that Iona wouldn't betray the truth of it if the redcoats came. It was the new constant fear. If the redcoats came . . .

She was still uneasy in her mind on that early May day while Iona chattered on, her small arms filled with wildflowers and grasses. The day was a mild one, and the glen was verdant and lovely in its early summer mantle of green, the surrounding hills still wreathed in an ethereal, lingering blue-gray mist. It was almost possible to believe that the past months had been no more than a terrible nightmare, instead of the turbulent and bloody struggle for a Jacobite revival. Almost . . .

Mairi caught her breath, realizing suddenly that Iona was no longer a little magpie. She stood motionless a short distance from her mother, staring into the distance, a puzzled frown on her face. Too young to be really afraid, but unsure.

Mairi's heart pounded for a few reckless seconds as visions of Cumberland's redcoats leapt into her mind. They were alone in this part of the glen, a woman and a child. She shielded her eyes against the sunlight, trying not to let her hand tremble. She followed the line of Iona's gaze, seeing now the two limping figures emerging slowly out of the hazy distance, as if every step were a gigantic effort—a tall, broad-shouldered man in dun-colored clothes and a slighter figure, with a wild tumble of coppery hair, untamed as ever, about her face.

With a sudden strangled cry, Mairi came to life as though a spring had been released inside her. The wildflowers fell from her hands, and she was running, stumbling. Her eyes were blurred with tears of disbelief, and Katrina's name was on her lips. Somehow she had covered the distance between them on feet that seemed to have wings, with Iona racing along behind her. And then she was clasping Katrina to her breast, hardly able to believe she held her in her arms.

Katrina wept, too, for now the tears would not be held back. The last two days had been the hardest. The food had been difficult to find, and their feet almost too sore and blistered to search for it. The need to give up, to lie down and sleep, had been almost irresistible . . . but they'd both known that they had to resist.

Jamie had wanted to carry her, but she'd known that he was exhausted, too, and she had insisted on walking the last miles alongside him. Now her mother's arms were around her, and it was too much to comprehend. As Iona suddenly saw the identity of the strangers, she gave a great childish whoop of joy and was swept up in Jamie's strong arms. Ahead of them, the distant shape of Frashiel House was secure and solid and welcoming, and the sight of it was almost more than Katrina could bear in the emotion of the moment. There had been so many times when she had doubted that she would ever see it again.

Her limbs seemed to be fast turning to water as her tears mingled with her mother's. All this while she had sworn to Jamie that she'd not swoon or scream or resort to women's tears, but now all that need was gone, and she could only react like the child she felt herself to be.

She had so longed for home . . . and now she was here, clinging to Mairi like a wee bairn, insensible to the fact that her mother's reactions were almost identical to her own. For the first time in her life, Katrina felt totally inadequate, unable to function on her own, needing to be told what to do, how to behave. The enormity of the journey, of the dangers, and of finally reaching home safely under the very nose of the redcoats, was too much . . . too much. . . .

"Mammie!" she managed to croak at last. "Mammie, we're home. Do ye forgive us?"

Mairi's arms still held her close. "Hush, my bairn, 'twas all forgiven a long while since." Mairi's voice was as choked as her daughter's. "You're home, and that's all that matters, to see ye and Jamie safe."

The glen seemed to spin before Katrina's eyes then, a swirling glitter of green and gold and blue. She reached out to Jamie, clutching his arm.

"Jamie . . ." she said faintly.

Her senses reeled, and as her head rolled back and her knees buckled, Jamie caught her up in his arms and carried his wife the last half mile home.

CHAPTER 18

For the first time in many months, Frashiel House was a place of rejoicing. Once Jamie and Katrina had been welcomed inside its walls, word was sent quickly to Callum Mackinnon, and within the hour the two families were reunited. Callum was not too proud to let the sheen of tears show in his eyes at the pleasure of seeing his son and daughter-in-law again.

" 'Tis like the answer to all our prayers, laddie." He was gruff with emotion. "There's been so many nights when we've all lain abed with heavy hearts. There were times when we sorely wondered if we'd see either one of ye again."

"Now, Callum, let's have no more gloomy talk!" Mairi said. "The young ones are home safe, and that's all that matters."

She looked across at Katrina, as if suddenly aware that home to her daughter was now the home of her husband. The flickering emotions were crystal clear to Katrina at that moment, and she knelt with a swift movement at her mother's feet near the peat fire that burned now, despite the May month. She laid her head on her mother's hand for an instant, feeling the slight tremble.

"Mammie, can Jamie's father not stay here the night, along with Jamie and myself? I'd wish dearly that we could all be under the same roof this once, to share the luxury of being all together again."

She glanced at Jamie as she spoke, her eyes mutely pleading with him to understand this need. Her world had changed, along with Charles Stuart's. His dream had ended, but theirs had barely begun. She could begin to pick up the threads of her life now as Mistress Mackinnon; but just for this one last night, she felt the need to be in her old home, under her parents' roof. He gave a small nod, understanding the need in her.

"It minds me of the night of Mistress Fraser's birthday," Jamie said, "when we were all together like this, and I'd wish us all to be as happy again."

"Then so we shall," Duncan declared. He shouted for whiskey to be brought, for food to be prepared. Eyeing his daughter, gone now to sit close by her husband, her hand in his, he covered his own emotion in tones as gruff as Callum Mackinnon's. " 'Tis time Katrina had proper food in her, by the looks of it. Have ye been starving her, laddie? 'Tis no way to start a marriage, by letting your lassie go to skin and bone. She needs fattening up!"

"Oh, Faither!" Katrina smiled through a mist of tears at his nonsense. He must know very well that their gauntness was due to the conditions they had endured the past weeks. Her own fine cheekbones were more sharply contoured, and the gown Katrina wore now—since they had arrived home they had discarded their rags for tidier clothes and washed the grime from their bodies—hung over her curves, where it had once fit snugly. Jamie showed the same evidence of hunger and fatigue, but none of it mattered. They were home and all together again. She swallowed back the tears that seemed to threaten so often now.

"Ye've all changed, too!" she went on with a little catch in her breath, seeing how the months of worry had bowed her father's shoulders a little and had cast a fine dusting of silver on her mother's brown hair. They had suffered in a different way.

"Nobody stays the same, lass," Duncan grunted. "We all move on. And now that ye've done your wandering, I daresay ye'll be moving into Mackinnon House as a good wife should!"

Mairi shook her head in slow disbelief. "I still canna think of Katrina as a wife."

"Well, ye had better think of it, Mammie!" Katrina said, her face turning a fiery red. "Because I've been Jamie's wife since before the turn of the year! Mammie . . . was it a terrible shock to ye to get my letter? And—and my Aunt Janet's, too?" She bit her lip, waiting for the expected censure and knowing she couldn't put off the moment of reckoning indefinitely.

"A shock—aye!" Mairi's eyes gleamed at the memory. "But we've had plenty time to get used to the idea. I know there's no sense in worrying old wounds, nor taking away the joy of your homecoming. You're safe now, and I thank God for it, and I'd rather see ye safe wi' Jamie than unhappy, lassie, even though ye did your mammie out of the wedding celebrations."

"We'll have them now!" Duncan declared expansively, seeing his wife's eyes grow a mite wistful. "We'll have singing and music, and plenty food and drink, and pretend that this is Jamie and Katrina's wedding night! And the two of ye will dance a wedding jig!"

Katrina looked at Jamie, then down at their swollen feet, where the blisters had rubbed the skin raw. They began to laugh, then Jamie held out his hand to her as Duncan reached for an old fiddle and played a madcap tune on it. Katrina rose painfully, and together they moved very slowly to the music. It was a mere shuffling acknowledgment to dancing, but to the watchers who clapped and cheered it was the sealing of the marriage.

Later, full of good home cooking and Duncan's best whiskey, they went to their bedroom, where clean nightclothes and a tub of warm water awaited them. Katrina had asked especially for this, for the need to feel clean and fresh after the nights of traveling and the days of sleeping in squalor had become almost an obsession with them both. They were almost too weary to bother, but somehow it helped to wash away the weight of anxiety and desperation that had accompanied them on their journey. Finally they tumbled into the cool sheets together, warmed by each other's arms, and knew no more until morning.

It seemed as if the gods smiled on them for the next few weeks. The sun continued to warm the glen, and their physical scars healed under Mairi's care. They stayed at Frashiel House another four days before going on to Jamie's home. By then they could walk without wincing; the hollows in Katrina's cheeks had begun to fill out, and the gaunt gray look in Jamie's face had lessened.

Katrina had started to show a feminine interest in clothes again, in all the things that had seemed of little importance compared with the greater need to survive. And despite the anxiety they still felt as to the fate of the prince, and the various tales they heard of his movements, Katrina felt the gladness of being alive.

News that the couple were home had spread farther afield, and neighbors had come to visit. It was Christmas and birthdays all rolled into one. Old Margret Blainey didn't come to Frashiel House, but it wasn't long before Katrina made the gentle walk from her new home with Jamie and his father to visit her old nurse.

It was then that her thoughts began to dwell more seriously on Charles Stuart again, and she realized that his image had never really been far from the surface of her mind after all. His cause had been too much a part of her life for her to be able to dismiss it so easily. The cause was past but not forgotten. She caught sight of old Margret's scarlet shawl in the distance. The old woman was returning to her cottage with armfuls of twigs for the fire to kindle the peat blocks, and Katrina called her name.

Margret turned, her parchment skin creasing in a wide smile as she saw her favorite lassie approaching her. The twigs were forgotten as she hugged Katrina to her bosom, though there was no great look of surprise on her face. Margret was ever the enigmatic one.

"Oh, Margret, 'tis so good to see ye!" Katrina cried joyfully. "Had ye heard that Jamie and me were home?"

"Aye, lassie, I'd heard," the old one said dryly. "But I dinna need the telling. I knew ye were coming, though 'twas a knowledge best kept to myself and my man. 'Tis foolish to raise hopes in such troubled times."

"But not so troubled now, Margret?" Katrina said, bending to gather the fallen twigs. "The Stuart is safely away and is mebbe on his way to France even now."

"Nay, lassie." Margret shook her head, her expression doleful. Katrina felt the old thrill of excitement that Margret used to instil in her. She caught at the old nurse's hand as they walked toward the cottage together.

"What do ye know, Margret? Is the prince near? Is he safe?"

"He's harbored in croft and castle, lassie, and will continue to be until he's safely away, and I can tell ye no more than that," she said in her mysterious way that said nothing and everything. "The English are fools if they think the passion the Stuart roused in the Highlands can be bought by the insult of a reward!"

They had reached the cottage and went inside. It was the same as Katrina remembered. There were the familiar smells of peat and wool spinning, and old Angus's clay pipe in its rack by the fireplace, the whiff of the evil-smelling stuff he smoked still clinging to it.

Margret threw her shawl on the back of a chair and bade Katrina sit down, saying she would make her some fresh barley water. Katrina seized the woman's hands.

"But is he *near*, Margret? The redcoats canna be far behind now. Jamie and me found it hard enough to reach home safely, and Jamie was more sure-footed about the lie of the land. But they'll come, Margret. They'll not give up, and ye must know it as well as me. They want Charles Stuart's blood." She shivered as she spoke. "He'll not stand a chance, one man against so many."

"Were ye not listening to me, lassie?" Margret chided her. "One man, do ye say? The Stuart still holds the heart of Scotland in the palm of his hand, and there's no true clansman who will betray him."

The words were said as a comfort, but it was no real answer. Katrina was still wracked with unease, as if she herself had the sight at that moment and the future stretched ahead into an endless void, filled with shadows.

" 'Tis not the same Scotland he came to less than a year ago, Margret. The people have changed. Mebbe not in their passions and fervor, but circumstances have changed them. We're used to looking over our shoulders and fearing shadows. Some of our rebels were so desperate for food at times they would have killed for it—and probably did."

Her eyes grew sad at the memory of the blackened wastes,

burnt bracken with its acrid stench, and the dead, shriveled heather, where once the mountainsides had been ablaze with glorious color. A tremor ran through her at the sheer destruction of the butcher Cumberland's vengeance.

"The grass will grow again, dearie." It seemed as if Margret could read her thoughts. "As long as there are brave hearts left in Scotland, she will never die. Ye have one of those brave hearts, lassie, and so does your man."

Katrina smiled wanly, and a sudden longing to be with Jamie overcame her at that moment. They had rarely been parted in the days since Culloden, and she was almost fearful to let him out of her sight now. It was something she had to conquer, and she knew it. One minute she was fearful, lost, uneasy . . . the next as stalwart as any rebel. She felt somehow off-balance, as if the whole purpose of her life, and Jamie's, was drifting aimlessly. The one certain truth was that Cumberland's army was marching over the Highlands toward them, combing the hills and glens, burning and plundering and slaughtering.

By the time she left Margret's cottage the chill of her own thoughts was unsettling her again. She and Jamie had glimpsed the redcoats on too many occasions to forget them easily, and she froze inside at the very thought of them coming here to their glen, their peaceful and beautiful glen. It was a nightmare that she dreaded, but she knew that they would come.

Established now in Mackinnon House, Katrina and Jamie tried to live as normal a life as possible, as though their lives had been unaltered by a fair-haired young man of noble blood, as though marriage between two who had been betrothed since childhood was the ultimate end to a fairy-tale beginning.

But life rarely followed the pattern of fairy tales, as Katrina knew only too well. Added to the brief calm following their arrival home were too many hasty meetings in the house and too many whispers in corridors. Anxiety showed in their faces as they scanned the landscape for the telltale red uniform of the English soldiers. There was an unending feeling of expectation, of dread.

Angus Blainey appeared at Mackinnon House very early

one morning, wheezing with the exertion and leaning heavily on his shepherd's crook.

"Come inside man, before ye expire," Jamie said as soon as he saw him, noting the old man's florid color. "Ye'll take a dram before ye tell me the news."

Katrina felt her heart leap. It was not what Jamie said but the inflection in his voice that told her he had been waiting for news. She sensed it instantly, and as Callum Mackinnon came limping heavily to join them, she knew something of importance was to be told. Angus drank deeply of the whiskey Jamie gave him, and it was obvious that the two Mackinnon men were taut with expectation.

"Now then, Angus, out wi' it," Callum growled at once. "Do ye have the news we've waited to hear?"

"Aye." The old man nodded. "Ye'll know of the caves at Loch nan Uamh. The treasure trove is there and will remain so awhile before being removed to the isle of Skye as soon as possible."

Katrina looked from one to another of the grim-faced men. What childish nonsense was this! Why did they not speak the prince's name! They were all friends here, and she did not need to be clairvoyant to know that the treasure trove was Charles Edward Stuart!

She felt a stab of pity for the young prince, hunted down like a stag, wandering on foot in this harsh, bleak country— the land that had welcomed him as its hero and in which his cause had ended so ignobly. She heard Jamie say that he would leave for the caves at once, and a wave of anxiety swept over her. Of course he must go . . . but it didn't alter her fear.

"Ye'll do well to go wi' caution, Jamie, and stay hidden when ye can," Angus went on. "I doubt there'll be any movement for some days before the move to Skye. Food and clothing have been taken care of for the time being, I'm told. A chain of helpers has seen to it, but there have been reports that the redcoats are very near. Ye'll know that, o' course. And I've seen evidence o' their camps from my sheep watches—aye, and already lost a few sheep to them, which I'll be accounting to ye for in a wee while."

" 'Tis no fault of yours, Angus, and none will blame ye for it," Callum said. "But ye should know that Jamie will'na hide away from the English."

"Why should he not? If the bonnie prince hides himself away, then why not all of us?" Katrina was stung to say. She saw Callum's words as a reproof of his son. She knew now what she had been surmising for days—that news of the prince and of the redcoats' movements were known to some, if not to all. Jamie had known, by the sound of it, and had refrained from telling her. And after all they had shared together, been through together, Katrina felt slighted at the knowledge.

Jamie's hand closed over hers. "Hush now, lassie, and leave men's talk to the men," he said, and by the roughness of his voice she guessed that he knew very well how she was feeling.

"My thanks to ye, Angus," he went on, "for bringing me the news. Ye're well enough to go back to your work?"

Angus shrugged. "When 'tis my time to drop, I'd as soon drop beside my sheep or my good woman as anywhere," he said. His old face crinkled into a broad smile. "Dinna fret about us old 'uns, maister. Yon Margret can give as good as she gets. She's already had a few verbals wi' the redcoats on her wanderings and treated them to a taste o' her tongue. Seems they thought her a mite frivolous in her scarlet shawl."

"Oh, Margret must be careful," Katrina gasped. "They'd as soon run her through."

"Naw, lassie." Angus shook his head. "They keep well clear of her now, since she started on wi' her long screechings. They take her for a wild one and won't take the risk o' stirring up a spell on themselves!"

He went out, cackling in his throat at the thought of it, but his blathering was soon forgotten as Jamie faced his father and began discussing the situation.

"I'll not leave in the daylight," he decided. "I'm well used to being the night owl now, and if the redcoats are near, ye'll need my protection."

"What of our protection after ye've gone?" Katrina found herself saying. "Will it be for an hour or a day, or are we never to see ye again! I canna bear the uncertainty, Jamie. I thought we were safe now. I canna bear it.''

To her own horror, her shoulders began to shake, and Jamie took her in his arms. She seemed to be mumbling incoherently against his chest and realized sharply that she had been living on a knife edge ever since they'd returned home—wondering where Charles Stuart was hidden . . . eyes ever-watchful for the first sign of the English soldiers . . . never knowing if they were the next ones to be murdered in their beds or to smell the burning if the soldiers took it on themselves to raze Mackinnon House to the ground. It was a nightmare that went on and on.

A glass was pushed to her cold lips, and she tasted the fiery liquid and involuntarily swallowed the whiskey. Swift shame at her loss of control made her hide her heated face against Jamie's shoulder a moment longer. Then he tipped up her chin with his finger, forcing her to meet his eyes. He looked down at her, understanding and not condemning.

"Ye'll bear it, Katrina, as we all have to bear it," he said quietly. "A Mackinnon bears all disaster with dignity."

She gave a small nod, trying to hide the trembling of her lips. "And so I shall," she promised him in a whisper, and he never knew what it cost her to say so.

She was not meant to be strong like a man was strong! She had imagined a golden future, living and loving, and bearing Jamie's children, wee bairns to be dandled on their grand-parents' knees. Simple lives, uncomplicated by the passion of a prince from over the water come to claim his homeland, or by the brutal fury of an English army.

Even as the thoughts sped through her mind, Katrina knew that if her strength was not physical, then she, too, must use that inner strength, the need to survive. A crooked smile touched her mouth as she realized she was already thinking of those unborn children as flesh and blood, part of her and Jamie, though they only lived in her dreams as yet. Thoughts of their future stabilized her fluctuating emotions, and she reassured Jamie that she was not going to crumble.

" 'Tis odd to think how we welcomed the bonnie prince and rallied to his cause," she said painfully. "And now we do everything we can to get him safely away from Scottish shores."

Jamie folded her to his chest, knowing that with her words she gave him her blessing to go to the Stuart's side whenever the need came.

But it was decided he need not go yet. The prince was safely hidden in the caves, and it was thought that Jamie's presence might be of better use at Mackinnon House if the soldiers came searching. By now they had already visited Katrina's old home, such a little distance away, and it seemed that they played a cat and mouse game among the clansmen and neighbors—watching and waiting for any false moves.

Katrina awoke in the predawn gloom a few mornings later. The sounds of her own heartbeats were loud in her ears, as though she had awakened from a bad dream, yet she could remember nothing. She reached out a hand to touch Jamie, needing his reassuring presence, and encountered nothing.

She told herself that he was probably wandering the house in the darkness, as he was apt to do these days when he was unable to sleep. But the fear in her gut wouldn't go away, and she reached for the candle at the side of the bed. When it was lit she saw the note with her name upon it. Quickly, she pulled a bed wrap around her shoulders to keep out the early morning chill and opened the piece of paper.

"Forgive me, dearest," Jamie had written. "I thought it best to leave you while you were still sleeping. I have to go to the place where the treasure trove is hidden. You understand me, Katrina. I pray for the prince's safety, and for yours, my dear one, while I am away. Say nothing, admit nothing. Act the simpleton if need be, while always keeping your wits about you. My love will be your talisman, as yours is mine. Keep safe for me. Jamie."

Katrina felt tears sting her eyes as she finished reading. Jamie was gone, away at the caves or on his way there, ever alert for the redcoats, scrambling over hill and glen in the darkness until he reached the caves and found where the prince was sheltering.

As children, she and Jamie had played among the caves of the Loch. What Jamie was doing now was far more dangerous than a childish game. The sobs stuck in her throat until it ached unbearably.

Finding it impossible to sleep, Katrina slid out of bed. A pearly gray light was turning the sky to silvery pink above the distant mountains as she drew back the curtains. In a little while the mountains would be bathed in glory as the dawn sun rose in the east. And where would Jamie be by then? What did he hope to achieve—he and the others who were gone to be at the prince's side? To protect him if danger threatened? To be ready to ferry him from the loch to where it joined the open sea, to where, hopefully, a French ship would be waiting for him?

To get him away from the mainland to yet more hiding, as had been suggested, over the sea to Skye, to the islands beyond. And still more living the life of a fugitive instead of a prince of noble blood. . . . The swirling thoughts were suddenly clamped shut in her mind, and her heart leapt dizzily in her breast.

There were stealthy movements among the grasses in the glen some distance from the house. A glimpse of red here and there was just visible if Katrina strained her eyes hard. Or was it just a trick of the dawn light? Was she imagining it all, so tense with anxiety that she thought she saw a redcoat behind every clump of bracken, every tree stump? Her heart beat uneasily, pounding so hard she thought she would faint. It was so hard to tell if her eyes were playing tricks on her.

Suddenly she flew back into the room, a gasp of real fear escaping her lips and dilating her eyes. She had been so intent on looking into the distance, her face pressed close to the window glass, that she had missed what was right beneath her nose. And now she knew that it was not her imagination.

The distant redcoats labored steadily onward in their route to Mackinnon House, but others were already here. Even as Katrina leapt back from the window, the eyes of an English soldier, unkempt and filthy, leered up at her from the ground below. Even from here, in the early daylight, she could see the sudden flare of interest in the man's face. She could see the way he nudged the man next to him and muttered something in quick heavy undertones. She felt a new and different fear.

Even before she heard the heavy front door of the house kicked open, Katrina's mind was winging frantically ahead. The Mackinnon servants were few and feeble. Callum would defend her to the death if need be . . . but he slept in the back part of the house and slept heavily of late, taking sleeping draughts to ease the gnawing pain of his leg. She was virtually alone.

But not only that! As Katrina's heart drummed wildly, she realized that she still clutched the note Jamie had left her. If the redcoats caught sight of it, Charles Stuart's chance of escape would be gone forever. His hiding place would be known, and the caves would be swarming with English redcoats, every one of them greedy for the price on the prince's head. They would show no mercy . . . and Jamie was there with the prince.

Katrina looked desperately around the room, wishing she could spirit herself away before the redcoats reached her. She was numb with dread. She had no need of guesswork. Rape, murder, the burning of one more house. . . . Yet all of these were of minimal importance to her scattered senses. The vital thing was to destroy the note—and quickly. But where?

The stumbling footsteps were already storming through the house. It would be but moments before they reached her room. They would take her as one more prize for England and be rewarded by the greater prize of Charles Stuart's whereabouts. She was almost frantic.

They were outside on the stairs. The candle was on the other side of the room—and even if she tried to burn the note, it wouldn't burn in time. They would know it was of importance. They would retrieve it, and they would know. She was terrified. She seemed unable to move.

"Find the wench, me boys! There's a fine bit o' rumping for the lot of us. Age before stamina, buckos, though I wager I'll give her a piece to remember."

If she hid the note in the bedclothes, they would find it. She had heard tales of wild orgies where beds were overturned and women were left raw and bleeding.

"Kick the door in! Find the beauty!" The gutteral voices turned her bones to ice, and then a sudden deafening pistol shot somewhere in the house seemed to bring her out of her temporary frozen state. She jumped violently, her body shaking from head to foot, and then she did the only thing possible with Jamie's note. She stuffed it in her mouth and began chewing as fast as she could, choking and gagging on the thick paper and feeling the blood rush to her face as she tried not to vomit. Her eyes streamed. Her skin was clammy.

The door burst open, and it seemed as if a sea of leering faces hovered there before they came into the room and separated into half a dozen gaunt and stinking soldiers who had clearly been tramping the countryside for a long while and were ready for a different kind of sport. She shrank back, her hands still covering her mouth as she tried to force the paper down her throat. She saw the men glance uncertainly at each other for a second or two.

"Not such a pretty sight as it looked from below, mebbe," one grunted in disappointment. "But 'twill do. Any rough piece o' meat tastes like honey to a starving man."

"Put a pillow over her head, and you'll not see the fever face," another sniggered. "Let's get her, boys. Strip the wench and spread her."

"Keep back!" The words were torn from Katrina's throat in a hoarse gasping voice. At the redcoat's words, sudden inspiration came to her, and she clutched at her body, hardly needing to make it shake more than it already did but exaggerating the spasms as much as she could. Her eyes still streamed, and perspiration made her hair cling damply to her forehead. And at her jerking movements, the soldiers paused. In those moments, Katrina acted as she had never acted before.

"Cholera," she gasped out. "Right through the house! If ye want to take it with ye, then ye're welcome to share my bed, my brave ones, but ye'll not like the pain of it, I promise ye. It tears your guts wi' a fire that burns like a furnace! Come to me, then, if ye've the stomach to be the first."

As she spoke she gagged on the shreds of paper, retching violently. Fragments of the sodden stuff oozed from her mouth with her spittle, and the sight of it was enough for the redcoats. They were as ignorant of the symptoms of cholera as Katrina herself, but seeing such a madwoman, apparently in the throes of convulsions, was enough.

"You filthy bitch!" the spokesman shouted, backing against

the other redcoats as Katrina stumbled toward them. Had they but known it, she was so near to fainting she could hardly stand, but to them she seemed a demented, disease-ridden hag.

If Katrina had felt like it, she would have laughed out loud at their frantic scramble to get out of her room and out of the house. But she felt further from laughing than anything else. She felt drained of all feeling, scarcely able to believe that she had been successful in getting rid of Jamie's note, and the redcoats at the same time. She swayed on her feet, almost delirious with relief.

But there was still danger. They might well burn the house. Katrina's heart leapt with new fear. She could hear them barging about below, arguing loudly among themselves.

''Move, me boys, and let's be away from here.''

Katrina heard the shouts of assent, and minutes later the sounds were receding and the house fell silent again. Except for one sound—sobbing. Deep, racking sobs that she suddenly realized were coming from her own throat, releasing her from the terrible tension of the ordeal.

She was alone, and never had she felt it more. Callum must have been oblivious to all that had gone on that morning, or he would surely have come storming about to see what was happening. The servants were probably cowering somewhere, and she couldn't blame them for that. Who would not cower to save their own skins when the redcoats came?

Katrina stood in the middle of the room, limp, not knowing what to do. Her mind wouldn't work. There *was* something she had to do, something with a desperate urgency, but the thought of it wouldn't penetrate her senses. Her body felt boneless, her mind frozen.

A faint sound outside her door tightened every nerve in Katrina's body in a second. She breathed harsh, despairing sobs. One of the soldiers had come back after all, braver than the others. It was all useless, useless. . . . The door opened a fraction, and the pallid face of old Robert, Callum's manservant, peered in at her. His voice was a hoarse rasp of fear when he spoke.

''Are ye unharmed, mistress? If they've harmed ye, Maister

Jamie will have my hide. They were everywhere, mistress. I could'na get to ye.''

Jamie! Jamie, and the prince! They must be warned. She must warn them now, at once. Mentally, Katrina moved like the wind, as if her feet already flew across the wild landscape. Physically, her feet remained wooden, refusing to react to her needs.

Old Robert's face seemed to loom back and forth, bobbing like a candlelight in front of her, dazzling her. She was forced to close her eyes, and as she did so she lost all sense of balance. She was falling, falling, into a deep velvet blackness. . . .

CHAPTER 19

Katrina *tasted the whiskey on her lips as Robert tried to* make her drink. Seeing the old man's distraught face, she realized that her ruse had been convincing enough to fool Robert as well as the redcoats. She took deep breaths, struggling to speak as calmly as she could, though her words sounded labored to her own ears.

"Dinna fear for me, Robert. 'Tis not the cholera or any other ailment. 'Twas all part of a plan, but God willing, it succeeded. This house will'na be bothered by the pigs again.''

Katrina pulled her bedwrap more closely around her shoulders and tried to subdue the panic that threatened once more. She spoke in a high, urgent voice.

"Listen to me, Robert. Jamie has left this house to be with friends. Ye know well who I mean. They must be warned.''

"At once, mistress,'' he said stoutly, misinterpreting her meaning. Katrina's eyes misted a little. She wondered if Charles Stuart himself knew what loyalty he commanded even now when all seemed lost.

"Not you, Robert," Katrina said at once. "But ye will tell Mr. Mackinnon all that's happened when he wakes, and that I will return here when I can. I have another plan."

It was as though something was telling her exactly what she must do, as if all the pieces of a puzzle were slipping into place in her mind. She had to reach the caves where Jamie and Charles and the rest of the group were hidden, and she dare not risk being seen.

If the redcoats saw her, she would be fair game for their wenching, but there was far more at stake than her own safety. If the same redcoats who had come to the house saw her, they would know at once that she had deceived them. Instead of warning Charles, her movements might very well lead the enemy straight to him. She could not wander about freely . . . but old Margret could.

She kept her plan to herself. If Robert were unaware of it, there would be less danger of him unintentionally betraying it if the soldiers came back. And neither would he be able to dissuade her if he was unaware of her intentions.

"Go about your business in the house as usual, Robert," Katrina told him. "But stay inside the house, and tell Jamie's father to do likewise. They'll not expect to see people wandering about if we're supposed to be struck down with the cholera. But first prepare some food for me to carry." It was very likely that the group would be glad of any extra food she could bring to them, Katrina thought. The task also gave Robert something to do and would stop his mithering about the folly of a young woman taking on such a dangerous mission.

The danger of it was furthest from Katrina's mind. It was a job that had to be done, and she was the only one who could do it. But she was thankful that Callum would be sleeping for a while yet. She doubted that he would make any objections, but the less talking and the more action now the better.

By the time she had dressed in a sober-colored dress and shawl, Robert had brought the parcel of food to her. She knew she must move cautiously, careful to keep the old shawl over the brightness of her hair. There was always a chance that she could reach the caves like this, but there was a better way.

By now the redcoats were quite used to seeing old Margret wandering the hills in her distinctive scarlet shawl, gathering the gift fleece and the berries. She remembered how Margret had told her of the times she had waved her arms at the soldiers when they'd taunted her, and how some of them had turned pale when she'd gabbled on. They most likely thought she was a witch . . . or at the very least, an eccentric old crone. Whatever the reason, they didn't bother her now, as if word had spread quickly among them that she was either harmless or a dangerous old biddy who could do them evil with her chantings. And Angus had thought it comical that the redcoats preferred to keep clear of his Margret than risk finding the truth of it.

The plan had come swiftly to Katrina's mind: She would go to Margret's cottage and beg the use of her scarlet shawl. She would adopt the old woman's stooping gait and make her way down to the caves alongside the loch. Margret would not fail her, she was sure.

The hardest part was reaching Margret's cottage. It was not so far from Mackinnon House, but the route was fraught with dangers. Time and again, Katrina dropped soundlessly to the ground, heart beating painfully fast as distant shouting and occasional gunfire sent the sweat prickling over her skin. The faint crackle and smell of fire was wafted on the air, the way it always seemed to be these days. She crawled the last yards to Margret's cottage and ached with the raw fear of being seen.

She burst through the cottage door without warning and was rewarded by seeing old Angus scramble to reach for the gun he had hidden in his roof thatch. It was doubtful that the old man would ever be quicker than a redcoat's aim if the need arose, but like them all he would defend his own to the death.

"Miss Katrina, what are ye about?" Margret gasped, clutching the old man's arm to stop his wild searchings. "Has aught happened at the house or to your own dear ones? Och, tell me 'tis not so, but I see that something's amiss."

"No, Margret, no one is hurt, though the redcoats have been to Mackinnon House, but 'tis not that that I'm here about. I need to beg a favor of ye—to help . . . a certain person.''

Was she as mad as the rest of them to speak of him in guarded language like this? Angry at herself, yet unable to do otherwise, Katrina licked her dry lips. It was as if the very mention of Charles Stuart's name were going to bring the enemy running.

"Ask away,'' Margret said at once.

"I've knowledge of his whereabouts, as Angus knows full well. But he needs to be warned that the redcoats are so near. They—they—''

"Did they touch ye, lassie?'' Angus said fiercely. "If they did . . .''

She shook her head quickly. Why did they bother with such trivial questions when the greater need of getting Charles Stuart to safety was of far more importance?

"I made them think we had the cholera there,'' she said rapidly. "They'll not bother us again. But Margret, they must not see me outside the house when I'm meant to have a fever. I mean to go to the caves to warn them there. Would ye give me the use of your scarlet shawl to cover my head and shoulders? If they think 'tis yourself wandering the hills, they'll not bother me.''

"Take it and welcome, if ye think 'twill work. But take care, my lamb. There's some that think it fine sport to bait an old woman. If any approach ye, wave your hands about ye like a mad thing.''

"I'll remember, Margret.''

She removed her own shawl and replaced it with the one Margret handed her, shaking a little as she adjusted it to cover most of her slight body. The shawl was thick and warm, and inside it Katrina was in a bath of clammy perspiration. It didn't matter. Nothing mattered but reaching Jamie and the prince before the redcoats did.

She pressed the two pairs of gnarled hands tightly as Margret and Angus wished her God speed, and then she slipped out of the cottage. There was no time to think or fear, no time for anything but to reach the caves.

But she must go slowly, Katrina reminded herself. She was now Margret, hobbling among the bushes and the bracken. At the last moment, Margret had thrust her old canvas bag at her, which Katrina used now as she remembered to snatch at the gift fleece from time to time, in case any soldiers were watching.

She stuffed the coarse bits of sheep wool in the canvas bag the way Margret did, she picked berries, and she paused now and then to rest, rocking slightly back and forth the way Margret did. She never saw anyone on what seemed a painfully slow walk toward the loch, yet she could not rid herself of the feeling that there were eyes everywhere, watching, waiting.

If she lost concentration for a moment, if she straightened or moved with the lithe easy grace of a young woman, she might be pounced upon. It unnerved her far more than if she had seen soldiers in the distance.

At last, at last, she reached the slopes leading down to the caves, and her heart was almost bursting with thankfulness to know she had arrived safely. But she still felt far from safe, even though this place was known to her while the enemy wouldn't know of its hidden caverns.

She and Jamie both knew this loch. It was long and deep and led out to the open sea. Along its shores of gritty sandlike substance the caves were a wonderland of hiding places. As children she and Jamie had come here often, inventing weird and magical tales of what might lie within the mysterious caves. It had been exciting then to run in and out of the mist-laden entrances, where it was always shadowed and damp, and smelled of dead vegetation no matter how bright the sunlight outside.

It was no less unnerving to Katrina now. Her mouth was as dry as it had ever been on those long-ago days when coming here to the loch had been part of the games they had played. But this was no game, and her heart beat with a sickening fear as she slithered down the grassy slopes to reach the ground below.

Her boots crunched on the stony surface, and each step she took seemed to sound like thunder in her ears. She had that eerie feeling again that eyes were watching her. She longed to call Jamie's name, to tell him she was near, to warn him, but she did not dare. She might have been followed out of sheer curiosity by curious redcoats wondering why the old woman strayed so far from home. She must continue to playact for the present, until she found the cave.

Katrina's hands were clammy as she clutched the scarlet shawl around her more closely. The loch stretched away in either direction, the waters still wraithlike with the morning mist that hadn't yet cleared. She had no way of knowing which of the many caves here hid Charles Stuart. There were no guards in evidence, nor had she expected there to be.

She chose the direction to the right. If it was the wrong way and she found nothing, she would simply have to turn back and begin all over again. She moved slowly, in Margret's heavy gait, bending now and then to pick up a pebble or a few roots, as if searching for treasures or for something edible for her table.

She edged gradually nearer to the cave entrances, though her eyes were unable to penetrate their dark interiors. There was a strange silence here, yet it was a silence filled with the sound of her own breathing, her footsteps, the drumming of her heart; the scuttling of loch-side rodents, and the scream of seabirds overhead.

Her progress along the loch side was painfully slow, as if her feet were weighted with lead. She couldn't have run now if she tried.

Suddenly, Katrina stifled a cry as a figure appeared from the shadow of the caves. She was terror-stricken for a moment, wondering if she had conjured him up out of her own imagination. The man was unkempt, his beard straggly, his garments unclean as though they had been slept in. Like those remnants of Charles Stuart's army in the desperate hours of retreat at Ruthven barracks. But before she could pursue her milling thoughts, the man's hand had clamped over her arm.

"What's your business here, lassie?" He spoke harshly. "I've been observing ye a while, and ye had best have a good reason for acting the ancient one when 'tis clear from your face that ye're but a bairn and a weed picker."

A fragment of the fear receded from Katrina's mind. This was a highlander, not a redcoat. And what was *he* doing in this place unless he was on the Stuart's business?

She was no bairn, nor a weed picker! Her chin lifted with

some of her old arrogance, and her shoulders straightened. The shawl slipped from her hair a little, and the man was under no illusion as to her age and beauty now. But Katrina cared nothing for the flicker of admiration he couldn't quite conceal. It barely tempered his suspicions of her, anyway.

"My business is with a certain person I believe to be in these caves," she said as calmly as she could, considering how she shook inside with the sustained ordeal of reaching the caves. "And as ye so rightly say, I am not the ancient one, but the wife of Jamie Mackinnon."

"Mackinnon, ye say!" His eyes narrowed.

"And the daughter of Duncan Fraser of Frashiel House," Katrina went on. "And if ye don't wish it to be thought odd for us two to be standing here blathering the day, will ye please take me to the place I seek? Other eyes may be watching us."

She felt an odd light-headedness as she spoke in the guarded manner. She had thought it nonsense to be so cautious of using the prince's name, yet here she was using the same ambiguous terms at the first meeting with a stranger! She felt the man's grip on her wrist lessen a little as he gave a short nod, apparently satisfied of her identity.

"Ye'll understand the need for caution. I've observed ye for a while and from a distance your bright shawl made me wary. 'Tis the redcoats' color, but I've no' seen the redcoat yet who favors lassies' skirts to white trews! Ye'll follow me, mistress."

She presumed now that the man had been on watch, so the cave she sought must be near. Some of them were obvious, no more than gaping, shallow indentations in the rock. Others were more cunningly concealed, their entrances a narrow, grass-covered slit, through which the twisting tunnels led to a larger cavern beneath the hillside.

The clansman looked keenly about the loch and the area for an instant, then pulled her behind him. What had seemed to Katrina no more than a steep grassy bank was now revealed as one of those concealed entrances. She squeezed through after the man and felt the brief panic of claustrophobia as the darkness enveloped her and the dank coldness of the hard-packed rocky earth pressed on either side of her body.

"Stay close, mistress. 'Tis but a short squeeze like this, and then 'tis easier."

Katrina prayed that it was. She could hardly breathe, and how the bulkier forms of the clansmen had gotten through here, she couldn't think. Unless desperation gave them a strength and determination they didn't know they possessed. She knew that was possible. She knew it only too well.

To her relief the man was right about the short squeeze. The passage opened out quickly, but it still took some minutes to reach the inner chamber where a dozen or so men sat or sprawled, intent on the maps they studied by the light of candles. The air was foul, almost fetid, with just enough from the cave entrance to keep them all from suffocating, though much of the air was used up by their very breathing and by the candlelight.

Katrina felt her head spin like a top. She willed herself not to act the softie now, when she had come so far. If ever there was a time when she must not resort to women's tears, it was now when she had a purpose, a mission.

She hardly registered the fact that Jamie was among the group of clansmen with the prince, except to throw him a quick glance of recognition. Her purpose now was to warn the prince that he must get away from this place and from the mainland *now*. He rose to his feet at her approach with the clansman, and she tried to smother her momentary shock at his appearance.

He was still regal, even in the humbler garments he wore now, a sharp contrast to the silks and velvets of Glenfinnan, but he was thinner and his face was gaunt with fatigue. Yet he retained a dignity that touched her. In this appalling cave, he was still their prince. There was an aura about him that the past months hadn't dimmed, that could make his fervent followers still scorn the reward offered for his head.

Yet in that instant when Katrina's eyes became accustomed to the scene inside the cave, she also noted that none of the clansmen wore the kilt. The English victors had already proved their dominance. None dared flout Cumberland's orders after seeing the consequences to their neighbors, but the resentment of the outrage to their own identity still festered and burned.

271

Among all the faces turned to her, Katrina saw one face only, it was to him that her words were spoken.

"Sir, I come with a warning that the redcoats are near and will be coming this way. They have reached our glen, and I beg ye to take heed of my words. 'Tis urgent that ye get away as quickly as possible."

She felt the prince take hold of her shoulders as her voice grew shrill and knew that she was babbling like a burn in the glen. She bit her trembling lips, not wanting to appear a gibbering idiot in front of him.

"Calm yourself, Katrina. Breathe deeply for a moment." He spoke quickly, too, and with authority, although his voice was laced with kindness. But how could she breathe deeply in an atmosphere such as this!

"Sir, the soldiers were at Mackinnon House early this morning," she went on more slowly. "There were more than I could count. I saw them in the distance, like a red tide on a beach. And there were some that came right to the house."

Now she could not be unaware of Jamie as he gave an expressive oath and leapt to his feet to seize her cold hands a moment, unable to restrain himself.

"Did they touch ye, Katrina? Or my faither? Was anyone hurt? Tell me at once, lassie."

She shook her head quickly, her wild hair flying about her face and shoulders. She turned to her husband briefly.

"None of us was hurt. Your faither slept through it all wi' his sleeping draught and knew nothing until Robert informed him after they had gone."

She turned again to the prince.

"I was away from the house before Jamie's faither was roused, sir. It seemed the only way I could warn ye quickly, to borrow the old woman's shawl and do the playacting."

Her voice cracked a little. To her own ears it sounded as brittle as splintered glass. Now that she was here, involved at last in Charles Stuart's cause, her plan seemed threadbare. It could have come to disaster at any moment if a stray redcoat had been curious enough to follow the scarlet-clad woman to the loch. Her wits seemed in danger of deserting her, and her brain seemed made of a substance resembling the gift fleece in Margret's canvas bag.

"Sit beside me, Katrina," the prince ordered, as though he could sense how distracted she felt. He drew her down to sit beside him on one of the rocks strewn about the cave. "Now tell us as clearly as you can. How long ago did the soldiers come to Mackinnon House?"

She thought quickly. Hours or days? It seemed like a lifetime ago. She fought to remember.

"Just at daylight, sir, because I could just make out their red uniforms like a haze in the distance at first." She subdued a shudder at the memory. "I did'na see the ones right below the house at first, and when I did so I was feared that they would see the note Jamie had left for me and would know he had gone to ye. They would know ye were near."

"And did they find it?" Charles spoke urgently, but he was calmer than she, and Katrina shook her head vigorously.

"No, sir! They found their way to my bedroom, but by then they found a demented lassie, gagging and choking as if from a fever as I stuffed the note in my mouth and tried to swallow it down. I dared them to come near a woman wi' the cholera."

"Cholera!" One of the clansmen leapt to his feet. "Ye're no' telling us, mistress—"

"You can see that she's not!" Charles rounded on him impatiently. "She's telling you of her quick thinking, man, if you'll but listen. Mistress Mackinnon does not have the cholera, but she does have all my admiration! I would reward you handsomely for it, mistress, if it were possible."

"I dinna want rewards, only your safety, sir!" She felt suddenly awkward, her face reddening.

"You acted with great courage and ingenuity, Katrina," Charles went on. "But what of the consequences? The house was not damaged?"

Her heart still beat in painful stabs against her ribs at the memory. "They laughed and taunted, thinking it would be better to leave us all to a slow death rather than hastening our death by burning us."

"Thank God the ruse worked," Jamie said, close to her now. She felt his anxiety and his pride in her. She had saved his home and her honor, yet all of that seemed of less importance to Katrina now than saving the prince. He needed to know every detail, and she still had his rapt attention as he bade her go on with the story.

"When the soldiers went back to join the others, I managed to reach my old nurse's cottage and borrow her scarlet shawl. The soldiers leave her alone while she gathers the gift fleece. They think her a harmless biddy, or else a witch. Either way they leave her alone to pick the fleece that she spins for herself and her man."

She stopped, suddenly embarrassed at speaking of such homely and menial tasks to a prince.

"So you hid yourself beneath the scarlet homespun to reach us here," Charles finished for her. He glanced at Jamie. "You've a wife to be proud of, man, and now we must think what's to do."

At Charles's bidding, someone gave Katrina a dram of whiskey from a leather flask. She drank quickly, feeling the fiery liquid spin her head again, and she looked down at her trembling hands as the men's talk flowed around her. It had been more of an ordeal than she had expected, but she would do it again if she had to. Almost at the same instant that she knew she had fulfilled some inner need to aid the cause, she realized that she was weak with hunger. She had eaten nothing since last night, and there was still the journey back home. A fine thing it would be if she fainted on the way back. She had not thought of going back, and her thoughts veered away from it now. As the talk waned a little, she foraged in the bottom of the canvas bag.

"I brought some food wi' me, sir. 'Tis little enough, but 'tis fresh-baked pies and bread and good crowdie cheese."

"Then we'll eat it, and you eat, too, mistress, or you will collapse before giving us more of your useful information," the prince said at once.

More? She thought she had said all there was to say, but for the moment she must sink her teeth into one of the pies and try not to appear too ravenous. The men ate and drank, too. There were supplies already there. It was clear that here, at least, Charles Stuart did not go hungry. There was no respite in the questioning while they ate. But before eating, Charles turned to her. He held a drinking vessel in his hand.

"I drink to you, Mistress Mackinnon, my loyal scarlet rebel! And I'd ask all here to do the same."

Katrina flushed with pleasure now as the rough-hewn men did as they were bid, including her Jamie. It was but a small moment of pageantry, so grand a name in the dark confines of the cave, yet nonetheless poignant to her. But the moment was brief and quickly passed for more important matters.

"So, Katrina," Charles said keenly. "The English soldiers are in the area, and they are apparently increasing in numbers. They have obviously deduced my movements. Summer will have lessened their hatred of our wild Highland country, and also lessened our chances of staying undetected. Do you have exact knowledge of their direction?"

She looked at him dumbly. No, she had no real knowledge! Her flight had been an instinctive one, with no proper information behind it. After all the prince's praise, he was going to realize it at once. He prompted her as if he guessed at her feelings.

"Think carefully, Katrina. Some of the greatest military strategy was planned from snippets of news. You'll know which way the redcoats came from. You'll know the lie of the land around Mackinnon House and these caves. Was it a direct way for you to get here, and would they be able to follow it as directly? Or did you take a devious route?"

His questioning clarified her thinking. It seemed little enough that she could tell him, but she pieced the story together, surer of herself now.

"I've told ye of their numbers, sir, and my mammie says they have already visited my old home once or twice, so to reach Mackinnon House they must be coming this way, toward the coast. As to my route, sir, 'tis not an easy landscape, but I took the quicker route over the mountain, because I know of it. The redcoats wouldn't—"

"Were they on horseback? How did they travel?" Charles was clearly used to extracting the information he needed with well-used expertise.

"I did'na see any horses, but those away from the house may have had some. I'm sorry."

"There's no need." Charles smiled for the first time. "You've done well, Katrina."

275

"I'm alarmed at the news of a great body o' men near Jamie's house, sir," one of the clansmen said roughly. "Ye must get to the islands quickly. There are many friends to hide ye there, and the redcoats will be mazed by the number of islands."

"And although these caves are fairly safe now," another put in, "if the redcoats made a real search along this loch and discovered them, we'd be trapped like rats in a hole."

"Then our next plan must be put into operation quickly," Charles said, his face grim once more.

"Would ye leave soon, sir?" Katrina asked him, as if she expected the redcoats to storm into the cave at any moment. He gave a short laugh.

"I wish it were so simple, but my good friends assure me it would be madness to risk it in daylight. We await the darkness, and for some bad weather to hide my departure. I'm assured it will not take long."

"Aye," growled a clansman. "A good blustery night, and then the services of our loyal fishermen will be put to better use than carrying a cargo o' fish!"

Katrina heard the frustration in his voice at the enforced waiting. The urgency was all around them, tangible in the pungent air, but they could not act yet. The daylight was too risky. They must wait . . . wait . . . and the longer they waited, the nearer the redcoats came.

"I'll pray for your safety, sir," she said quietly. "And once safely among the islands—what then?"

She wished she could take back the question at the wave of sadness that crossed the prince's handsome face.

"A return to France would seem the only course open to a prince without a kingdom, mistress! A ship will come for me. I have every faith in my French supporters."

Katrina sensed the glances between the clansmen then and knew that the prince had more faith in the French than they had. But they were too canny to say so as they prepared to wait out the day. Charles Stuart was still their prince, and therefore a man to be respected. He was also a man apart. Katrina realized, as she had done once before, what a lonely figure he seemed.

With his fair good looks and the ability to fire a country

with his own enthusiasm, he was still very much alone. How comforted Charles might have been to put aside his princely heritage for a while, Katrina thought briefly. To be as other men, and to weep on the shoulder of a woman, as Jamie had once wept unknowingly on hers.

CHAPTER 20

There was no thought of Katrina leaving the cave that day. It would be too dangerous if the English soldiers had begun to find the route to the loch and were combing the hills nearby.

"My guess is that they'll search farms and cottages first," Charles commented dryly. "They'll expect me to want the comforts of life."

"Aye, and enjoy the plundering and seeing the poor folk cower," Jamie couldn't resist adding, with the threat to his own family so acute in his mind.

As it wore on, the frustration of the day began to affect all of them. That and the growing fear of being discovered. This cave was better hidden than most, and there was always a guard at the entrance, each of them taking turns to keep watch; but the danger was ever there. Other Highlanders came and went during the day, and Katrina realized that the Mackinnon men had been only a small part of the loyalist group aware of the Stuart's movements. The Jacobite supporters were as strong a force as ever, only now the fervor in them was to get their prince away from the mainland as soon as the time was right.

There were moments when Jamie and Katrina could sit together and exchange private words. When he could tell her in a low voice of the new pride he had for her.

"I did what was needed, Jamie," she whispered. "And no more than ye would have done."

"But for a lassie to face a group o' redcoats alone and pretend to have the cholera was more than I'd have thought up! Did ye no' think what would happen if they'd disbelieved ye, dearest?"

She shivered. "Aye, I thought, and it made me act all the more! I dinna want to think of it, Jamie."

"And then to make the journey here took another kind of courage," he went on quickly, seeing the pallor in her cheeks. "Ye were always a lassie of spirit, Katrina, but now my heart fair bursts wi' pride for ye."

She gave a quick smile. "Will ye stop, Jamie, before my head swells so much I'll never get back through the cave opening?"

Gradually the long day passed. From time to time each of them moved cautiously outside to one of the shallower caves. They were still sheltered, but they were able to breathe in fresher air and stretch their limbs a little. At last the shimmering waters of the loch began to change color in the dying rays of the sun and were tinted a silver-rose hue.

Behind it, the hills took on a glowing purple magnificence, but those who watched and waited cursed the calm beauty reflected in the depths of the glassy water and wished for stormclouds to gather so that their prince could be spirited away to the islands under cover of darkness.

Then, almost unbelievably, as if in answer to that prayer, a chill wind sprang up from the direction of the sea, whipping up the surface of the loch to angry ripples and then surging waves. What moonlight there was became hidden beneath a blanket of heavy oppressive clouds, and almost at once the onset of stinging rain drew a muted cheer from the waiting group within the cave. A man was sent off to await the approach of the fishing boats. This was the night they had been waiting for, and the fishermen would be alerted by the approach of the storm.

As it worsened, it was welcomed by those who guarded the prince. The danger of a small boat on a storm-tossed ocean was less than that of the pursuing redcoats, and all knew it. The boats tied up at the loch, and it was time for the prince to embark. All that was left to do was assist him on his way as swiftly and silently as possible, as they had vowed to do.

"Ye'll not go with him, Jamie?" Katrina whispered as some of the clansmen stepped into the flimsy boats with Charles. Her stomach turned. She wouldn't stop him, but she didn't want him to go.

"I'll not go," he said roughly. " 'Twas not my luck. We drew lots for it, and once the boats are safely away we'll make for home, hen. I'd be there during the darkness, and I've no wish to spend further time in a rat's hole!"

No more did she. The daytime vigil had been bad enough, but the night was cold, and her face was streaked with grime and fatigue, mingling with the rain and the hot gush of tears as she watched the fishing boats silently move away with their precious cargo. She wondered if she would ever see Charles Stuart again. It was unlikely.

Those that were left at the loch dispersed quickly. The night grew colder as Jamie and Katrina struggled to reach the safety of Mackinnon House over the shorter mountain route she had used. Wind and rain tore at their faces and hands, and it made talking between them impossible. Once when they crouched together to listen for alien noises in the howling wind, he said roughly in her ear that they must bless their Highland weather this night.

"At least it will speed the prince on his way and keep the wet-nosed English indoors."

"Aye, and any Highland folk with any sense would be following their example," Katrina retorted with the ghost of a smile. He didn't answer, except by a squeeze of her hand.

All their concentration was needed for battling with the elements. It was doubly exhausting to be ever alert in case a redcoat patrol should be lurking about, even in the misty, blinding rain. They were not all idiots.

The scarlet shawl about Katrina's shoulders was already sodden. She was freezing, wet, and miserable, and already it seemed no more than a dream that Charles Edward Stuart had drunk to her as his scarlet rebel. For an instant the name had charmed her. Now she only wanted to be rid of the shawl and all the other clinging garments, to be safe and warm in bed with Jamie's arms around her.

But Jamie was pulling at her hand and urging her to keep up. Katrina was unable to think clearly and merely followed where he led. She had had no sleep, and no more had he, she presumed. She was like one of the sheep that roamed the hills, and if he were to drive her unwittingly to the edge of a precipice and tip her over, she could do nothing to resist. That such a ridiculous thought should even flit through her mind was one more frightening part of this terrible night.

"We're home!" Jamie's voice was right in her ear as she stumbled on, hardly knowing how to put one foot before the other. She jerked up her head and saw the dark shadowy mass of Mackinnon House looming ahead of them. The moment almost surpassed the joy Katrina had felt on arriving home after the endless journey from Ruthven barracks. Almost.

She gave a violent shudder as Jamie's arm tightened around her, helping her over the last short distance. Would this nightmare never end? Or would the fear continue until Charles Stuart and his like were exiled forever? The twist of fate was poignant. So much rejoicing at a new Jacobite rebellion . . . so much fervor now to be rid of their hero. . . .

She almost fell, jarring her ankle and leaning heavily against Jamie with a sharp cry of pain.

"I'm sorry," she mumbled hoarsely. "I'm sorry."

He half carried her the final distance. The household was sleeping, but Jamie kicked open the door and roused it quickly enough. Old Robert came running, his eyes filling up as he saw his master and mistress safe, the quavering candle in his hands threatening to fall.

"Thank God ye're both safe," Robert said thickly.

"Aye, we're safe, and we'll recover the better when we've some hot broth and drink inside us, Robert," Jamie told him quickly, seeing how Katrina swayed into a chair as though she were boneless. "Will ye first inform my faither we're home, and then see to it, please?"

The man moved away at once, and minutes later Callum stumped down the long staircase. Though he had been in bed, he'd taken no sleeping draught, too tense with worry about his son and his wife. He embraced them both, heedless of their damp state and the ache in his leg.

"Thank God." He spoke with a gruffness that hid his

emtoion. " 'Twas a long day of wondering. And what of the other? Did he get away?''

"He did,'' Jamie said. "The final destination is not known to me, though probably one o' the far islands will be the choice. 'Tis no doubt better that we're ignorant of his movements now.''

Callum nodded. "Aye. What we don't know, we canna tell.'' He looked down at Katrina's once glorious hair, sodden streamers now. "Ye'll know of your lassie's cleverness, Jamie? She's proved to be a canny one, and ye'll be as proud of her as myself.''

"That I am,'' Jamie said softly. "And so, too, is Charles Stuart this night.''

Katrina's weariness lifted briefly, and a warm glow of pleasure ran through her at this muted praise.

"Ye'll want to talk together,'' she said to the two men, "and I want to rid myself of my wet clothes before I eat.''

She rose stiffly and left Jamie with his father as she went up to their room to strip off the offending clothes and rub herself dry. She refused to remember the last time she had stood in this room, in fear and dread of the soldiers leering at her. She slid a nightgown over her head and put her arms through a bed wrap, and as she was ready Jamie appeared to change into nightclothes as well, saying that he and his father had done their talking, and Callum, now able to sleep, had gone to his bed with his sleeping draught. Robert would bring the food and drink to their bedroom.

When it came, they drank the hot broth eagerly, glad of its reviving sustenance. The whiskey-laced hot chocolate, too, was a reviver to the spirit, and at last some of the tension began to leave Katrina. It was a good feeling to know that this house still stood solid and safe, and that there was still a sane world beyond the needs of a fugitive prince.

Jamie couldn't forget the dangers still ahead for Charles quite so quickly. He still felt tight within himself, and Katrina's own arrival at the cave had been a shock to him.

Katrina finished eating before he did and said that she must lie down and sleep. Jamie drank more of the whiskey and wished that half his thoughts were not still on that hazardous journey in a flimsy fishing boat between the loch and the islands. Part of him wished he was there, too . . . and another part was filled with guilt that he had left Katrina alone to face the bastard redcoats—here, in this very room that was so private to them both.

He felt an impotent rage that the bastards had come here, had seen his wife half-clothed, and had lusted after her. . . . They had invaded his territory, and he had not been here to prevent it.

By the time he moved unsteadily to the bed, Katrina was already sleeping. In the soft glow of candlelight, the curving dark lashes were two crescents on the whiteness of her cheeks. Even in her sleep her soft lips trembled slightly, as though the memory of the long day had not left her yet. Her hair was half-dry, fanned out against the pillow in burnished strands about her face. His woman . . . his love, whom he needed with a sudden longing. . . .

Katrina barely stirred when she felt the sweet invasion of her flesh as he entered her. It hardly mattered to either of them that Jamie was half-drunk with the whiskey and exhaustion, or that Katrina was still in the hazy fantasy world of a lovely dream. What mattered was the love that flowed between them and the mingling of his seed with hers. It was a brief avowal of love, and when it was over they clung to each other as if neither could bear to pull away.

"I should never have left ye to face the bastards alone," he murmured against her cheek at last, and she knew that he was still tormented by the images of the redcoats here at his house. She stilled his words with a kiss that was softly passionate.

"Jamie, have ye not thought how different it would have been if ye had been here? Ye'd have challenged them, and there would have been bloodshed and death. They may have spared me—and for what? We both know the answer to that! They would have burned the house, and another loyalist base would be lost forever. Do ye not see the truth in it, Jamie? It was so much better that ye weren't here!"

"Aye, I see that ye're right," he said slowly. "But lassie, ye took such a risk in pretending to have the cholera. What if they had not believed ye? And there are those who survive it,

Katrina. If one of the redcoats had had the disease and was immune, did ye never think that he might have scorned your tauntings? If one of them had risked coming near ye, they may all have seen through your ruse, and then . . .''

She knew his fears for her and grieved for them. But it was in the past now, and there was no sense in brooding over it. She held him more tightly, as though he were a child.

"Jamie, 'tis over. The prince is safely over the water, and we, too, are safely together. Sleep, my dearie, and try to forget. Please, Jamie, try to sleep."

She felt him gradually relax in her arms and breathed a sigh of thankfulness. She held him until he was deep in sleep, and only then did she ease her aching arms away from him and fall into an exhausted sleep herself.

When she awoke she was alone again, and the unspoken fear rushed back. Not again . . . please God, not again! Her eyes sought almost feverishly for another note, as if Jamie's earlier absence were to be repeated. There was nothing. She felt light-headed and feverish. She was on fire, from the top of her head to the soles of her feet.

Thoughts seemed to tear through her head. She had willed herself to have the cholera! And people died from cholera, in agony, in disgusting, vomiting filth. Jamie's last memory of her would be as a mad thing, stinking and violent with pain, instead of his lovely Katrina. . . .

The very idea of it set up a paroxysm of nerves in her, so that she shook so hard her teeth seemed to rattle in her jaw. Where seconds before she had burned with fever, now she was piercingly cold. She seemed to have no control over her muscles. Tears streamed down her cheeks. She had always been so strong, and now she felt no more than a newborn babe, helpless and alone.

Was she already dead? Otherwise, why did no one answer when she cried out? Was she to watch them all file past her in a while, with long, sad faces, while she tried desperately to cry out that she still lived and breathed and felt pain? The heat raged through her again, stabbing like needlepoints, reminding her of the cushion case she had stitched for her mother in old Margret's cottage a century ago.

Her ramblings churned on inside her head. Old Margret

and Angus would be here soon to pay their last respects. Her mammie would be red-eyed and weeping, and so would her faither, though he'd hide it more. The bairns would be feared of death, or mebbe Hamish would think himself too much a man now to be so affected. Iona wouldn't understand what was happening to her sister. Callum would be saddened, and so would old Robert, who was so protective toward her.

And Jamie . . . her Jamie . . . how would he feel, gazing down at her, so waxen and cold, knowing he would never again feel her in his arms . . . never know the warmth and passion of their love?

"Jamie, Jamie, dinna let me go!" The words were suddenly screaming from her lips in terror, as if the ghostly shape of herself were like a gray wraith before her, weaving and beckoning . . .

"Jamie, I canna bear to be alone in this darkness. Hold me, Jamie, hold me!"

There were arms holding her then, substantial and comforting, but she was sure they weren't Jamie's arms. The gray haze still clouded her vision, and she couldn't see through it. She didn't know whose arms held her, or where she was. She was still not sure that she was really alive, and she was near to swooning with the sheer terror of it. Her body was bathed in sweat, her fingers clawing at the arms that held her.

She thought she could hear the buzz of voices, like irritating bees in a garden, but the ringing in her ears seemed to distort the noise. She had screamed, but no one seemed to hear her. God was punishing her for pretending to have the cholera. She had willed it on herself. She was dying—or she was already dead. . . .

A cool hand smoothed her brow. It was definitely a human hand. Katrina moved her own hand to cover it, to intimate that she was alive, to let someone know; yet her fingers moved with agonizing slowness. If she didn't hurry, the other hand would be gone. The person would go away and never know that she lived. She wept inside, almost despairing of hope, and then her fingers met other fingers and curled around them. The gray cloud swirled a little less densely, and she could make out strange moon shapes in front of her, floating back and forth.

"That's the way, my lassie," said a gruff male voice she seemed to know. She fought to match the rest of the man to the voice—a man who had coaxed her through childhood ailments and given her medicine to make her better. "I think the worst is over, Mistress Fraser. She'll be wanting plenty care, but the fever's broken at last."

Mistress Fraser. That wasn't her name. She was Mistress Mackinnon, Jamie's wife. . . . A faint scent of womens' clothes filled her nostrils, familiar, safe. One of the moon shapes became a face she knew and loved, and was dear and familiar, too.

"Mammie," Katrina croaked. "Oh, Mammie. Am I alive?"

Mairi Fraser hid her emotion at the question. Now was not the time to tell the lassie how near she had come to leaving them for that other world. She hugged Katrina carefully, as though her daughter were made of glass, and Katrina knew at once then whose arms had been holding her and willing her back to life.

"Yes, my dearie," Mairi said huskily. "Ye're alive, though ye've given us a time of it this past week."

"A week? I've been like this a whole week?"

A week had gone from her life, and she had no recollection of it. It was frightening, and yet she felt detached from the worry of it.

"Mammie, have I had the cholera?"

Mairi laughed now, though there was still a catch in her throat.

"Nay, my lamb, not the cholera, but the worst chill that even Dr. Grantley has seen. Ye've had such a delirium I was sore afraid for ye, but 'tis all behind ye now, and ye're going to recover."

"Mammie, where is Jamie?" She couldn't seem to concentrate on anything for long, her hands moving restlessly on the bedcovers still. "Is he here?"

She saw now that she was in their bedroom at Mackinnon House, so her mammie was only visiting. It seemed to be the middle of the day—a week later than it ought to be.

"Jamie's sleeping at the moment, my bairn," Mairi told her. "He's been sitting with ye night and day, until the doctor

insisted he must sleep, or he'd be in his deathbed before ye.''
She bit her lip, seeing the look in Katrina's eyes.

"Have I been so ill?" she whispered.

Mairi nodded wordlessly. It made Katrina feel very strange.
It felt as though she had been reborn, and her life was
beginning from this moment. She wondered if everyone who
had been near to death felt the same way. She saw the doctor
hovering in the doorway. Pleased that his patient had recovered,
he was preparing to leave, but he was unable to resist a tidbit
of news to tell her, in the hope of cheering her up.

"Ye'll have missed a wee bit excitement, lassie." He
chuckled. "The redcoats came back this way a few days ago.
Your Jamie could'na stop them rampaging through the house,
despite the fact of your mammie and wee sister being here
with ye at the time and being told that this was a house full of
illness."

Katrina felt the slow pounding of her heart as she listened
to his complacent words.

"Well, the redcoats came barging into this room and took
one look at ye, Katrina," the doctor blathered on, "and then
scuttled away like scared rabbits, shouting and bleating about
the cholera. Your Jamie shouted after them that they'd best
stay away from your mammie's house as well as this one,
since she'd be carrying the disease back and forth wi' her in
the nursing of ye."

Doctor Grantley was still laughing at the thought of it as
Mairi left the room with him, and Katrina heard the sound of
her own weak laughter echoing it. Just as suddenly, the
laughter changed to tears—weak, healing, natural tears. She
wasn't going to die. She was going to live, and the redcoats
had had their second taste of fright at her hands. A woman
could do little in battle, but there were other ways in which to
fight for a cause!

A movement at the door made her turn her head, and then
through a blur of tears she saw Jamie. He was gaunt and
unshaven, and she saw the anguish still in his eyes, as though
he couldn't quite believe that she was whole again. Katrina
held out her arms, not seeing how they trembled, and he
crossed the room in swift movements, to hold her close to his
heart.

* * *

She seemed unable to fight the weakness from her illness. For two more weeks she was listless, and Jamie treated her like a fragile plant. The very fact of it was beginning to irritate her. Katrina wasn't used to being ill and didn't like it. Physically, she recovered quickly, once the fever left her; but the strange apathy took longer to go. Jamie's tenderness roused her a little, but to both of them it seemed an interminably long time for her to be the Katrina she used to be.

She knew she should try to take some interest in what was happening around her, but somehow it all seemed too much effort. There were still strangers calling at the house from time to time, and she knew well enough what that meant— news of Charles Stuart or of the redcoats. Once, Katrina would have been annoyed that Jamie didn't confide in her. Now, she hardly cared, and even though they might all be knee-deep in some new conspiracy, unless one of them actively came and told her so, she would let the outside world drift along without her.

There was still enough of the old Katrina in her to be faintly alarmed at herself for letting this lethargy take control of her. She knew it was happening, yet she was content to sit back as though she watched it all from a distance. She was detached from life. It was a strange and rather pleasant feeling.

It meant she needn't trouble herself about Charles Stuart. She had been ill, and others could carry the burden of his safety. His life was now nothing to do with her. She hardly realized how immersed she was becoming with her own state of health, introverted to the exclusion of all else.

Jamie might have helped her more by storming at her the way he used to do when their verbal battles had been heated and abrasive. Then they had never failed to end their arguments in laughter, because it was so time-wasting to fight when all they really wanted was to be in each other's arms.

But Jamie seemed perplexed by her moods. He had watched her struggle with the fever and had thought his heart would break if she died from it. He had watched the strength in her combat it all and had seen her emerge as this pale being he didn't know. It was as if she had used up all her strength in the fight to survive and had not yet wholly returned to him.

Jamie wanted his own natural, passionate wife restored to him, not this strange, remote body.

Part of him was torn with guilt, too. If he had not left her on that night to go to Charles Stuart's side, then she would not have used the scarlet shawl and braved the mountains to reach the caves. She would not have had to fight her way back through the terrible storm the next night, and she would not have been struck down by the fever that almost killed her. If he traced everything back, it tormented Jamie enough to know the guilt was at his own feet.

He had tried to tell her so once, though it was hard for a man to speak of guilt, and Katrina had flushed with anger at the very mention that he might be to blame for her illness.

"I'll not listen to such talk, Jamie," she said fiercely. "How many times have ye put yourself at risk for the bonnie prince? And would ye have me such a milksop that I'd be afraid to do the same? Would ye rather I had done nothing that night, but cowered in my bed after the redcoats had gone, knowing that they would be tracking ye down? Dinna spoil it all for me, Jamie. Dinna make me think I did wrong."

He caught her in his arms, feeling the trembling in her and feeling how fragile she was now. He smoothed the silky strands of hair from her forehead with gentle hands.

"I'm not meaning to, my dearie! Ye filled me with pride for ye then, and I'll not forget it. No more will Charles Stuart, I think. 'Tis not your wrong I fret about, but my own. If I had not left ye that night."

"Jamie, we've argued this out before! Please let's stop it! Ye make my head spin, and what good does it do us to go over it and over it? Let's both be grateful that as far as we know the prince is safe—at least, we've heard naught to the contrary. And we're both well and together again. Is that not enough—more than some folk have got?"

"Aye," Jamie said heavily, guessing which way her thoughts were going. "Ye heard my faither tell of the farmlands that were burned to ashes not twenty miles from here, then?"

"I heard it," she said quietly, suppressing a shudder. "I think we should be counting our blessings, Jamie."

He knew it. He knew more than he told. The English soldiers were combing the hills and glens now and becoming more incensed by the day at the way the prince still managed to elude them. There were Highlanders who openly mocked them and paid dearly for it if they were caught. It was becoming an embarrassment to Cumberland and his army that one man should be so adept at losing himself among these inhospitable mountains, and that all the resources of the English army could not track him down.

It was even more galling to know that despite the privations imposed on the Highlanders, the threats, the burnings and the killings, none was ready to betray the prince. Had he bewitched them all?

If Katrina was a long time returning to her old verve, it was perhaps ironic that it was Iona, the little counterpart of herself, who put the first real spark of normality back into her older sister's eyes. Katrina had begun walking daily in the glen near Mackinnon House, walking farther each day and gaining more strength with each stroll. The summer sunshine was warm now, and she rarely strayed too far from the house. At least she kept within sight and sound of it, and old Robert was never far behind her, unobtrusive but watchful of his young mistress.

It touched her to know it, and to know that Robert would be hard put to defend her from any redcoat's attack if it came. He was too old. But then, Katrina thought, she would hardly attract any redcoat's attention now!

Her lovely hair was lank, and she had scraped it back from her head into a knot to stop it falling over her face when she stopped to gather wildflowers. The severe style defined the slender lines of her face and the pallor that still lingered despite the warmth of the sun.

The fragrance of the flowers was heady that morning, the scents delicate and fresh, and Katrina buried her nose in their velvet softness. Suddenly a rustle in the grasses nearby made her heart lurch and her senses swim, and the fear was back with such swiftness it almost made her cry out. But even before she could do so, or make her feet begin to run, she caught sight of the small figure flying toward her, arms waving like windmills to catch her attention.

"Iona!" Katrina dropped the flowers at once, seeing the

wildness in her sister's face. The flowers scattered, dancing on the breeze, but Katrina never noticed them. Even from the short distance away, she knew something was wrong.

She ran toward the child and seized her shaking shoulders. Now she could clearly see the frightened look in Iona's eyes, and she knelt beside her at once so that her face was level with the child's.

"What's happened, Iona? Tell me at once!" Katrina rapped out the words, for the child seemed momentarily unable to speak and needed to be ordered to do so. With some of her old impatience, Katrina shook the small shoulders a little.

"It was—it was the soldiers—the redcoats . . ." Once the words began they spilled out one after the other. Iona's eyes were huge now, dilated with fear, darting from side to side as if the hated redcoats were about to pounce on her at any moment.

"They came to the house, Katrina! And Mammie—Mammie said they were drunken pigs. She told them so, and Hamish shouted that they'd best get away from us if they did'na want to catch the cholera. But these redcoats were nastier ones, Katrina. They said—they said they'd want to see a body sick wi' the cholera before they'd believe it. I was so feared, and Faither was away from the house . . ."

Katrina shook her again as she began stuttering and stumbling over the telling. By now Robert had come panting up to them and was listening with alarm as Katrina coaxed the story out of her sister.

"Then what happened, Iona! Ye must tell me!"

"I cried, Katrina!" She was almost sobbing now. "And Mammie shouted at me to stop, because ye know that when I cry too much I'm sick, and she hissed at me that 'twould be a disgrace to be sick in front o' the redcoats! But I could'na help it! I was sick and sick and sick, and the redcoats said I was a stinking little bitch!"

Katrina forced back the laughter that threatened to overflow as Iona's voice became shrill with indignant remembering. It was too soon to laugh until she had heard all of it. But a wild hope sharpened her voice.

"Then what happened? Tell me quickly now!"

Iona drew a shuddering breath. "Hamish got all red in the

face like a ninny and asked them what more proof they needed. He shouted at them, and Mammie shouted back at him and told him to be quiet, but he would'na. He said that if Faither was'na home, he must do the man's work, and he faced them in front of us, Katrina, and I thought they were going to shoot him——''

Her voice broke again, and Katrina hugged her shivering wee body close. But she needed to know it all still, and she tried to make her voice more gentle now.

"Hush now, my bairn, ye're safe wi' me and Robert. Just go a wee bit slowly, and tell us if the redcoats hurt anyone."

She swallowed dryly, suddenly vizualizing her brother standing straight and tall and fearless, and aching with love for him, and for them all.

"Nobody was hurt, Katrina," Iona went on quickly. "But even Mammie got all red-faced as though she would cry, and Mammie never cries."

"For heavens' sake, what *happened*!" Katrina lost her patience and glowered into the child's face as though she would will the truth out of her. Iona sniffed loudly, trying to calm herself.

"Well, then Hamish told them to go and see our sister at Mackinnon House, because 'twas she who was spreading the cholera. He dragged me forward, and I was still wanting to be sick, and he hurt me so that I cried again. And Hamish said couldn't they see that it was spreading to his little sister as well? And I dinna want the cholera, Katrina!" She suddenly began to wail loudly.

"Hush, my lamb. Ye dinna have it, and no more do I," Katrina said forcefully in her ear. " 'Twas only your usual upset, and thank God the soldiers don't know of it!"

Robert wanted to know more, his voice gruff at the bairn's distress.

"Did the soldiers go away then, my dear?"

Iona looked up at him, nodding very fast. Her small face suddenly broke into a gleeful smile as she remembered.

"They got all funny after Hamish pushed me near them. They almost fell over each other, and they started shouting bad words. They said they had best get out o' the house as fast as they could. They remembered ye, Katrina. They'd heard the tale from some other soldiers, it seemed, and they said our glen must be fair filled wi' the disease by now, and they wanted to get away from it as fast as they could. They were going to wash themselves in the loch. And then they said ye must be dead by now, Katrina, and good riddance to ye. And I did'na want ye to be dead! Mammie said I must stay in the house, but I had to come to see . . . and ye look so different now, I canna be sure if ye're dead or no!''

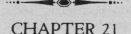

CHAPTER 21

Iona's *young voice rose, and Katrina could sense her panic.* Especially to ignore their mammie's instructions and come running out here by herself. Wasn't it just the way Katrina would have behaved? The wayward Katrina . . . She saw the small rebellious ghost of herself in Iona's wee tense body. She hugged the bairn to her, stifling her emotion and making her voice brisk and amused.

"Well, ye can see that I'm no' dead, ye ninny! Ye can see that I'm very much alive, and I'm taking ye right back home before Mammie starts fretting over ye. And ye'd best stop that snivelling this very minute, before ye're sick again over your nice clean clothes, or ye'll be in more trouble!''

The scolding restored some of the confidence to the child, who began to breathe more easily. She clung to Katrina's skirt.

"Will ye stay at home, Katrina? I won't plague ye, I promise! I'll be as good as an angel, and Faither's always saying how quiet the house is wi'out ye!''

Katrina laughed out loud now, the sound of it as bracing as a tonic. It seemed so long since she had laughed, even though she guessed wryly that Duncan Fraser's words may have been said with his tongue in his cheek!

"I canna stay, dove," she told Iona gently. "Not for always. My home is wi' Jamie now, but I'll come back with ye and stay awhile, then ye'll know for certain I'm not dead!"

"Is it wise, mistress?" Robert intervened now. "There's a wide stretch o' glen between here and Frashiel House."

"I'm hardly unaware of that, Robert," Katrina retorted. "But I'll not be stopped from taking my wee sister home, and 'tis hardly safe for her to be wandering about by herself at the present. I'll take her back to my mither's house this instant!"

She held Iona's hand, and the child was now clutching her tightly. She spoke in the imperious tones old Margret would have frowned upon, but she did it as much to reassure Iona as to make sure Robert was not going to stop her.

"Ye can either come with us or go back and inform Callum Mackinnon that I've gone visiting my kinfolk, Robert. I've a need to visit my own kin again. I've neglected them too long."

"Then ye'll do me the kindness to remain in this spot while I go back to tell Mr. Mackinnon, mistress," he growled back, clearly not too pleased at the way this short stroll was changing. "The young maister holds me responsible for ye, and I'll not see ye wandering off down the glen wi' the redcoats still somewhere about."

"Be as quick as ye can, then, Robert. If Mammie has missed Iona by now, she'll be worrying."

He stumped off back toward the house, still ruffled by her attitude, but Katrina knew she had taken the first positive action of any sort for weeks. Not since she had tricked the soldiers at Mackinnon House and then gone stealthily away to Margret's cottage and thence to the caves had she felt the blood flow so freely in her veins—not with fear, but with energy because she was in control of her own actions once more. The dead, dull lethargy was lifting at last.

Besides, who would be interested in the wraithlike woman with the small child who sat waiting now among the tall grasses of the glen? She had cared nothing for her appearance of late—she, whom her mammie had sometimes accused of being too vain!

A twist of remorse brought some of the color back to her face. How impossible she must have been then! And how dreary a companion for Jamie lately. Jamie . . . her Jamie. She couldn't blame him for his strange treatment of her lately, when she had hardly known herself! She must seem like a different person from his passionate Katrina of old.

Iona's small hand curled impatiently inside hers, and Katrina realized she had been gripping it too tightly. They were well hidden among the grasses, and sensibly so. Robert was wise to instruct them to wait for him, and Katrina knew it well. She saw now that Iona was looking at her uncertainly, for this was not quite the caustic Katrina she had always known, nor the romantic sister who had run off to wed Jamie Mackinnon. This was a different Katrina.

"Are ye still doing your lessons well for Hannah, Iona?" She had to force herself to recall the tutor's name, and Iona looked at her in amazement.

"Hannah went away a long while since! Did ye not know of it, Katrina? Mammie teaches me herself now, and some days Margret comes to the house to keep me in order!" she finished with a mischievous smile.

Katrina bit her lip. Had anyone told her of this? They must have done. And if they had, then the knowledge had slipped from her mind as easily as the waterfall slid over the rocks at the far end of the glen.

Her mind seemed to be full of holes still, unable to retain anything for long. The thought of it frightened her more than she realized. Was she ever to regain the intense enjoyment of life she had always taken so much for granted? She seemed so incapable of real deep feelings anymore. She was as insubstantial as a shadow.

Iona's fear of the redcoats and her excitement at finding her sister alive and well had dwindled away, and her incessant chatter had dried up. Katrina wished Robert would come soon so that she could see for herself that her family was safe at home. She needed to talk to her mammie and to warn her brother to be careful of taunting the redcoats. Though she thought ruefully that Hamish was as hotheaded a Fraser as the rest of them, prone to acting first and thinking later! It was a trait Katrina understood well.

At last Robert appeared, with the message that Katrina was to stay with her family until Jamie came for her that evening.

"Once I've delivered ye two lassies, I'll return to Mackinnon House," Robert said doggedly, obviously determined that they shouldn't go alone. Katrina didn't argue. She realized that she was weary, and that despite the surge of exhilaration, she had only taken the first step back to real health. She still had to go slowly.

Impatience warred with acceptance in her head. She knew she acted more like an old biddy than a young bride at times these days. Poor Jamie. . . .

The three of them walked away from Mackinnon House and across the long stretch of glen separating the two homes. When they got within sight of Frashiel House, each of them saw the gray pall of smoke at the same instant.

Iona began her shrill wailing at once and raced away from the others. Robert shouted at the child to wait as he lumbered after her. Katrina stood numbly for a second, as if totally unable to believe what her eyes told her was true. Frashiel House had been fired by the redcoats! Her feet seemed to be fastened to the ground, her throat closing with fear so quickly that she wondered if she would die from suffocation . . . as if the flames and smoke already choked her.

Then she gave a loud, agonized cry, and she was running, running, gathering up her skirts as she went. They were still some distance from the house, but she screamed out the names of her family as if they could already hear her.

"Mammie! Mammie! Faither—Hamish! Don't die. Oh, please don't burn, don't burn! Mammie—Mammie—"

A sawing pain in her side went unheeded. She forgot that she was still weak from the fever. There were greater needs than her own at stake now. She was filled with hate toward the soldiers who could do these terrible things, and she desperately needed to see her family safe.

She passed Robert, hearing his wheezing, labored breathing as he ran. She passed Iona's sobbing little figure and rushed through the gates of the house and straight into the dining hall where the acrid smoke and the heat of the flames reminded her instantly of other homes she and Jamie had seen burning. But this was her own. This was where she had been born, where her mammie lived.

The haunting, terrible memories wouldn't leave her as she

rushed through the blinding smoke. Then there had so often been the unmistakable, nauseating stench of burning flesh to add to the horror. Her eyes began to stream as the smoke stung them. It filled her nostrils, choking her within seconds.

She had to draw breath, hard though it was. She needed the breath to scream. . . .

"Mammie! Mammie! Faither—where are ye? I canna see ye!"

Tongues of flames licked the walls, where the claymores gleamed red and gold in the heat. Katrina coughed and gagged with the asphyxiating fumes. She was unable to find her bearings as the smoke enveloped her, and then she felt rough hands pulling at her and thrusting a container into hers.

"God knows what ye're doing here, Katrina, but since ye're here, then *help*!" Duncan Fraser roared at her. " 'Tis no' so bad as it first appeared, and we're near to getting it under control. Fling the water and I'll pass ye more."

Through the blinding gray murk, she could make out the shapes of her family now, together with a few servants. They formed a human chain of water carriers, and it was the effect of the dousing that sent the smoke billowing. But it had to be done, and it seemed that the fire was being contained in this one room. With God's help they would save the rest. Katrina grasped the container of water and threw its contents toward the fire, moving back quickly to reach for another and then another. . . .

Her arms began to ache appallingly from the continued effort, but she dared not stop. Her eyes were red-rimmed, her throat a raw channel through which she could only rasp. The room seemed to be full of people who were screaming, shouting, blathering obscenities at the redcoats who had done this and hardly knowing they did so.

The people and the heat were suffocating her. She felt that she would surely drop soon, and no one would even notice it among the chaos. There were others who had seen the smoke and come to the Frasers' aid, but none worked more frenziedly than Katrina. In her fever to help, this day's work seemed almost like a penance to her.

She had deserted them, all those months ago when she had run away from her aunt's house to wed Jamie Mackinnon, but now she was here, adding her weight to save them all. It was like a small seed of sanity in the muddle of her mind.

Now that she had a definite purpose, she no longer acted like the shuffling old invalid of the past weeks, almost uncaring whether she lived or died. She was eighteen years old, and she was young and alive. She was strong, and she had everything to live for. All the vitality that had been so dimmed of late seemed to be miraculously back again. Even through all her exertions she was aware of the change in her.

"Don't tire yourself, Katrina," she heard Mairi shout at her in a hoarse voice. " 'Tis almost done here now. Get outside with Iona and rest a wee while."

"I'm no' tired, Mammie," she croaked back. "When ye all rest, then so will I."

Her feet paddled in the water-strewn floor, but she gave no thought to it or whether she was in danger of getting a new chill on top of the old. There seemed an inner strength in her that told her she would survive—that they all would. She had come this far, and she never doubted it.

"I think we've beaten it!" Duncan's voice hacked in her ears. "Outside to be accounted for, every one of ye now, and to get some clean air into your lungs."

Once the command was given, the bedraggled group stumbled outside the house. Duncan rasped at a servant to bring whiskey for everyone, and the stinging liquid gave relief to raw and aching throats.

The helpers, sprawled out on the grass, were a sorry sight, faces blackened and weary with exhaustion, clothes sodden and filthy, totally spent. Yet Katrina felt a great love for all who had rallied, her family, friends, and neighbors. She closed her eyes for a moment and felt the welcome warmth of the sun on her face. After the searing heat of the fire it was gentle and caressing on her skin.

A pair of small arms were suddenly hugging her tightly, and she felt Iona's soft kiss on her cheek.

"Do your hands hurt bad, Katrina?" asked her sister. "Ye were so brave to go into the house. Robert would'na let me go."

Her hands? Katrina looked down at them in surprise. They lay, palms upturned, on her lap. Why should they hurt? She had given no thought to them. Now she saw how reddened and blistered they were, and she gradually began to distinguish the pain in them from the ache that enveloped the rest of her.

"Let me see, Katrina." Her mammie was by her side now, tenderly examining Katrina's hands. Mairi had worked as doggedly as the rest of them, yet here she was now, with a bowl and water and cloths to wipe away the grime, and salve to apply to burns and blisters.

"It's no' so bad, Mammie." Katrina couldn't hide the pain of it in her voice all the same. "See to the others."

"I'll see to ye first, my darling," Mairi said quietly. "These hands need binding, so sit still and I'll be as gentle as I can."

Callum Mackinnon appeared beside her, as blackened as the rest of them.

"Ye should'na be here, lassie! Ye should be safely under lock and key!"

She gave a small laugh, the sound of it cracking a little.

"Is that the only way ye think to keep me safe, Mr. Mackinnon? I'm no caged bird, nor ever could be! And I could say the same for ye, riding all this way with a leg that's paining ye to help a neighbor. Don't censure me, Mr. Mackinnon. Do ye think Jamie would want a puppet for a wife?"

She winced then as Mairi's attentions to her hands began. She had not thought of Jamie until that minute. There had been no time to think of anything but fighting the fire and saving the house.

Katrina drew in her breath a little as Mairi gently salved her poor hands and began to bind them. When she finished, Katrina looked down at the bandaged stumps at the ends of her wrists. She smiled wanly at her mother, to disguise the throbbing pain of her hands.

"How am I to hold my Jamie now, Mammie?" she whispered.

Mairi spoke gently. "I think 'twould be best if ye remained at Frashiel House a few days, my lamb, so that I can attend to your needs. Ye must choose for yourself, but 'tis what I strongly advise."

Katrina nodded slowly, seeing the sense of it. Her father

came to look at her, to assure himself that she had suffered no other ill effects from the ordeal.

"I was sore afraid I was seeing a wee ghostie when ye appeared in the midst of the fire, lassie," he said in a taut voice, and Katrina knew how feared Duncan had been for her and for them all. If they had not been able to get the fire under control so quickly, they might all have been homeless by now.

"Not a ghostie, Faither," she said huskily. "Though I feel as useless as one with these great lumps of my hands!"

"I never saw a ghost yet wi' bandaged hands," Duncan retorted, squeezing her shoulder to hide some of his emotion. "'Twas a reckless thing for ye to do, to come to our aid, lass, but no less than I'd have expected of ye. For a wee while the spirit was knocked out of ye, but it does'na stay down for long, and 'tis glad I am of it."

He bent to kiss her cheek and went quickly away to help organize the salvaging of the dining hall, leaving Katrina with the sheen of tears in her eyes. She sensed the pride in her father that in this trouble they had been all together again. They had been a family, fighting to survive, and the thought gave her great comfort.

Others came to sit with Katrina, as though she were the only one to have suffered. It was not so! She had to beg them all not to make such a fuss of her and to say that she would much rather be left alone to lie down and rest in the sun.

The truth of it was that apart from the searing pain in her hands, in spirit she felt better than she had in weeks. She felt whole again, alive, as though she belonged to the world once more and wasn't hovering in that half world where Jamie seemed afraid to touch her. Yes, her body was exhausted from racing to Frashiel House and from sharing in her family's ordeal, but if she were not so very tired, she would be helping her mammie put the house to rights as well. Maybe she would just close her eyes a wee while. . . .

She dozed longer than she realized, for when she next opened her eyes, there was a cushion beneath her head, and someone had placed a light covering over her. Her bandaged hands lay on top of it. There was a shadowy figure blotting out the sunlight from her vision. She squinted up at it, and it took on shape and form. At the same instant she was gathered up in a powerful embrace and rocked to a broad chest.

"Jamie, oh, Jamie!" She felt the weak tears in her eyes as she leaned against him.

"Am I cursed wi' a madwoman for a wife?" Jamie said harshly. "Scarcely out of her sickbed, and she comes courting disaster by rushing into a burning house."

"Would ye rather I had let my kinfolk burn wi'out doing what I could to help them?" The old passion was roused in her at his words. She moved back from him to stare into his eyes, and then she saw the anxiety for her there and realized how afraid he must have been for her. She swallowed back the bitterness as he pulled her close to him again.

"I'd rather have the feel of ye here in my arms, witch!" he said gently. "Even though it seems ye'll not be able to hold me properly for a while. Does it pain ye very much, my dearie?"

"Not too much," she lied. "But what of the damage inside the house, Jamie? I've seen naught of it yet. Mammie made me stay out here, and I fell asleep."

"And rightly so. Ye've hardly recovered your strength yet, sweet. But dinna fret yourself over the house. There's a small army of helpers seeing to it all, and walls and chairs can be replaced. If ye feel strong enough, then we'll go inside and ye can see it all for yourself. The worst of it is over now, I promise ye."

She made to stand, but as she swayed a little Jamie scooped her up in his arms as though she were weightless. She leaned her head against him. She was careful not to let her hands come into contact with anything at all. They smarted so badly now that even the glow she had felt on seeing Jamie seemed to have made the sting of them worsen.

Jamie set her down carefully in the dining hall, and Katrina felt the lump return to her throat as she looked around the once fine room. The huge table was blackened and singed and still smoking a little. Several chairs were no more than charred skeletons.

The surge of fury against the redcoats who had done this enveloped her anew. The floor still seeped with water, though much of it had been mopped away now, and her mammie was pushing a weary hand across her forehead. Hamish was furiously cleaning the claymores to their earlier perfection, as if to assert their clan's identity in what little way he could. Duncan was still passing around the whiskey to all who needed it and to those who didn't. At this rate they would all be insensible by nightfall.

Katrina looked dumbly at the drinking glass held out to her. She didn't want whiskey, but Jamie took the glass from her father's hand and gently instructed her to drink. She took a few fiery sips to save argument. If her face paled as much as she felt it did at that moment, however, it was not at the sight of her once lovely home reduced to such rubble—it was the sudden realization of just how helpless she was. She couldn't even hold a glass to her own lips, because of the bundles of cloth around her hands. For a moment she felt utter panic. An expression of bewilderment must have crossed her face, for as though her mother understood exactly what was going through Katrina's mind just then, Mairi came to her and put one arm loosely around her shoulders where she stood in Jamie's embrace.

"Jamie, I think 'tis best that Katrina remains here until her hands heal," Mairi said. "Ye'll understand that she needs a woman's attention, and I am the one to give it. I hope ye'll agree to the suggestion and let me care for her."

For a second, Katrina thought Jamie was not going to agree to any of it, and then he saw the sense of it and nodded slowly.

"Aye, 'tis probably for the best, though I shall miss my wife."

"I'll not be a hundred miles away, Jamie! I hope ye'll take the time to come and visit me!" Katrina said with a short laugh, although the thought of their parting was as strange to her as to him. This whole day was fast becoming unreal again. Jamie laughed with her, but it was a strained sound.

"Of course I will, hen. 'Twill be just as though we're courting again!" Only it would never be the same as that ever again, and they both knew it. He broke the small silence by turning to Katrina's father.

"I came to the house wi' some news for us all, though

what with all the excitement, I thought it best to wait until later to tell it. 'Tis naught that affects us directly, but still news about a certain person. . . .''

Katrina's irritation flared. "Why do ye not say his name, Jamie! We all know 'tis Charles Stuart of whom ye speak! Only bairns speak in such riddles."

Jamie's handsome face flushed darkly and his eyes flashed.

"I see the pain in your hands does not improve your temper, lass. I'm glad to see ye restored to normal, even if it does mean I'm to get the sharp side of your tongue."

"I think we'll move to a more comfortable room, Jamie," Duncan intervened in an attempt to avert the rousing passions in these two. Unconsciously his hand went to the loosened cravat at his neck. It was straggly now, but he absently tucked it into a buttonhole.

The gesture may have been no more than a wish to tidy his appearance, but it was also the old sign of the Jacobite supporters. And Katrina saw it with a feeling of bitter irony. Even now, when his house might have been burning all about him, Duncan would still be as loyal as ever.

While she . . . There was a guilt deep inside her, that this day's work by the redcoats on her own family home had done more to shake her loyalty than she had ever dreamed it would. But she dared not speak of it, and in her heart she prayed that it would only be a passing thing. She waited eagerly to know what news Jamie had to tell them.

"The prince has been wandering the far islands these past weeks." Jamie threw his wife a glance as he stopped speaking in guarded terms. "There are still many loyalists who will hide him, and there's no fear of that, despite the hordes of redcoats hunting him down. But we've heard now that he's back on the mainland."

"Then the French ship has been sighted, lad?" Duncan said quickly. "Ye've seen the prince and verified all this?"

Jamie shook his head impatiently.

"No to both, I'm afraid. His whereabouts are constantly changing and are not known to me at the present. The tale is being widely told now, though, of his escape from Benbecula Island to Skye, wi' the aid of a young lassie of the MacDonalds, one named Flora. The lassie thought to disguise the prince in women's clothing as her maid and to bring him in a rowing boat to Skye. Once safely there, they went to Flora MacDonald's kinsman's house in the north of the isle. He hid there awhile, and he was finally brought back to the mainland at Mallaig.''

"Then he's still safe, thanks to God and Flora MacDonald!" Duncan said quickly.

Jamie shrugged. "As far as I know, Duncan. He's sheltered on the mainland now, but I've no real knowledge other than what I've just told ye. He'll not be properly safe until the ship comes to take him to France. God knows why it does'na come, but there's no other way open to him now.''

The sooner the better. . . . The words were so fervent in Katrina's mind, she was afraid she had said them aloud. But they had all been inside her head, and she did not think them for entirely loyal reasons.

Was it treasonable for her to feel this way? she wondered. To wish Charles Stuart safely on his way back to France so that the lives of every Scottish family could resume some kind of normality? Surely it was not!

What was treason anymore? To uphold the ideals of a lost cause or to succumb to English rule, as they were forced to do whether they chose to or not? Those families that hadn't been devastated by Cumberland's redcoats were still under his control and the control of the English government. Every man here now wore the trews instead of the kilt according to the new orders. The Gaelic tongue was never spoken except in privacy, or unwittingly in anger, and then was all too often silenced by a musket shot from a redcoat. The playing of the pipes was never heard. The sadness of it was infinite, but though outwardly some Highlanders were totally crushed by the new regime, others still maintained the fiercest loyalty. Katrina knew instinctively that the Frasers and the Mackinnons here were some of the latter, and she kept her own wavering thought to herself.

"A constant watch is being kept at all points, the lochs and mountains,'' Jamie went on. "Fishermen will alert the chain of loyalists the moment the French ship is sighted. Word of mouth moves faster than the wind at times, and when there's aught to tell, we'll learn of it soon enough.''

"Meanwhile, we wait," Duncan stated.

"Aye," said Jamie grimly. "We wait."

They were all silent for a moment, as though willing an imminent signal to appear. Mairi cleared her throat with some impatience, sharing a little of her daughter's edginess. Her dining hall was still singed and stinking, her poor Katrina's hands blistered and painful. Those were more urgent matters to Mairi Fraser than surmising the lot of a fugitive prince. More than one of the helpers at the fire had suffered injuries and burns, but the lassie seemed to have taken the worst of it. At least they were all alive, the roof remaining over their heads, and to sit about gloomily debating Charles Stuart's fate was not helping anyone.

The day had grown late, and long shadows had replaced the bright summer sunlight. These men would be wanting food in their bellies, and Mairi remembered her duty as she rose stiffly and suggested it to them.

Callum Mackinnon beamed at her. "Aye, bonnie Mairi, if ye're including Jamie and me in that invitation, then I'll confess that I'm fair ravenous. A good fight or a bit o' danger always did set my belly to rumbling."

"Aye, we'll stay and gladly, Mistress Fraser," Jamie put in. "I thank ye for the offer, and I'd see Katrina safely to bed, too, before I leave."

Katrina felt herself redden as the words sent an odd feeling of embarrassment creeping over her. How strange it all sounded! Her mammie would see to all her needs and help her into bed, attending to all the personal things she couldn't manage for herself; but it was still Jamie's right to remain with her as long as he wished.

And here in her parents' home, it suddenly filled her with a new restraint. As though all the past months of intimacy between herself and Jamie, of feeling closer to him than to any other living person, were suddenly wiped out, and he was the stranger who insisted on having access to her bedroom!

She opened her mouth to say she would help her mother prepare the food, then closed it again. How could she help with these useless hands? She knew she should be hungry, too, but she had lost the taste for food. She could still taste the smoke from the dining hall, acrid and bitter. It was making her nauseated.

She heard Mairi insist that they eat in the proper room, and that no redcoats were going to drive her away from her home or the proper order of things. Katrina wished it could be elsewhere than the dining hall, but her father was jovial with the whiskey now and agreed with his wife.

"We'll throw open the windows and doors and let the fresh air into the place," he said heartily. "Iona, ye'll fetch a cloth to throw over the table, and 'twill hide the damage."

The meal was a strain for Katrina. Jamie insisted that she eat a little of the meat and bread, though she managed to protest that while he was feeding her he paid little attention to his own needs, and in the end he gave up trying to coax her. Tomorrow, she promised him, she would feel more like eating.

At last it was over, and Katrina said she wanted to go to bed. Her head swam, and she was very pale. Jamie got up at once and helped her up the long staircase to her old room. Mairi followed and bade Jamie wait outside until his wife was decently in bed.

"Thank you, mistress." Jamie spoke with a touch of mockery as their eyes clashed. He wasn't sure whether to be annoyed or relieved at this enforced separation. He admitted that he had been more disturbed than he realized by Katrina's strange, ethereal state these past weeks—especially because it had prevented him from touching his wife in the way he wanted to, with all a man's needs. Still, Jamie couldn't rid himself of the faint resentment at the way Mairi Fraser was taking over his Katrina, even while he knew the sense of it all too well.

When Mairi told him his wife was ready, he went back to the bedroom. Katrina lay against the pillow, her face almost as white as the bedcovers. The only color was in the burnished gleam of her hair around her shoulders and in the blue-green brilliance of her eyes. Her skin was almost translucent. She looked like a waxen doll, with her poor bandaged hands placed at her sides.

"I won't break, Jamie." Katrina spoke huskily, as if she

could read the confusion in his mind. "Ye can hold me a moment or two, if ye've a mind."

"Is that all?" He laughed shortly. "A moment or two?"

He crossed the room quickly, leaning over and taking her into his arms, gathering her up to his embrace. It was as much to hide the guilty expression in his eyes as to express his love for her. He needed to so badly, and yet he couldn't, not in the same sweet way that seemed to fuse them into one person, one love.

"Mammie says I'm to get as much rest as possible for a few days, Jamie," she whispered. "I'm to have the doctor to see to my hands, but I'm sure 'tis not necessary. All I need is a little rest, and I know I'll get all the care I need here. Ye—ye do understand, Jamie?"

He muttered his agreement, but all the time he was wishing she'd say passionately that she wouldn't stay here one more minute, that she'd demand to go home to Mackinnon House this instant! To be the old Katrina—wayward, passionate, with a mind of her own, and to blazes with any other considerations. . . .

Even while her eyes were mutely begging him to understand, he didn't want to understand. He wanted her home with him. But his practical side told him how foolish it would be. Her mammie was the person to care for her now, for however long it took.

"I'll come to see ye tomorrow, my dearie," he murmured against her soft cheek. "Sleep well."

He left her room, remembering those times when he had left her side to fight for Charles Stuart. She had always said then that she couldn't sleep properly without him by her side. He waited for the words to come again, but when he looked back into the room she was already asleep. He watched her for a moment longer and then went quickly out of the room.

It was Jamie now who had the thickening in his throat and a chill feeling, like the east wind blowing through the glen, gripping his gut. A man didn't weep for a woman, but the sight of his lassie, so vulnerable and alone in the bed there, made Jamie feel very near to weeping.

CHAPTER 22

T*he few days Katrina intended staying at Frashiel House* stretched into weeks. Regardless of her daughter's wishes, Mairi sent for Dr. Grantley to take a look at her.

The doctor looked at her keenly after he had made his examination and put new dressings on her hands. She remained stoically silent while he did so, even though they felt raw and painful.

"Ye've had some distressing times lately, my dear, and ye know the old saying about a hen coming home to roost. This is the best place for ye for a wee while longer yet, Katrina, and I'm sure Jamie can do wi'out ye a mite longer wi'out going to pieces. Take comfort in having a loving family to look after ye, Katrina, and if there's aught else that troubles ye, then let me know about it. Promise me now."

"There's nothing to tell," she murmured. "Thank ye for your concern, Doctor."

He eyed her keenly. The hands were beginning to heal, despite the fact that attention to them could make the lassie's mouth pinch with pain. And the shadows beneath the lustrous eyes still remained, as though there were still something more. A lovely young lassie like Katrina should respond quickly, even to all that she had endured these last months. She had a resilience that was rare, even in these hardy Highlanders. He ran a professional eye over her slender shape.

Katrina had been wed to Jamie Mackinnon for seven months now, and Dr. Grantley would have wagered there'd be a bairn in her belly before this. They were a lusty young pair, and if it was the thought of that that ailed Katrina . . . But maybe it was not. A lassie as fearless as this one wouldn't fear the pangs of childbed, or be wary of telling her doctor through any false modesty!

He bade her good-bye and went riding away through the glen. She saw him pause to speak with another rider coming toward Frashiel House. Her heartbeats quickened. As though she were a thought reader now, she guessed that Jamie would be told that his wife was in the best possible place for her to regain her health, and Jamie would be none too pleased to hear that there was no mention of her returning home yet.

When he slid from his horse to come to her side, Katrina smiled up at him from her seat in the garden. He was smiling, too, but she saw that the smile was forced, the hint of impatience not far behind it.

"Well then, the doctor wants ye to stay away from me yet, my dearie." He bent to kiss her, careful to avoid her hands.

"Aye, unless ye're going to play the heavy husband wi' me and insist that I come back where I belong!" She spoke teasingly, but a sudden sweet longing for him to say just that made her words sharper than she intended. For an instant she wished that Jamie would sweep her up in his arms, sit her on the horse in front of him, and carry her away this minute.

"I'd not go against your best interests, now, when I'd have your mammie and the good doctor after my hide," he said shortly, seeing a mild rebuke in her words. He sat beside her, his arm around her shoulders, yet his eyes seemed distant. It was as though Jamie were with her physically, but his thoughts were far away.

She swallowed back the words that had been brimming on her lips. Secret words she did not even intend to confide to a doctor yet, that were for her husband alone to hear. But her own tingling suspicions as to why she made such a slow recovery should be greeted joyously. And to whisper to Jamie now that she thought she might be carrying their child in her womb seemed out of place, especially since he acted more like the polite stranger than her loving husband!

Once before, Katrina had thought she might be with child, but this time she was more certain. There was a difference in her feelings, an inner glow, despite the precariousness of her health. She believed that a child lived and breathed inside her, and in the idling days of recovery she had traced back to its likely conception.

One night alone seemed the most likely—the night she and Jamie had struggled back to Mackinnon House in the terrible storm that had taken Charles Stuart away to the islands. A momentous night in many ways, when so much had been shared and endured. And this the most momentous result of all. . . .

But it was not confirmed yet, and for the time being it still seemed a secret best kept to herself, Katrina decided. The moment for telling had to be so right, and this was not it. She had said nothing, not even to her mother. The nauseating morning feelings were soon gone, providing she moved slowly for an hour or so after awakening, and that was deemed perfectly natural at the present.

"Is there any news, Jamie?" she asked him quickly.

He shrugged. "Very little. Thank God the redcoats seem to be leaving us in peace for the moment, and some other poor bast—folk—are receiving their attentions."

"Since when did ye have to mince your words wi' me, Jamie! I've heard ye curse before!"

"But not in your mammie's earshot," he said dryly, and she saw that Mairi was walking toward them from the house. They seemed to be rarely alone for very long. If her mammie wasn't seeing that she was comfortable, then Iona or Hamish sat with her, sometimes reading to her as she had once read to them.

Margret came to the house at times to teach Iona her crafts, and there seemed to be a constant flow of visitors to the house, to inquire after Katrina or to chat with neighbors about the fire, and to compare tales of the soldiers' visitations to other homes and farms.

Sometimes it seemed to Katrina that she and Jamie would never be alone again. She yearned for that time, and yet the old intimacy they had known still seemed like part of a distant dream, something that they must learn to share all over again. The learning would be sweet . . . and yet she could not picture it. Where once the sweet imagery would come to her in an instant, it was always hazy now, and it filled her with panic to know it.

Jamie came to her mammie's house at least once a day during the time Katrina stayed there. He was attentive, caring, but he still seemed to treat her like some remote being, and she knew that his thoughts were far away, even when he sat with her.

When her hands were healed enough for the bandages to be removed, he gently kissed each pink palm and held her close, but it was still as though he were afraid of hurting her. Maybe the fervor she had always known in him was taken up with the doings of another, Katrina thought with a surge of anger.

She asked him pointedly one evening. The strange lull over the prince's movements of late was more unnerving to her than the constant speculating among the menfolk. Katrina demanded to know if Jamie had definite news of him. They had seen no soldiers in the vicinity these past ten days, and that, too, was unnerving. It was like the calm before the storm.

He answered cagily enough. "Well, 'tis rumored that he still remains on Skye, and 'tis clear that the redcoats firmly believe it."

"But he's here on the mainland. Ye told us so a while ago on the night of the fire, Jamie!" She stared at him with narrowed eyes. "Am I to guess that he's not so far away?"

Jamie gave a brief laugh. "Do ye have the second sight now, then? I'll not deny that he's on the mainland, but he's not close. 'Tis better that ye don't know the full facts."

"Why is it better? Am I a bairn, not to be trusted with secrets!" She had her own secret, but she still couldn't bear it when Jamie kept this secret from her. Had she not won the right to be trusted, from the day Charles Stuart had dubbed her his own scarlet rebel?

"What use will it be for ye to know?" Jamie said roughly.

"It may prove that ye still have a fondness for me, Jamie!" The quick hot tears stabbed at her eyes. "A *fondness*, indeed! 'Tis a poor word compared with all the love and passion I thought we shared."

"Dinna be foolish, woman. A man does'na need to prove his love for his woman," Jamie growled at her.

She changed direction quickly. "The prince canna doubt my loyalty, Jamie. Why do ye, by not telling me what ye know?" She may have questioned it herself, but she dared anyone else to do so!

"If ye must know, lassie, the prince is safely harbored in the mountain refuge of the Macpherson chiefs and will remain there for the time being. When we get news of the French ship coming to these waters to speed him away, then he'll be brought nearer to the coast. Does that satisfy your woman's nose?"

It was a tease, but Katrina felt her cheeks flush as she tilted her chin higher.

"At least ye're not treating me like one of the bairns and keeping things from me! I've a right to know what keeps my man so occupied, Jamie."

Without warning he pulled her closer into his arms, so quickly he all but knocked the breath out of her. She could feel his heart beating against her own. His hand slid up behind her head and held it fast, and then his mouth was on hers, forceful, demanding. Katrina's head spun dizzily with the unexpectedness of it. But he moved away from her just as quickly, his voice still teasing but with an edge to it now.

"I'm thinking 'tis near time ye returned to your husband's home, then, if ye've such a need to know of his movements. Your hands are almost healed now, and any help ye need I'd be the one to give it. Think carefully, Katrina, and mebbe the next time I come visiting, 'twill be to hear that I'm to take ye home where ye belong."

Her mammie joined them then to see if Katrina needed anything, and her approach broke the small brittleness between them. Katrina knew that he was right. A spark of her old rebellious nature made her wish he would sweep her into his arms there and then, and say she was going home with him this very minute. But he did not. He had more respect for her mother's wishes.

But after he had gone that night, Katrina told Mairi firmly that she must go home to Mackinnon House with Jamie the very next day. Mairi hugged her daughter.

"Ye're right, Katrina. I see it in Jamie's eyes each time he comes visiting. Ye've stayed away from him long enough, and 'tis unnatural for a married pair to be parted like this."

The next evening, Callum Mackinnon looked around his dining table with real joy in his heart. The two people he

Jean Saunders

loved best in all the world were together again, and they were a family once more. Once the evening meal was over, he went off to his bed early, as he so often did these days, but tonight it was as much to leave these two alone as to rest his aching leg.

It was good to get some peace and quiet, Callum thought, and maybe Jamie would be in a better humor now that Katrina was home again. Not that there was so much peace and quiet to be had if one began roaming far from the house, he ruminated. The English had deduced now that they were playing a fool's game in wandering about the far islands looking for the fugitive prince, and many had returned to the mainland. They were as ruthless in their searchings as ever, and with such a reward for the prince's capture none could blame them. But it made the loyalists' task of sheltering the prince that much more difficult.

"I think I'll go to bed, Jamie," Katrina said some while later. "I'm very tired."

She looked up at him in the firelight, and he thought how very lovely she was. She wanted, and expected, him to take her in his arms and carry her up the wide staircase to their room. She wanted it and was almost shyly hesitant at the thought. They were like newlyweds all over again, yet as unlike those two who had loved so passionately on their wedding day as any two people could be. In her heart Katrina wept for those two, who had suffered so much since that day, and she prayed that they could recapture that ambience again.

And once the old, easy relationship was back between them, she could tell him the words she longed to say. When the time was right, and she was folded in his arms and felt truly loved, she would tell him that their love had been fruitful and that she was sure she was nearly two months with child.

It might even be more. The signs were all there, and if it were so, then she hadn't conceived on that storm-filled night when the prince had gotten safely away to the islands, but long before it, when they had shared more of the nighttime hours together than they had of late . . . when they had been together in every sense of the word.

Katrina mourned the fact that Jamie was still so occupied in

312

that other world of his, the man's world, which she couldn't enter. For a while she had been so much a part of it, in the shared journeys, in the hazardous night when she had gone to the caves to warn the prince, and in the journey back to Mackinnon House. Since that time, she had felt shut out of whatever it was that Jamie did, and not only because of her illness and the subsequent injuries to her hands. Now, she put a tentative hand on his arm as though to remind him that his wife was here, wanting him. . . .

Jamie's fingers trailed around the curve of her neck.

"I wish I could come to bed with ye, my dearie," he said huskily. "But 'tis not a night for sleeping or loving just now. I've a task to do, and ye should know that we may have a visitor for a wee while."

Katrina's surge of disappointment was halted by his guarded tone.

"A visitor? In the middle of the night?" It could only be one person. Her heart began to beat more quickly. She saw the wary look come into Jamie's eyes.

" 'Tis wisest that ye don't ask the identity, love."

Her eyes flashed with anger. Of course the visitor was to be Charles Stuart. Why was Jamie shutting her out again? The prince was almost like a dream to her now, but she was still willing to do what she could to aid him. She realized instantly that her loyalty was still intact after all, and the thought warmed her. But her thoughts whirled then. Jamie was to bring the prince here, and she was to be hostess to him in her own home! It might have been a hasty decision, as so many of the arrangements were, but how casually Jamie mentioned it! A burst of feminine anger made her rail at him.

"Have ye become so unthinking that ye canna inform me properly when I'm to have a guest at my table?"

"I beg your pardon, mistress." She heard the heavy sarcasm in his voice. "I was of the opinion that it was still *my* table, and the day when Jamie Mackinnon comes under petticoat rule is the day I'll see the lochs dry up into deserts!"

Their glances locked, until Katrina realized she was clenching her hands so tightly she was making the still tender palms sore. It was all so foolish, when they both wanted the same thing, to keep Charles Stuart safe. She moved quickly toward Jamie and put her arms about him.

"Go in safety, Jamie," she said softly, as dignified as though she sent him off to battle with his clan plant badge tucked in his blue bonnet. He pressed her close to his heart a moment longer.

Then he was gone, and she stood in the middle of the room, thinking how different this night was from the homecoming she had expected. And yet that strange feeling of exhilaration was stirring inside her anew. It was time to resume her proper role as Jamie Mackinnon's wife, and if that meant sheltering a fugitive prince, she would do it unquestioningly.

Her thoughts began to race on more coherently. Of course Charles Stuart would not come here as any ordinary guest! These were no ordinary times, and the visit would be furtive and secret, lest the English soldiers came searching again. She thought sensibly now. There was one room in the house where Charles would be safe. Like most other houses of its size, Mackinnon House had a secret room, with access known only to the family and a few faithful servants. Clearly this was the room that must be made ready for the prince.

Katrina took a candle from the dresser and went out of the dining room, to mount the long winding staircase and go through the twisting corridors to the room with no visible door and no windows, a room ventilated only by the cunning use of slits in the stonework.

It was a room that was rarely used but surely never put to such valued use as now. She told no one of her movements, as she knew would be Jamie's wish, but went methodically about her task. She put fresh linen on the narrow bed and made the sparsely furnished room as comfortable as she could. She piled many cushions on the floor in the assumption that the prince would have friends accompanying him.

Katrina was rewarded many hours later when she lay sleepless in bed, too tense to close her eyes. The arrival of the men had been so silent she had been unaware of it until she heard Jamie open and close their bedroom door. He leaned over her and pressed his lips to hers. They were cold, and he smelled of the night air, and she could hear the tiredness in his voice.

"Ye've done well, my dearie. Our visitor and his companions are safely away upstairs. I pray 'twill not be too long a visit, and then we may all breathe easier again. Now I must crawl into bed before I drop with weariness. I've taken longer journeys without sleep, but there's none so tense as those near the end of a dangerous road."

Katrina knew he spoke with a double meaning. The prince's departure to France must be imminent, and she felt a great thankfulness in her heart. Whether the cause was lost or won, Charles Stuart must be kept safe, and she restrained herself from asking any more questions of Jamie now as he climbed wearily into bed beside her.

Once she might have demanded to know everything at the instant, but a new maturity told her this was not the time. Now was a time to be silent, and to be glad that Jamie curled into her, seeking her warmth. He was asleep in seconds, his arms around her, his cold cheek against her soft one.

Someday soon, all the nightmare would be over. Katrina prayed for it fervently. She prayed for the bonnie lad's safe escape to France and prayed in thankfulness for her own bonnie lad's return to her arms.

Neither of them slept for long. Katrina awoke to find Jamie already dressing. He told her that there were four men in the hidden room who would be wanting breakfast.

"No more than that?" she asked with a glimmer of humor. "I had expected half an army marching through the house!"

Jamie gave a grim smile. "There's a fine network of loyalists ready to pass the word if any danger threatens the house, hen, and to check on whether we were followed in the night. We're but one link in a chain to speed the prince on his way. Dress now, and let's see to his needs."

Charles might be a fugitive, but he was still a prince, and Katrina suddenly felt as nervous as the first time she had spoken to him at Moy Hall with the Lady Anne. She dressed and tidied herself, then went with Jamie to the secret room. Inside, the three men sprawled on the cushions she had provided, but Charles Stuart paced about the small room, his natural energy and impatience evident even now.

Katrina saw at once that the prince was weary and haggard. His clothes were dusty and torn in places, but he was still her prince. She gave a small curtsey and received a warm smile in response as he took her hand, touching it to his lips in the foreign way he had.

"My thanks again, Mistress Mackinnon, for your hospitality," Charles said quietly, as though this were an everyday occurrence.

"We are the honored ones, sir," she said awkwardly.

Charles smiled again, more strained this time. "I trust you'll always think so, Katrina. I fear I bring more trouble than glory to my friends."

She spoke quickly. "Will ye remain here for breakfast, sir? It may be wiser, and it will be a pleasure for me to serve ye and your companions."

She saw Charles shake his head.

"We'll not put you to so much trouble. If you will lead the way, we'll follow you downstairs."

Jamie spoke uneasily. "Sir, it may be best to stay here. The fewer who know of your presence the better, and who knows if the redcoats got wind of our movements last night."

"If I cannot trust the household of a friend, then I'm probably already doomed," Charles retorted. "I have little time left to me to enjoy the hospitality of my homeland, Jamie. A meal at your table will soon be no more than a memory, so do not deny it to me."

Katrina was moved by his quiet dignity. His cause had been doomed a long while since, but somehow Charles had never lost his own fervor, nor failed to inspire it in others. He still held them all in the palm of his hand, and it was uncanny to know it. As he spoke of his departure, it was a poignant thought to Katrina that this might be one of his last hiding places in Scotland.

"We have been left alone this many weeks," she said quickly. "And it should still be safe enough."

Jamie nodded, though he knew that the longer the redcoats left them alone, the sooner it would be their bad fortune to be searched again. Even the most ignorant of Cumberland's soldiers could not believe the cholera infection lasted forever!

Jamie led the way down the stairs. It was evident to Katrina now that he had informed his father of their guests, for Callum awaited them in the dining room. Robert, too, had been roused early to prepare the room and the table, and a small breakfast feast was ready. Katrina ate little herself. The uneasy feeling in her stomach was accentuated that day by the feeling of anxiety. It was almost as though she waited for something, yet she didn't know what. She looked across the table at Charles Stuart and knew in her heart that he still wanted something of her. She knew it as surely as she recognized the slow, heavy heartbeats in her chest. But it was to Jamie the prince turned when the meal was finished.

"You have a lovely and accomplished wife, Mackinnon. I almost hesitate to ask you to let her do this one last dangerous thing for me. I do not command it."

Katrina's heart beat more quickly. Why did he not ask her himself? It was as though Jamie echoed her thought.

"I canna answer for my lassie's movements, sir. She has a mind and will of her own. Ye should know by now that I'll not stop her if she agrees to it!"

Charles turned to Katrina, watching her steadily. She heard his words as if in a dream.

"I need my scarlet rebel once more, Mistress Mackinnon. The English soldiers have begun firing haphazardly at any man they see wandering about at dusk, and I need someone to go this night to the old caves to bring news of my ship. We have word that it nears these waters, but it may be risky for the fishermen to leave their boats tied up at the loch too long while they venture so far inland. Between here and the caves is a dangerous stretch, where we have little communication except from the fishermen. But the old woman in the scarlet shawl can move about freely and without arousing suspicion."

Katrina's mouth had gone dry as Charles spoke, and now she felt him reach across the table to take hold of her cold hands. She had almost lost track of days, weeks, since her illness, and summer had already gone without her really noticing it. There was an icy fear in her now that had nothing to do with the onset of the cooler weather.

"You have the right to refuse, Katrina," Charles went on. "I don't command you to do this for me. I merely ask this one last favor of you, to go out at dusk wearing the scarlet shawl, to bring me news."

"I canna refuse ye, sir," she whispered. "No true loyalist would say nay to her prince."

But she felt her head swim for a moment. It was as though she spoke her own death sentence. She saw the prince rise. She saw the fatigue and tension in the faces of the men with him and knew there could be no other answer. He came around the dining table and drew her to her feet, leaned forward, and pressed a light kiss to her cheek.

"Think hard, Katrina. I know I ask much of you, and if you have any doubt in your mind . . ."

Her whole body was one massive doubt, but she swallowed the fear as best she could.

"I've given my word, sir," she said quietly. "I'll not fail ye."

She caught the look of pride then on Jamie's face; he had looked that way before when she had undertaken a similar mission, unknown to him. Had he suggested it this time? It didn't matter to her. What did matter was that Jamie and Charles Stuart believed in her loyalty enough, and trusted her enough, to ask her to do it again.

"I have every confidence in that, Katrina," Charles replied, confirming her thoughts. "But I urge you to take every care. It's even more vital than the last time."

And this time she would be all too aware of the dangers, the heart-stopping moments when she thought she was about to be discovered, the small night sounds that were magnified in her head to gigantic proportions as she strained for any alien movements among the mountains. . . .

"Katrina knows the route well, sir," Jamie said tersely, as though he sensed her mounting panic.

So she did, but taking a carefree walk in summer, in sunlight and in freedom, was very different from the risks after dark, when a lone traveler was as likely to be shot on sight as questioned. The redcoats fired first and queried later. She pushed the fears away from her, not wanting all those here to know how her woman's heart quaked at the thought of venturing to the caves all over again. She squared her shoulders and nodded in answer to Jamie's words.

"Then I'll outline my journey for you." The prince moved away from her side to talk more briskly to the men, once

318

more the leader. Through the long window, the morning sunlight glinted on the prince's fair hair and the elegant set of his shoulders, evident even now in the rags he wore. No one could deny his stature or the aura of nobility surrounding him.

"The ship has been sighted, as we know," Charles went on. "It's still a fair distance away, and our movements from here must be carefully chosen. I don't want to put your house at risk any longer than need be, Mackinnon. You've already done much to further my cause."

He glanced toward Katrina as he spoke, and she was warmed by the look. So the ship had already been sighted, which was presumably why Charles had been brought nearer to the point of departure. But there was still the dangerous journey over the mountains, and clearly there must be little delay in the timing; the prince and the ship must reach their destination at the same time.

And Katrina must be the one to go to the caves to glean what she could from the fishermen or by her own sight. She must don old Margret's shawl once again and make her way to the caves by the loch. Her heart still thudded, but this was her final chance to prove herself a rebel worthy of the name . . . Charles Stuart's scarlet rebel. . . .

Last time it had worked, but then she had been driven on by her own desperation and the need to warn Jamie that the redcoats were in pursuit. Then, there had been no time to think. Now it was different. She had to wait until dusk to move from the house, all day long, with nerves stretched taut.

There was another consideration, too, one of which Jamie was unaware. With a child growing in her belly, she should be taking extra care of herself, not putting herself and the unborn one in danger. She had always been physically strong, but recent weeks had undermined that strength. It was unbearable to think that she might risk doing harm to the bairn that had been made from love.

But Katrina clung to that last thought. If the child in her womb grew out of the love between her and Jamie, then surely it must survive, since what she was about to do grew out of an even greater love—that for her country. Even though the child's protection was her greatest wish, Charles Stuart's life must be protected, too, for he symbolized all that

Scotland held dear. His safety was all that was left of the cause that had seemed such a shining star.

She caught the prince's glance again, and she moved out of earshot to sit at the window seat while the men's conversation droned on. Loyalty to prince or to self . . . this time the decision was totally hers. There was no question in her mind, not for a second.

···•——◆——•···

CHAPTER 23

A *swift dizzying sensation made Katrina rise swiftly and* murmur that she would leave the men to their talk since she had things to attend to elsewhere. She felt suddenly stifled by the weight of her own destiny, uncertain though it was. There were many, many others who had played as great a role in Charles Stuart's escape from the English, but the thought of it didn't diminish her own part in it one bit. She stepped outside the house, breathing in the clean morning scents in the glen and fighting off the waves of nausea.

Was it ironic that the glen had rarely looked so beautiful to her as it did then? She captured the picture of it in her mind for all time, as if today would be her last real look at it. The distant blue-misted hills, majestic and timeless, the sweeping loveliness of the glen, the rush of the waterfall, and the babble of the incessant waters of the little burns. . . . Her throat thickened at the wild perfection, dazzling in all its glory in the morning sunlight.

Abruptly, she went back into the house. Callum was coming from the dining room, and she decided against disturbing the grim-faced men inside.

"I'm going to pay a visit to Margret this morning, Mr. Mackinnon," she said, as casually as though he didn't know just what that visit entailed. "It's been a while since I sat wi' her."

"Dinna be away too long, lassie," he grunted. " 'Tis best that ye're not seen abroad; we've too much at stake to rouse the redcoats' suspicions now."

Katrina nodded, wondering if there would ever come a time when they would be able to talk freely again. She left the house with her own dark shawl around her shoulders, for even though the day was sunny, the September days were fresher, and she must still take care of herself. She scanned the horizon, seeing nothing untoward, and hearing nothing but the distant chorus of bleating sheep.

She shivered, wrapping her shawl around her more tightly. The day was cooler than she had thought. She walked briskly through the glen toward the old woman's cottage. As always, the sight of it, as solidly square as ever, gray smoke spiraling from the chimney into a cloudless blue sky, reassured Katrina a little. The world might change, but old Margret and Angus were as indestructible as the hills.

Margret opened the cottage door to her at once, tut-tutting as she saw the pallor in Katrina's face. It was an uphill walk from Mackinnon House, and the old woman assumed the climb had been too much for Katrina. As she fussed about her, Katrina quickly told her to stop mithering.

"Ye've more than a touch of your old impatience back, then, lassie," Margret said tartly, eyeing her up and down. "I was wondering how long ye were going to let yourself wallow in the sickness, though I've a wish to see more color in those pale cheeks."

"I'll be better in a minute or two, Margret," Katrina said, fighting off the nausea that still plagued her.

"Well, since ye've seen fit to come and visit, at least sit ye down and take a hot drink and some fresh-baked scones. Time was when ye'd never say no to my baking, and I daresay ye've not got too grown for that."

Katrina took deep breaths, but as she did so the warm smell of the baking began to turn her stomach still more. At any other time she would have welcomed Margret's scones, and she had been unable to take more than a bite at breakfast. But not now . . . not today. . . .

To her horror she felt the bile rise swiftly in her throat, and she rushed to the stone sink in Margret's scullery. She retched over the sink and was humiliated at the sound of her own vomiting, but the touch of Margret's rough hand on her brow was oddly calming. After a few minutes of the heaving Margret was wiping her mouth with a washcloth and helping her back to a chair.

"There, my lassie, ye'll no doubt feel better now ye've got that out of ye," the old woman told the trembling girl. "It often takes a lass this way in the first few months, and if 'tis ailing ye so much, then ye should have come to old Margret sooner. I'll make ye a concoction that will ease the morning sickness."

Katrina looked searchingly into Margret's face. She trusted the old woman implicitly and had always done so. If she carried a child in her belly, Margret would know, with that innate wisdom of hers. Katrina felt her heartbeats, erratic once more, almost pounding in her chest, the blood soaring in her ears. But the wretchedness of the nausea was passing.

"Margret, do ye believe I'm with child?" Katrina asked, her voice husky and intense. "All the signs are there."

"Aye, I think it, lamb. I thought it the last time I saw ye at your mither's house, and if ye had'na been acting so huffishly with me, I might have told ye then."

A glorious feeling of warmth swept through Katrina at the words. She gave the old nurse a hug with all her old verve. She never doubted Margret's instincts, any more than she doubted her own, but in her mind now they were doubly confirmed. The child grew within her, a living part of her and Jamie, created from their love. . . .

"Oh, Margret, 'tis what I've wished for," Katrina whispered. Tears of joy shimmered on her dark lashes, and she wiped them away with a shaking hand.

"And your man, too, I hope!" Margret spoke in the caustic tone she used to cover her own emotion at seeing happiness in Katrina's eyes. " 'Tis a business between two people, hen, and the last I saw of your Jamie, he looked anything but content. All I saw was a glowering face and a temper to match. Ye dinna need to forget your wifely obligations so soon, lassie, if that's the trouble between ye both!"

Hot color replaced the earlier pallor in Katrina's face. Margret was as outspoken as ever, no matter what the subject. Katrina was still her bairn, to be taught the ways of a man and a woman as well as the schoolroom lessons.

" 'Tis naught like that, Margret," Katrina said in a rush. "The truth is . . . I have'na told Jamie yet."

Margret stared at her in disbelief.

"What kind of a ninny is this?" she demanded. "Of all the folk who need to be told when a bairn is expected, 'tis surely a husband's right! Do ye think yourself some sort of divine being, to have conceived a bairn wi'out your man's help?"

"Of course not!" Katrina said angrily. She was feeling a wee bit giddy again, and the purpose of her visit was eluding her. She must remember its importance, even though there was no great hurry, since the plan couldn't be put into practise until dusk.

"I merely wanted to be sure about the bairn," she went on doggedly, hoping Margret would believe her. "I did'na want to disappoint him, and I wanted the time of telling to be right, that's all."

"There's no better time than lying in your husband's arms," Margret said bluntly.

"But sometimes there are more important things to attend to first, and 'tis for that reason that I've come to see ye, Margret." Her voice took on a different tone. "We've a special guest briefly at Mackinnon House, one who needs our sheltering."

Margret's old eyes narrowed at once and she gave a small nod. "So he's come. Tell me what's needed, lassie."

Katrina drew a deep breath. "I need to borrow your scarlet shawl again, the same as before. 'Tis just for tonight, Margret. I'm to go on an errand for this someone."

She stopped abruptly. The ambiguous talk was so commonplace now that even Katrina did it without thinking, even while it irritated her so. A body really needed to read minds at times to follow half of it, but in old Margret's case that was never a bother.

"And is this why ye're so keen not to tell Jamie about his bairn?" Margret wanted to know. "Because he might stop your wanderings if he knew of it? I dinna think he would, but

323

I'm no' so sure I should'na stop ye myself, Katrina. There's a burning in your eyes I dinna like. I've seen others obsessed with the desire to help this someone, to their own destruction at times.''

Katrina gripped the woman's hands, the light in her eyes blazing with concentration.

"Margret, ye canna stop me. Ye musn't try! Nor must ye breathe a word to Jamie about the bairn until I'm ready to tell him myself. 'Tis my right to tell him. Ye said as much. And—and all this canna go on much longer. The French ship is believed very near.'' She bit her lip, saying more than she intended, yet Margret had probably known or sensed as much even before the prince had. "It can only go on a wee while longer. Let me do this last thing for Scotland!''

Margret's eyes softened. "For Scotland, lassie? Mebbe so. But ye must also think to yourself and remember 'tis part of Scotland's future that ye shelter inside ye. But aye, I'll lend ye my shawl and bag, and I'll keep myself indoors wi' the spinning for the day if 'tis your wish. But I beg ye to be careful, my dearie.''

"I will, Margret. I've that much to be careful for.'' She touched her hand protectively to her belly as her voice faltered a little.

"When do ye leave on this errand?'' Margret asked.

"Not until dusk.'' She couldn't help a leap of her heart as she said the words. "Your usual time for the fleece gathering at the end of the day, Margret. The twilight will aid me if I encounter any soldiers.''

"Pray God that ye don't,'' Margret muttered. "And ye expect your guest to be leaving your house very soon, then?''

"I hope so. I confess I'm uneasy the longer he stays there.''

"Instruct Jamie to bring him here as soon as 'tis dark,'' Margret said decisively. " 'Tis that bit nearer to the sea loch, and any news that ye have, ye can bring here as well as to Mackinnon House, and 'twill be less of a journey for ye to take back. I'll feel much easier in my mind to see ye back here safe and sound, Katrina, and ye'll have noticed that the redcoats leave this cottage severely alone. They're sore afraid of being spell cast if they dare do damage to a stick or stone of it. My wild cacklings and arm threshings have served me well!''

''I'll tell Jamie. He'll be grateful, Margret.''

''I want no gratitude, only your safety, lassie,'' Margret retorted. ''And the knowledge that we can all play a small part in getting our bonnie lad to his safe destination. Ye'll see to it, then, and now ye'll sit quietly and take that hot drink and a scone if your innards have settled, and we'll speak of other things. There's women's talk to be done, and a new life to discuss, and 'tis no less important.''

Katrina put her hand on the old woman's arm.

''Just so long as ye'll promise me ye'll not tell Jamie about the bairn, Margret. Your promise, please!''

''Do ye need to hear me say the words to know I'd respect your wishes, now?'' Margret said in an aggrieved tone. ''Aye, then, ye have it. I'll no' breathe a word to Jamie, providing ye tell him yourself, just as soon as ye can. Some joyful news will put the sparkle back into his eyes as well as yours.''

''I'll tell him,'' Katrina promised. ''When the time is right, I'll tell him.''

Dusk had never seemed so long in coming as it did that day. There had been occasional sounds of shooting that had all their nerves jumping, as if even now the prince would not get away in time. Whether the firing was close at hand, magnified by the mountains, or from a distance, it was enough to send the sick fear pounding through Katrina's veins.

The prince spent much of the day with his companions in the secret room, to Katrina's relief. Twice he insisted that they must go outside for some exercise or they would be permanently cramped, and those times were anxious ones, while a careful watch was kept. But as ever, the prince would have his way, with that stubbornness of which Lord George Murray and some other officers had so despaired.

But at last the sky grew heavier, turning from hazy pink to a deeper purple in the lovely gloaming of evening. The time came for Katrina to don the scarlet shawl and for the mission to begin. The shawl covered her head and shoulders and much of her back. She was thankful that Margret made her shawls so voluminous. She held it tightly around her body, the canvas bag slung about her in the way of the old woman. She hoped that the men waiting here to see her leave would not guess how she trembled inside.

Before she went, Charles touched his lips to her hand one more time. He spoke gravely.

"My prayers will follow you, Katrina. I'll not forget the courage of my scarlet rebel as long as I live."

"Thank ye, sir," she mumbled, swallowing hard.

Jamie took her in his arms, holding her close in a fierce embrace as his father and the Stuart's men turned away from them.

"Take no undue risks, dearest," he said tensely. "Watch every step and come back safe."

She almost gave an hysterical laugh; the entire venture was a foolish, terrible risk! If she failed and the soldiers stumbled across her, they would know at once that she was a fraud. They would begin asking questions, and she doubted that her courage was enough to stand the kind of brutal questioning they would employ. If they were to wring her true identity out of her, then they would surely come to Mackinnon House.

She couldn't think further. She clung wildly to Jamie for one last moment.

"Ye'll do as Margret suggested and await my—my return in her cottage, Jamie?" she stammered. "It makes good sense to do so."

"Aye, have no fear, love. In an hour from now, when 'tis darker, we'll go to the cottage one by one. The plan is already made. Ye'll go back to the cottage when ye've gleaned what news ye can. The fishermen will be at the caves, God willing, and on the watch to pass on any news."

"Just so long as I'm not mistaken for a redcoat in this garb!" She smiled crookedly. Jamie himself had thought her a redcoat for a few seconds that first time in the cave. That time she had given no thought to herself, but she had had a chance to think this time and to fret.

"When did ye ever see a lone redcoat, Katrina?" Jamie continued to encourage her into cheerfulness. " 'Tis thought that there's more safety in numbers for rats!"

He was outwardly more cheerful than he felt inside. He knew the risks of letting his wife go alone on such a mission, and the consequences if she was discovered by the soldiers. But Katrina had chosen to go, as he had known she would, and his fierce pride in her outweighed the fears.

"Take the honor of the house with ye, Mistress Mackinnon," he said softly against her cheek before he let her go.

She nodded swiftly, too full to say more. Good-byes were only prolonging the moment when she must slip out of the back of the house. She did so unobtrusively now, waiting and listening a moment for the slightest sound on the night air. The night was as still and calm as if it, too, were waiting, and waiting and watching. . . .

Katrina couldn't rid herself of the uncanny feeling that she was surrounded by invisible eyes. She moved forward into the bracken-filled glen, and every crackle of twig and thistle beneath her feet seemed louder than a drumbeat. She wasted no time in adopting Margret's stooping posture and the clawlike plucking of the gift fleece. Even if she could see no one, and the gloaming was giving her precious cover, there was no guarantee that she was alone in glen and hillside.

There was a good distance to travel before she reached the caves. She prayed she would reach the loch that led out to the sea in safety and find the fishermen who kept vigil for a bigger fish than usual moving into the glassy waters.

If only she had Margret's reputed second sight and could know that the French ship was moving stealthily along the Scottish coastline to receive its royal cargo. Not even Margret seemed able to tell anyone as much, but the ship must be very near for Charles to have sent her on this perilous mission.

Katrina's heartbeats became more erratic. Her mouth was as dry as dust as she plodded on, frustrated at doing so because her own youthful steps would have taken her to the caves far more quickly. But she dared not race. She must go slowly, carefully. . . .

She stopped as infrequently as she dared to catch at the fleecy wisps on bracken and gorse and thrust them inside the canvas bag as Margret would have done. Just enough to allay suspicion, if indeed she was being spied upon. She covered the distance in haphazard fashion, mumbling to herself the way Margret did. It wasn't hard to mumble. She began to think herself a little crazed to be taking this journey, instead of sitting cozily by her own fireside, dreaming of the bairn she and Jamie had created.

But she must not think of it. Not the bairn, nor Jamie, nor anything but the task she had been given by Charles Stuart. Of all the women in the world, he had chosen her, and it was a thought that sent her doggedly on.

She seemed to be entirely alone in the Highlands and the feeling was too eerie to be believed. The giant mountains loomed up like gray crouching monsters all around. Shadows moved and changed shape in the slightest rustle of the breeze. The whole panorama darkened whenever the moon slid behind the clouds.

Her nerves sent the sweat running down her back in rivulets. If only she could make her mind a complete void as she stumbled on. There was no visible sign of danger, and she tried to cling to that fact. She must keep calm. There could come a time when she would need all her wits.

Suddenly Katrina's foot caught in a rut, and she almost cried out, biting her tongue hard to stop herself. Any small sound would carry on the still air, and her normal voice was so different from Margret's it would alert any redcoats at once. Her eyes stung with tears from the swift turn of her ankle and the soreness of her tongue.

She tested her step and breathed a trembling sigh of relief. It wasn't sprained or broken, and although she could feel the wrench quite acutely, at least it meant she could hobble with more reality now. She peered through the dusk to get her bearings. She was within the shelter of the mountains between the glen and the loch. She felt a little less vulnerable among the craggy rocks and could align the direction of the loch by the twin hillocks to the north of it.

A minute later some sixth sense put her on her guard. She had leaned against a rock to catch her breath. It overlooked a small grassy hollow, and the instant she glanced down into it a group of English redcoats leapt up from their lounging positions, hands reaching for their pistols. She guessed instantly that they hadn't been there long, for they had not lighted a fire. If they had, its smoke might have warned her.

"Be it one of our boys?" she heard one of them mutter.

"Can't be. We're all here, so give the bastard a blast to

remember, if he's stupid enough to be wandering on his own and disobeying orders," another of them yelled.

Katrina began to act as she had never acted before. There was no time to think or plan. Though terrified, she seemed to hear old Margret's cackling laughter as she told of how the redcoats were afraid of being spell cast.

With one piercing screech, Katrina lifted both arms in the air, flailing them about like wind sails, and issued a torrent of unintelligible gibberish dredged up from the panic in her mind. There was just enough sense in the screechings to put the fear of the devil into the soldiers.

"Ye flibbery flaggerty nighthawks, disturbing the peaceful pickings o' wise 'uns! Ye death-wishers, scurvy-lumps, cattle-turds, and cholly-rumps! A curse on the first one to dabble wi' things o' the night. Who dares to come near me or try to touch me or harm me will find the droppings o' vermin scabbin' his flesh. Who'll be the first to take hold o' my skeinin'? 'Twill spin ye a fine winding-sheet, sweet laddies, if ye've a hankering to share old Margret's cot. Who'll be first to come share my secrets?"

She hollered the words in a hoarse caterwauling, driven on by her own terror. As she screeched she pulled wisps of the gift fleece from her bag and began scattering it down to where the soldiers stood transfixed at the unearthly sight above them and the sudden tirade that seemed to come out of the night from nowhere.

"You filthy old hag! I'd slit your belly through if I got my hands on you," the bravest of them bellowed back.

Katrina beckoned him forward with talonlike movements in the fading light. The shawl hid her face, shrouding her in a gossamerlike mantle of blood-red hue against the backcloth of the mountain.

"Come and touch me, sweet boy," she cackled. "'Twill be a fine night for breakin' in a young buck."

"You dirty old fleabag!" One of the redcoats, less impressionable than the rest, started scrambling up the slope toward her. She was done for, Katrina thought hysterically. In desperation she suddenly clasped the edge of the huge rock alongside her, flinging her arms around it, and began intoning loudly, in the weird deep voice that Margret once used in the nursery for telling witch stories.

"I call on this stone to render me invincible. Mother-stone, protect your handmaid from the evildoers."

One of the younger soldiers suddenly screamed out in terror.

"Don't get near to her, Tom! These old witches can't be killed. If you touch a hair of her, she'll turn you into something putrid and stinking. Get back down here, for Christ's sake, and let's get away from this place before she curses us all. I'll not wait to be scabbed by the old crone!"

"No more will I!" said another, slithering back down the hillside as if all the demons in hell were after him.

Their fear was as contagious as their false bravado. When one fled, they all fled. For long, agonizing minutes Katrina stayed clinging to the rock, as though she believed in her own wicked blasphemies. Very slowly she realized she was alone on the hillside. Only then did she let the tears fall like a river, but she stopped them quickly. There was no time for tears, not yet. There was still the errand to be done.

She unfastened her fingers from the rock. It was as though they had been stuck there like limpets. Her limbs were shaking so badly she could hardly stand, and she was near to swooning. She steadied herself, taking long, deep breaths, and pulled the shawl around her tightly again. If she dared to believe in such things, she could think it was the scarlet shawl that had protected her—Margret's shawl, into which would be woven all the secrets of the ages. She pushed the thought out of her mind. Her own wits and her own determination had saved her, and they must not fail her now. She must concentrate on reaching the caves, and that must be her only thought.

Yet as Katrina struck out once more, fearfully peering through the gathering darkness, another thought was too poignant to be ignored. What normal woman with a new life stirring in her belly would venture out in the chill of night, screeching at soldiers and enacting a wild dance of destruction on a lonely hilltop? What damage was she doing to herself and the bairn? She had flung herself against the rock without thought to the gentle cradling of the child, and if the child was harmed because of it, Katrina knew she would feel

endless hate for the butcher Cumberland and his entire army.
She felt it now.

Fighting back the tight sobs in her throat, Katrina blundered on through the mountain passes toward the lower slopes
on the far side, toward the loch and its caves. It was almost
too dark to see properly now, but she knew the way unerringly.
How often had she and Jamie run these same sparsely grassed
paths over the hills, to collapse with laughter and love in
those same hollows where the soldiers hid? Quick tears stabbed
her eyes. If only they could turn back the time to those
halcyon days!

She abandoned caution as darkness settled around her. The
hills took on deeper hues of purple and indigo, the veils of
mist rising around them. She fled now as the soldiers had
fled, the sound of her own ragged breathing like thunder in her
head. It seemed that she ran for hours, as if she would run for
all eternity and never reach her goal. . . .

Suddenly Katrina dropped to the ground like a stone.
Motionless, she crouched low as a new small sound reached
her ears out of the blackness. It was a mere crackling in the
bracken, a breaking of twigs . . . but Jamie's old instructions
served her well. They had crouched like this so many times in
the flight from Ruthven barracks, while the redcoats had
probed the hills and glens.

Was she to die alone after all, Katrina wondered with a
choking sob, when the scent of the sea loch was already
wafting toward her, the cool tang of it bittersweet now. She
was so near . . . so near. . . .

She stifled a sudden cry as a hand clamped over her mouth,
and the dark shape of a large male form sank down beside
her. She was almost too terrified to register anything but the
strong smell of fish that came from the man. Then she heard
the low voice coming from him—a voice she knew, thick and
guttural.

"Keep silent, lassie. I took ye for a redcoat at first, until I
stalked ye for a while, and no redcoat ever moved among the
Highlands wi' such a pretty sway."

Were his words meant to reassure her or give her time to
think before he removed the large damp hand from her mouth?
She couldn't think, ever again! Her shoulders suddenly felt

like heaving masses of jelly as she sagged against his body. It was so ludicrous to hear the rough flattery on such a night as this, in such a place, but she was agonizingly aware that the man could have knifed her first and discovered her identity later. She drew a deep shuddering breath, forcing her lips to move as the man cautiously took his hand away.

"Dougal!" She croaked out the name in a dry whisper. "Dougal Maclean. Do ye not know me?"

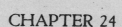

CHAPTER 24

The *fisherman peered through the darkness at Katrina. Had* she changed so much in fourteen months?

"'Tis the young Fraser lassie, by all that's holy."

"Jamie Mackinnon's wife these past nine months nearly, Dougal," she found the breath to say before she seized his great hands in her trembling ones. "I'm sent to bring news. I'm away to the caves at Loch nan Uamh. Will ye help me get there, Dougal?"

"And garbed like old Mistress Blainey!" She heard the edge of recollection come into his voice. "I mind being told of such a ruse before, lassie. It made a fine fireside tale."

Katrina moved impatiently. There was no time to crouch here blathering, except that she needed a few minutes to get her breath and gather her wits again. But now she must be away. Dougal held her arms fast, as though he sensed the tension in her every nerve end.

"Steady now. The hills are combed by the English redcoats, lassie."

"Ye dinna need to tell me! I've seen my share of them, but I must be away on my errand." If the redcoats couldn't stop her, then what was this old fool doing gabbing the night away when she had asked for his assistance?

"There's no need, for I've the answer to it," he grunted, as if he read her mind. "Why else would I be away from my boat this night unless 'twas on matters of greater importance? The ship we await is here in Scottish waters, lassie, and is ready to take the cargo aboard. We must get it there as quickly as possible."

The simple words were almost dizzying. Katrina could hardly believe she was hearing them. The French ship awaited Charles Stuart and it was almost over. The final journey. . . .

"He—he will be at Mistress Blainey's cottage by now," she stuttered through cold lips. "It was thought best for him to wait there with Jamie and his own companions. I must go back at once."

"And I'll accompany ye," Dougal said quickly. "Ye've done more than enough by the looks of ye, and your man can be proud of ye this night."

He rose carefully from the bracken, listening for a few minutes, and then beckoned her silently.

"Tread carefully, lassie. Follow in my footsteps and do as I do. Ye still have the strength for it?"

She had strength for nothing. She was a leaf in the wind, a shadow, a raindrop in a vast ocean. She nodded, squeezing his hand in silent assent.

They began to move as swiftly as possible, back the way Katrina had come. Several times they saw and heard the soldiers and smelled the fires, lighted now that darkness had fallen and giving the two loyalists a sure guide on which paths to avoid.

Taking endless detours, Katrina and Dougal crept on, and to her it was a journey of sheer fantasy. She felt as though she had been wandering these mountains for all eternity, and only the occasional warm grip of the fisherman's hand held any reality. She went where he led and was numbed and exhausted by the time they neared Margret's cottage at last, not daring to take the time to rest. The cottage loomed up in front of her quickly, and Katrina was hardly aware of stumbling inside, of being welcomed with a dram of whiskey, of being held fast in Jamie's arms. Held there, while the murmuring voices went on all around her, ghostlike.

The tiny cottage was filled with the large shapes of men.

Margret and Angus seemed to dwindle into the background, as did the brawny Highlanders guarding the prince, and even Charles himself, peering at her as anxiously as Jamie. She need not have gone after all; the wild realization of it was threatening to turn her weak tears to hysterical laughter. If they had waited, old Dougal would have brought the news in time. But where would he have taken it? A sliver of sense checked the hysteria as Jamie chafed her cold hands.

"Thank God ye're safe," Jamie said harshly, over and over. "I should'na have let ye go. 'Twas my place to go, not yours."

"Tis all right, Jamie. Dinna fear for me now I'm back safe," she whispered.

"Sit down and rest, Katrina," Charles was saying. "And thank God my trust in you brought its own reward in your safe return. My thanks are inadequate, but I thank you from my heart."

She didn't want his thanks. If he thanked her too much she would begin to weep and she would fail Jamie even now by showing women's tears. She gave a brief nod instead and made herself breathe steadily.

"We should go at once, sir," young Macpherson said in a low and urgent voice. "We must not delay another minute now."

She felt Jamie's grip on her hand tighten and knew then that he, too, would escort the prince to the end of the journey.

"We'll take the detours Mistress Mackinnon and myself followed," Dougal Maclean said swiftly. "If ye'll follow my trail . . ."

"I must go, Katrina." Jamie gave her a quick hug. "Once the prince is safely delivered to his ship, ye'll have your husband home again, I promise ye that."

Margret's face appeared out of the gloom at the back of the cottage as the men prepared to leave one by one, with Charles protected to the front and rear of them.

"Katrina will stay wi' Angus and me this night, Jamie. I'll see to her comfort, never fear."

And if there was anything amiss with the child she carried, then Margret would know what to do, Katrina thought, a great lump welling in her throat. She couldn't bear to think the bairn was harmed. But it was Jamie now who was going into danger. . . . He had the right to know of his child, but there was no time for the telling . . . no time at all.

Charles came to her side, his hand on her shoulder for a brief moment.

"Good-bye, my scarlet rebel. I won't forget you."

He said no more but went out swiftly and silently into the night. Jamie and the others went as silently after him, and the thought came into Katrina's mind that there could be no greater contrast than between the way Charles had arrived to the pomp and ceremony in Edinburgh to proclaim his father king, and this furtive hustling from a poor cottage in the night.

With the prince and the Highlanders gone, there were only the three of them in the dim candlelight—old Angus sucking heavily on his clay pipe, Margret, and herself. And it was Margret who caught at her as Katrina got to her feet and then began to sway.

"Steady now, my lamb. Your task is over, and ye'll rest properly. They asked too much of ye this night."

"If Charles Stuart had asked it of ye, would ye have refused?" Katrina retorted in a small voice, in a semblance of her old spirit.

Margret edged her gently toward the rumpled bed in the corner of the room and bade her lay down on it at once. Katrina did as she was told as Margret eased off her boots and covered her body with a blanket. Margret didn't answer Katrina's question, but they both knew that neither she nor any other true loyalist would have refused to do the Stuart's bidding.

"I'm away to mix a potion that will help ye sleep, Katrina, and 'twill also relax your tense muscles. There's no sense in fretting over your man now, and it will'na help ye."

Katrina looked into Margret's canny old eyes, and her own eyes burned into them as if she would read Margret's very thoughts.

"Do ye think all's well with the bairn, Margret?" she asked hoarsely. "I could'na bear it otherwise."

"If 'tis not, then the next hours will show it," was all the old woman would say. "And the calmer ye stay, the better 'twill be for ye, so do as I say now and rest."

It was impossible to rest. How could she, when her tormented imagination was following the silent group of men taking Charles Stuart to the French ship? They all played a dangerous game . . . and Jamie was in the heart of it. Her hands trembled, knowing she would never be able to sleep until he was safely home again.

"Drink this down, Katrina. Every drop now," Margret instructed, holding the cup to her lips, her voice allowing no arguments. She drank obediently, and the potion was bitter and dark.

It was daylight when Katrina awoke. At first she was totally unable to collect her muddled thoughts. She felt heavy and tired, and it was an effort to lift her eyelids. The scent of a peat fire was pleasantly strong in her nostrils, and as her focus became steadier she saw a bent figure tending it. Unconsciously Katrina's hands went protectively to her belly.

"Margret." Her mouth was too dry to speak properly, but the woman heard her and turned. "Is all well wi' me, Margret?"

The woman came to her at once, and her look was reassuring.

"Aye, lassie, if ye mean ye and the bairn, all's well. Ye've a good strong body and an even stronger spirit."

"And Jamie?" Her eyes sought for more reassurance from Margret.

"There's been no word yet, but that does'na mean anything. Mebbe they were forced to hide during the night, and then there's no knowing when they'll risk taking the Stuart to the ship!"

Katrina had so wanted it to be over and done with that she had given no thought to any delay.

"Ye never did too well wi' the patience, did ye, lassie? But ye've no other choice now, and 'twill doubtless be a while before we hear any news."

Frustration swept over Katrina. Her own mission had been so frantic, so fraught with danger and risk, and now she was to lie here twiddling her thumbs in a fever of anxiety and foreboding. She heard Margret give a sharp sigh.

"Remember what I told ye in the night, Katrina. The bairn ye carry needs a calm haven."

"Because it may be all I have left of Jamie?" She hadn't meant to utter her darkest fears, but the words were out before she could stop them. The risks weren't over yet, and this child could be doubly precious if she were to lose her man. She felt clammy just thinking of it. She tried not to think, to be as strong as Margret thought her to be.

But at that moment she had no wish to be strong! She had need of being a woman, with her man's strong arms to protect her. She closed her eyes briefly, as the morning nausea flooded through her.

"Drink this, lass," Margret instructed now, pushing more of the dark liquid toward her. " 'Tis a milder draught than before. It will calm ye, not make ye insensible. I know ye'll want to be fully alert when Jamie comes back to take ye home."

Katrina drank obediently. A thread of hope ran through her at the old woman's words. If Margret was truly the oracle she half believed, then she was surely telling Katrina to have faith that Jamie would return safely.

Katrina's body was beginning to recover from the aches and pains of the previous night. The draught calmed her as Margret had said, and later she felt well enough to move about the cottage, taking some porridge and barley water and gazing through the thick glass windowpane as though her eyes would penetrate the dense mist of the morning.

By the middle of the afternoon the mist had lifted, and Katrina wasn't sure whether to be glad or sorry. It would have given cover to the prince and his men and would have been a hindrance to the redcoats in the unfamiliar country. She wished desperately that Jamie would come striding over the hills toward the cottage. Margret left the girl alone for a while, tramping the hills in her usual manner, the more to find out any further news; but there was none. When Margret told her so, Katrina almost stamped her feet in frustration.

"I canna stay here longer, Margret," she cried out. "I feel the need to be in my own home, where I feel Jamie's presence most. I'll away to Mackinnon House, and if—when—he comes here, ye'll tell him where I've gone. I dinna think he'll expect to find me still here, Margret. And his faither will be wondering about the two of us, wi' no news.''

"Calm yourself, lassie. Angus saw to it all. He went to the house early today, and Callum Mackinnon knows how ye fare and what's afoot. But mebbe what ye say is right." She gave a slow nod. "Your man has a right to find his lassie waiting in his own house. A man's home is the dearest place to him. Go in safety while the sun shines, Katrina."

The sun wouldn't shine for her again until Jamie, too, was safely home. Katrina bit her lips to stop herself from saying the words out loud. She had given Margret enough trouble without pouring out more of her heartache. She hugged the old woman before winding her own dark shawl about her shoulders, and then she started the gentle walk down the hillside toward Jamie's home.

She made her way casually, as though she had been merely making an afternoon visit to an old friend. She saw no one on the way, but not until she was inside Mackinnon House and clasped thankfully in Callum Mackinnon's arms did she feel truly safe.

"Thank God, lassie," was all he said in a deep gruff voice, but she knew how worried he must have been for her.

"I'm well." She answered the question in his eyes. "But I'll be better when Jamie gets back."

"So will we all, my lass. So will we all."

Katrina went to bed as early as Callum that night. The day had been long, and with every hour that passed the two of them felt a stirring of hope. As long as no bad news was relayed to them, they could assume that the prince was still being ferried out to the French ship or was awaiting a suitable time for the final escape from the mainland. As long as there was no bad news . . .

She went to her bedroom, but Katrina knew she wouldn't sleep, nor did she try. She wanted the room to be snug and warm for Jamie's return. She had asked Robert to light a wood fire in the hearth, and as she watched it crackle and burn with a fierce brightness, she recaptured the memory of the tiny cottage near the border and the first beautiful hours of her marriage. She knelt by the fire to warm herself and to brush her long hair into a burnished sheen. She was glad of the fire's heat. The September nights were chill, and already it was the twentieth day. A day that Scotland would long remember, she thought, if their bonnie prince was leaving its shores forever. . . .

Katrina sat by the fireside for a long time, but at last she climbed wearily into bed, stiff and uncomfortable from sitting by the hearth. Jamie had not come home, and darkness had settled over the house. The fire still burned with welcome cheer, but as she blew out the candle she felt the sick fear and disappointment wash over her again. There seemed no end to it, no end. . . . She closed her eyes tightly, as though to push away the hated images of Jamie in danger. Jamie, Jamie. . . . She didn't know that she slept from sheer exhaustion, nor how she moaned in her sleep.

"Hush now, my dearest one!" Jamie's voice spoke roughly in her ear as she thrashed on the pillow and cried out his name in her sleep. She was still struggling to awaken from the nightmare when she found herself rocked tightly in Jamie's arms, and the cry became one of joy instead.

For a moment she couldn't speak, nor could she quite believe that he was real. But his face was cold against hers, and the salty aroma on his clothing instantly reminded her of his night's work. He was no illusion. He was real, he was her man, and he was here in her arms.

"Oh, Jamie, Jamie, I was so feared for ye!" She wept now, unable to control the pent-up emotions another second. "I dreamed that ye were dead, and I had'na told ye."

"Well, I'm no' dead, woman, but I'm fair likely to be if ye dinna stop trying to strangle me!" he growled at her, disentangling her arms from his neck with an effort and trying to cover his own emotion with a short laugh. "Did ye have so little faith in our plans, my sweet?"

She heard the edge of raw male arrogance in his voice, as though to imply that men's plans were superior to the woman's panic that had sent her running to the caves in Margret's scarlet shawl that first time. She heard it, but none of it mattered. There was a more important need in her.

"I had every faith, Jamie, but it did'na alter my fear for ye and the prince," she said tremulously. "Did it all go as ye planned it?"

"Aye. He'll be on the way to France by now."

She felt a rush of thankfulness at his words, yet she knew at once that he was still troubled. He should be rejoicing. She watched him move from her side and begin to strip off the damp clothes, still tense in his movements as he went nearer to the fire to warm himself.

She felt her throat tighten. She had made a little love nest in the room for him to come home to, and he seemed totally unaware of it. She sat up in bed, hugging her knees, and wondered how she was ever to tell this cold and distant stranger that their child lived and breathed in her body.

"Then 'tis all over, Jamie," she said, suddenly needing all his attention as he gazed unseeingly into the fire. He turned to glower at her. It was as though he didn't really see her at all, Katrina thought in bewilderment. She sensed that in spirit Jamie was very far from this room they shared. He was away somewhere on that dangerous sea journey between Scotland and France, unable to separate himself from all that had led up to this night. How could she have been so insensitive not to know that it would be so?

"Over?" Jamie said harshly. "Have these fourteen months meant so little to ye that ye can say 'tis over because we've sent our prince into exile like his faither before him? We've failed, lassie. We bear the shame of it."

"There's no shame!" Her voice was vibrant with suppressed anger. His attitude frightened her. He had always been so strong in mind and body and determination, but this Jamie she saw now had withdrawn into some private world of his own. She couldn't follow him there.

"There's shame," he repeated bitterly. "Tomorrow the news will spread through the glens that the prince has escaped safely, and there'll be rejoicing. *Rejoicing!*" He slapped one large hand into his other palm in a savage fury. Against the glow of the fire, his back seemed to be in spasm. Katrina could see the muscles and sinews tightly corded.

"Why should they not rejoice! Ye've all striven to get him safely away. So many have fought for this day as hard as they fought for the cause, Jamie.'' She hated to see him so hostile. And then all the tension seemed to leave him.

"They should weep," he said tiredly. "For ye're right, my dearie. 'Tis over, and Scotland will never see his like again. Does the thought of that not make ye want to weep?"

He stared into the flames, as though all the hopes and dreams of Scotland burned there. Katrina's eyes stung with tears. She ached to comfort him, but he was still so remote from the Jamie she loved. He still grieved for his fair and bonnie prince, and his lost cause. Jamie would never forget . . . and no more would she. She had so many special memories. She was Charles Stuart's scarlet rebel, and she cherished the memory.

But Charles Stuart, their Bonnie Prince Charlie, would by now have taken his last sight of the receding, mist-shrouded mountains and glens of Scotland. His cause was finished, and his loyalists' task was done. Were their lives to be saddened forever by the ghost of his bid for a throne? And was her own laddie never to be her passionate Jamie again? She couldn't bear to see him like this, so far away from her in mind and spirit. She wanted him back. She wanted her man, and she wanted him now.

Katrina left the warmth of her bed and moved softly across the room to sink down beside Jamie on the hearth rug. She touched her soft hand to his arm, then stroked his beloved face with her fingertips. His flesh remained granite hard, and it seemed as though she would never reach the loving heart of him. She drew in her breath on a small sigh.

"Does the scent of the woodsmoke please ye, Jamie?" she asked in a quiet voice, praying that he would remember.

"Aye." He gave a grim smile. "Like the barracks at Ruthven, or the thatch on burning cottages and farms at the redcoats' hands, lass. That's what it does for me."

She felt the tension back in him and the echo of it in herself. But like a sudden illumination, Katrina knew instantly what ailed Jamie, by the bleakness in his eyes that he was unable to hide. His whole life for the past fourteen months had been dedicated to the cause, and with Charles Stuart's escape all the purpose in Jamie Mackinnon's life had drained out of him. The cause was over . . . and what was there left?

"Jamie, listen to me." Katrina placed herself in front of him, so that the firelight gleamed on her hair. He looked at her, still unwilling to drag himself back from the despondency he didn't fully understand himself. He felt Katrina take his hand. She moved it to the gentle swell of her belly and held it there.

"We have something very special to live for, my dear one." She spoke quietly still, as if afraid to break the spell between them now that she had gotten his attention at last. She moved his hand very gently against herself. "The wee one made from our love is growing there, Jamie. I've wanted so much to tell ye, but the time was never right. Now is the time for it, dearest, and I pray that your heart will be as full of gladness for it as my own."

She saw the dawn of understanding on his face as she spoke, his beloved face, now slowly changing from the hard mask she didn't know to her own, her darling Jamie. . . .

His hands were suddenly warm on her shoulders, his eyes searching hers, as if unable to believe that what she was saying was really true.

"Ye're sure of it, sweet? We're to have a bairn?"

"I'm sure, Jamie!" She was laughing and crying at the same time. "And I pray that it will be a boy. It *must* be a boy! A laddie that we can name after another special laddie."

She could say no more then, for he was hugging her so tightly she could hardly breathe. She was in the circle of Jamie's arms, cradled in love . . . and he could no more explain the complexity of his feelings at that moment than explain the changing of the seasons, but it was as though her words rekindled all the life in him—as though he were emerging at last from an endless nightmare.

He held her close, whispering words of love. Her eyes shimmered bright with the thrill of his reaction to her news; he thought he had never seen them blaze so brilliantly as they did now. He had never seen her look more beautiful, he thought wonderingly as he held her sweet face close to his. It was as though he had never seen her before, not like this, the mother of his bairn. . . .

"Oh, Jamie." Her voice was a soft sigh against his shoulder. "We have everything in the world now. So many times I wanted to tell ye, but always the words seemed to trip on my tongue. It was as if they were meant to be held until the time was right. Do ye forgive me for it, my love?"

She held her breath as his hand moved to touch the gently trembling mouth, to trace its contours and follow his fingers with a kiss of infinite sweetness. She felt the wildly beating pulse in her throat and saw the leap of passion in her man's eyes as he held her close against him.

"Forgive ye? Forgiveness is a word that does'na exist between us, my dearest one." He spoke huskily, and then she knew for certain that he hadn't forgotten any more than she had. Together they had survived, and out of despair they had sowed the living proof of their love.

"Hold me, Jamie," Katrina whispered. "Oh, hold me, love me."

Her face was fiery against him, and he gloried in its warmth. "It will'na hurt the bairn if I lie with ye?" He felt obliged to ask, his voice half-teasing.

Katrina felt the laughter welling up inside her, together with a tingling happiness. It felt so wonderful to laugh, to feel free and young and alive! So wonderful to tease and know there would be only one ending to the teasing, in each others' arms. . . . She wound her arms about Jamie's neck and looked deeply into his eyes.

"No, it will'na hurt the bairn," she said with an instinctive wisdom. "But it will mebbe hurt your wife if ye do not show her how much she means to ye, Jamie Mackinnon. I mind how ye once told me it was a wondrous thing for a man to pleasure his woman. Do ye remember that day, Jamie? So long ago—"

Her words ended quickly as he caught her up in his arms in one swift movement and carried her from the fireside to the bed. He laid her gently down between the sheets and slid into bed beside her. For a long moment he gazed down at her, loving her beyond imagination, new life soaring inside him at the thought of the new life they had created from their love.

Katrina sensed all the love in him, wild as the night, matching her own, and she knew that he was restored whole to her again. She blessed her woman's instincts that had told her to keep the telling until a special time . . . this precious time.

Jamie bent forward to kiss the softly rounded belly.

"Sleep softly, my bairn," he murmured against her flesh.

Her eyes moist, Katrina pulled him to her then, with a fierceness and a joy, and the belonging was as exquisite as the first time. In some strange, inexplicable way, this was the first time—a new beginning, as she and Jamie were joined in love. All they wanted, all they needed, was here in that warm, firelit room with the scent of woodsmoke, fragrant and sweet. Now, at last, they had all the time in the world.